Praise for these other thrillers from *New York Times*
bestselling authors
Iris Johansen and **Roy Johansen**

Sight Unseen

"The stellar team of Johansen and Johansen is back with
the next installment of this clever and terrifying suspense
series . . . Filled with frightening twists and terrifying turns,
the book ends on a cliff-hanger. The reader's heart will
be racing the entire time, so waiting for the next book is
going to be difficult!" —*RT Book Reviews* (4½ stars)

"The Johansens do a page-turning job of tying up all the
loose ends in this complex cat-and-mouse game, but they
always manage to leave one thread dangling: just the
kind of ploy designed to keep loyal series fans eagerly
anticipating the next installment." —*Booklist*

"A thrill-a-minute, chill-a-minute thriller that keeps
reader[s] on the edge of their seat[s]. Each character is
minutely defined and believable; the good guys, the
victims, and the executioner. Iris Johansen and her son
Roy Johansen are true masters of page-turning terror
guaranteed to shock and awe you." —*Reader to Reader*

"Edgy . . . : a flashy romantic thriller."
—*Publishers Weekly*

"Shocking . . . with a vibrant cast of characters."
—*Fresh Fiction*

THE NAKED EYE

IRIS JOHANSEN

&

ROY JOHANSEN

St. Martin's Paperbacks

THE NAKED EYE

Copyright © 2015 by Johansen Publishing LLLP.
Excerpt from *Hide Away* copyright © 2016 by Johansen Publishing LLLP.

All rights reserved.

For information address St. Martin's Press, 175 Fifth Avenue, New York, NY 10010.

Library of Congress Catalog Card Number: 2015013655

ISBN: 978-1-250-07901-5

Printed in the United States of America

St. Martin's Press hardcover edition / July 2015
St. Martin's Paperbacks edition / January 2016

St. Martin's Paperbacks are published by St. Martin's Press, 175 Fifth Avenue, New York, NY 10010.

10 9 8 7 6 5 4 3 2 1

For Sherry Kappler Cooley
Who took as much love and joy
from life as she brought into it.
We miss you every day.

CHAPTER
1

SHE WAS FLOATING. FLOATING IN a pool of blood.

No, now it had become a river of blood.

What in the hell . . . ?

Of course.

This was a dream. The same horrible nightmare that had haunted her for months. Why hadn't she realized it before?

Because the terror was real, and she was always afraid the nightmare was real, too. Colby was a demon. Couldn't a demon make a nightmare come true?

She was back at the gully in Coachella Valley, the place where she had beaten him. Yet here he was, night after night. He crouched on a rock at the gully's end, waiting for the blood river to carry her to him.

No!

Colby laughed and raised his two large knives. "Here we are. Just me and you, Kendra. The way it was meant to be."

He swung his blades at her.
Darkness. Darkness. Dark—

GOT ONE FOR YOU.

Kendra Michaels jerked wide-awake at the jangle she'd programmed to signal the text messages on her phone.

Damn.

She threw her legs over the edge of the bed and studied the message header. It was from Martin Stokes, a San Diego Police Department homicide detective. He'd included an address and a few details.

She took a few minutes to steady her breathing, trying to gain control. She was still trembling from her nightmare, and her face was covered with sweat. She'd be okay in a minute. Every night the nightmare came, and every night she survived it.

Just as I survived you, Colby.

I won't let you drag me back to that time, and someday I'll fight off this damn nightmare.

But here in her hands, a real-life nightmare beckoned. She didn't have to go, of course; a glance at the crime-scene photos and a reading of the case file would probably tell her everything she needed to know.

Probably.

Who in the hell was she kidding? She knew she was going.

No matter how horrific the scene was, it couldn't compare with the beast still taunting her in her dreams.

A quick shower and she'd be out of here. She reached for her jeans and headed for the bathroom.

She stopped short as she glanced in the vanity mirror. She reached up and touched one of the dark circles beneath her eyes.

Those nightmares again. There was no strength in that face at this moment. She appeared delicate, breakable.

She was *not* breakable. She was the one who had broken Colby that night in the gully four years ago.

Colby had been her first case as an FBI consultant, and she had been so horrified at the brutality of his kills that she had become obsessed with catching him. The cat-and-mouse search had culminated with her almost dying in that gully and Colby going to the hospital with a fractured skull. He had found that defeat intolerable. His ego couldn't bear the thought that she had triumphed and sent him to prison. She had become the focus of his hatred and obsession, and he had let her know; he had been a dark shadow behind her all those years he had spent on death row.

You're out there waiting, aren't you, Colby?

I can feel it.

So wait, you bastard. And when you get bored, come after me.

I'm waiting for you, too.

And I'm not standing still.

She turned and jumped into the shower.

"I DIDN'T THINK YOU WERE going to show." Detective Stokes lifted the police tape for Kendra to duck under and join him in the driveway of the one-story craftsman home. Four squad cars were parked on the street, flashers pounding the house with out-of-sync strobes of red and blue light. The scene was crawling with uniformed officers, detectives, and forensics experts.

Kendra shrugged. "What else would I have to do at three-thirty in the morning?"

"I could think of lots of things. Especially since you don't *have* to be here."

What did he know? She felt the familiar chill. "I do have to be here."

She'd tried to suppress the shudder, but Stokes's narrowed stare told her the effort was unsuccessful. "Sure, but you should be thanking Detective Kael. He's the one who beat it into my brain that I should contact you if I encountered any killings of a serial or ritualistic nature. He thinks you're the real deal."

Did that mean Stokes did not? She gazed at him appraisingly. Thirtysomething, receding brown hair, pleasant enough features. No sign of belligerence or cynicism. "Kael is a good man."

"He's a rotten softball player, but other than that . . ." He motioned for her to follow him up the driveway. "But I trust him most of the time. I was actually glad when I had an excuse to call you on this case." He grimaced. "I'm very curious. But you know I've heard so many incredible things about you that it's hard to separate the truth from the bullshit."

She half smiled. "Bank on the bullshit."

"I don't think so. Tell me, were you really blind for the first twenty years of your life?"

"Yes."

"Completely blind?"

"Yep. I'd never seen a thing in my life."

"That's amazing. Kael says you got your sight from some kind of stem-cell surgery."

She nodded. "In England. They did a lot of the early work in corneal-regeneration techniques."

"I've always heard that blind people developed their other senses to compensate. And that's how you pick up on stuff most other people don't."

She wished he'd just drop it. Patience. At least he was

pleasant enough, and she might need him to notify her again if he ran across one of the target murders. "I guess so. But I don't think my senses of hearing, smell, taste, or touch are better than anyone else's. I just had to use them to make my way in the world."

"Yeah. And afterward you used your eyes, too." He smiled. "You don't remember me, but I was at the Van Buren crime scene a few years ago. It wasn't my case, but I was curious as hell about you. So I just stayed in the background and watched."

"Really? I hope you were entertained."

"Did I say the wrong thing? I didn't mean—I was impressed. You cracked that case by reading the lips of a suspect when he was talking on the phone to his wife. It was amazing . . . and surprising. It made me want to go out and learn it myself."

"Did you do it?"

"No, it was like a lot of things in my life. It just somehow slipped away as time passed." He paused. "But I think I should let you know, Kael isn't the only one who thinks you're the real deal. I do, too, Dr. Michaels."

He was sincere. Sincerity deserved politeness as well as patience. "Thank you. I appreciate your calling me. I hope you'll think of me again when something like this comes up."

"You can bet on it." They had reached the front door. "Let's hold up here for a second." Stokes held up his hand as he looked inside the open front door. "The photographer's doing his thing."

"Sure."

Stokes crossed his arms in front of him. "I think this is going to be one of those cases when you'll have to concentrate on being pretty sharp about things you see."

"Whatever." She was feeling the tension start. She didn't like standing out here waiting. "I never take things for granted. Things I see aren't just details to me. They're *gifts*. They're part of the world that was closed off to me for so long. I guess I just want to take in everything."

"I'm afraid you'll get more than you bargained for in there." He shook his head. "It's not a pretty scene."

She just wanted to get to it, dammit. Kendra glanced at the driveway next door, where another detective was talking to a distraught-looking bald man in sweatpants and a Padres T-shirt.

"That's the husband?"

"Yeah. He fell asleep watching TV upstairs in bed. A little before two, he came downstairs and found his wife's body in the kitchen. It's a mess."

"He has no clue who could have done this?"

"No. His wife was an elementary-school teacher, no enemies that he knows of."

"Maybe *he* has the enemies. What does he do?"

"Residential mortgage manager at a bank." Stokes glanced back inside. "All clear."

Kendra followed him through a small living room, carpeted with a thick burnt-orange rug that probably wasn't even in style when laid fifteen years before. She scanned the room. Photographs, vacation souvenirs, and two watercolor prints probably purchased from a cruise-ship auction.

Through a doorway on the far wall, she heard at least half a dozen pairs of footsteps. No, she self-corrected, more like eight.

Stokes motioned her through the doorway. Kendra walked through and nodded her greeting at the seven men and one woman working the crime scene. She recognized most of them from other recent investigations. They'd become much more at ease with her now that they knew she wasn't interested in grabbing credit from them.

That's never what this was about.

Two forensics men were crouched in front of the open refrigerator. Upon seeing Kendra, they stood and moved away to reveal what had brought them all there: Thirty-five-year-old Marissa Kohler, lying in a pool of her own blood.

Kendra had seen many murder victims over the years, many at much more gruesome scenes than this one, but it still hit her like a kick in the stomach. She hoped she'd never become too callous to not feel that horror. This woman had probably just gone through the motions on her last day on Earth, with nary an idea that it would all soon come to a horrific end.

Detach. Focus.

Time to see if *he* did this. The monster.

Kendra crouched next to the corpse, trying to avoid the splatter trails on the tile floor. Dressed in sleeper shorts and a long T-shirt, the victim was lying in front of the open refrigerator as if attacked while getting a midnight snack. Her hands were near her face, suggesting a defensive position even after falling. A pair of round spectacles rested on the floor about five feet away. Obviously, the victim's glasses, confirmed by the distinctive mark on her nose that matched the spectacles' arched bridge.

Stokes pointed toward the open back door, which was splintered as if kicked open with a fierce kick. "Point of entry over there. No curtains on the back windows, so the killer could have spotted her in here."

"Maybe." Kendra leaned over and examined the victim's wounds. The woman's throat had been opened in five horizontal gashes, plus over a dozen punctures to the torso.

Who did this to you, Marissa? Could it really have been . . . him?

Show me. Give me something. Anything . . .

Her eyes flicked from Marissa's face to the back door. Of course.

Kendra stood up and brushed herself off. "Thank you all. I'm sorry for disturbing you." She turned and walked out of the room.

Stokes ran after her. "Wait. That's it?"

"Yes."

He grabbed her arm. "You didn't find out anything?"

"Yes, I found out what I needed to know."

He gazed at her in frustration. "Well, are you gonna let me in on it?"

"Of course." But she might not have notified him until the next day. She just wanted to get out of here right now. She stopped in the living room and looked back through the doorway. "This isn't the work of a serial killer. Certainly not the one I'm looking for."

"Then whose work is it?"

"Her husband's."

Stokes lowered his voice. "What?"

"That scene in the kitchen was staged. Check upstairs. She was killed there."

"How do you figure that?"

"The smell of blood is wafting down that staircase. Sickly sweet and more than a bit metallic. Plus a useless attempt to cover it up with a half a can of Lysol Powder Fresh."

He sniffed the air. "I smell the Lysol . . ."

"I'm sure you smell the blood, too. You just don't realize it. Send your forensics team up there with Luminol. The victim also has faint rug burns on the back of her heels. She was dragged down the stairs, posed, and maybe even stabbed a few more times postmortem. It looks like there are punctures without much bleeding."

"And the door?"

"He knew enough to go outside and kick it in to give the appearance of forced entry. But he obviously didn't go any farther outside than the patio. The ground in the yard is a muddy mess, but there are no footprints out there."

"Are you sure? It's dark."

"The porch lights give at least fifteen feet of visibility. Trust me, no one approached the house from the yard. And I spotted a tiny shard of orange rubber on the splintered door frame."

He stared at her. "Orange rubber."

She nodded. "Surely you noticed the obnoxious orange rubber soles of the athletic shoes her husband is wearing?"

"Holy shit," Stokes whispered.

"I'm done," she said wearily. "Good night, Detective. I'm sure you'll have no trouble taking it from here."

Stokes didn't answer as he dashed out the door.

Kendra left the house and walked slowly down the driveway. She was in no hurry to get home. She was disappointed and tired, but there might be only nightmares when she got back to sleep.

She cast a glance back at Stokes as he approached the husband, who was still playing the part of the bereaved widower. The guy was an amateur; he'd undoubtedly left many more clues behind, and the cops would have their case against him sewn up in a matter of hours.

"Finished already?" A familiar voice called out mockingly to her from the street.

She let out an exasperated sigh. "Adam Lynch . . . Seriously?"

"Hey, I don't like your tone. You're hurting my feelings here."

She turned back and saw Lynch leaning against her car. While everyone else on the scene was middle-of-the-night bedraggled, Lynch's every dark hair was in place. Probably just the way he rolled out of bed, the bastard. He wore jeans, a pullover sweater, loafers, and a sexy, high-wattage smile that seemed terribly out of place at a grim murder scene. But then, everything about Lynch was high wattage. He was a paid freelance operative who worked for any agency or nation who could afford his services. Those services were both deadly and innovative, as Kendra had found in the past year. But there had been times when she was grateful for both his skill and that cool intelligence when cases had thrown them together. And other times when she had only been wary of how Lynch managed to stir her emotions when she knew how dangerous that could be. It had become a complex relationship that bound them together, and she never knew from one minute to the next how she would feel toward Lynch.

"Feelings?" she said. "Why would I think you actually have feelings?"

"You got me there." He checked his watch. "By the way, you wrapped up this case in about two and a half minutes. That's a new record, isn't it?"

"I didn't come here to wrap up the case."

His smile faded. "I know that, Kendra. I hear you've been visiting a lot of murder scenes lately."

"Not because I enjoy it."

"I know that, too."

She let the silence hang between them. "He'll be back, Lynch. We both know it."

"It's been four months."

"Colby's methodical. He's had years to plan his next move. What's another few months to him?" She was speaking only the truth. Colby was very patient. He was a serial killer who had murdered at least twenty people in various terrible ways before he and Kendra had come together that night in the gully. He had taken his time with all his victims and made sure their deaths were agonizing. "He's driven. He has to kill. He just has to do it his way."

Lynch's gaze slid away from her. "You've got a point."

"You don't believe me, do you?"

"I didn't say that."

"You don't need to. It's obvious you don't believe Colby is really still alive."

"If you believe it, I believe it."

She slammed her palms onto her car hood. "That's one of the most patronizing things anyone has ever said to me. And believe me, when I was blind, I heard a lot of patronizing things."

His gaze shifted back to her. "I mean it, Kendra," he said quietly. "I do trust your judgment."

"Even if the California Department of Corrections doesn't."

"Colby was their prisoner, and it was their responsibility to put him to death. For them to admit that they might have botched it and let a convicted serial killer escape, well, that's asking a lot."

"The prison's attending physician and his wife were found dead less than forty-eight hours later. I can't believe they still think that was a coincidence."

"It appeared to be an accident. And even you couldn't find any evidence to prove otherwise."

Kendra nodded. "Colby and his partner were too smart to leave behind any evidence. The doctor administered a drug to slow Colby's heart and pronounced him dead in front of a roomful of witnesses, and a rented hearse drove him right out of the main gates of San Quentin State Prison."

"If you could offer any proof of this, I guarantee you that a lot of people would listen.

"I tried." Her fists clenched in frustration. "No one cared."

"I cared, Kendra."

"To a point."

"You weren't able to get anywhere with the cremation service?"

"No. A body with the correct paperwork was delivered to them that night. The crematorium didn't fingerprint the body or do anything to confirm the corpse's identity. The system doesn't account for the fact that there are monsters out there who can drive to skid row and easily come out with a dead body no one will miss."

"Again, still no proof."

"Even you have to admit that there was enough to follow up on. Colby's partner, Myatt, had that medication they called the zombie drug in his possession, and he had the prison physician's name in his notebook. Before he died, he as much as told me Colby was still alive."

"He could have been taunting you. He had a history of that."

"That's what the FBI thinks." She shook her head wearily. "I thought you were on my side."

"I am. That's why I'm out here at four in the morning."

"So the FBI sent you to tell me to stop making waves and lay off—"

"No. For God's sake, I'm not the FBI's errand boy."

"Funny you should say that, when you're the go-to errand boy for any government agency that decides to pay your fee. Who is it this week? FBI, CIA, NSA?"

"None. This is all about you, Kendra."

"Is it?" She stared at him for a long moment. She'd gotten to know Lynch well during the course of their two previous cases together. So well that she'd found herself confused about how much was sexual attraction and how much was the stimulation of working with a tough, intelligent partner who managed to strike a rare note in her mind and soul. In this moment, she was feeling a little of both but principally she was aware of a new vibe from him. He was . . . truly concerned. Concerned about her. The surge of warmth she felt at the realization made her smile. "You didn't look this worried even when you thought a killer was stalking me."

"This may be worse. Colby has gotten under your skin. In your head. Are you still having the dreams?"

She looked away and didn't answer. He was the only one she'd told about her nightmares. He'd been there for her in those moments of weakness following Colby's supposed execution, when the nightmares had started.

"You've been having that dream for months . . . He pulls you back to that gully night after night. But it shouldn't be a nightmare. That's the night you caught the bastard. That's where you beat him, Kendra. Literally, I wish you'd killed him with that rock instead of fracturing his skull."

"I thought prison was the best place for him. I was wrong."

"Come back to my house. You'll feel safe there."

"I can't hide out in your suburban fortress for the rest of my life, Lynch. And if you remember, that's where those awful dreams began."

"Maybe that's where they can end."

"Besides, your Asian, bikini-model girlfriend might not like me hanging around."

"Ashley is almost never in town these days. Her career has taken off. She actually wants to meet you."

"I might say that she just wants to size up the competition, but women that beautiful don't really have competition."

Lynch stepped closer to her. "You're every bit as beautiful as she is, Kendra."

She looked up at him. His sudden closeness was disturbingly intimate.

Too disturbing, she admitted to herself. Damn him.

She made herself look away. "Now I know you're patronizing me. I don't have all that many fashion designers jetting me off to the French Riviera for photo shoots." She smiled. "I've seen her picture in a few magazines lately. Ashley has branched out from swimsuits to cocktail dresses and athletic wear."

"Enough about her," he said roughly. "You're the one I'm worried about."

"Don't be."

"Then stop this."

"Stop what?"

He waved his arm toward the crime scene. "This. Dropping everything and running at the first sign of a bloody corpse. There was a time that the cops and the FBI had to beg you to come help them out on their cases. Now they can't keep you away."

"I assure you that they make me feel very welcome," she said wryly.

"You know what I mean."

"You're damn right, I do." She stared him in the eye.

"It's because I know Colby will be back. He *needs* to kill. It's part of who he is. He can hide for only so long. When he resurfaces, I need to be there."

"And you will be. But for now, just let the cops and the FBI do their job. They're good at it. They have labs, worldwide databases, and lots of manpower. Trust them."

"How can I? When they don't even believe he's alive? They're not even looking for him."

"He may not even be in the country. You can visit every crime scene in the state, but it won't mean anything if he's killing people in Budapest."

Kendra leaned wearily against her car. "I know. I've been spending a lot of time combing the Web for any sign of him."

Lynch shook his head. "You need to take a step back. Please. This isn't good for you. God, you look tired."

"It's almost 4 A.M. Of course I look tired. You're the freak here for looking so damned chipper."

He slipped his hands into his pockets and shrugged. "Let's go to breakfast. Ever been to Brian's 24?"

She laughed. "I'm going to bed."

"That's even better." His smile was both intimate and mischievous. "Whatever you want, Kendra."

"By myself. In my own place."

"Okay, fine." He nodded toward the detectives, who were putting the husband in the backseat of a squad car. "But the next time you feel compelled to barge in on someone else's murder scene, give me a call."

"Why? So you can stop me?"

"I know better than that. So I can go with you. Which is a hell of a lot better than trailing after you." He turned and moved away. "Think about it. I always thought we made a pretty good team . . ."

* * *

THE SKY HAD BEGUN TO LIGHTEN BY the time Kendra made it back to her condo near the Gaslamp District. She was already wound up by the double punch of the crime scene and Lynch's unexpected appearance, but the sunlight's psychological effect would soon make it even more difficult for her to get any sleep. The first year she'd had her sight, she'd covered her bedroom windows with aluminum foil to keep the daylight from poking around her curtains and nudging her awake. She had moved beyond that, but once awake, it was still tough for her to go to sleep once it was light outside.

Might be time to invest in blackout curtains, or at least a jumbo roll of aluminum foil.

It would be more difficult to put Lynch out of her mind. How in the hell did he know she'd be there?

Of course he knew. He was Adam Lynch, and he had connections everywhere.

A light flashed on the phone in her living room, indicating a message had been received while she was gone. Between three thirty and four thirty in the morning. Probably someone from the crime scene she had just left. Or possibly her mother, who was presently at a conference in Amsterdam and frequently forgot to take into account the time difference.

She picked up the phone and checked the caller ID: Olancha Police Department.

Another murder scene? Olancha was over two hundred miles away; she hadn't cast her net that wide. She tried to remember if she even knew anyone on the force there.

No, she was sure she didn't.

And if there was an active scene, they had to know there was no way she could get there quickly. So why call in the middle of the night?

Kendra retrieved the voice mail, and there was only a brief message asking her to call Sergeant Hank Filardi at the Olancha PD at her earliest convenience.

She stared at the cordless phone in her hand.

No.

Lynch was right. She needed to step back. Whatever it was, it could wait a few hours while she tried to salvage what was left of this night.

She put down the phone.

Todos Santos, Mexico

VICTOR CHILDRESS

He stared at the name on the ID card he had just purchased. Victor Childress. Not a name he would have chosen for himself, but it would do.

He pocketed the passport and turned toward the pounding surf. He couldn't see the waves crashing on the dark beach though he could hear them. He took a deep breath. It should have been refreshing, but it wasn't. It was like inhaling salt and dirt.

He couldn't wait to leave this place.

Less than an hour from San Diego, yet a world away. A shit hole, to be sure, but it suited his purposes. No one knew him here, and no one would even think of looking for him. And after all those years in that prison, he needed the time to recharge his batteries and make preparations for his return.

It was time. Years of planning had finally led to this moment.

At his feet, a chunky Mexican man struggled to catch his breath as he rolled in a puddle of his own blood. The man's lungs had collapsed, and he would survive only another minute or so.

He pocketed his knife and took another look at the forged California driver's license, and then at the other items he'd been furnished. All the documents he'd ordered were superb. He slipped them into his pocket. The dying man had done magnificent work, but he couldn't be allowed to live. Things had progressed too far to be derailed by an overtalkative tradesman.

He stepped over the dying man and walked across the warm sand. The wind suddenly kicked up, as if heralding the start of his journey.

He felt a surge of exhilaration. It was all coming together.

The waiting was over.

Eric Colby smiled. "This is it, Kendra," he whispered. "Can you feel it? You will soon. This will be our masterpiece . . ."

CHAPTER
2

"DR. MICHAELS? KENDRA MICHAELS?"

Still groggy, Kendra sat up in bed and adjusted the phone against her ear. Had she been more awake, she probably wouldn't have picked up. She glanced at the clock. 7:25 A.M.

"Depends on who's asking?"

"Sergeant Hank Filardi, Olancha Police Department."

It took her a moment to make the connection. "Olancha . . . Right. You left a message on my phone."

"Yes, ma'am. I apologize for the calls, but I was wondering if you could help me out with something."

"I see. A homicide case? Is there something about the killer's M.O. that makes you think I would have special interest in—"

"No," he interrupted testily. "Dr. Michaels, we're quite capable of handling our own homicide cases here. We don't call on outsiders to—"

"Then why did you just wake me up?"

"I'm calling about a young woman named Beth Avery. Do you know her?"

"Beth." Kendra tensed. "Is she okay?"

"Is she a relative of yours?"

"Is she *okay*?" Kendra repeated harshly. "Answer me."

"She's fine. Is she a relative?"

"No." Kendra threw off the covers and stood up. "She's the sister of a friend. Eve Duncan. What's this about, Sergeant?"

"I wish to hell I knew." His voice was surly. "I have a Beth Avery in my jail, and I don't know what to do with her."

"*What?*"

"She's been in lockup since last night. She was arrested on assault and battery charges."

Kendra shook her head. This conversation was getting more surreal by the minute. "Repeat that . . . You think that *she . . .*"

"There were witnesses. It happened outside a bar called Blitzed just down the street from here. She worked a guy over pretty good."

"A guy? There has to be some kind of mistake. Beth Avery isn't much over middle height and she's not that strong. Besides, she's not a violent person."

"Tell that to the six-foot-two guy she put in the hospital."

"This is crazy."

"I agree. And what's crazier is that she could have posted bail and been out before midnight, but she's made no effort to do that or even make a phone call. She doesn't appear to be an indigent, and she drives a nicer car than I could ever hope to own."

Because Beth was a multimillionaire, and that car was

one of the few indulgences she'd allowed herself since she'd decided to stay here in California. *What in hell have you gotten yourself into, Beth?*

"Look," the sergeant continued gruffly. "I'm just trying to help her and get her out of our jail. She doesn't belong here. We tested her for drugs, and she's clean. Harley Gill, the guy she beat up, is a local and has a history of violence and misdemeanors. She seems like a nice woman, real friendly. I'd like to process her and send her on her way before he's released from the hospital and this escalates into something out of control."

"I second the motion. How did you find me?"

"I found your number in her phone under In Case of Emergency."

Kendra nodded. The last time she'd seen Beth, six months before, she'd grabbed the phone and typed in the number herself. They had spoken several times since then, and Beth always seemed happy and well.

"Okay. Can I speak to her?"

"She doesn't seem interested in talking to anyone. She said that she didn't want anyone to know she's here. I think she'd refuse to speak to you. You say you're friends with her sister?"

"Eve Duncan, but she lives in Georgia. She probably couldn't make it there before tonight." She paused. "And Beth wouldn't want Eve to know she's in trouble. Eve really wanted Beth to stay with her and let her take care of her."

"Not a bad idea," he said sourly. "Look, I don't know how you want to handle this. I can help you process bail for her, but I'm not sure if that's what she wants or will accept even if—"

"I'll come there," Kendra said quickly, before even

thinking it through. "I think I can be at your town a little after noon."

"Well, she could definitely use a friend even if she won't admit it. She's being held at the Inyo County Jail in Independence. You got a pen?"

Kendra jotted down the address and prisoner number. "Thanks, Sergeant." She hung up the phone.

She shook her head in bewilderment.

Beth Avery. In jail.

It was all wrong.

Beth had been illegally imprisoned for years by the corrupt director of a mental institution, and was only now beginning to taste the freedom that had been denied her for so long. Was it too much for her?

Possibly. Kendra remembered her own chaotic few years after she had first gained her sight. What she always referred to as her "wild days." A world of sights and colors had finally been revealed to her, along with more freedom and independence than she ever imagined possible. She'd worried her friends and family sick in her relentless pursuit of every variety of sensory stimulation she could soak in.

A few nights in jail had also been part of her own package, Kendra remembered. As much as she said she didn't regret anything in her wild days, she could have done without that particular experience. Or at least modified it a bit.

She picked up her phone and glanced through the calendar app. It was supposed to be a research day, compiling data for a music-therapy study she and a colleague at Tulane University were conducting.

It would have to wait.

Beth Avery needed her.

Inyo County Jail
12:30 P.M.

KENDRA SETTLED INTO THE tiny conference room, which usually hosted meetings between prisoners and their attorneys. The Inyo County Jail was located in the rural community of Independence, California, where miles of desert scrub brush collided improbably with a line of snowcapped mountains. She'd never had any reason to visit the place, and she doubted she ever would again.

The door swung open, and Beth Avery stepped into the room. She looked different than the last time Kendra had seen her. She liked the change. Beth was thinner than Kendra remembered her and wearing calf-high boots, jeans, and a blue plaid flannel shirt. But it was her demeanor that had undergone a transformation. Her color was high, and her blue eyes sparkled with energy. Despite her present situation, she was walking with a confident stride, altogether different from the hesitant gait she'd had after her release from the mental institution. Her shoulder-length dark hair flowed behind her with a healthy luster that had a vibrance of its own.

"Hi, Beth."

Beth froze in her tracks as she caught sight of Kendra. She shook her head emphatically. "No. Only in case of emergency . . ."

"It seemed like it might head that way." Kendra stood to give her a hug, but the guard gestured for her to back away.

"Does Eve know?" Beth asked.

"Not yet. I didn't want to worry her until I found out what you've gotten yourself into."

"*Then* you'll worry her."

"Probably."

"No, it's not necessary." She took a seat at the small table, and Kendra sat across from her. "I'm sorry they called you, Kendra. I really wish they hadn't."

"Beth . . . Why in the hell are you here?"

"I'm making a point."

"They're about to process you. The woman up front says you're about an hour away from getting a jumpsuit and joining the general jail population."

Beth smiled as she looked down at her clothes. "Maybe you should have waited. A bright orange jumpsuit would have been much more striking."

"I didn't come here for a fashion show. I'm here to help you."

"And I appreciate the effort, but I can help myself."

"Not in here you can't. What happened?"

Beth took a deep breath and looked away, as if deciding whether or not to tell her.

"Beth."

"Okay, I was at a bar in Olancha last night. A place called Blitzed. There were two UCLA girls there who were on their way to Tahoe. Nice kids. One of them stepped out to make a phone call, and I saw a scary-looking guy slip out a minute or so later. So I went out there just in time to see the asshole trying to force himself on her. I told him to stop, but he didn't." She shrugged. "So I made him stop."

"How exactly did you do that?"

"I put him down face-first into the parking lot," Beth said casually, as if it were an everyday occurrence.

Kendra nodded. "You drew a weapon on him?"

"No." Beth was clearly insulted by the suggestion. "I

used his weight against him. I dislocated his shoulder and most likely cracked a rib or two."

Kendra stared at her for a long moment. "Where in the hell did you learn to do that?"

"Bakersfield. I was there for a couple months, and I spent almost every day taking self-defense classes from this amazing older woman."

"You studied martial arts?"

"I studied everything that works. After all those years of feeling helpless in that mental hospital, I decided that I'm never going to let myself feel that way ever again. I'm still learning. I have a bunch of her videos on my iPad, and I practice every day."

Kendra could understand her need for independence. The staff of the hospital had orders to keep Beth weak and drugged, and they'd done it for the years she'd been kept there. Falsified reports and diagnoses by corrupt doctors and officials had assured that she remain almost in a zombie state. Now, free of those drugs, there was nothing in the least zombielike in her personality or vision of life. She'd taken control with a vengeance.

"I see." Kendra's lips turned up. "So you've become The Terminator."

Beth grinned. "Nah, I liked the way Linda Hamilton put all the bad guys down in those movies. She used brains and not superhuman brawn." Her smile faded. "The guy had it coming. That college kid was just there to have a good time, and he tried to make a victim of her."

"I don't doubt he had it coming. So what happened next?"

"The girls freaked out and hit the road. Bubba-Joe's friends came out of the bar and—"

"Bubba-Joe is the guy you put down?" She frowned. "That's not the name the police gave me."

"I didn't pay much attention to what the police called him. I was too busy arguing and trying to keep from being thrown into jail. He looked like a Bubba-Joe, so that's how I think of him."

"Gotcha."

"His friends came out, and it must have occurred to him how bad it looked to have his ass handed to him by little ol' me. So he made up this story about him enjoying a smoke outside and me attacking him from behind with a heavy metal beer sign. By the time the cops got there a minute or so later, his friends were claiming to have witnessed the whole thing, just the way he said it."

"Nice. And the UCLA girl was nowhere to be found."

"Exactly."

"You could have made bail, Beth. For God's sake, you're a wealthy woman. Besides your family money, I know you got a fortune in your settlement from that Seahaven mental health institution. When the state board found out about the corruption there and what they'd done to you, they couldn't recommend a high enough compensation in the courts."

"I don't want bail." Her jaw clenched. "I want to stay and fight. I want everyone to know what he did. And I want everyone to know I don't belong here."

Kendra could understand. As tough as Beth appeared to have become physically, she was still carrying emotional scars from her years as a prisoner. "We'll get you a good lawyer. The best. Put this behind you, and let's get out of here."

"Not yet, Kendra."

"Seriously?"

"I know I could make bail, get some super-duper lawyer, pay the guy's medical costs, and be done with it. I don't want to do that. I'm not paying him a dime. I'm going to stay here and get a good local attorney and maybe a private investigator. We can't let scum like that bully people."

"You can fight him from anywhere. You can hire an army of lawyers and investigators to make his life miserable forever. You don't have to stay here to do that."

"It will put more pressure on the locals to do the right thing. 'Wealthy heiress detained in small-town jail' will attract a lot more attention than 'Entitled Rich Bitch Victimizes Local Man.'"

"I have a third headline for you: 'Former Mental Patient Might Be Crazy After All.'"

"Very funny."

"I'm not trying to be funny. If Bubba got his hands on a sleazy lawyer, that's what they'd make people think."

Beth gave her a questioning glance. "Not people like you."

"Of course not. It's just . . ." Kendra struggled to find the words. "I told your sister I'd look after you. Eve would have loved for you to move to Georgia to be near her, but she understood that you needed your space. I thought the same thing. Now I'm thinking I didn't do a very good job."

"A good job looking after me? I don't need or want to be looked after. I had that all those years I was in the institution. I wanted freedom. I always knew you were there, Kendra, just a couple hours drive away. That's all I ever needed." She leaned forward in her chair, her gaze holding Kendra's. "The choice was never yours or Eve's. I just wanted to be on my own for a while. I thought you understood that."

"I do. When I got my sight, I didn't want anyone hovering over me for those first few years. I *wanted* you to have space, Beth. I think I understood that better than Eve. But

I know she wants to get to know you better. You were separated your entire lives until she found you."

"And I want to get to know her. But I want to be a complete person when we come together again. Not a victim.
A year ago at this time, we didn't even know each other
existed." She shook her head. "Hell, I *didn't* exist. I wasn't
me with all those drugs they forced down me. But the next
time I see Eve, I'll be complete with experiences and a personality that's totally my own. And I won't see her again
until that happens. That's why you mustn't tell her about
this. Do you understand?"

"Yes, I understand." She understood the passion and
the struggle that Beth was going through better than ever
before. She had thought that her own battle for independence and discovery were similar to Beth's, but that wasn't
true. Kendra's wild years were principally exploration.
Beth was also having to go through a painful element of
creation. "And I won't call Eve into this."

She gave a relieved sigh. "Thank you."

"But that doesn't mean you're not stuck with me."

"I don't need you to—" She stopped as she saw Kendra's
expression. "You're not going to give up, are you?"

"It won't be painful if you'll just work with me. Let's
look at the situation. You're a guest of the Inyo County Jail.
We both know I'm not going to abandon you. But it will
be a real drag to have to stay here at this jail and hold your
hand. I have a life, you know."

"I believe I've heard rumors to that effect."

"Then I have to satisfy your idealistic goals in order to
get on with it. I promise that I'll do that." She looked her
in the eye. "But first you have to let me bail you out." She
held up her hand as Beth opened her lips to protest. "I
know. I know. But trust me. Before we leave town, I'll find

this guy—your Bubba Joe—and see what I can do for you."

"Like what?"

"I'm not sure. I have a few ideas, but I may have to change with the situation. That's where the trust comes in."

"That's not very reassuring."

"Trust me," she said again.

Beth gazed at her for long moment. "I do trust you." She suddenly smiled impishly. "And if you don't get me what I need from Bubba, I can always do some more damage to him and end up right back in jail."

"Yes, that's always an option." She smiled. "But you'd better start thinking of him as Harley Gill and not Bubba if we have to deal with him."

"I like my name for him better. You know, it might be fun working this out with you."

"Another experience?" She shook her head. "Where can I find him?"

Beth tilted her head, thinking. "I have a pretty good idea . . ."

Highway 395
Olancha, California

AFTER A HEFTY STACK OF PAPERWORK and the transfer of $2,500 in bail money, Beth and Kendra made their way to what passed for Main Street Olancha—a gas station, a bar, a diner, and a fresh beef jerky stand, all on the same side of a lonely stretch of two-lane highway. As Kendra stood and took in the scene, a tumbleweed literally blew across the road.

"What *ever* made you come here?" Kendra asked.

Beth shrugged. "I've been to lots of places like this in the past few months. Big cities still kind of freak me out. For now, I'm comfortable in places where you see the same people every day."

"Until you move on to the next town?"

"Well, I don't want to get too comfortable. But I've met a lot of nice people along the way."

"And at least one rotten one." Kendra nodded to the bar ahead, identified by the faded, sand-blasted sign that read BLITZED.

Beth suddenly slowed her pace. "Yes. But I'm not going to be a victim anymore. I can take care of myself."

"You've already proved that. But part of taking care of yourself is knowing when to let people help you. It took me a while to learn that one."

"You've already helped me, Kendra. You and Eve both. I don't know what I would have done if you hadn't—" She stopped dead in her tracks. "That's him."

Kendra looked ahead to see a beefy man wearing a Transformers T-shirt that didn't quite cover his bandaged torso. A black extension sling held his arm at an awkward angle before him, and he had a massive bruise over his right eye that resembled a patch. He stood next to the bar's front door, smoking a cigarette.

Kendra squinted. "Did you give him that black eye, too?"

"Oh, yeah. I forgot about that."

"Jeez, Beth. You *are* The Terminator."

The man's sunburned face practically turned white when he saw Beth. He dropped his cigarette and stepped back. "Stay away from me."

Kendra smiled. "We're just taking a walk, Harley. Care to join us?"

His gaze was still on Beth. "No."

"Too bad," Kendra said. "Nice day."

Beth nodded. "Beautiful."

Harley glared at Beth. "I'm pressing charges against you, bitch."

"Oh?" Beth said. "And I thought I spent the night in jail for the turndown service and exquisite cuisine."

"Just keep sassin' me. You'll see where that'll get you."

Beth stepped toward him, and he instinctively recoiled so quickly that he nearly stumbled. He winced in pain.

"I'd be less worried about her and more concerned about yourself," Kendra said.

"Why's that?"

"Because you lied to a police officer. And your friends did, too. And if this goes to trial, are you willing to per- jure yourselves?"

"Oh, it's going to trial. And it's her word against all of ours."

"Not just her word," Kendra said.

"What do you mean?"

She pointed to the roofline of a defunct, graffiti-ridden Laundromat next to the bar. A small security camera was aimed toward the sidewalk. "These days there are eyes everywhere."

"What . . ." He took a few tentative steps toward the camera, as if it were a bomb that could go off at any moment.

"Yeah, I talked to the building owner this morning," Kendra said. "I guess he got tired of vandals, so he put this camera up a few weeks ago." She reached into the pocket of her jeans and produced a USB flash drive. "I got video of the whole thing. You attacking that college girl and Beth here kicking your ass all over the sidewalk. Once your friends know we have this, do you really think they'll stick to their stories?"

Harley stared at the flash drive in her outstretched hand. He moved toward it, but Beth menacingly blocked his path. Kendra fought the urge to either laugh or shake her head in amazement at this slender young woman getting away with threatening a man who easily had a hundred pounds on her.

Harley glared at Kendra. "And who in the hell are you? Her lawyer?"

"Never mind who I am. All that matters is that I'm holding an HD video file that makes you look pretty damn ridiculous. We all know this woman didn't sneak up from behind you with a pole sign. She came right up into your face with nothing but her bare hands. Not only will your buddies run for the hills when this surfaces, they'll know that this sweet young thing mopped up the sidewalk with you. Is that really something you want them to see?"

Harley looked like a deer caught in the headlights.

Kendra rolled the tiny USB stick across her open palm. "And it's not just your buddies who are going to be laughing their asses off. I've already uploaded this to my YouTube account, and I set it to go live in a little less than two hours from now. Then the whole world will see what happened out here last night. But if you're cool with that . . ."

"You *bitch*."

She ignored him. "It's just the kind of thing that could go viral, don't you think? A big, beefy bully getting pounded into the sidewalk by a cute little woman. I'm sure that every evening news program in the country will pick it up to show right before the last commercial break. You'll be famous, but not the kind of fame you'll like."

His face was now the color of a radish. He gathered himself as if he was about to lunge at Kendra.

But Beth wagged her finger at him. "Careful, Harley." She pointed back at the camera. "You have an audience."

"Shit." His hands clenched into fists at his sides. "What do you want?"

"I want to get the hell out of here and never lay eyes on you again," Kendra said. "And that's what Beth feels, too. So we're going to hit the road." She checked her watch. "But in the next hour and forty-nine minutes. I want to hear that you called the Inyo Country Sheriff's Department and told them that you had too much to drink last night and were confused and Beth Avery is completely innocent. You'll tell them that you're not pressing charges and would like to put this behind you. You want it so badly that you're going to furnish them with a signed written statement to that effect and drop it off with Sergeant Filardi. If I get that call from the Sheriff's Department, I'll take the file off my YouTube account before a single person sees it."

He pointed to the USB stick in her hand. "What about that video?"

"We keep the video." Kendra smiled. "Maybe we'll pull it out once in a while on girl's night out when we're looking for a good laugh after a few glasses of wine. But other than that, no one will see it."

"How do I know you'll keep your word?"

Beth shook her head. "I have no special desire to be known all over the world as 'that girl who beat up the redneck dumbass.' Why would I? It would just get in my way. Sure I'd do anything I had to do to show you that you can't get away with this kind of bullying. But if I win the battle, all I'll want to do is turn my back on you."

Kendra shrugged. "I'd actually love to see *The Today Show* gang giggling over it some morning next week, but the ball's in your court." She glanced at Harley, who was glowering at them. "Personally, I hope that Harley is stupid enough to fumble around and blow it." She tapped her watch as she and Beth turned and headed back to her car. "Tick-tock, Harley."

KENDRA AND BETH HAD JUST RETRIEVED Beth's car, a silver Mercedes SLS AMG roadster, from the impound lot when a call came to Beth's mobile phone from Sergeant Filardi at the Sheriff's Department. Beth put the caller on speaker.

"Harley Gill is dropping all charges. He just came by with a written statement," the officer said. "Mind telling me what you said to him?"

"Nothing much," Beth said. "Just a little commonsense wisdom."

"Ma'am, I've known Harley most of his life, and 'common sense' and 'wisdom' are two things that aren't usually mentioned in the same sentence as that guy."

"Well, in the cold light of day, I think he realized it wouldn't be too good for his rep for people to know that he'd been beaten up by a woman half his size."

"That I can believe. In any event, the case is now closed. Have a good day, ma'am."

Beth cut the connection.

"You didn't mention the video," Kendra said.

Beth's eyes narrowed on her. "Well, I didn't think it was a good idea to lie to a cop. Which is what I would have been doing, right?"

Kendra smiled. "Would you?"

"I may not have your powers of observation, Kendra . . . But I'm pretty sure that camera wasn't there last night."

Kendra feigned a look of total innocence. "Really? Hmm. I guess you were too busy pounding that guy's face into the ground to notice."

"Kendra . . ."

"Fine." Kendra shrugged. "I might have dug an old webcam out of my closet before I left home in case I needed it. And I might have stuck it under the roofline with some double-sided tape."

"When?"

"Just a little while ago, on my way to the jail to see you. I wanted to take a look at the scene before I got your story."

"You did more than take a look."

"I know you. I knew you weren't guilty. I thought it wouldn't hurt to be prepared if push came to shove." She made a face. "No big deal. If it wasn't necessary, all I'd have lost was an old camera that hadn't worked in years."

"Well, I'd say it worked pretty well just now."

"I guess it did. Most bullies don't like to broadcast it when they get pummeled by one of their victims."

Beth pointed to Kendra's pocket, where the USB stick still bulged. "And what was on the memory stick?"

"Data for my music-therapy study. Good thing I didn't have to show it to him. I might have bored the guy to death."

Beth threw back her head and laughed. "Good thing."

"You won't have to worry about him anymore. As long as you leave town, I think he'll be happy to forget about the whole thing."

"That makes two of us." She paused. "After you tell me how you managed to play Bubba so cleverly. I was watching you and you were able to meet his every response almost before he made it."

She glanced away. "You described him. He wasn't hard to analyze."

"Kendra."

"He was the easiest mark imaginable." She looked back at Beth. "Nicholas Marlin would have considered him totally unworthy of using him."

"Mark?" Beth's eyes were suddenly eager. "And who's Nicholas Marlin?"

"Someone I knew from my unsavory past. A friend of a friend." She sighed. "He was a con artist. He was fairly despicable, but I learned a lot by watching him. He was truly amazing. He could read things about his marks that were totally incredible just by observing body language and facial expression."

"Then I can see how that would be useful to you."

"It was. My other senses were honed, but my visual acuity had to be sharpened. I had to know what I was seeing. I learned a lot. Not all of it good. It's incredible how the human mind can be manipulated if you study just how to push the buttons." Her lips tightened. "In the end, I tried to forget him and the more sinister aspects of what I'd learned by watching him."

"Sinister?"

"Drop it." She smiled with an effort. "And forget it as I've done. Except when I need to pull something out of the hat as I did with Harley."

"Interesting. But then you're always interesting."

"Forget about me," Kendra said firmly. "We obviously have some catching up to do. What have you been doing with yourself, besides morphing into a one-woman army?"

Beth tilted her head. "Why don't you tell me?"

"What?"

"Come on, Kendra. You don't have to pretend with me."

"What do you mean?"

"You can probably tell more about me and what I've been doing than I could myself."

"That's ridiculous. I'm not psychic."

"You're better than psychic. You're *real*. I knew it before, and after today, it's more clear than ever." She grinned. "Come on. You start, and I'll fill in the blanks. If there are any."

"I told you, I tried to forget about that con artist for a reason. Now you're trying to—"

"Except when you choose to use what you learned. Choose it now. Heck, there's nothing sinister about me. I just want to see what you can do."

No, there was nothing sinister or dangerous about Beth, but she could be damnably persistent. "I don't know what you think I can possibly—"

"Please? Spill it."

Get it over with.

"Okay. Well, I know you've been all over the northern half of the state in just the past couple of weeks. You've been in Bear Valley in Colusa, all the way up to northern California, where you spent some time at the Yurok Tribe reservation."

Beth's eyes widened. "Wow. Keep going."

"Somewhere in there, you tried rock climbing, maybe a bit of rappelling in Yosemite?"

"Castle Rock."

"You drove back on the coastal route. You saw Seahaven. It must have been strange seeing the place that holds many horrible memories for you. Did you actually drive onto the grounds?"

Beth nodded. Her eyes were suddenly glistening, and Kendra could see the tough veneer she tried to assume softening. "As close as I could get. I couldn't resist going back. It was . . . drawing me. It's closed now, and the gates were all locked. It's actually very beautiful. I never saw much of the outside when I was there."

"Their license was revoked. I don't know what's going to happen to the place."

Her face tightened. "Good. The sooner it's gone, the better."

"I agree." It was better to change the subject. "You spent some time at or near the beach before cutting across to this part of the state. You made the drive just yesterday."

"Very good. See, I didn't have to tell you anything."

"It's nothing. I still don't know how you've been thinking and feeling about your new life. I know it's been an amazing time for you."

"It has. Mostly good, but not all." She waved her hands in a "let me have it" motion. "Okay, how the hell did you know all that? Start with the Indian reservation."

"Your shampoo is very fragrant. A mixture of yucca, soap root, and a bit of vinegar. Only the Yurok tribe makes it quite that way, and they sell it on their reservations."

"You're an expert on every shampoo out there?"

"No. Most Americans use one of six shampoos. Anytime I've gotten a whiff of one that smells as unique as yours, I've made it a point to ask what it was. When you can't see, how a person smells becomes very important. It's a big part of that first impression."

"But you just reeled off my entire route. I know my shampoo didn't tell you that."

"It didn't. Your car did."

"I already thought of that." Beth turned back toward her Mercedes. "There are no brochures, no tacky bumper stickers, nothing that could possibly tell you where I've been."

"Your front grill and headlights tell me pretty much everything I need to know."

Beth crouched in front of her car. "There's nothing here but a whole mess of squashed bugs. Unless you're telling me . . ." She looked up at Kendra. "Really?"

"Even if you're not into bugs, it's pretty easy to spot the phosphorous yellow-green splat of fireflies on the front of your car. I've never seen fireflies this far south. It tells me you've been to a cooler, wetter area. Northern California has them. It also has the biggest Yurok reservation in the entire country, up in Humboldt County."

"That's the place."

Kendra rubbed her hand over the hood and showed Beth the yellow and pinkish dust on her hand. "Pollen from both California poppies and creamcups."

"You can tell that from just looking?

"And from smelling." Kendra held her hand up to her nose. "Although the pollen starts losing its scent as soon as it separates from the flowers. The time of year also makes it easier to zero in on them. Plus, I see that your boots are stained from what I suspect were adobe lilies. One place nearby that all three are found in large numbers is the Bear Valley Wildflower Meadows."

"Very good. You've been there?"

"Many times, but not since I've been able to see. My mom used to take me there and to the fields in Antelope Valley when the poppies were in bloom. Such amazing smells . . . It's like fireworks to a blind person."

"And I did try rappelling." She held up her hands. "My

fingers took a beating, but that could have been from any one of a number of causes."

"Not really. The back of your fingers are sunburned from just above the knuckle. You were obviously wearing climbing gloves. Your fingers are cut and bruised in a way that suggests that you were pulling yourself up by some jagged rocks. And the palm of each hand has a faint lateral burn just about where you would grip the rope. Even though there was a glove between the rope and your hand, heat from the rope's friction was enough to leave a mark."

"It's an exhilarating sport. I can't wait to do it again."

Kendra smiled. "Take me with you when you do. I'd love to try it."

"Well, that brings me almost all the way back here. Except how you knew about the coastal route and my visit to Seahaven."

"The squashed bugs again. There are some fairly fresh kelp flies splattered on your headlights and front license plate. Those are found along the coast. The few splotches of fresh seagull excrement on your car helped confirm it. And since you took the coastal route back, there's no way you wouldn't have at least seen your old hospital since it looms over the highway."

"Just as it loomed over my life," she said moodily. Her smile was forced. "Impressive as always, Kendra. As usual, you've met the challenge." She glanced back at her car. "And most of all, you've shown me that I really need to find a car wash. First order of business."

"What are your plans? After the car wash, of course."

"I'm not sure." Beth glanced up the long highway. "I met some people who live in Fresno. I think maybe I'll go there."

"You also know someone who lives in San Diego."

Beth looked away and shifted uncomfortably. "I've been meaning to visit you, Kendra. I really have."

"Then come back with me."

"Now?"

"Why not?"

"I'm not sure . . . that I'm ready."

"You don't have to stay with me though you're welcome to. If you still think you need some space, we'll set you up in a spectacular hotel. Or if you're more comfortable in some fleabag, San Diego has those, too."

Beth made a face. "Whoa. I may have spent some time in some less than desirable places lately, but that doesn't mean I still don't appreciate the finer things in life."

"A nice bayside hotel will work, then." She put her hand on Beth's arm. "No pressure. If you want to spend some more time on the road by yourself, I understand. Trust me, I've been there."

Beth thought about it for a moment. "I'll tell you what. I'll start following you back. If I decide to peel off between here and there, no offense. Okay?"

Kendra watched her as she moved around to the driver's door and unlocked it with her key fob. She understood. Just one more way of clinging to the control that had been stolen from her so long ago. "Sure, Beth. No offense."

EVEN WITH HEAVY TRAFFIC ON the I-5 freeway, Kendra and Beth arrived at Kendra's condo less than three hours later. As Kendra opened the building's front door, she smiled back over her shoulder. "I thought I was going to lose you in San Clemente."

"I thought about stopping there . . . But not today."

"I'm glad. We'll have fun here, for however long you can stay. If you're up to it, I'd love for you to meet some friends of mine. One of them lives right here in the building."

"Sounds great."

They took the elevator up to Kendra's floor, and as they approached the unit, Kendra saw a business card wedged in the doorjam. Kendra took the card and glanced at it.

"Let me guess," Beth said. "A maid service. A pest-control company. A cute guy down the hall who wants to take you to dinner."

"No. It's from an online journalist. Sheila Hunter, a writer from The Kinsley Chronicle."

"I read that on my iPad every morning. Good reporting, once you get past all the celebrity stuff."

Kendra turned the card over, where a brief message had been scrawled.

She froze.

Beth leaned closer. "Are you okay?"

Kendra's mouth went dry, and she could feel her heart pounding. "I—I need to call her. Right away." Her hand shook as she unlocked the door.

"Kendra, what's wrong?"

"I'm sorry, I just—" She turned to Beth. "I'll explain. But first I need to—"

"Make your call," Beth finished. "Sure. Do you want me to wait out here?"

"No. Come in."

Kendra pushed open the door, already punching the number on her mobile phone.

The reporter answered on the first ring. "Sheila Hunter."

"This is Kendra Michaels. I just got your card." She

drew a deep breath. "Is what you wrote on the back of that card true?"

"Dr. Michaels, thanks for getting back to me. I'd like to meet with you and ask some questions about—"

"Never mind that. *Is it true*?"

Sheila was silent, then answered, "Yes. It's true. I have proof that Eric Colby is still alive."

Kendra felt her chest tighten. "You're not lying? You're not just trying to get some story?"

"I don't lie. I'm a reputable journalist. Of course, I'm trying to get a story, but Eric Colby *is* the story. If you'll meet me at the rooftop at the W Hotel in an hour, I'll prove it to you."

"I'll be there." She hung up.

Her heart was beating hard, her hands were cold. She was excited, and yet it was a strange, chilling excitement. Close. Was she close at last?

"Kendra?"

She'd almost forgotten that Beth was standing there. She smiled with an effort as she turned to face her. "Sorry." She moistened her lips. "I'm going to have to go out for a while. Something is . . . happening."

"And it's not good. You look like you've seen a ghost." She took a step closer. "How can I help?"

"It may be good. It might be bullshit. I don't know yet." But that remark about seeing a ghost struck Kendra to the soul. It was too close to the truth about the call she'd just received about Colby. "I won't know until I meet with this Sheila Hunter. She has the information. I'll try to be back as soon as possible."

Beth shook her head. "You're upset. You're one tough woman, and this isn't like you. I'm not going to let you go by yourself. I won't interfere, but I'm going to be there for you."

"I don't need you to be there for me. I just have to talk to this woman."

"You talked to her for two minutes, and your hand was shaking when you hung up," Beth said quietly. "I'm going."

"I was just surprised. I don't need you."

"Just like I didn't need you when I was in that jail cell. I've not had much experience with friendship, but I thought it went both ways." She paused. "Unless you're regarding me as a duty and not a friend."

Dammit, Kendra thought helplessly, the last thing she wanted was to involve Beth or anyone else she cared about in this hunt for Colby, even in this small way. But she couldn't reject Beth or make her feel she was less than a full person. She'd had to go through too much of that in that mental hospital.

"Okay." Beth started to turn away. "I guess I was wrong about this. You don't want or need my help. I'd probably just be in the way."

"I didn't say that."

"No, but it was implied. Look, you're too busy to bother with me right now. It's okay, I understand. I'll just go to Fresno as I planned." She smiled faintly. "If you need me, just give me a call." She headed for the door. "And like it or not, I'll be here for you."

Kendra could have stood whining or arguments. She couldn't take the dignity and graciousness. And she couldn't take the idea of Beth's driving out of town when she'd just made this fragile contact with her again. "Don't you pull that on me," Kendra said. "In case you didn't know, people try to protect their friends, and that's what I was doing." She smiled. "But I wasn't being fair to you by not letting you do the same. So let's get out of here and get a drink at that bar before we meet the reporter. I think I could use one."

CHAPTER
3

KENDRA GLANCED UNEASILY AROUND the rooftop bar at the W Hotel just a few blocks from her condo. Decorated with a tall, bonfire-themed fire feature, beach chairs, and several tons of sand, the whimsical nature of the area couldn't have been more out of tune with Kendra's edgy mood.

Beth came back to the table with a glass of cabernet for Kendra and a tall green concoction for herself. "Here we go. Though you obviously could use something stronger."

"What's that?" Kendra nodded toward Beth's drink.

"It's something I invented myself. I call it the Angry Leprechaun. It's mostly Midori, with Frangelica and a kick of spicy rum." She shrugged. "I spent a few weeks tending bar in Mammoth Lakes."

"I see."

Beth sat down. "You've been seriously freaked ever since you talked to that reporter we're meeting. Are you going to tell me why?"

Kendra sipped her drink and looked away. "It goes back to my first criminal investigation. I helped catch a serial killer named Eric Colby." She paused. "He's the most terrifying man I've ever known."

Beth wrinkled her brow. "But he was executed a few months ago, right? I couldn't turn on a TV or go onto the Web without seeing his face."

"He was officially put to death by lethal injection in front of a roomful of witnesses. But I don't think it really happened. We know he was working with another killer on the outside. I think this man might have kidnapped the prison physician's wife and pressured him to administer a drug to simulate Colby's death. The doctor and his wife were found dead in their car in the Angeles National Forest a few days later."

"Murdered?"

"It was ruled an accident. I went to the site myself, and the scene had already been so trampled by cops and rescue workers that I couldn't prove otherwise. It hadn't been protected as a crime scene."

"Incredible."

"It would be if I could prove any of this. He was supposedly cremated that very night, but I also have doubts about that. I've been searching for some sign of Colby ever since, but he still hasn't resurfaced."

"And this reporter thinks she has the proof you've been looking for?"

"That's what she says." Kendra shook her head. "I've been here skimming some of her other investigative pieces on my phone, and she looks like the real deal."

"I take that as a compliment, Dr. Michaels." The voice was brusque but pleasant and came from behind them. They turned to see a slender woman wearing a dark blue suit. She was attractive, with large brown eyes and shoulder-length brown hair. She extended her hand. "Sheila Hunter."

"Kendra." Kendra shook hands and motioned toward Beth. "This is my friend, Beth Avery."

Sheila gave Beth an awkward glance. "I see. What I'm here to tell you is extremely confidential. I'm only prepared to discuss it with you alone."

Beth moved to stand up, but Kendra motioned her to stay. "Ms. Hunter, I understand, but anything you want to talk to me about you can also say in front of my friend. I assure you that she will keep it entirely confidential."

Sheila didn't look happy to be thrown a curve. "I'm sure your friend is trustworthy, but in my business, information is currency. And the more people who have the information before I can publish my stories, the less valuable it is to me."

"Beth has no interest in scooping you. Please sit down and let's talk."

Sheila looked searchingly at both of them for a long moment, then finally joined them at the table. "Very well. I'm going to trust you to make sure there's no leak, Dr. Michaels. Thank you for meeting with me."

"Kendra, please."

"Kendra . . . I have some law-enforcement sources who have told me about a theory you have. A theory that Eric Colby is still alive."

"Now it's my turn to be concerned. Not that I expected it to stay a secret. I thought that the more people who knew there was a possibility, the more chance I had of catching the bastard."

"So it's true. You don't believe Colby was really executed."

"I don't. Even though our state penal system and forty witnesses will tell you different."

"It so happens that I was one of those witnesses," she said quietly. "I was in the observation room at San Quentin that night."

Kendra's brows rose in surprise. "Then you won the lottery. Journalists all over the world were vying for those tickets. I think it was easier to win the Powerball than to get into that witness chamber."

"Won isn't the right word." Sheila drew her arms close, almost in a defensive position. "I still think about that night."

Kendra nodded. "It's not easy to watch a man die."

"Oh, it wasn't that. It wasn't that at all."

"What was it?" Beth asked, obviously drawn from silence by Sheila's sudden wave of emotion.

"It was Colby." She drew a deep breath. "I'd seen pictures and courtroom footage, but nothing could compare with actually seeing him in the flesh. Those dark eyes, his thin lips . . . It was chilling. Everyone in that room could feel it. I tried to communicate that sickening chill in my story, but I know I failed miserably."

"Words were empty where Colby was concerned. You had to experience him," Kendra said. "No one has ever frightened me more. He knows exactly how to push the buttons of anyone with whom he comes in contact."

"Well, you would know. You're the only one to face off against him and survive."

"He was toying with me. It was a game to him. He was still trying to involve me in his game right up until his execution day."

"And you believe he still might be doing it."

"He'll never stop. Sooner or later, he's going to show

himself. He'll find some way to prove to me that he hasn't been beaten."

Sheila raised a file folder from the handbag on her lap. "I think he already has."

Kendra went still. "What is that?"

"You tell me." She placed the folder on the table in front of Kendra and opened it.

Kendra leaned over it to examine the folder's contents; half a dozen color-photo printouts, detailing a crime scene that looked vaguely familiar to her. There were two bloody corpses, a man and a woman, sprawled across a large bedroom featuring floor-to-ceiling windows overlooking the ocean.

"Redondo Beach, six weeks ago?" Kendra said.

"Yes," Sheila said in surprise. "You were there?"

"No, but I read the report and saw some of the crime-scene shots. But it didn't look quite like this."

"What was different? Can you tell me?"

Kendra turned the photos around in her hands, examining them from different angles. "Hmmm. I glanced at the materials a few weeks ago, but there's something about these that—"

She froze.

It couldn't be.

But, dear God, she was afraid it was.

"Kendra?" Beth said.

"The corpses," Kendra whispered. "They're positioned differently than they were in the crime-scene shots I saw."

Sheila nodded.

"They were posed?" Beth asked.

"It's more than that." Kendra's stomach churned as she studied the body positions. "These are military ground-force arm-and-hand signals."

"Remind you of anyone?" Sheila said.

"Colby." The battery-acid taste returned to her mouth as she spoke his name. "He decapitated his victims and positioned them to give us messages and taunt us. Some of the later ones even gave clues where and when his next victims would be killed."

"Positioned . . . like this?" Beth asked.

"Yes." Kendra pointed to the arrangement of the corpses' arms. "Look. The woman's right arm is raised over her head, palm out, elbow bent at a thirty-degree angle. That's the ground-force call for attention."

Beth looked queasy. "His message to the agents investigating the case?"

"That's what it meant last time. As the case went on, the messages were directed more at me."

Beth pointed to a male corpse with his right arm extended in front of him, hand tilted back. "What does that mean?"

Sheila answered the question. "It's the sign for 'Are you ready'?"

Kendra looked up at her. "That's right. These hand signals were definitely Colby's M.O. Where did you get these pictures?"

"I have a source."

"I have sources, too," Kendra said. "Very well placed ones. And the photos I saw of the scene didn't look like this."

"It's because you saw the official crime-scene photos."

Beth was gazing in bewilderment between the two women. "Are you saying that the officers on the scene were trying to hide the fact that these bodies might have been Colby's victims? That they might have actually repositioned them before taking the official crime-scene photos?"

"I don't know," Sheila said. "What do you think, Kendra?"

Kendra stared at the photos for a long moment before glancing up. "I don't understand this. Why would anyone want to hide actual proof?"

"I've been wondering the same thing. My investigation led me to you and the suspicions you've been tossing about." Sheila gathered the photo printouts and placed them back into her folder. "No one else is willing to even entertain the idea that Colby is still alive."

"I'd like copies of those."

"That's not possible."

"Sure it is. Slide those over to me. I won't tell anyone where I got them."

Sheila pulled the folder closer to her. "It's not me I'm worried about. I have to protect my source."

"To hell with your source. There's a killer out there."

"Yes, and that's why my source took such a risk to give me these. But I can't let them out of my possession or even let anyone else see them. I had to get permission to show them to you."

"Permission from whom?"

"Really, Kendra, you should realize I wouldn't be at liberty to say. But in light of your suspicions about Colby, I thought you should know about these. I'd appreciate it if you wouldn't mention these to anyone else at this point."

Kendra stared with frustration at the folder, considering the prospect of grabbing it and running like hell to the elevator. Sheila tightened her grasp and lowered it to her lap, almost as if she'd read her mind.

Damn.

"Fine," Kendra said. "No, it's not fine. I won't mention

your name, but I won't guarantee I won't tell anyone that this cover-up exists."

"I wish you wouldn't." She shrugged. "But I always understood the risk I was running by contacting you."

"Tell your source I want to meet with him. Or her."

"I really don't think—"

"Just ask," Kendra interrupted. "Get me a face-to-face meeting, and I'll take it from there."

Sheila shrugged. "Okay, I'll ask. But I want something in return for all this. I need all the background on this case from your angle and your reasons for believing Colby is still alive." She glanced at Beth. "And I want your word that your friend here isn't going to—"

"Ask me for my word," Beth said quietly. She had been listening with obvious fascination by the battle of wills between the two women. "Kendra is my friend, not my custodian."

"Custodian," Sheila repeated. "A strange choice of words."

"I'm not a writer like you. But I know about custodians," Beth said. "But you have my promise that I won't reveal anything I've heard here today as long as my silence won't hurt Kendra."

"That's good enough for me." Sheila turned back to Kendra. "Well, will you give me the details?"

Kendra slowly nodded. "Fair enough, Sheila. But you might want to get yourself a strong drink first."

HALF AN HOUR LATER, KENDRA and Beth were walking back to the condo. Kendra was so lost in thought that she realized she hadn't said a word during most of the ten-minute journey home. She looked up at Beth. "Sorry. Rotten host I'm turning out to be, huh?"

"Not at all," Beth said. "I'd have to be crazy to think you'd bounce right back and be chatty after having to re-live your experiences with that monster." She shivered. "I needed a little time to recover myself."

"I didn't want to expose you to Colby." Kendra shook her head. "You know, Colby grew up as a child of privi-lege, with all the advantages in life. He studied metallurgy at MIT, and by all accounts, he was brilliant in his field. He was always a loner, though. No friends, no romantic relationships as far as we can tell. There's no evidence that he ever hurt anyone until he was in his thirties, but then something seemed to snap. He killed over twenty people in just a few months. No regrets. No excuses. It was as if the monster he'd kept hidden all those years had suddenly broken free." Her lips tightened. "And is still free; it's ter-rifying that he's still out there."

"This time I hope you're wrong, Kendra. I hope he's dead."

"I'm not wrong."

"And you're trying to save the world from him." She walked in silence for a few moments. "I'm starting to re-alize just how much I've been missing out. You and my sister lead incredibly interesting lives. While I've been on the road looking for adventure, this is where the real ex-citement has been."

"I don't know," Kendra said dryly. "Beating up that beefy redneck must have been pretty exciting."

"That was nothing. This is life and death. I always thought you should do this full-time."

Kendra snorted. "Me, a full-fledged FBI agent? It would never work."

"Sure it would. I know how much you're in demand. Eve told me that the FBI and various police departments are falling all over themselves to get you to consult for them."

"But I get to say no, which is exactly what I do 95 percent of the time. I wouldn't have that option if I were their employee. Besides, I love my music-therapy work. It's what I live for."

"But wouldn't you rather be saving lives?"

"I like to think that my music-therapy work makes life worth living for some people." Kendra glanced over and smiled at Beth's skeptical expression. "I don't expect you to understand, but during all those years I was blind, music is what gave my world color. It was something I could share with everyone else . . . A way to connect."

"So your patients are blind?"

"No, almost none of them have been. The blind usually don't need me. A fair number of the people I help are autistic and quite a few have been senior adults suffering from dementia. People who have difficulty connecting with the world around them. It's still an emerging field, but we've had success using music to draw them out. It actually helps them make emotional and intellectual connections that language, for whatever reason, can't make for them. When it works, there isn't a better feeling in the world."

Beth stopped as they reached the front of Kendra's building. "I didn't mean to sound cynical, but I spent a lot of time in that institution, where so-called therapists did nothing but hurt me. I'm glad there are people out there like you. People who really care."

"Trust me, Beth. There are a lot of people who care." She hesitated before continuing. "And while we're on the subject . . . Have you talked to anybody about what happened to you at Seahaven?"

"Talked to anybody . . . like a therapist?"

Kendra nodded.

Beth laughed. "You're kidding, right? I've heard that a few times since I got out, but I never expected to hear it from you. I thought you understood me."

"I do. It's just that . . . You've been through hell. You can't just shrug off an experience like that. It could sneak up behind you and ambush you."

"Believe me, I'm not pretending it didn't exist. I'm still working through it. As crazy as it sounds, there are days I wish I was back in that institution, medicated out of my mind. Sometimes it's easier to not feel anything than to face real life."

"But have you actually even started to face real life? It doesn't seem like you have. At least not yet."

Beth looked away for a long moment. "I'm facing it as much as I can right now. Okay? I need to ease back into things."

"Sure. Just remember that there are people in the world who have your back. People you can trust."

Beth smiled. "I remember. Thank you, Kendra."

"I just wanted you to know." She stopped and took the condo keys off their ring and handed them to her. "I hate to do this, but I need to leave you for an hour or so."

"You're ditching me?"

"I need to talk to the head of the local FBI field office."

"Now?"

"Yes, I texted him while we were still sitting there with Sheila. I don't think he's very happy with me right now, but he agreed to meet at his office."

Beth looked down at the keys in her hand. "I don't suppose you'd let me go with you?"

"Not this time. Griffin isn't into sharing with unauthorized personnel, and he's not as easy to manipulate as Sheila Hunter. He'd probably throw you out."

She made a face. "Pity. It would have been interesting." She turned toward the door. "Okay, see you."

"Beth . . . You'll be here when I get back, right?"

Beth grinned. "Depends if I get a better offer. I guess that means you'd better get back here soon."

"I will." She shook her head in amusement. "I promise."

FBI Field Office
San Diego

KENDRA STOOD UP FROM THE BENCH in the main lobby and moved toward Special Agent in Charge Michael Griffin. He had just come from the parking-garage stairwell and looked irritated as hell.

"Thanks for meeting with me."

"I had just gotten home, Dr. Michaels."

Now she knew he was annoyed. He only called her "Dr. Michaels" when he was genuinely pissed.

He continued, "I was sitting down to dinner with my family, thinking about the Chargers-Cowboys game on my DVR . . ."

"It was a rout. Cowboys trounced the Chargers forty-seven to six."

His face fell. "Great. You had to take that away from me, too."

"I'm kidding. I didn't even know there was a game tonight."

"Oh, you're hilarious."

"I didn't come here to entertain you. I think I may finally have some evidence that Colby is still alive."

He sighed. "I liked you better when you were ruining my football game. Let's go to my office."

They took the elevator to Griffin's spartan office on the fourth floor. They passed a half dozen agents in cubicles, some working late, others toiling away on their evening shifts. Griffin closed the door behind them. "Now what do you have for me?"

Kendra raised a lined notepad and tore out two pages. "Sorry this couldn't be more polished, but I drew them down in the lobby while I was waiting for you."

Griffin took the pages and studied the hastily drawn sketches. "Hmm. You're amazing in many things, Dr. Michaels, but freehand drawing isn't one of them."

"I'm still learning. Schools for the blind don't have 'crayon time.'"

"Are these glorified stick figures supposed to be people dancing?"

"No. They're dead people. This is how the corpses were posed at a murder scene in Redondo Beach a few weeks ago. I drew them from memory based on some crime-scene photos I saw just an hour or so ago."

He smiled. "You couldn't have just brought me the photos?"

"Not an option. My source wouldn't let me have them. My rotten drawing aside, do those poses mean anything to you?"

He stared at the drawings a moment longer. "I get it," he said quietly. "Military signals . . . just like Colby's victims."

"And what's more, they don't appear this way in the official police crime photos. Just the photos I saw."

"What, exactly, are you saying?"

"I'm not sure. I don't know what the cops could possibly have to gain by rearranging the corpses to hide Colby's possible involvement."

"I don't either," Griffin said. "No reasonable person would. Careful how you tread here."

"You've been telling me to be careful for months now."

"And you haven't been listening. It's one thing to accuse the California Department of Corrections of botching an execution and allowing a serial killer to escape, but when you start hinting at a police conspiracy . . ."

Kendra dropped down in a straight-backed chair in front of Griffin's desk. "I think I've been pretty low-key about Colby."

"Depends on your definition of low-key."

"Okay, as low-key as I can get."

"In any case, Colby is dead."

"I wish I could believe that."

"Believe it." Griffin circled around, and instead of sitting behind his desk, he took the seat next to Kendra as he did every time he was trying to show empathy or gently break bad news to one of his underlings.

She just found it annoying.

"Two different law-enforcement agencies investigated your claims," Griffin said. "They couldn't find any proof. And neither could you."

"Colby had help on the outside. If you remember, I was there when Myatt, Colby's psycho partner, took his last breath on Earth. I talked to him. I found his shopping list that included purchase of that zombie drug that would make Colby appear dead if administered. And we found actual traces of the substances that would make the plan possible."

"Products of a delusional, diseased mind."

"That diseased mind concocted plans that allowed him to kill half a dozen people while he was working to free Colby from that prison. He worshipped Colby and was the perfect copycat. He would have done anything to free him."

"Which is why we took it seriously enough to investigate. Listen, if I thought Colby was really out there, I'd have every agent, every specialist, every secretary on the clock to hunt him down. Hell, even I would be out there pounding the pavement."

"If you'd done all of that four months ago, we might have him now," she said baldly.

"Tactful, as usual. You've been on the alert all this time, and it hasn't brought you any closer."

"He's planning something."

"So you keep telling us. But again, no actual proof."

"I know how his mind works."

"*Worked.* Past tense."

"No one will be happier than I if you're right. But I think he's spent years laying the groundwork for this."

"Laying the groundwork . . . from death row?"

"Other people have underestimated Eric Colby. Almost all of them are now dead."

"Two of his victims were my own men. Believe me, I don't need you to remind me."

"Look, I don't want it to be true. But that's no reason to just look the other way."

Griffin impatiently pushed back the chair with the backs of his legs. Empathy time was obviously over. "That's not what's happening."

"The hell it isn't."

He turned away from her. "We're done here."

"You won't help me with this? That's it then?"

He picked up the two note pages she'd given him. "Yes. Unless you want me to send these out on the wire."

"You son of a bitch."

"Don't be disrespectful." He smiled, obviously pleased to have gotten such a rise from her. "Okay, I'll reach out to Redondo Beach PD and see what's going on with the crime photos. Happy?"

"For now."

"It's all I can do for you. You really haven't given me anything else to work on."

No one knew that better than Kendra. She supposed she was lucky with this much response. "I know that, Griffin." She got to her feet. "I'm trying, dammit."

El Cajon Boulevard
City Heights

IT WAS LIKE THEY WERE ALL moving in slow motion.

Or perhaps underwater, taking their evening strolls in the deep side of the pool.

Moving slower, talking slower, their tiny brains unable to function at the same level as his.

Imbeciles.

Colby glanced around the busy street in the East San Diego neighborhood of City Heights, surrounded by people, yet struck by the sensation that he was occupying a different physical space than the rest of these dim-witted souls. He'd felt this way years before his incarceration, but the feeling had lately become more pronounced.

No wonder he was always several steps ahead of the rest of the world. At this rate, it wouldn't be long before everyone would appear to be standing perfectly still. Amazing. Had Einstein and Newton felt like this?

Colby turned the corner. The neighborhood had changed. Many of the empty storefronts were now populated by ethnic restaurants, and he could see that there had been some effort to revitalize this gang-infested hellhole. Nice try, he thought, but no way this place was coming back.

But it would suit his needs for the next couple of weeks.

He approached a shuttered storefront and pressed the doorbell. Did this damned thing even work anymore? He glanced up and saw curtains rustling in the second-story apartment.

A wrinkled old woman's face appeared, frozen in its perpetual scowl. Some things never changed. She pointed behind her, then disappeared. He walked down a narrow alleyway between the buildings, sidestepping two syringes and a condom as he made his way around to the well-hidden rear entrance. The door creaked open before he even reached it.

"Get in here. Get in here!"

Colby smiled as he stepped inside and closed the door behind him. "Don't worry, Pamela. I didn't let the germs inside."

Pamela Gatlin lowered the surgical mask she held over her nose and mouth. She was in her late eighties, but she always looked the same—wrinkled, freckled, and no eyebrows. "Been awhile," she said. "Wasn't sure you were coming back."

Poor ignorant Pamela, he thought, amused. Of course she had missed the news of his arrest, conviction, and execution. She had no phone, no TV, and read only her Bible day after day. The perfect caretaker.

"I told you I'd be back," he said. "But I wasn't sure you'd still be alive. I thought you might be decaying in that floral chair with flies buzzing around you."

She cackled. "That'll happen one day, but not anytime soon. I still got a lot of kick left in me."

"I believe it."

"When the time comes, you'll take care of me. You promised."

"Yes, I did. At the Ruiz Cemetery, next to your son."

"Yes. That's right."

Never mind the plastic tub and jugs of hydrochloric acid that were waiting in the cellar for her, Colby thought. Where, he remembered with amusement, her arrogant son had actually endured his final, terrifying moments on Earth.

"You take care of me, Pamela, and I take care of you. That's always been the deal." He looked up the dark staircase that led to the upstairs apartment. "Everything okay here?"

"Yep. Guess you've been paying the utilities on time, 'cause they haven't tried to shut anything off."

"I've made arrangements. Everything will continue to be paid by the Euripides Trust until after you're gone. Probably until after I'm gone. Has anyone been asking for me?"

"Not personally. I've had some people who've been asking for the owner, 'cause they want to buy the place. You never gave me a way to get hold of you, so I couldn't even let you know." She frowned. "You really ought to tell me your last name."

Colby smiled. He'd covered his tracks well. There was no way anyone could trace this place to him. "The less you know, the better. Safer for you. Safer for me. Go on upstairs. I have work to do in the cellar. I'll look in on you before I leave."

She climbed the stairs, mumbling something to herself all the way. He'd have to check out the apartment later, to make sure no one else had been there. Highly unlikely, he thought. Colby turned to the boarded-up cellar and pried loose the large sheet of plywood. It was painted black, rendering it almost invisible against the dark walls of the empty stockroom.

Colby entered what appeared to be a small closet. In the back of the compartment, he gripped the built-in shelves and pulled them toward him, revealing a steep stairway that led down to the windowless cellar. Stale, musty air wafted upward. God he loved that smell. He felt for the switch, pressed, and light flooded the room below.

Each step creaked as he made his way down. He hadn't been sure if he would ever see this place again, but it now seemed inevitable that he should return. He finally reached the bottom. He turned.

Ah, at last.

A plastic-lined embalming table centered the room, equipped with nylon wrist and ankle restraints. Acoustic panels covered every inch of the walls and ceiling, rendering the room virtually soundproof.

A row of heavy plastic bags lined the back wall. They contained his tools and instruments, sealed and waiting to be pressed into service. He smiled. He knew he had several hours of work ahead of him, but he didn't mind. He was back in his element. He had to prepare his chamber for a very special guest.

Ah, there was no place like home . . .

CHAPTER
4

KENDRA SPENT THE NEXT MORNING conducting three back-to-back music-therapy sessions in her office studio, and the last appointment ended with a difficult conversation with the wife of an eighty-eight-year-old Alzheimer's patient. It had become apparent that the man would never respond to this type of therapy, and Kendra couldn't waste his time when he could pursue other courses of action that might actually help him. His wife was still clinging to hope, trying to convince herself that he was showing improvement.

It just wasn't happening.

The woman fought back tears as she led her husband out of the studio.

Kendra slowly sat down on the piano bench. Shit. Some days, her successes weren't enough to erase the disappointment of her failures.

"You handled that very well," Adam Lynch said as he stepped out from the small observation room. Kendra had been aware of his entering from the hallway outside, but she was too involved in her conversation to pay him much mind.

"My sessions are private, Lynch. You can't just barge in here like this. I know for a fact that the hallway door to the observation room was locked."

"Really? So how did I get in?"

"You picked it, of course. Well done. It's supposed to be a tamper-proof lock."

"No such thing." He crossed the studio, which was outfitted with a piano, a drum set, a xylophone, and a pair of guitars on stands. "I would have rung the bell, but I didn't want to disturb you."

"How very considerate."

"I heard you went to the FBI field office last night. You talked to Griffin."

"Word travels fast. So you probably know as much about the conversation as I do."

"I figure he pissed you off, you pissed him off, then you went your opposite directions. Does that about sum it up?"

"Yeah, that's about the shape of it."

"I also know about the case in Redondo Beach."

"Is that supposed to be significant? As far as I know, Griffin was supposed to reach out to the local PD."

"He already did. That's why I'm here."

Kendra stood up. "So why isn't Griffin talking to me about this himself?"

"To be honest, he doesn't consider it worth his time."

Her half smile was bittersweet. "So what else is new?"

Lynch pulled out a flash memory stick and motioned toward a tablet computer sitting on one of the music stands. "May I?"

"Knock yourself out."

He picked up the tablet, inserted the stick, and pulled up a series of photos. He showed them to Kendra. "Look familiar to you?"

"These are the official police crime photos for the Redondo Beach murder scene. I've already seen those."

"Probably not all of them. Redondo Beach PD sent over everything the photographer had. This is exactly the way the bodies looked when the building manager found them. No military hand signals, nothing like that."

"How are you so sure?"

"I talked to the building manager myself less than an hour ago. I e-mailed a couple of these to him. And there was a whole crowd of people there. You know what it's like at those scenes. I seriously doubt they were repositioned."

Kendra took the tablet and swiped the photos. "I'm telling you, yesterday I saw half a dozen photos that—" Kendra stiffened, her eyes glued to the screen. "No way."

"What is it?"

She swiped through a few more of the crime-scene pictures. "I don't believe it."

"What?"

"The pictures I looked at yesterday . . . They weren't of this room."

"I'm not sure I understand."

"Neither do I." She showed him one of the photos with a long shot of the apartment interior. "The room's layout and furnishings are identical in these and the pictures I saw yesterday, so it may be the same building. But the pattern of the crown molding is different here. And I believe the lamp shade is a slightly different shape. This is a cone, and the one I saw yesterday was more tubular."

He studied the photo. "Are you certain? You didn't notice the difference when you looked at those photos yesterday?"

"The differences may not have been visible in the official police crime photos I saw. There are a lot more shots here. And even if they were visible, it's been a few weeks. They're not details that would have necessarily stuck with me at the time."

He nodded. "Okay, so we're back to the original question. What does it mean?"

Kendra paced across the room. "There are only a couple possibilities. Either someone went through the trouble of staging those pictures to bring to the reporter . . ."

". . . Or the reporter staged them to present to you," Lynch finished.

"But why? In either of those scenarios, why would someone go to the time and trouble? Unless . . ." Her gaze flew to meet Lynch's. "You don't think . . ."

He took the tablet from her hands and quickly navigated to The Kinsley Chronicle.

"Shit," he said. He turned the tablet around to show her the news site's page one headline: "Deluded FBI Consultant Believes Executed Inmate Still Alive."

Kendra felt her face flush with rage. "She screwed me. Unbelievable."

"It's extremely easy for me to believe," Lynch said. "But I've always been a hell of a lot more cynical than you." He turned the tablet back around and skimmed the article.

"How bad is it?"

"Really bad." He read in silence for a few more moments. "She's painting you as a nutjob. There's a healthy sprinkling of nasty quotes from police sources, both named and unnamed. Probably every cop you've made look bad over the years. The 'deluded' quote comes from one of them. And you're quoted all the way through, but in such a way to make you appear as hysterical as possible. Why in hell did you give her an interview?"

"I didn't." Kendra snatched the tablet from him and quickly read the story. It was packed with snarky, half-truths and outright lies. "That reporter, Sheila Hunter, played me. Under any other circumstances, I never would have talked to her. She found just the way in."

Lynch nodded. "She presented herself as an ally in a situation where allies have been scarce for you. And what's more, she came to you seeming to have evidence that you've been sorely lacking." He shrugged. "As much as I join you in despising her right now, I have to admire her strategic abilities."

"Spoken like the master of manipulation you are. They don't call you 'the Puppetmaster' for nothing."

"Have I ever told you how uncomfortable I am with that nickname?"

"Only because it reveals an ability you'd prefer to keep hidden. And at this moment, your comfort really isn't all that important to me, Puppetmaster." Kendra grabbed a stack of notebooks and shoved them into her leather satchel.

"What now?"

"I'm going to talk to Sheila Hunter."

"Like hell you are."

"Just try to stop me."

"I will." He grabbed her wrist as she tried to push past him. "I'm telling you, it's a bad idea. You can't win."

"You think I should just shrink away without a word of protest?"

"I'm not saying that at all. But you don't want to give

her fodder for a follow-up story. Trust me, you've given her too much already."

"Well, what I'm about to give her, no news organization could ever print."

"Wanna bet? If you go at her like a lunatic, not only will she pick out some choice quotes, she'll record the whole thing. Just as I'm sure she did yesterday. And if you sound sufficiently deranged, that audio file will be all over the Web by the end of the afternoon."

"I can't let it go, Lynch."

"At least let me go with you."

"No, this is between me and her."

"And possibly hundreds of thousands of readers. You're not used to dealing with the media."

"I usually just ignore them."

"Excellent strategy. That's exactly what you should be doing right now."

She thought for a moment. He was probably right. She knew all wisdom dictated he was right. But what about justice, dammit? Didn't that count for anything?

She turned toward the door. "Sorry, I just can't do that. I'm talking to her alone. Lock up behind you, won't you. You obviously won't need a key."

She left the studio.

"SHEILA . . . SHEILA HUNTER!"

Kendra ran across the plaza that fronted the Imperial Avenue headquarters of Hobart News, the media conglomerate that owned The Kinsley Chronicle. Two phone calls from her car was all she needed to know where to find Sheila, and the reporter was now practically sprinting from the building.

Sheila pretended not to hear her, but Kendra cut her off. "It was all a big lie," Kendra said fiercely. "That picture that you showed me yesterday."

"Dr. Michaels, I have a meeting I need to—"

"Tough. You have a meeting with me right here, right now."

Sheila pulled her phone from her pocket and tapped it. "Look, I'm running late, so whatever you want to say to me—"

Kendra grabbed her hand and turned it around to look at the phone's front screen. A recording app was working away, with two graphic spools slowly spinning. Kendra pushed the apps red STOP button. "You do not have permission to record this conversation. Just as you didn't yesterday."

"I stand by my story," Sheila said.

"Stand by it, don't stand by it, I really don't give a damn. The core of your story is correct. I believe Eric Colby is still alive. But until your piece appeared, he didn't know I knew. That was a major advantage I had over him. He didn't know I was looking for him, and now there's a strong possibility he does."

Sheila's lips curled in a disbelieving grin. "Dr. Michaels, everyone but you seems to know that Eric Colby is dead. I really did watch him die."

"And yet you mocked up those photos to offer me proof that suggested otherwise."

She shrugged. "I knew it was the only way I could get an interview with you. It was a gaping hole in my story."

"How did you even do those pictures?"

"A friend of mine is a real-estate agent, and she got me into an identical unit in that building."

"*Almost* identical," Kendra said.

"Close enough. A bit of Photoshop helped out, too."

"That's why you wouldn't let me have copies. You didn't want me to be able to study them for too long."

"Well, they did their job."

"Your 'story' doesn't even qualify as news. It's gossip mongering."

"I beg to differ. The woman who captured one of the most notorious serial killers in our state's history now insists that his execution didn't really happen? If that's not news, what is?"

"It will be news when I find him. And your half-baked story is only going to make it more difficult. Does your employer know that you lied and manufactured evidence to get me to talk to you?"

"The Kinsley Chronicle doesn't want to know. Do you really think they care what their reporters do to get stories? In this case, they handed me the story and told me the slant they wanted on it. They want buzz, page hits, and advertising dollars, not necessarily in that order. Your story will give them all those things."

"My story? Don't you even care that—" Kendra stopped, then said, "I can't believe you. What if I'm right about Colby, and if he kills again before I can find him? How will they feel then? How will you feel?"

"Didn't you read the story? Didn't you see that every law-enforcement official I interviewed is positive that Eric Colby was put to death?"

"I read it." She took a step closer and got into Sheila's face. "You made me believe you were into a much bigger, much more horrible story that I really didn't want to be true. I actually thought you were helping me to save lives."

Sheila lowered her voice to a hiss. "But you do want it to be true, Kendra. You're not fooling me or anyone else.

You want it to be true so that you can prove you're right and the rest of the world is wrong. Even if it means that people have to die."

Kendra was stunned at the sheer malevolence of the woman. "You're so wrong. You couldn't be more wrong."

"Couldn't I? Well, it doesn't matter. Do you think I care? I have the power of the press, and everyone will believe me anyway."

Sheila whirled and strode away.

EVEN IF IT MEANS THAT people have to die.

The words were still pounding in Kendra's head as she drove back to the condo. It wasn't true, but that's exactly what those cops thought, she realized. They thought she only wanted to prove herself.

Lynch was right. It had been a mistake to talk to Sheila.

But she'd probably do it again.

Shake it off. Nothing that horrible woman wrote or said made a damned bit of difference.

If only that was true.

Even if it means that people have to die . . .

As Kendra entered her parking garage, a text message appeared on her phone from Beth. THE PARTY'S AT OLIVIA'S.

This made her smile. Beth was making friends. Her years in virtual isolation certainly hadn't impeded her abilities on that count.

She went to the third floor and immediately heard the pulsing music coming from the condo at the end of the hall.

Kendra rapped on the door and let herself in. Beth and Olivia Moore were seated at the dining-room table with half a dozen shot glasses lined up in front of them.

"Wow," Kendra said. "It *is* a party."

Beth raised a glass in her direction. "Why didn't you tell me your friend was so cool?"

"I knew you'd find out soon enough."

Olivia smiled. "How are you, Kendra?"

They knew about the story, Kendra realized. Olivia's stunning, olive-toned face gave it away immediately. She had known Olivia since they were children together at the Woodward School for the Vision Impaired in Oceanside. They had been close since the day they'd met, and when Kendra had been granted the miraculous gift of sight, her only regret was leaving her friend behind in the darkness. Olivia was never anything but supportive of her friend, but Kendra knew that her deepest wish was to find a way to regain her own sight someday. Sadly, the stem-cell technique that had worked for Kendra wasn't an option for Olivia.

"You know about The Kinsley Chronicle story," Kendra said. "Don't try to pretend you don't."

Olivia turned toward Beth. "I told you she'd know. That's one problem with being friends with Kendra Michaels. It's tough to keep secrets."

Beth nodded. "The story popped up on my iPad. I couldn't believe it. Olivia here had to talk me out of driving over and pounding that wench into the ground."

Olivia shrugged. "Didn't think it was a good idea."

"You're right," Kendra said. "One assault and battery charge is enough for the week."

"But I felt exactly like Beth so I dug out my magnetic dartboard, and Beth and I set it up with an appropriate target." She gestured to the wall in the living room. "Care to take a go?"

Kendra turned and burst out laughing. Sheila Hunter's official photo had been pulled from the Web site and blown up to cover the dartboard, which emitted a pinging sound to allow blind players to zero in on its location. The target was covered with feathered darts, the most on the reporter's smiling, lying, mouth. "You've been busy. I love it."

"We needed to let out our frustration," Beth said. "Olivia is much better at it than me. She's got that magnetic stuff down to a science. Want to try?"

"No, thanks all the same. I vented in person."

"So everything she told us was a lie?" Beth asked. "She just wanted an interview?"

"Pretty much." Kendra filled them in on her conversation with Lynch and her follow-up with Sheila Hunter.

Beth's fists clenched into fists. "Now I really want to pound her into the ground."

"She's not worth it. I've already given her more attention than I should have."

Olivia nodded. "I'm sorry, Kendra. I know this is the last thing you need right now."

"My mistake. I wanted it too much. I trusted her."

"You know, The Kinsley Chronicle's parent company tried to buy my site last year. It would have made me pretty rich."

Kendra raised her brows. "Really?"

Olivia's Web site, Outtasight, had quickly become a major online destination for the blind, who browsed its pages with one of several screen-reading applications. The site featured product reviews, interviews, and news stories, mostly written by Olivia herself. In a little over a year, what had been a spare-time hobby now afforded her a comfortable living.

"Yeah, I turned them down. What would I do, retire? Anyway, after seeing the number they pulled on you, I would never want to sell to a company like that."

"I'm sure it's just things the cops and FBI have been

saying about me all along. They can say whatever they want about me, but as I told that reporter, I don't want the investigation to be compromised. And I guess . . ." Kendra paused. "I guess I'm thinking of the families of Colby's victims. They thought they had at least some measure of closure. This is just picking at the wound."

Beth shrugged. "Hey, don't worry about that. Whatever closure they had, they still have. Anyone who reads that article would have to believe you're crazy."

"Thanks a lot."

"Anytime."

Olivia gestured toward a chair at her dining-room table. "Have a seat, Kendra. Beth has been treating me to some concoctions of hers that will make you forget all your troubles. And probably your own name."

Kendra chuckled. "Then I'm surprised you hit the dart-board at all."

"I had motivation. That bitch hurt my friend."

Kendra was touched. Their affection and support was soothing away the stinging indignation and outrage and putting the wound in perspective. "As appealing as that sounds right now, I think I'm going to pass. I'm just going to head back to my place and catch up on some paperwork."

"No." Olivia shook her head. "I've already promised to take Beth out and show her some of the San Diego hotspots. And you're coming with us."

"Not tonight, okay?"

Kendra expected Olivia to fight her on it. But after a long pause, she finally responded. "Okay. I'm not sure if the town could handle the three of us tonight. We'll just bombard you with embarrassing texts to update you on our progress."

"Do that." She smiled. Olivia might still be blind, but

she was the observant one, the person who always knew what the people around her needed. Kendra turned to Beth. "Will you be okay?"

"We'll see. I'm not sure if I can keep up with Olivia here, but I'll give it my best."

"Oh, I have faith." Kendra moved to the door and stepped into the hallway.

Beth was right behind her. "Kendra . . . Hold up for a second."

She stopped. "Yes?"

"Look, this has turned out to be a horrible time for you to be playing hostess and tour guide for me. May I just hit the road and get out of your—"

"No."

"Are you sure?"

"Damn sure. Beth, your coming here is the only good thing to happen to me this week. Stay." She smiled. "Please."

"Okay." She lowered her voice. "About Olivia . . . She's supercool but I haven't spent a lot of time with people that are . . ."

"Blind?"

"Yeah. Anything I should know?"

"Well, you probably shouldn't let her drive. Other than that, you're good to go."

Beth smiled. "Okay, I deserved that. Thanks for the tip."

"My pleasure."

"OPEN THE DAMNED DOOR!"

BAM BAM BAM.

"Kendra!"

She snapped awake. What in the hell . . . ? She checked the time—10:40 P.M.

She was on her living-room sofa. She'd spent a couple of hours writing her day's sessions, then curled up for what she thought would be a quick nap.

BAM BAM BAM.

"Kendra!"

Lynch's voice.

Still groggy, Kendra hurried to the door and threw it open. "At least you didn't jimmy the door this time. Though how the hell did you get past my entry buzzer downstairs?"

He pushed past her. "You went to see Sheila Hunter today."

"Yes, you know I did. Is that why you're here? To rub it in? You were right, okay? I should have just left horrible enough alone."

"No. I'm not rubbing anything in. There were people who saw your blowup with her in front of the Hobart Building."

"Good news travels fast."

He glanced around, then grabbed her jacket from the back of a dining-room chair. "Here. Put this on. We're going down to the marina."

"It's been a hell of a day, Lynch. The last thing I want to do is—"

His lips tightened. "We're going."

Normally, she would have been angered by his insistence. Not now. He wasn't bullying her. She knew the difference between Lynch just wanting to have his own way and Lynch worrying.

And that worry was beginning to scare her.

"Why?" she asked. "What's in the marina?"

"Sheila Hunter's dead body. Or at least what's left of it. She's been murdered."

CHAPTER
5

KENDRA SHOOK HER HEAD IN disbelief as she buckled herself into the passenger seat of Lynch's Ferrari. "I can't believe it. I just saw her a few hours ago." She turned toward him. "You don't have any details at all yet?"

"Next to none. A source of mine at the FBI field office just tipped me off. I didn't wait for details."

"So the FBI wants my help on this one?"

"No. Nobody asked for you."

"Oh. Good to know."

"As far as I know, the case is still under the jurisdiction of SDPD. But it's a hell of a coincidence that she's killed just hours after posting a story about your serial killer."

"Since when did he become *my* serial killer."

"Since you started tilting at the Colby windmill and became the only one who's convinced he's still out there. Though I guess he really became yours the night you put him away. He was obviously preoccupied with you."

She looked down, remembering the chill she felt in Colby's cell at San Quentin. Every inch of the place papered over with hundreds of photographs of *her*. He knew just how to burrow into her psyche.

And stay there.

Lynch's car stereo was tuned to the local police band, and the speaker crackled with dispatches directing officers to the murder scene. Lynch turned down the volume with his steering-wheel control. "Anyway, if we waited around for you to get an engraved invitation to join the case, it might be too late for you to do any good."

"So much for me taking a step back."

"I figured this is one you need to be there for."

"You're right. Thanks, Lynch. I do need to be there." Her eyes narrowed on his face. "But you meant something else, didn't you?"

"We need to wrap this up before the police decide that you thought Sheila Hunter might do enough damage to your career to warrant killing."

Her eyes widened. "What?"

"It's a possibility. You came out of this as an obsessed crazy woman, and she came out as a squeaky-clean journalist."

"Not quite."

"From the outside, that will be how it looks."

"Only until you look a little deeper." She took out her phone and handed it to him. "Play the last recording."

He pressed the button.

Sheila Hunter's voice was suddenly there in the car with them.

He listened for a few minutes and turned it off. "You recorded that last conversation with her. You're right, she came off as an unscrupulous bitch, framing you to get a story and not caring whom she hurt." He paused. "You didn't tell me."

"She tried to record me again, and I stopped her. I was so angry that she probably didn't think I had the composure to record her instead." She looked at him. "You didn't, Lynch. I wouldn't have confronted her if I hadn't had an ace in the hole to protect myself."

"My apologies." He shook his head. "I should have known."

"Why? It was pure instinct. I was angry and emotional, but I knew that I couldn't walk into another trap. So I made her say a few things that would put an end to any other articles she might write about me."

"You could have told me afterward."

"I was sick about the whole mess. I just wanted to forget it." She looked down at the phone. "But I don't believe anyone would think that Sheila came out on top. I could have caused her career more damage than she could mine. I might have come off as obsessed to find a killer. She came across as callous and crooked. I definitely wouldn't have killed her out of fear or frustration."

"I think I might borrow your phone recording and let San Diego PD have a listen. It might stop a problem before it begins."

"Whatever. I just hope that it doesn't get in the way at this murder scene."

In a few minutes, they passed the airport and drove down Harbor Village Drive to Marina Cortez. The choppy bay water glittered from the lights of the city and work lights and squad car flashers immediately pointed the way to the crime scene. It was a houseboat on the marina's outer edge.

As they drove closer, Kendra's eyes narrowed in shock at a sight so horrible that it just didn't seem real. "Shit. Did you know?"

Lynch jammed on the brakes and just stared at the grisly scene for a long moment. "No. No idea."

The work lights were trained on the top of the house-boat's tall mast, where Sheila Hunter hung from a guide rope wrapped around her neck. Blood oozed from her throat, down the front of her clothes to the deck below.

A fire truck had pulled alongside the dock, and its extension ladder soared over the mast, where a police photographer was snapping shots of the corpse.

Lynch gave a low whistle. "How would you like that job?"

"I'm going up there."

"Yeah, right."

"I'm serious."

Lynch glanced over at her. "Of course you are. Sorry, I forgot who I was talking to."

"It's the only way." Kendra felt that familiar chill again. "Look at her eyes."

Lynch nodded. "Wide open."

"Unnaturally so. Almost like . . ."

". . . like the top of her eyelids had been glued," he finished. "Just like Colby's victims. But he decapitated his kills."

"It may not be Colby's work." Kendra pushed open the car door. "I need a closer look."

Kendra swiftly climbed out of the car and hurried toward the fire truck.

Lynch was right behind her. "Be real. You can look at the photos he's taking."

"Photos can't show me everything, you know that. And

if looking at pictures was enough, I could have stayed home."

Lynch pointed up at the photographer. "In case you hadn't noticed, the ladder is occupied. Do you plan to share that perch with him?"

Kendra jumped to the fire engine's rear running board. "Of course not. The second he climbs down, I'm going up."

"The hell you are," a voice called from the other side of the rig.

Kendra looked over to see Detective Martin Stokes, whom she had met at the domestic murder scene less than forty-eight hours earlier. "Dr. Michaels, get off the fire truck."

"Not you, too." She let out a long breath. "Fine. I'll sign a waiver. If you're worried that I'll fall and—"

"That's the least of my worries right now. I need you to immediately step away from the area."

"I don't think you understand. I met this woman just yesterday, Stokes. I find it very disturbing that—"

"I understand more than you think." He raised his phone, which had The Kinsley Chronicle displayed on its screen. "Interesting reading. Especially when it's written by a woman who lambasted you just a few hours before she's murdered on her houseboat."

Kendra stared at him. "You actually think I may have had something to do with this?"

"At this point, I'm not ready to think anything."

"Obviously."

He ignored the jab. "Okay, no, I don't think you killed the woman. I respect my own judgment. I've been around long enough to sift out the bad guys. I'd let you go up there if I could. Look, you helped me the other night. You made me look good."

"I take it you took full credit."

He shrugged. "I might have left a few things out of my report."

"I don't care about that. Just let me climb this damn ladder."

He shook his head. "Can't do it. My captain would say you're definitely a person of interest. Your, shall we say, contentious relationship with the deceased means that I can't let you contaminate the crime scene. But I do need to get a statement from you."

"Now?"

"I'm a little busy at the moment. Stand back and let us do our job."

She shook her head in disbelief as Stokes turned and walked toward the houseboat.

Lynch took her arm. "Come on. I'll make some phone calls. We'll set that guy straight."

Kendra's eyes were still fixed on the houseboat's tall mast. "Give me a minute."

"What do you see?"

"Nothing yet. But if I can just . . ."

The sheer horror of the crime scene was preventing her from truly comprehending what she was seeing, she realized.

Block out the terror and the pain that was etched over this woman's face.

Detach. Concentrate.

She scanned the houseboat, Sheila's still-bleeding corpse, the dock, the surrounding area . . .

"Anything?" Lynch asked.

"The houseboat was her home. She didn't stay there last night, and probably not the night before. Her car is the Volvo over there. She was killed as she walked from the parking lot."

Lynch turned toward the lot. "Are you sure?"

"Yes. No one is even paying attention to the real murder scene, though a couple of the cops have already traipsed through it. They'll realize it after sunrise tomorrow."

"Do you mind telling me how—"

"On the window by the houseboat's front door, there's a small decal. The exact same decal that's on the lower left corner of the back window of that white Volvo."

Lynch studied the three letters on the houseboat window. "ONA?"

"It's possible she was a fan of the former Grand Duchess Ona of Lithuania, but I'm guessing she was actually a proud member of the Online News Association."

"Smartass."

She turned toward him. "You did a trick for me once. When we first met, you secretly hacked my phone and pulled information out when it was still in my pocket."

"Correction—I put information into your phone while it was still in your pocket. My name and phone number."

"How could I forget? Smooth, real smooth."

"My info is still there, isn't it?"

"Actually, I deleted it."

"Really?"

"I reentered it later myself. I got a weird feeling whenever I looked at the entry you made. I felt like I'd been violated."

"In a world where we live and die by our wireless devices, it's hard not to expect a few incursions."

"Sheila Hunter's phone is probably still in the area. Can you pull her address or recent call log?"

He raised his phone. "Already done."

Her eyes widened. "You're full of shit."

"I did it while you were sparring with Detective Stokes. I didn't think you were going to have his cooperation in any meaningful way and made a preemptive strike. It's all right here."

"How did you know you were hacking *her* phone?"

"Because I got her cell number . . . off *your* call log."

She bristled. "You hacked my phone again?"

"You called her yesterday and today, right?"

"I am not believing this . . ."

"Yes, you are. It's what you wanted, isn't it? I live to oblige. By the way, who keeps calling you from the 310 area code? Someone I should be jealous about?"

"Says the guy with the supermodel girlfriend."

"I wouldn't say she's a *super*model. At least not yet."

"I think I need to take my phone and have it scrubbed in bleach."

"It's the world we live in. I can help you secure that phone with just a few—"

"No thanks. You'd probably leave yourself a back door. I'll handle my own security."

"Because you've been doing such a stellar job of it so far."

"We'll discuss all your flagrant privacy violations later." She lowered her voice. "Let's take a look at her car."

They walked the fifty yards away to the parking lot, where Sheila Rogers's white Volvo XC90 SUV was parked. Kendra turned on her phone's flashlight as they drew closer.

"Looks like we have first crack at this," Lynch said. "The cops haven't pulled her car registration yet."

"I have a feeling they'll be over here the minute they see us. We need to make this fast." Kendra shined her flashlight through the driver's side window. "The driver's seat is set for Sheila's height. The passenger seat is all the way back, probably for a taller man." She moved the light over the vehicle interior. "Sheila was a nonsmoker though. I noticed that after I met her."

"It's amazingly clean," Lynch said.

"Yes. As a matter of fact . . ." She suddenly stepped back.

"What is it?"

Kendra looked up to see Stokes and a pair of uniformed officers approaching. "I . . . think Sheila Hunter's killer was in this car."

Stokes stopped a few feet away, staring at her. "Did I hear you correctly?"

"It depends on what you heard. I wasn't trying to hide what I was thinking."

"I'm not certain of that. I came over here to bust your chops about contaminating another part of my crime scene."

"Fine. Bust away."

"It can wait. What makes you think her killer was in here?"

Kendra shined her light back into the car. "Look for yourself."

Stokes glanced inside. "I'm sure you're gonna try to make me feel like an idiot in a few seconds, but I don't see a thing."

"I don't see anything, either," Kendra said.

"That's a relief. So what's your point?"

"It's pristine clean. I'll bet forensics won't find a single fingerprint on the dashboard, the console, the door handle, the control touch screen, or even that glossy mahogany steering wheel. Not one. Unless she suffered from an acute obsessive-compulsive disorder that compelled her to totally wipe down the interior of her car every time she arrived at her destination, I'd say her killer was in here, and he wiped it clean. One way or another, this is where the abduction took place. She was killed somewhere between here and her houseboat."

Stokes nodded. "Very good guess. But I'm sure forensics would have told us that once we turned them loose on it. I'll tell them what to look for. Or not look for. I'll need you to step back and keep out of the way now."

Kendra raised her hands and took a step back. "Your gratitude is overwhelming."

"Sorry. Just doing my job."

"Ready?" Lynch asked Kendra.

"In a minute." Stokes wasn't being overly cooperative, but he hadn't entirely closed her out. She watched him call for forensics, her gaze on the houseboat. When he finished the call, she nodded toward the dock. "Pretty pricey home for a journalist."

"It appears she lived there alone, but it wasn't hers. The marina has it registered to another name."

"What name?"

He didn't answer.

"Look, Stokes, you don't really think I had anything to do with her death. There's no way I could have gotten her up on that mast. Yes, I had no liking for Sheila Hunter. She lied and attacked me. But I've worked with you guys before, and you know that I'm not stupid enough to kill someone just for being a bitch. I do want to work at clearing this up. Help me out, okay?"

He hesitated, then looked down at his notebook. "I guess you could find this out just by checking the registration. Kevin Burnett."

"Boyfriend?" Lynch asked.

"We're still trying to find out. We just got it a few minutes ago."

He was still reluctant. Ask questions fast before he closed down again. Kendra glanced around at the growing crowd of onlookers. "Who found the body?"

"A private security officer on his scheduled patrol. He didn't see anybody else out here. We've already started a canvass, but very few of these crafts have anyone living on them. There aren't many guests at the moment."

"The killer chose his spot well."

Stokes moved closer to Kendra. "Suppose I let you in on something, Dr. Michaels. I've helped you, now you help me. You probably couldn't see from where you were, but the victim was posed in a very specific way. The fists were balled up with glue, probably the same glue that was on her eyes. Her wrists were turned, with elbows slightly bent."

"I could see," Kendra said. "It was another hand-and-arm signal."

"And you know what it means?"

"I'm afraid I do. It means 'stand by for further messages.'"

"A threat?"

"A promise."

Stokes's gaze shifted back to the body on the mast, which two firemen and a forensic tech were finally pulling over to the ladder. "I know what you're thinking. Everyone knows you show up at our crime scenes because you're looking for that creep Colby. Some of our people think you're nuts. Maybe they're right. But, me, I take help where I can get it." He glanced back at her. "But this doesn't really mean anything. It could be just a copycat, riled up by you and your theories."

She shook her head. "I've been pretty damned quiet about my suspicions as far as anyone but law enforcement is concerned. It was that reporter who took it public." As Kendra spoke, she glanced up and happened to lock eyes with Sheila's horrific, glued-open gaze.

She was riveted, frozen in place.

"Kendra?" Lynch said softly.

"Yeah." She finally tore her gaze away. "Let's get the hell out of here."

THEY DROVE IN SILENCE FOR A few minutes before Lynch finally spoke. "Do you think it was him?"

Kendra glanced up from looking out the passenger-side window. "I don't know. Colby's influence was definitely there, but Stokes was right. It could have been someone imitating his crimes."

"I guess we'll have to wait for the DNA."

"There won't be any. At least not if it's Colby. All those murders he committed, he never left behind a shred of his DNA."

"That's incredible."

"Almost unheard of in this day and state of technology. Evidence collection has improved in the last few years, but I'd still be surprised if he left anything behind."

"Maybe in the car. Criminals sometimes leave behind skin cells when they're trying to wipe away prints."

"Colby knows better. But if it's somebody else . . ." She shrugged. "Who knows?"

"So what you're saying is if it's Colby, there won't be

any evidence. With that kind of logic, it won't be easy for you to convince the cops that he's still out there."

"If he's out there, I won't need to convince them. All I'd have to do is wait. As clever as he is, he won't be able to help but show himself. It's his nature. This may be only the first sign."

They drove in silence while Kendra gazed out at the lights of Harbor Drive. Lynch finally said, "Look, I want you to stay at my place for a while."

"I'll bet you do."

"Unfortunately, no lust involved. I won't be there."

"What?"

"I'm leaving for Luxembourg tonight."

She tried to read his expression as they passed a streetlight. "You're not kidding."

"No, I wish I was. There's a matter that needs finessing. I was hoping like hell it could wait, but things have come to a head."

"This is getting to be a nasty habit of yours, bailing on me in the middle of an investigation."

"I know." His tone was suddenly savage. "Do you think I'm happy about it?"

"You're the one who came on so strong, telling me what a great team we were."

"We are, Kendra." He was staring directly into her eyes. "In every way imaginable."

She instinctively backed away from the intensity in that last sentence. "But you have important people to see and situations to handle," she said flippantly. "No problem."

"It *is* a problem, dammit."

"Look, you don't owe me anything." She moistened her lips. "I didn't mean to give you a guilt trip. I was just surprised. We both know that's not what our relationship is about. I'm grateful that you've been there for me in the past. You're one of the few people who doesn't look at me like I'm crazy when I talk about Colby's possibly being alive. That's enough for me."

"It's *not* enough. I'd feel better if you stayed in my house while I was away."

"We've been through this. And besides, I have a friend visiting from out of town."

"She can stay over, too. Hell, invite Olivia, your mother, and anyone else you want. Make a party of it. There's enough room for all of you. And you're already familiar with the security system there."

"I am. It's like living in a vault."

"A beautiful vault. There's not a safer place in the world for you right now."

It was beautiful, she remembered. And in those horrible weeks after she first suspected Colby was still alive, it was the only reason she could sleep at all. Lynch had built that fortress because of the multitude of enemies he'd made during his career. He had to be constantly on guard. It was the only place he could truly relax. She knew how that felt during her time there. His home's perimeter motion sensors, security cameras, and retractable steel window shutters guarded her from any and all threats lurking in the outside world. But the longer she isolated herself from that world, the more frightening and daunting it became. It hadn't taken long for her to realize that it couldn't become a way of life for her.

"I can't hide behind those walls right now, Lynch. I have to be out here."

"Fine. Hide behind them when you sleep."

"Not now."

"When?"

"When and if I think it's necessary. In case you haven't noticed, I'm fairly in tune with my surroundings, even while I'm sleeping. No one's getting near me without my knowing about it."

He reached out and touched her cheek. "I'd feel a lot better if I knew you were there."

She felt the familiar heat start to radiate beneath that touch. As usual, she was too aware of him. Lynch was fully capable of using that sexual chemistry between them to catch her off balance and try to get his own way. She moved her head to avoid his hand. "My primary focus isn't to make you feel better while you're traipsing across Europe."

He let his hand drop away from her face and let out an exasperated breath. "Okay. I'll e-mail you a custom app. The electronic locks in my place perform a key change every six seconds. The only way the app can unlock any of my doors is if you swipe your thumb across your phone's fingerprint reader."

"Ah. An upgrade. And foolproof, unless someone steals my phone and chops my thumb off."

He grimaced. "Don't even say that. Besides, it wouldn't work. Without blood circulating through your fingers, there's no way that—"

She interrupted him. "I was joking. My severed thumb is one thing I'd rather not contemplate. E-mail me the app. I doubt I'll use it, but it's nice of you to offer."

"I've already installed it in your phone."

She shook her head. "Damn. I *knew* you were going to say that."

"JEEZ, KENDRA." BETH STOOD UP from the sofa in Olivia's condo. "Did you have to kill her?"

"You've acquired a dark and disturbing sense of humor in these past few months." Kendra slid out of her jacket. "Sorry that I can't laugh about this."

"The story about Sheila Hunter's murder just broke online," Olivia said as she stepped out of the kitchen. "When we couldn't reach your mobile, we figured you were there."

"I was. It was horrible."

Beth made a face. "I guess you're right. Not at all funny. I was just so angry about the way she treated you that it's hard for me not to be callous."

"Was it . . . him?" Olivia asked.

"Don't know yet. There were some similarities between this and Colby's kills, but I can't really come to any conclusions. If you ask the cops, they would say no."

"But they brought you into the case anyway."

"They did nothing of the sort. They'd rather I stay as far away from this as possible. Lynch took me there."

Beth wore a puzzled expression. "So they expect you to sit on the sidelines and twiddle your thumbs while they conduct their investigation?"

"I don't know if they expect it, but it sounds like what they'd prefer."

"So what are you going to do?"

"If there's a chance Colby is involved, I'm working this case. With or without the cooperation of the San Diego PD. Lynch had to leave town, so one of my few allies is out of the picture right now." She looked at Beth. "You've already gotten more than you bargained for on this visit. I'm sorry. I wanted things to be different."

"Why are you sorry? You're feeling bad that you can't take me to the zoo, Sea World, and Museum Row? Puleeze."

"I wanted us to be able to spend time together."

"Who says we won't?" Beth shrugged. "It looks like you might need me on this."

"What?"

"Well, you said you're going rogue on this case. I've been studying rogue for a long time."

"Going rogue? You make me sound like a vigilante."

"That's kinda what you are." Beth tilted her head. "Isn't it?"

"No, I mean . . ." Kendra turned to Olivia. "Help me out here."

Olivia nodded. "Definite vigilante."

"Thanks a lot."

"It's not an insult," Beth said. "Just the opposite. But you shouldn't be going it alone. You're used to having backup from all those cops and FBI agents."

Kendra's lips twitched. "So you're my backup now?"

"Hey, I'm bringing the muscle."

"Whoa-whoa-whoa. Tracking a man like Colby is a chess game, not a boxing match."

"Fine. You play chess, but it's still good to have a friend in your corner."

"You're using boxing metaphors again."

"I don't know how to box. Maybe I should learn."

"That didn't seem to matter to the guy you put in the hospital this week."

"Exactly. Proof that I'm an excellent person to have by your side."

Kendra smiled at her. Beth was definitely different than the unsure young woman who had ventured back into the world only a few short months before. Different, yet the same. That determination had always been there, even when her grim situation offered little hope. "Your sister will kill me if she finds out I've pulled you into one of my investigations."

"Leave Eve to me. Besides, this is one thing I think she might understand."

"For herself, yes. But she's fiercely protective of the people she loves. If she thinks I'm putting you in danger, she'll never forgive me."

She grinned. "You're now on record as trying to talk me out of it. Olivia, you're her witness."

Olivia held up her hands. "Leave me out of it. This isn't a game or a match. Kendra, if you're right about this being Colby, this is different than your other cases. He's had you in his sights ever since you put him away."

"That's why I have to do this."

Olivia shook her head. "No. You don't."

"I can't sit back and just let this play out. He'll keep killing until he's stopped." She added bitterly, "And at the moment, I'm the only one who believes he's out there."

Olivia sighed resignedly. "Okay." She moved into the adjoining living room, which was dominated by a large, L-shaped desk where she spent most of her waking hours. "I know better than to try to change your mind, so I want you to do something for me."

"What's that?" Kendra asked warily.

Olivia picked up a box and carried it back over to Kendra. "Take this. I know you're not fond of guns, but maybe one of these things will work for you."

Kendra peered into the box. "What is it?"

"I just reviewed some self-defense products for my Web site. Some of these might come in handy for you."

Beth reached in and pulled out a chrome, cylindrical-shaped object. "Self-defense products . . . as in weapons?"

"Yes. Tasers, pepper spray, flesh-colored brass knuckles, among other things. But whatever you do, don't touch the silver tube."

Beth froze.

"I'm kidding." Olivia chuckled. "It holds pepper spray refill cartridges. I heard it roll around when you picked it up."

"I'm going to get you for that." Beth returned the cylinder to the box. "Very funny."

"I kinda thought so. By the way, did you know Ohio actually issues handgun carry permits to blind people?"

"Is that another joke?" Beth asked.

"I wish it were. I just found out about it when I was writing the piece for my Web site. I'm all for equal rights for the vision impaired, but that's one I hope California doesn't pick up."

"You and me both," Kendra hefted the box. "Thank you, Olivia, but this really isn't necessary."

"Take it. There might be something in there you can use."

"Sure." Kendra gingerly picked up a small black handgrip with two prongs at the top. "I feel like James Bond getting my gadgets from Q Branch."

"James Bond is indestructible. You're not. I think this is a great time for you to get away from here. I don't suppose I can talk the two of you into joining me at the Hawaii Hot Springs Spa and Resort on the big island for the next week or two? Balmy breezes and wonderful scents."

"Later," Kendra said. "I promise."

"Beth? You still have a chance to be the sane one."

Beth laughed. "You do know I've spent the last few years in a mental institution, right?"

"Here's your chance to convince me that you still don't belong there."

"Most people tap-dance around that subject with me. Not you."

Kendra moved toward the door. "Don't expect anything else. Olivia is the most direct person you'll ever meet."

"I'm beginning to see that." Beth hugged Olivia. "And appreciate it. Rain check on that spa vacation?"

"We'll see." Olivia smiled faintly. "Depends on if I can round up some more sensible friends to go with me instead."

After the door slammed behind them, Kendra and Beth walked down the corridor. Beth glanced back. "She's amazing."

"That's the word I usually use for her."

"Was she born blind?"

"No. She lost her sight in a car accident when she was a child. We've known each other since we were seven years old. She helped me through some tough times."

"I'm sure you helped her, too."

"Maybe. I think she was always the stronger one, though."

"You've gotten your sight back so completely . . . Is there nothing that can be done for her?"

"Not so far. I lost my sight from a degenerative corneal disease in the womb. A stem-cell procedure basically grew my cornea back for me. Olivia has different issues that medical science can't tackle yet. She's hopeful, though. We all are."

"Has she ever shown any resentment?"

Kendra smiled. "Never. Not once. She knew I had never seen colors, the sky, or a person's face, and she was thrilled for me when it finally happened. The problems were on my end. I felt guilty for leaving her behind in the dark. She sensed that, and she pulled away from me for a while. She thought I needed room, and I guess I did. That was the start of my wild days. But now we're closer than ever."

"That's great." She was silent for a moment. "I haven't reconnected with my old friends yet, but I will. I was sent to that mental hospital when I was only seventeen and just starting to make firm friendships and memories. Most of the people I grew up with have moved on and probably forgot I existed."

"Maybe not. Perhaps there's someone out there who would like to hear from you."

"That life all seems so far away. The only thing that seems real are the people I've met, the friends I've made since I left Seahaven. The past holds a lot of pain and bewilderment. I'm just not ready yet, you know?"

Kendra nodded. "I know. I just wanted you to think about it. I don't want you to be cheated of anything that might be out there for you. No pressure. It's good to take time for yourself right now."

They stopped in front of the stairway that would take them back to Kendra's floor.

"Well, now that we've bonded and settled my immediate personal issues, isn't it time we got down to business?" Beth asked with a grin. "So where do we start with this case of yours?"

"You're not serious."

"Of course I am."

Kendra shook her head. "I was hoping that you'd just drop it. And that's your idea of taking time for yourself?"

"Absolutely. Look, I know there's no way you're going to let me get near Colby. You try to leave me free, but you're almost as protective as Eve. But there's no reason I can't help and sort of skate around the edges while you keep me from breaking through the ice. If I get in your way, tell me to get lost. But, as long as you're not investigating in an official capacity, why can't I help?"

"I . . . don't have an immediate answer for that."

"Good. Don't search for one. Where do we start?"

"*I'll* start by looking at Sheila Hunter's call logs and phone directory."

"You really have those things?"

"Yes. Don't ask how. Anyway, that will give me an idea where to go next."

Beth nodded. "I'll head back to the hotel and grab a few hours sleep. I'll see you back here at seven thirty tomorrow morning."

She was probably making a mistake, Kendra thought. But if she sent Beth away, there was no telling if she would be back on her doorstep anyway. Beth could be very determined. And Beth had been right, Kendra would never put her into a position where she would be in danger.

So let her help and keep her skating around the edges?

Surely Kendra could tolerate that amount of participation if she never let Beth too close.

Maybe.

She looked away for a long moment. What the hell. "Sure. See you here."

"Right." Beth flashed a bigger and more brilliant smile than Kendra had ever seen from her.

Then she turned and practically flew down the stairs.

CHAPTER
6

AFTER RETURNING TO HER CONDO, Kendra spent forty-five minutes searching the recent phone numbers in Sheila Hunter's incoming call log. She pulled together a preliminary list, separated by the known and unknown callers. Her office accounted for the vast majority of calls, followed by a man named Robert Schultz. Probably a boyfriend, judging from the length and late hours of their conversations. There were still several others that needed some follow-up, but that could wait for the morning.

She leaned back in her desk chair. Lynch's illegal tech skill had finally come to be of some use to her. A hell of a lot more useful than anything she had been permitted to see at the crime scene, that was for sure.

Lynch. As he had done so many times before, he had swept into her life with gale force, whipped everything into a frenzy, then vanished. She had no idea when she would see him again. Days? Weeks? A year?

Why did she care? Yes, she always felt as if life took on more brilliant hues, that his mind was always in sync, that in a world where she'd opted to stand alone, she could lean on his strength . . . if she chose.

Not that she would choose.

It was just that life was always a little emptier when he left her. It was strange to think that she couldn't reach out and call him when she had a thought, or needed to tap him for information or influence.

No matter. There was no doubt she could handle everything by herself without help from Lynch. She had enough to occupy her without—

GIVING UP SO SOON?

The words appeared on her laptop screen, one letter at a time, right in the middle of her document.

How the hell . . . ?

The cursor jumped to the next line. Again, words appeared one letter at a time, as if being written by an invisible typist: SURELY YOU'RE NOT GIVING UP, KENDRA . . .

Of course.

She typed furiously. NOT FUNNY, TOO FAR, LYNCH.

The answer came back immediately, again in her in-progress Word document: I'M NOT WHO YOU THINK I AM.

She froze, then typed: WHO IN THE HELL IS THIS?

SOMEONE WHO'S BEEN WATCHING YOU.

She stared at the words on the screen, then typed: WATCHING ME WHERE?

EVERYWHERE. I'VE BEEN WATCHING YOU FOR A LONG TIME, KENDRA.

She instinctively glanced around, feeling that there were eyes on her at this very moment. She typed: WHO IS THIS?

TIME FOR THAT LATER.

Her mind raced. Sheila Hunter's story had just gone on-line that day. Had some sicko read the story and hacked into her computer?

She was just about to type a response when more words appeared on the page: I SAW YOU AT THE MARINA TONIGHT.

Kendra went still. She typed: WHY WERE YOU THERE?

YOU KNOW WHY.

She typed: TELL ME.

FOR SHEILA HUNTER. YOU'LL BE HAPPY TO KNOW SHE WAS SCARED OUT OF HER FREAKING MIND.

Kendra's hands shook as she moved her fingers over the keyboard. YOU KILLED HER.

MY GIFT TO YOU. DON'T PRETEND. I KNOW YOU WERE HAPPY.

She stared in disbelief at the unfolding dialogue on her computer screen: NO, THAT'S NOT TRUE. WHO IS THIS?

YOU KNOW WHO. YOU'LL NEVER BE DONE WITH ME, KENDRA.

Her breath left her.

"*You'll never be done with me, Kendra.*"

Colby's last words to her, just days before his scheduled execution.

NOW YOU KNOW.

She used her index finger to punch her reply one key at a time: COLBY.

Ten seconds went by. Then fifteen.

YOU NEVER STOPPED BELIEVING, KENDRA. TOUCHED BEYOND WORDS.

It was him.

After all these months of wondering, of watching over her shoulder . . . He was back.

She flexed her trembling fingers over the keyboard. Stay cool.

Detach. Concentrate.

WHY SHEILA HUNTER?

His reply was immediate: DID SHE NOT DESERVE IT?

She replied: NO. NO ONE DESERVES THAT.

Except Colby, she thought.

EXCEPT ME. THAT'S WHAT YOU WERE THINKING, WASN'T IT? I KNOW YOU, KENDRA. TOO WELL.

He did know her, she realized. All those years in prison, he was studying her, making his sick plans. She felt another surge in the pit of her stomach.

Hold it together.

She typed: THEN YOU KNOW I'VE BEEN EXPECTING YOU.

He fired back: OF COURSE. I'VE BEEN COUNTING ON IT.

She believed him. He did know her too well.

YOU NEVER DISAPPOINT, KENDRA.

She held her shaking hands over the keyboard, weighing her next move. Bold, decisive strokes were the only things that ever worked against Colby, but did she want to go this far? She finally typed: I'M THE ONE YOU WANT, COLBY. BRING IT ON. NO ONE ELSE NEEDS TO SUFFER FOR WHAT I'VE DONE TO YOU.

Long pause. Had she thrown him off balance? He finally responded: I'VE ALREADY BROUGHT THE FIGHT TO YOU, KENDRA. YOU JUST DON'T KNOW IT YET.

REALLY?

He shot back: OH, YES. I LEFT YOU A PRESENT INSIDE SHEILA HUNTER'S HOUSEBOAT.

She went still. She could only imagine what constituted a present from Eric Colby. She made herself respond: IF YOU WERE REALLY THERE, YOU WOULD KNOW I COULDN'T GET NEAR THE PLACE.

I SAW. YOU'LL JUST HAVE TO TRY HARDER, KENDRA. I HAVE FAITH IN YOU.

Before Kendra could reply, he quickly signed off: ENOUGH. YOU HAVE WORK TO DO. PLEASANT DREAMS, KENDRA. I CAN'T TELL YOU HOW MUCH I ENJOY THEM.

The document went blank. A moment later, her laptop screen went blank and the fan shut off.

She stood and backed away from the computer, still trembling.

He was back.

Her first instinct was to turn the computer back on, but she stopped herself. Best to leave the system undisturbed until she could get this thing to an expert who could figure out how in the hell Eric Colby had tapped in.

Which expert?

She wasn't about to involve Lynch, and if she tapped the FBI forensic computer specialists, it would probably mean boxing up her laptop and shipping it to D.C. There was always a backlog for anything except national-security issues, and Colby's future victims didn't have the luxury of time.

Kendra stared at the laptop. She did know someone who could outgeek the FBI experts any day of the week. He was based in San Francisco, but his talents were sought after by clients all over the world. Even the Defense Department had their agents keep an eye on him because he was so valuable in protecting their sites from foreign hackers. But even if he was in the country, there's no telling if he was available to help her.

One way to find out.

She picked up her phone and punched a number. Within seconds, her ear was blasted by blaring rap music and the sound of a boisterous crowd.

"Kendra!"

She recognized Sam Zackoff's voice immediately even

though he was shouting into the phone. The tension in her body eased slightly. It was good to be reminded that there was a happy and carefree world out there, far from the grim reality that had suddenly pummeled her.

"Sam? Where the hell are you? A dance club?"

"No, better. I'm at a video-game trade show, and one of the companies is throwing a killer party. Free booze and dozens of hot young ladies dressed like the scantily clad characters in their new game. It doesn't get much better than this."

"I'll take your word for it."

"You don't have to. You can always join me."

"Actually, that's what I wanted to talk to you about. Where in the world are you right now?"

"I'm at the E3 computer-game trade show."

"That's supposed to mean something to me?"

"Sorry, I forgot you're not as big of a geek as the rest of the people in my social circle."

"That's a relief for me and very depressing for you."

"The E3 show is always in L.A. I'm at the convention center downtown."

"That's the best news I've heard all day. I need to come see you."

"It's getting loud in here. Did you say you needed me?"

"I said I need to see you."

"Okay, I heard you that time. You need and crave me with every fiber of your being. Got it."

"God, you're a geek."

"Sorry, the connection dropped out for a second. Did you just say I was a god?"

"You wish."

"If you really want my help, you're not being very persuasive. What's up?"

"My computer just got hacked, and I don't know how. I was working on a Word file, and someone just started typing into it. They could see everything I was typing."

"Easy peasy. A kid could do that. There are plenty of free software packages out there that can give anyone remote access to your computer. Tech-support people use them all the time to make adjustments to customers' settings."

"But something would still have to be installed on my laptop, right?"

"Again, child's play. If your computer touches the Internet, all notions of security and privacy go right out the window."

"Comforting. I wouldn't bother you if it wasn't urgent, Sam. This is a killer on one of my cases. I need you to look at my computer and see if there's anything here that could possibly help me find this sicko. Could you do that?"

"Sure. You want to meet tomorrow?"

"Tonight. I'm driving down right now. This time of night, I can be in L.A. in less than two hours."

"Whoa. I plan to be totally hammered by then."

"I'll take Sam Zackoff hammered over anybody else stone-cold sober any day of the week."

"Now *that's* how you get a guy to help you."

"Where do we meet?"

He thought for a moment. "There's an all-night diner just a couple blocks from the convention center. It's called Riff's. It's on Figueroa Street. I'll be there chugging coffee like a madman."

"Thanks, Sam."

"No worries. We go way back. If the only way I can touch base with you these days is to do an occasional favor, I'm here for you. I can never tell when your gratitude might overwhelm you. See you soon."

ON THE HOUR-AND-FORTY-FIVE-MINUTE drive down the I-5 freeway, Kendra glanced several times at her laptop on the passenger-side floor. She almost felt it was Colby himself down there, watching her, taunting her, and plotting his next move.

As she fumbled with the car stereo's volume knob, she realized that her hands had never fully stopped shaking since her dialogue with Colby.

Enough.

She had beaten him once, and she would do it again. As much as he liked to boast that he knew her, she knew him, too. She would use his confidence, his arrogance, against him.

You're going down, Colby.

KENDRA PARKED HER CAR AND entered the narrow diner. It was a freestanding building, but was clearly designed to emulate the railroad car diners of the Northeast, with a long counter and a wedged-in row of booths. There were only two people visible at first glance—a medical worker in pink scrubs eating chili at the counter and a homeless man facedown in the last booth.

Wait. Not a homeless man, she realized as she glanced at his tousled brown hair and brown bomber jacket. That leather jacket was lambskin and very expensive.

"Wake up, Sam."

"I'm already awake." He didn't lift his head or make any other move to look at her. "I'm just trying to summon the will. I wish you had called about two hours earlier."

"Never mind. I shouldn't have imposed. The FBI has experts who can deal with this sort of thing."

He snorted and finally sat up with a lopsided grin. "You're playing me, woman. If you really believed that, you wouldn't have driven all the way down here in the middle of the freaking night."

"You're the best, Sam. And I'm not playing you when I say that."

"I know you're not. You're the one person who has always held *all* my abilities in appropriate regard."

He smiled again with that wonderfully cockeyed grin. Sam was thirty, thin, and his thick mane was everywhere no matter how long or short it was at any given time, complementing his brilliance with a distinct mad-scientist vibe.

She and Sam had a brief, stupid fling during her wild days, but they both quickly realized that romance wasn't in the cards for them. But through all the years, he had always been there for her in a way that no lover ever had. She wouldn't trade that kind of friend for the world.

Sam picked up the pot of coffee on the table and emptied it into his cup. He waved the empty pot at the waitress who had just emerged from the kitchen. "Keep 'em coming please. Be assured that my friend here tips *insanely* well."

Kendra turned back toward the waitress. "I do. Make sure he gets anything and everything he wants."

She sat across from Sam and put the laptop on the table between them. "Here it is. I'm not sure what you can do, but I'm hoping you can find out something that can give me some kind of trail back to him. Maybe through a software vendor or maybe an IP address . . . I'm not sure."

The mere sight of her computer seemed to give him a

jolt, making him more alert than the coffee had been able to do. "You never know. Even the most accomplished hackers are often terrible at covering their tracks. Let's see what we have here." He lifted her computer, then froze. "I thought you said you turned this off."

"No, I said I didn't turn it back on. It turned off by itself at the end of my and Colby's rap session."

He raised his eyebrows at her. "No, it didn't."

"What are you talking about? I saw it happen."

"No, you saw the screen and indicator lights switch off, and you heard the fan shut down." He ran his fingers across the laptop's underside. "It's still warm. It shouldn't still feel this way, not after two hours. You were meant to think it was off, but it's not. For all we know, your laptop's microphone has been transmitting our entire conversation back to him."

"Shit. What do we do?"

He quickly popped the laptop's battery off and placed it on the table. "There. That should take care of it."

She stared at her computer, once again feeling that eerie sensation she'd had in the car. "Why would he do that?"

"Don't know, but maybe we can find out." Sam reached into the worn leather satchel on the seat beside him and produced a screwdriver. He used it to remove the laptop's back cover, then the hard drive. He pulled his own laptop from his satchel and connected Kendra's hard drive to it via an interface cable.

As he flipped up his laptop's lid, Kendra saw an elaborately etched cartoon version of Sam on it, with the motto BORN TO BE BAD in a fiery font.

"You're kidding, right?"

He shrugged. "A gift from a grateful client. He's actually very talented. If I detached the top cover and put it on eBay, I could get thousands for it." He switched on his computer. "Let's see what malware your nasty friend put on your computer."

"Aren't you afraid of infecting your own system?"

He smiled and shook his head. "Please. This thing is bulletproof. I've had foreign governments try to penetrate my systems and totally fall on their asses."

Kendra had once dismissed Sam's pronouncements as mere braggadocio, but she now knew better. As proud as Sam was of his accomplishments, she was aware of the fact that there was far more he *didn't* talk about, especially where his security-sensitive clients were involved.

Sam glanced at his screen as it booted up. "The thing about firewalls I build for myself, I don't sell or license them to anyone. That way no one knows how to crack them. Trust me, my computer has nothing to worry about."

"So what's happening now?"

"I'm taking an inventory of the applications on your hard drive. I hope you don't have anything on there you don't want me to see."

"Like nude pictures of myself?"

"Pfft. Seen that. Old news." He shrugged. "Maybe compromising pictures of the new man in your life."

"There's no new man in my life."

"I heard you were living with someone. But if you don't want to talk about it . . ."

"There's nothing to talk about. I was staying there for my own safety. Nothing more."

"Uh-huh. And there was nowhere else you could stay?"

"Not like that. I'm telling you, it's like a fortress."

"You've butted heads with a lot of sickos in your time. You've never squirreled yourself away before, even when it would have been the prudent thing to do. There must have been something about this guy that made you feel safe. Protected."

"Yes. His house. I've already told you. What are you seeing on my hard drive?"

"Still scanning." Sam regarded her for a moment. "It's not a sign of weakness to lean on someone occasionally, Kendra. I'm actually proud of you. I wish you'd do it more often. I think you're so determined to show that you can now stand on your own two feet that you sometimes ignore the lifelines that people throw your way."

"If you don't mind, I think we have more pressing things to address right now."

"Can't you tell? We're multitasking. If you'd prefer, we can talk about the weather until your hard drive is finished. Or maybe how I've ruined you for all other men."

"Well, that might be the truth, but it wouldn't be in the way you're thinking."

"All right, the weather it is." He glanced back at the laptop screen. "Ah. Okay. Here we go. I can see that your system has been infected by some kind of remote desktop software. As long as you had an Internet connection, he was able to see everything you were doing. And that's how he was able to type his replies."

"Is this software anything you can trace?"

"Don't know. A lot of these things are traded freely on Web sites in the hacker community. But I was right about him not trying to cover his tracks. It's almost like . . ."

"What?"

Sam shook his head. "It's almost like he *wants* us to see what he was doing. Every line of programming code is on display here. As a matter of fact . . ."

He grabbed a napkin from the table dispenser and pulled a pen from his pocket. He quickly started jotting down letters, transcribing them from the screen. "Damn," he whispered.

"What is it?"

He turned the napkin around to show her. "This isn't programming code. It's a message."

"To whom?"

He tapped the napkin. "You."

She looked down.

It read: YOU ARE WASTING TIME, KENDRA. THE ANSWER IS NOT IN LOS ANGELES.

She shivered. "What in the hell . . ."

"There's more." Sam was already writing on another napkin. He turned it around to show her.

WHAT'S A NICE GIRL LIKE YOU DOING AT THIS SEEDY DINER IN THE MIDDLE OF THE NIGHT?

Kendra quickly turned toward the row of windows facing the street. "Could he be watching us?"

"I doubt it."

"But how do you know?"

"I don't know. But it's far more likely that he could have been listening to your side of our phone conversation. He may have been watching you using your built-in webcam. And even though this thing doesn't have GPS, he could have used the Wi-Fi radio to get a pretty accurate fix on your location when you brought it here. Remember, your laptop was on and under his control until I yanked the battery."

She felt sick. "The thought of him watching me . . ."

"I know." Sam grabbed another napkin and started writing on it. "There's one more here. I'm not sure what this one means." He turned the napkin around.

It read: I TOLD YOU WHERE TO LOOK. THE HOUSEBOAT, KENDRA. YOU'RE WASTING TIME.

She pushed the napkin away.

"This guy knows you, Kendra. He knew you'd have the computer analyzed, so he planned ahead of time to leave these messages for you in the code."

"Obviously." She took a moment to stifle the tension that gripped every inch of her body. "Colby is no computer genius. I don't believe he's ever even owned one. He had help."

Sam nodded. "Well, it was definitely someone who knows what he's doing. That's where I'd start. Known contacts with fairly sophisticated computer expertise."

"It could have been someone he corresponded with from prison. He's had fan letters from all over the world."

Sam grimaced. "Fan letters?"

"Disgusting, isn't it? He was a psychopath on death row. Yet he even had marriage proposals."

"Well, it's one thing to contemplate marrying a psychopath when he's about to be put to death. I wonder if any of those women would marry him now?"

"I wouldn't put it past them. The first order of business is to find out if he was pen pals with any computer experts. His stint on death row put him in contact with a huge network of disturbed loners."

Sam nodded toward the screen. "It also seems pretty important to him that you visit this houseboat."

"It was the scene of the crime. He killed a woman there last night." She looked down at the words on the napkin she had pushed away. "A woman who did her best to make a national joke of me. The police thought it best if I stayed on the sidelines for this one."

"Well, he really wants you to go there."

"Which makes me want to run the other way as fast as I can."

"The hell it does. You're just dying to get in there."

She started to deny it, but she stopped herself. Sam was right. Colby had known what he was doing when he dangled that carrot in front of her.

Sam pointed to her hard drive. "I hope there isn't anything on this you want to keep."

"Aside from every project I've been working on for the past year. Of course not. I back everything up and save it in the cloud."

"Good girl." He handed her his pen and slid a napkin over. "Now jot down your cloud storage account info and password."

"Seriously?"

"Yes. I'm going to scan every single file you own and make sure there aren't any nasty viruses lurking there. And you can kiss this hard drive good-bye. I'll give it a good look, sector by sector. And I'll see what I can do about tracing any malware I find."

She wrote down the information and handed it to him.

"Now give me your phone."

She handed him her phone. "You think he might have done the same thing to my phone as my computer?"

"I've no idea, but I'm going to find out." He plugged her phone into his computer and did a check. "No, it's clear." He handed the phone back to her. "But I may ask you to let me check it occasionally just to be sure nothing has changed."

"Anytime. And with extreme gratitude." She tucked the phone back in her pocket. "Thanks, Sam. I knew you were the right man for the job."

"The *only* man. In the meantime, it would be a good idea to find the computer geek who helped him with this.

Check mail and call logs at the prison, visitor information, whatever."

"Got it. I know he managed to obtain a cell phone in prison, so that may be the place to start."

"Good. And there's something even more important."

"Yes?"

He was gazing at her soberly. "Watch your back. This isn't just a hacker you're dealing with here. For this guy, hacking is just a means to an end. He wants nothing more than to get in your head. It's personal for him. I guess what I'm saying is . . . Don't be afraid to grab every lifeline you can."

IT WAS ONLY A COUPLE HOURS BEFORE dawn when Kendra pulled into her parking place at the condo.

She didn't move for a moment. She could feel exhaustion dragging at every limb. She had first experienced a rush of adrenaline, then pure shock. It had been hard to comprehend the scope of Colby's invasion into her space.

She'd felt violated.

Well, she had to comprehend it. She had known he was clever, even brilliant. She had to meet that dark, malignant brilliance and survive it. She glanced down at the place where she'd set her computer when she'd brought it to Sam.

Crazy. She felt as if the computer were still there, listening.

Good Lord, that *was* crazy. She was actually nervous, paranoid, feeling as if that machine might actually attack her.

Get a grip. That was the response Colby wanted from her.

She swung open the driver's door and got out of her car.

Five minutes later, she was unlocking the door of her condo. Another five minutes, and she was crawling into her bed and turning off the lamp.

Pleasant dreams. I can't tell you how much I enjoy them.

She went rigid. It was the first time she had even thought of those last words Colby had written. She had been too occupied with the shock of his main message.

And she'd been right to ignore them. It had just been another ploy to terrify her and make her remember a time when he was dominant, and she was weak.

Blood.

That knife shining in the moonlight.

That feeling of helpless terror.

He couldn't know, he was guessing.

But he knew her well enough to guess that she would never forget that night, that any panicky event would make it storm back to her.

He'd probably even realized that she would not be able to assess that last sentence until she was here alone, in her room.

Block it. She needed to rest, to plan, to sleep, so that she would be able to deal with the next few days. It was only a few hours before Beth would be pounding on her door.

Sleep.

She closed her eyes determinedly.

Pleasant dreams . . .

I don't hear you, Colby.

"YOU LOOK LIKE HELL." BETH GAZED AT HER appraisingly. "And it took forever for you to answer my buzzer downstairs. You okay?"

"I will be after I have a shower. I had a late night." She stepped aside and let Beth into the condo. "Twenty minutes. Get yourself coffee and orange juice."

"Those call logs paid off?"

"You might say that they did. But not in the way you might think." She turned and headed for the bathroom. "I'll tell you over coffee."

She held her face under the warm spray, letting it wash away all the cobwebs.

Not cobwebs. Blood.

Pleasant dreams.

Don't think of it. It may have been an uneasy sleep born of terror and nightmares but she'd take it. She couldn't control her subconscious while she was sleeping, so she'd use it to fuel her determination while awake. Just don't let the thought of Colby get in the way while she was wide-awake and searching for him.

Instead, think of what she was going to say to Beth and how she was to handle her response.

Lord, she was tired of trying to handle everything around her. As for what she was going to say, there was no question. The truth and nothing but the truth. Beth was no child and had suffered years of oppression. If she wanted to help, Kendra would never keep her in the dark.

Kendra knew the dangers of that darkness.

BETH GAVE A LOW WHISTLE. "DEAR GOD, Kendra, that sounds very, very weird. And downright scary." She had listened quietly while Kendra had related the events after Beth had left her last night. She lifted her cup to her lips. "And fascinating. I'd love to meet your Sam Zackoff. I remember you told me he helped you and Eve get me out of that hospital, but I've never had a chance to thank him.

And I never dreamed computers could be so interesting. Of course, I was in that hospital during the years when all those high-tech high jinks were being developed."

"I could wish these particular high jinks were a little less fascinating," Kendra said dryly. "It was a distinctly uneasy experience."

"I can see how it would be." Beth reached across the table and grasped Kendra's hand. "Sorry. The concept just interested me. It must have been terrible for you. I can imagine how it would be to see a message from a monster seemingly appear out of nowhere in front of you." She added gently, "But now you know that you were right, that Colby is still alive. I know that doesn't bring you satisfaction, but it should bring you vindication."

"Hollow victory."

"It's a step forward. I'm trying to be optimistic." She finished her coffee. "Now, let's go and see what's on that houseboat."

Kendra's brows rose. "I believe I mentioned that I might have a little trouble getting permission."

"You'll get around it."

"I'm going to go see Griffin at the FBI and see if I can get him to use his clout to get me inside."

"See, I told you that you'd get around it."

"And I'm not sure that I should take you along on an errand Colby is sending me on."

"Why not?" Beth met her gaze. "Are you afraid Colby will connect me with you? Too late. If he's spying on you through that computer, he probably knows who and what I am to you. Right?"

She nodded. "I'm afraid that's true. But I can keep you under the radar."

Beth shook her head. "It would only show Colby I'm important to you if you try to hide me."

"So much for skating around the edges. I'm sorry, Beth."

"I'm not. I'm beginning to dislike this Colby intensely." Her lips thinned. "That computer nonsense was really creepy."

"I would say the murders were a good deal more intimidating."

"Yes, but you're far more accustomed to violence and mayhem than I am. But he was trying to scare and manipulate you with that computer message. I don't like manipulation. I was manipulated most of my adult life while I was penned up in that hospital. I *hate* for anyone to try to do that to you."

Kendra could see how that would strike Beth. She would always remember those years and fight against their happening again. Even the karate lessons and physical training in self-defense were part of that battle for control of her life. "I'm with you. But that doesn't mean I've changed my mind about trying to keep you as much out of this as possible."

"I didn't think it would. It's your nature. I just wanted you to realize that it was useless to go overboard in that direction by hiding me in the cellar."

Her lips twitched. "I have no cellar."

She waved her hand. "See, total waste of time. So now that we've established that, do you have something for me to do that would prove useful?"

"You can check on the executive who is paying for the houseboat where Sheila Hunter was living." She gave her the name. "And find out whatever you can from the people where she works."

"Got it. Anything else?"

"The computer geek who might have been tapped by Colby while he was in prison. He's important. You can help me locate him."

"And may I go with you to the houseboat?"

She hesitated.

Beth shook her head. "No cellar, Kendra," she reminded softly.

She sighed. "Okay."

"Great." Beth got to her feet. "So let's see how we can go about manipulating that bastard, Colby."

Kendra pushed back her chair. "Slow down. First, I have to see about manipulating Special Agent Griffin," she said dryly. "And that's not going to be easy."

CHAPTER
7

"NO," GRIFFIN SAID FLATLY. "I'M not going to interfere with local·law enforcement. We have enough trouble maintaining harmonious relations."

Kendra tried to hold on to her temper. She'd been trying to persuade him for the last ten minutes and gotten nowhere. "I've shown you that computer message from Colby. He killed Sheila Hunter, and he's going to kill again."

"And I'm sure that you'll show that to the detective in charge, and he'll add it to the evidence. It's their case, not ours." He shrugged. "And there's no proof that message was from Colby. Copycat."

"It's not a copycat. He repeated the same words in that message he used to me when he was in prison."

"Really? I'm sure there could be an explanation for that similarity. San Diego PD just has to find it."

"Look, Griffin, I'm not going to disturb evidence. You

know me better than that. Just let me go in and see what the bastard wants me to see."

He just looked at her.

But he had an expression of sly satisfaction, and he hadn't kicked her out of his office. Was he enjoying this? It was possible. Their relationship was often conflicted, and he'd never liked the fact that he couldn't control her as he did his agents.

"I'm not going to beg you, Griffin. I'm sure you'd enjoy that, but it's not going to happen." She put her hands flat on his desk. "I'm just going to ask you what you want from me."

"Why, I don't know what you mean. We're both professionals, and we're merely having a difference of opinion."

"What do you want?" she repeated.

He was silent, then nodded. "What any civilized professional requests to settle a dispute. Compromise. If I do you a favor, it's only reasonable to expect a favor in return."

"What kind of favor?" she asked warily.

He smiled. "I haven't decided."

"What?"

"I believe I'd like to tuck that favor away for a rainy day."

"And let you hold it over my head for the foreseeable future?"

"That's about it." He leaned back in his chair. "After all, it's not as if I'm going to ask you to do anything illegal. Considering my position, that would go without saying."

"Would it? I don't know what you'll ask me."

"No, you don't. And that may bother you a little. But no more than the discomfort you've caused me on occasion. And this is going to be something of a headache. I'll have to make a call and back it up with my presence." He looked at his watch. "I have an appointment. But I could cancel it and call the superintendent in charge of the Hunter case. Should I do it?"

She hesitated. If she made the promise, she would be bound to keep it. She hated the idea of being obligated to Griffin.

She wanted to sock him.

She turned toward the door. "Make the call."

THE EARLY-MORNING SUN SHIMMERED ON the San Diego Bay as Kendra and Beth drove slowly toward Marina Cortez. They had stopped for coffee at Starbucks when Kendra had joined Beth after talking to Griffin. She had wanted to give Griffin plenty of time to get his ducks in a row. It should have been a beautiful drive, but Kendra couldn't shake the horrible image that had greeted her and Lynch there the other night.

It was now quieter, with a single TV news van parked nearby and a reporter from the local Spanish-language station doing his stand-up on the dock. The houseboat was still cordoned off with yellow police tape, and four men in their shirtsleeves were waiting nearby.

Waiting for her.

"Do you know them?" Beth asked.

"Yes. Three of them are cops, the other is FBI Special Agent Michael Griffin. He's the man I had to stop to see at FBI headquarters downtown. He's the only reason I'm being allowed in here today."

"Good of him to show up," Beth said. "I'm surprised. You were looking pretty grim when you came back to the car after seeing him."

"I was feeling pretty grim."

"But evidently he decided to come and smooth things over for you."

"That's the way it looks, doesn't it? More likely to make sure I play nice with the local cops. He stuck his neck out for me, and he wants to keep me from abusing the privilege."

"Will it work?"

"We'll know soon."

They parked and walked up the narrow dock to Sheila Hunter's houseboat. Kendra extended her hand to Stokes. "Detective, I do appreciate this."

Stokes shook her hand. "Thank my boss. Or my boss's boss." He grimaced. "Or whoever your FBI associate here strong-armed."

"Strong-armed?" Griffin smiled. "Is that really how we describe cooperation between our law-enforcement agencies? I merely made a request."

Stokes gestured to the two other men. "I believe you've met Detectives Ketchum and Starger. They've gone over every inch of this place since the night of the murder. If you would care to tell them what you're looking for, I'm sure they would be happy to—"

"I have no idea what I'm looking for," Kendra said.

The detectives exchanged a look. "No idea at all?"

"No."

"Okay." Stokes's tone was sour. "So much for cooperation between law-enforcement agencies."

Kendra turned toward Griffin. She wasn't sure how much information he'd given to their superior, and she wasn't anxious to share what probably would sound like a wild-eyed conspiracy theory.

"Look," Griffin said. "Dr. Michaels promised to share any observations she makes while in Sheila Hunter's houseboat. That was my deal with your superintendent, and she will honor that. Fair enough?"

Stokes motioned toward Beth. "Who's this?"

"Her name is Beth Avery. I brought her to take notes."

Stokes turned toward Griffin. "Was she part of your deal, too?"

"I suppose she is now."

Stokes handed Kendra, Beth, and Griffin pairs of latex evidence gloves. "If you wish to touch something, call one of us over to supervise."

Kendra snapped on her gloves. "No problem, I have a feeling you won't be too far away."

"We won't. This crime scene is still under the jurisdiction of the San Diego PD."

Griffin nodded. "And I'm sure you'll keep reminding us of that."

"Only if it becomes absolutely necessary. It's up to you," Stokes smiled. "Ready?"

Am I ready, Colby?

What have you got to show me in there?

You must have been here in this very spot, plotting, planning.

Killing.

She nodded. "Yes, I'm ready."

They stepped off the dock and walked through the doorway of the boxy one-story houseboat. Kendra was immediately struck by the luxurious interior that eschewed any hint of a nautical theme. The floors were covered by intricately patterned tile that looked like something out of a Beverly Hills estate. The lighting was soft, with several small ceiling spots highlighting framed art deco travel posters for European ski destinations.

Beth stepped around a large brown leather sofa. "Nice place. Very nice. I can see why you thought an online journalist wouldn't be able to afford digs like this, Kendra."

"I told you, it's registered to an executive of her media company." Kendra's eyes darted around the room. "Strange."

"What?" Beth asked.

"There are a few objects in here that have been wiped clean. Recently, in the last day or two." She turned toward Stokes. "I know forensics wouldn't have done it. Your men wouldn't have done it either, would they?"

He shook his head. "I don't know what you've heard, but our department doesn't provide maid service for murder victims."

She pointed to a guitar propped up on a black metal stand in the corner. "That guitar has definitely been wiped down. Its glossy finish would show every fingerprint and each speck of dust, but there are none." She pointed to a ceramic cigarette lighter resting on the countertop that divided the kitchenette from the living room. "Same story with that lighter."

"Lighter?" Beth turned toward the police officers. "Did she smoke?"

"No." Kendra answered before they could reply. "I would have picked up the odor on her, but someone was in the habit of smoking an occasional cigar in here. And the glass tabletop and the back of the chairs do have fingerprints. No one was concerned about wiping those clean."

Detective Starger spoke for the first time. "We lifted quite a few prints from the tabletop and elsewhere in here."

"Good," Kendra said. "I'd like to know what the story is with that guitar. Especially since she didn't play it."

"How do you know?" Griffin asked.

"Anyone who plays an acoustic guitar with any regularity develops calluses. I have them. It's actually necessary to play well. Sheila Hunter's fingertips were smooth, and her nails long and beautifully manicured."

"Maybe a boyfriend?" Beth suggested.

"Maybe." Kendra turned toward Stokes. "Was she in a relationship?"

"Not as far as we've been able to determine. We're still exploring that possibility."

Kendra scanned the kitchen. "Everything seems to be in place in here."

"There were two glasses in the sink," Stokes said. "Both had Sheila Hunter's prints and her prints alone."

Kendra nodded and turned back toward the living room. "Any sign of the area rug?"

"Area rug?"

"About six by eight feet, red and cream with gold medallions. It was in the middle of the living room, under the couch and coffee table."

Detectives Starger and Ketchum exchanged a look before turning back to face her. "There was no rug here," Ketchum said.

"Actually, there was. The only question is whether it was removed before or after Sheila Hunter's murder."

Stokes crossed his arms across his chest. "And how would you know that?"

"I saw it."

"You've been in here before?"

Oh, Lord, now they were suspicious of her again. "No, never."

"Then how—"

"You saw it, too," she said impatiently. "All of you did. You just weren't paying attention." Kendra walked back toward the entrance, where the wall was covered by a collage of framed photographs. She pointed to a group shot of Sheila and her friends in the living room wearing over-sized football jerseys. Some were sitting cross-legged on the rug, others were standing around it. "Right here."

The detectives, Griffin, and Beth followed her to the wall to gaze at the photos. "I'll be damned," Stokes said. "But there's no telling how long ago that rug—"

"Sixty days, give or take," Kendra broke in. "That's the most recent Super Bowl on the TV behind them. I have no idea who won, but those were the teams, right?"

Stokes studied the photograph again. "Uh, yeah."

In the photograph's glass reflection, Kendra caught Griffin smiling. He was clearly enjoying her display and the discomfort it was furnishing the detectives more than he did on his own investigations. That annoyed her, too. After that far-from-subtle holdup he'd maneuvered to get her permission to come here, she didn't like that he was getting any amusement from the situation.

She turned a warm smile on Stokes. "Actually, it's per-fectly understandable that you'd not notice the photo. You'd be surprised what Special Agent Griffin's team manages to miss, and they have all that expensive, technical equip-ment at their disposal. I'm sure you did a good job here, Detective."

Stokes nodded. "Thanks." He smiled. "It's good to be appreciated. Anything else you need to see?"

"Yes." She moved toward a rear doorway, passing Grif-fin, who was no longer smiling. "Bedroom?"

"Just a single bedroom and bath."

The group followed Kendra back to the bedroom, which, like the rest of the houseboat, was tastefully deco-rated. A queen-size bed headed one wall, and a closet and cherrywood chest of drawers anchored the left side. A small desk was pushed into the corner, where a laptop, printer/scanner combo, and a bulletin board formed Sheila's home office. Kendra motioned for Beth to capture the photo of the bulletin board contents with her iPad.

Beth crouched beside the desk and panned over the board. "Looks like she was working on a few different stories."

Kendra nodded. "It's likely she did a lot of work in her office downtown."

"We've been to her cubicle and spoken to her colleagues," Starger said. "Including some who witnessed your blowup in the plaza. It was quite the scene."

"Then I suppose you've read her story about me."

"We have. You're saying it's inaccurate?"

"No. My problem was that she lied and possibly used illegal means in order to get me to participate in a slam piece against myself."

"Yeah, the captain told us he'd received some kind of hard evidence that had happened."

Lynch. He'd told her that he'd find a way to do it, but she hadn't thought he'd had time yet.

Griffin shrugged. "It wouldn't be the first time that a journalist gained the cooperation of a source under false pretenses."

"She was scum," Beth said bluntly. "I had a front-row seat to the whole thing. Lying scum."

"Calm down, Beth. Her actions speak for themselves, as your captain will confirm, Detective," Kendra said. "I'll just leave it at that."

"That's all well and good," Stokes said. "But we may still wish to have you come in and discuss this with us a bit further, Dr. Michaels."

She stared at him, trying to decipher his tone. Was he threatening her? Or merely trying to check all the necessary boxes in the investigation? Or he might just be trying to pick her brains so that he would look good to his superiors. She was leaning toward the last option. It was what he had done at that first crime scene where she had met him. No problem. As long as he needed something from her, she might be able to get information. Cooperation would definitely be the correct course. She was probably going to have to live with suspicion until she was able to prove Colby had killed Sheila. She'd have to walk very carefully indeed. "Anytime."

She stepped through the bathroom doorway and froze. The shower was blocked by several lengths of police tape, pulled taut over the glass door. "What's this?"

Starger joined her in the cramped bathroom. "The forensics team has indicated that they might want to come back for another look there."

"Why?" Kendra said as she examined the white tile shower walls. "The only reason they'd do that is if . . ." Realization hit her. ". . . they think the killer might have cleaned up here."

Starger nodded.

Kendra knelt beside the shower to get a closer look at a tiny stain on the wall tiles. "Is that blood?"

"Yes," Starger said.

"Would you care to elaborate and tell me whose blood?" Kendra asked. "Purely in the spirit of our vaunted cooperation?"

Stoker spoke to Griffin as well as Kendra. "The blood is Sheila Hunter's. But we obtained other genetic material here. We're trying to push it through the lab."

"What genetic material?"

"We found some hair in the shower drain that wasn't hers."

Kendra moved closer and examined the toiletries on a small shelf above the sink. "Nothing out of the ordinary here. This is all the same shampoo, soap, and cologne she was wearing on the two days I saw her."

Kendra turned and stepped back into the bedroom. What in the hell had Colby sent her to find? It was easy to say that he only controlled her subconscious when she was sleeping and unable to fight him. But he *was* in her head, she realized. Baiting her, taunting her . . .

YOU'LL HAVE TO TRY HARDER, KENDRA . . .

Damn you, Colby.

I TOLD YOU WHERE TO LOOK . . .

The hell you did.

YOU'RE WASTING TIME . . .

Detach. Concentrate.

He was gone.

For now.

Stay sharp, she reminded herself. No good could come from having Eric Colby always in her mind.

She glanced around. "I need to look in every drawer, every closet. There has to be something I'm missing."

"Then we're missing it, too," Stokes said. "It's not a big place, and I was serious when I said we've searched every square inch."

"Please. I'll just be a few minutes more."

With Beth shooting video alongside her, Kendra examined every item of clothing in the closet and drawers. She held up each of Sheila's twenty-one pairs of shoes and turned them upside down to look at the soles. Then she moved to the kitchenette and living room, where she examined the drawers and cabinets.

Nothing.

Absolutely nothing.

"Satisfied?" Stokes asked.

Kendra shook her head. "No. I'm missing something."

"We can't allow you any more time." Stokes gestured toward the front door. "If you don't mind, Dr. Michaels."

She did mind. She wanted desperately to stay here until she was able to pinpoint the reason Colby had sent her here.

She turned on her heel and left the houseboat, with Beth following. Outside, they made their way down the dock to the parking lot. They turned to watch Griffin shake hands with the detectives.

All warm and fuzzy, Kendra thought. Griffin had given her exactly what she wanted, and she hadn't been able to follow through.

"You did a good job, Kendra," Beth said quietly. "You saw a lot in there. Things no one else picked up."

"It wasn't enough."

As the police detectives walked toward their cars, Griffin approached. "I'm sorry. I know that didn't go the way you had hoped."

"There has to be something else."

"Maybe there's a possibility you haven't considered yet."

"Like what?"

"Maybe your late-night hacker wasn't Colby at all."

"It was him."

Griffin shrugged. "Think about it. Sheila Hunter's story hit the Web, and just hours later, she was murdered. It became a worldwide news event. I don't have to tell you that there are a lot of weirdos on the Internet. A story like yours can inspire a lot of bad behavior. Her piece cast you as a lunatic, so maybe someone saw an opportunity to toy with you."

She said through her teeth. "I'm telling you, it was him."

"How do you know?"

"I told you, he used the same words he'd used to me before. No Internet prankster could know that."

"Are you sure? I've been thinking about that. These days, there are very few true secrets in the world."

"I'm positive. And it was more than that. I know the way he thinks, the way he expresses himself. That was Colby on the other side of that conversation. I'm positive."

"I know you believe that, Kendra."

He was patronizing her. "But you don't."

"I'm a pragmatic man. Truthfully, I'd like to believe you. It's just not in my makeup to do it." He smiled. "The feeling of frustration you're experiencing would miraculously evaporate if you could just find some proof." He nodded back at the houseboat. "And you sure as hell didn't find it in there."

"Maybe I did, and just don't know it yet."

He raised an eyebrow. "You're one stubborn woman, do you know that?"

"Yes. It's a curse. At the moment, a damned annoying curse." She turned to face him. "Oh, and I have another favor to ask."

"Of course, you do."

"It's not one that will cause you any inconvenience as this one did." Her lips twisted. "So you shouldn't demand a return favor."

"I'm listening."

"Your office still has copies of Colby's prison records . . . His visitor and call logs, and everything he left behind in his cell."

"Yes. We got a court order after his execution. There was some thought that there might be some victims that we didn't know about yet, so we wanted to cover our bases."

"I need to know if Colby was in touch with anyone with sophisticated computer skills. There was some FBI analysis done on those logs, wasn't there?"

"Some."

"Identifying his contacts, that kind of thing?"

"Again, some. But it hasn't been a high priority."

"I understand. But it would be a huge help if I could get that information."

He lifted his shoulder in half shrug. "I'll see what I can do. You're right, no real inconvenience connected to this favor, but you're still running up a serious tab in that department." He turned and strolled toward his car.

"It's like pulling teeth to deal with him, isn't it?" Beth murmured. "Will he do it?"

"Probably."

Beth turned back to Kendra. "What now?"

"Let's go back to my place. I want to take a look at the video you shot."

They climbed into Kendra's car and drove down Harbor Village Drive. They hadn't even gone half a mile when Kendra saw Stokes's unmarked car, flashers pulsing, turned perpendicular to the flow of traffic and blocking one of the two lanes. Starger and Ketchum were now standing in the road and waving cars through the roadblock.

Kendra pulled up to them. "What's going on?"

Stokes approached her. "I'm afraid this is all for you, Dr. Michaels. We need you to join us for questioning at the police headquarters on Broadway Street."

"What?" Her gaze wandered around the roadblock in bewilderment. "Why?"

"We can discuss it there."

"No, we can discuss it now. What's changed in the last five minutes?"

"Once we're at the station, we'll go into it in detail and—"

"We can discuss it now, or I'm not going anywhere."

He glanced up at the growing line of cars behind her. "Fine," he snapped. "We checked in on the lab results for the hair we found in Sheila Hunter's shower drain. They extracted the DNA, and we got a hit on the CODIS database."

"Good. Whose DNA is it?"

"*Yours*, Dr. Michaels."

Kendra stared at him, not sure she had heard him correctly. A car horn blasted in the line behind her. "You're trying to tell me that—"

"Your DNA. Your hair. Found in a place you just told me you've never been before."

She turned away, trying to suppress the sudden nausea that had hit her.

I'VE ALREADY BROUGHT THE FIGHT TO YOU, KENDRA . . . YOU JUST DON'T KNOW IT YET.

"Dr. Michaels?"

She finally looked back up. "Yes."

"We're going to need that statement immediately. Come with us, please,"

"Are you arresting me?"

"We just need to talk to you." His lips tightened. "And we need that statement."

"Kendra." Beth wore a stunned expression. "What the hell is happening?"

"It'll be okay, Beth."

"You heard him. You don't have to go with him."

"Of course, I do. We need to figure this out." She shifted into park. "Take the car. I'll ride with them and call you when I'm finished."

"No way. We'll both go."

Kendra was too upset to deal with comforting and explaining to Beth right now. All she wanted was to get this over. "That's not a good idea," she said impatiently.

"I'm going with you."

"Why? So you can be my lawyer? You're not qualified in that—"

"No," Beth said gently. "So I can be your friend."

Kendra immediately felt terrible for snapping at her. "I'm sorry, Beth. You're a great friend. But, trust me, it's best that I talk to them alone." She opened the car door and got out. "I'll call you when I'm done."

Kendra rode in silence in Stokes's car for the short ride to police headquarters on Broadway and Fourth. They didn't discuss the case again until they arrived at the small third-floor interrogation room and were met by Detectives Starger and Ketchum.

Stokes placed a bottled water on the table in front of her. "Anything else I can get you?"

She shook her head.

"Full disclosure, this conversation is being recorded, as is any conversation that takes place in this room." He pointed to the video camera glowing red in the corner.

She smiled. "Funny that you say 'conversation' when the sign on the door says 'interrogation.'"

"Tomato, To-mahto." He motioned for her to sit.

"Good one."

They sat around the small wooden table, where she noticed someone had managed to carve the words EAT ME, COP with the tip of a ballpoint pen.

"Thank you for coming, Dr. Michaels," Starger started. "In light of this development, we thought we should get you on record discussing your knowledge and personal contact with Sheila Hunter in the days preceding her murder."

Kendra looked down at the manila folder on Starger's lap, which was open to a photo of the shower drain. A clump of wet hair was caught in the grate.

Her hair.

She nodded. "Sure. Whatever you need."

"Okay, when was the first time you ever entered Sheila Hunter's premises at the houseboat?"

"At about ten thirty this morning."

"You're positive of that?"

"It was true this morning, and it's true now."

"Fine. And when was the first time you met Ms. Hunter?"

"Thursday evening. I'd never even heard her name before that day. She contacted me about a story she was writing."

"Please tell us about that meeting."

Kendra described their meeting at the W bar, the on-line news story that appeared a day later, and their confrontation in the plaza.

"And when did you see her next?"

"When she was dead and bleeding, hanging from the mast of her houseboat."

Stokes nodded. "You were there just a few minutes after we were. How did you find out about her murder?"

"Adam Lynch came to my condo and told me. He drove me to the scene."

"And how did he know?" Ketchum asked.

"He has friends in law enforcement everywhere, so

there isn't much he doesn't know. But you'll have to ask him."

"You can be sure we will." Ketchum's tone was biting.

None of the courtesy that Starger had shown her, Kendra thought.

Good cop, bad cop.

That was clearly how it was going to be played out.

If she permitted it.

She would try to hold her temper and let them do their thing. It was a bad situation, and the more accommodating she was, the more likely she was to get out of it.

Or at least mitigate the consequences.

"Time for the million-dollar question," Stokes said. He pointed to the crime-scene photo of the shower drain. "How did your hair get into the shower?"

"It was placed there. Obviously."

The detectives shared a quick glance. "Okay," Stokes said. "Placed by whom?"

"Eric Colby."

"Of course," Ketchum said sarcastically. "But can we be a little more real?"

Don't rise to the bait.

"He couldn't be more real."

"Okay," Starger said. "We'll get back to that later. Let's go back to Sheila Hunter. Will you repeat what you told us about your first meeting?"

"Why should I do—"

Patience.

She told them again.

And again.

They dug into every minute detail, then came back and did it again.

Hours passed, and the same questions kept coming. Her

answers became more clipped and sharp, but she didn't lose it.

Until Ketchum leaned forward, and said, "Why not be honest? We know this is a pack of lies."

She blew up. "You know nothing of the sort. You're just trying to wear me out, hoping to get lucky and find a fallacy in my statement. I've put up with it, but if that's the way you're going to speak to me, then we're done here."

Ketchum shook his head. "We'll tell you when you're done."

"Actually, no. Unless you're prepared to arrest me, which I know you aren't, or you wouldn't be trying to give me this poor man's third degree. This conversation is taking place by virtue of a Kendra Michaels grant. A grant of my time, and of my willingness to put up with your questions when I could be out there finding this person who *will* kill again." She looked Ketchum in eye. "Plus, I don't like being judged or called a liar by a man who's clearly cheating on his wife."

Ketchum reacted with a start. "What? What the hell makes you think that—" He looked at Starger and Stokes and started to sputter. "This is— This is crazy. Are we gonna just sit here and—"

"You know, I've just decided you're done, Detective Ketchum," Kendra said. "You can watch the rest of this conversation from the next room or wherever this camera feed goes. If you don't leave this room in the next thirty seconds, then I will."

Ketchum stared at her incredulously. "You're crazy. Do you believe we'd allow a person of interest in a murder case to dictate the way we—"

"Only if you want the conversation to continue."

Kendra grabbed her sweater from the chair back. "Twenty-five seconds. Your choice."

Another few seconds of silence. Stokes jerked his head toward the door. "Ketchum, take a break. It's gotten a little tense in here."

Ketchum looked at them all as if they were insane. He stood and stalked out of the room.

After the door slammed shut behind him, Starger leaned toward Kendra. "Just out of curiosity, how did you know he's cheating on his—"

"Let's not get into that right now," Stokes interrupted, nervously eyeing the camera. "Just a few more questions, Dr. Michaels."

"I believe that you've learned all you can from Kendra." Griffin walked into the interrogation room. "It's time to wrap this up."

"I think we have to make that decision," Stokes said. "And you're not invited in here."

"And I was politely keeping out of your way for the last hour. It was very interesting observing your interrogation techniques." He looked back at the door through which Ketchum had exited. "Or lack of it. But it appears Dr. Michaels is getting impatient. So I decided to step in and try to effect a compromise."

"Oh, yes, he's very good at compromises," Kendra said with irony.

Griffin ignored her comment. "She's right; you're not ready to arrest her, and it must have come to your attention that you're not going to get a confession out of her. I'm not sure you have any conviction that she really had anything to do with the killing. You just don't have anywhere else to go, and it's not making you look good."

"Her hair in the grate was—"

"A good reason to bring her in. I would have done the same. But we all know that DNA can be planted. Anyone with the abilities of Dr. Michaels would have known to safeguard herself and removed it from that grate. The FBI is assuming that it has to be a plant."

"And the San Diego PD isn't any too certain," Stokes said.

"And that's where the compromise comes in," Griffin said. "Let us have the strand of hair, and I'll have our labs fast-track any evidence about that DNA and any other evidence you bring to us on the case."

"We already have an ID on the hair. Why should we go any further?"

"Because if you don't search further, then you'll look like asses if we turn up something that makes her look like a heroine victimized by the hometown cops," Griffin added softly. "And we're very good at what we do. Let us help you tie this case up."

Stokes's gaze narrowed on his face. "Why are you doing this? She's not one of your agents."

"In the interest of justice. In the spirit of cooperation. You name it, Stokes."

He hesitated. "We remain in control of the investigation?"

"Of course."

Stokes slowly nodded. "Compromise is a good thing. Particularly when I come out on top." He pushed back his chair. "I was close to releasing her anyway. I can always pick her up again." He smiled at Griffin. "And I made a deal that the department will appreciate. We don't often get the chance to give orders to the FBI."

"Enjoy it." Griffin took Kendra's arm and nudged her toward the door. "It will be a rare pleasure for you."

Kendra only waited until they were out of the room before she turned to face him. "Why?"

"That sounded suspicious," he said. "When I'm only trying to do you a small service." He thought about it. "No, it was not small. Not huge, but considerable."

"Why?" she repeated. "Why did you come down here?"

"I heard you were having some difficulty, and I thought I'd see if it was necessary to step into the arena." He led her toward the elevator. "I thought you were handling them with admirable coolness until you decided to go on the attack. You had to bring up Ketchum's affair?"

"I just wanted him out of there. Those detectives were very aware of those cameras. Stokes, at least, is aware of my abilities. He probably didn't want another detective put on the spot and his private life revealed on that tape." She got on the elevator. "Why are you here? You wanted me to beg you for a favor that was less than this one. Now you show up and offer a bribe to get me off the hook."

"Merely a deal that will benefit all of us."

"Why?"

"I'll leave you to figure that out for yourself. Maybe it's because I have a real affection for you." He was smiling as the doors started to close. "Or maybe it was because I couldn't see how you'd be able to repay the favor you promised me if you ended up in a jail cell."

CHAPTER
8

"THEY KEPT YOU A LONG TIME." Beth was standing by her car, waiting, when Kendra walked out of the precinct. "By the time you called, I'd started to wonder if I needed bail and a defense attorney for you."

"I think it was a little close," Kendra said. "I changed from a person of interest to skirting the edge of being an actual suspect." She got into the passenger seat. "And if Griffin hadn't gone to bat for me and offered the facilities of the FBI to help in the investigation, I might have had to lawyer up to keep out of jail."

Beth pulled away from the curb. "Griffin helped?"

Kendra nodded. "Like Batman to the rescue. I was surprised, too." She looked out the window at the passing streetlight. "He pointed out that DNA could be planted and that a woman of my background and abilities would never make the mistake of leaving a piece of crucial evidence like that."

"And they said that everyone makes mistakes," Beth said. "I'm glad they decided not to play hardball."

"Me too." She leaned her head back and closed her eyes. "But Colby won't be glad. He went to so much trouble to set it up."

"You think it was Colby,"

"Who else? It would show how superior he was to me. How he could manipulate me to suit himself."

"Kendra," Beth said quietly. "Where did he get that strand of your hair?"

"I wish I knew." Her eyes opened. "The logical answer would be my hairbrush. It's also one of the most frightening. Did he find a way to break into my condo to get that hair?"

"Possibly. How is your security?"

"Very good. Is it perfect? Probably not." She shook her head. "It's not the only answer. I go to the hairdresser for hair trims every five weeks or so."

"That's not much scarier. He would have had to be watching you to know that was where he had to go to get what he wanted."

I'm watching you.

"That goes without saying. But I don't know how long he's been watching me."

"A minute is too long." She grimaced. "This really spooked me, Kendra. I didn't care about been thrown into jail myself, but I hated the idea that bastard was railroading you. I felt helpless. They wouldn't even let me see you."

"You couldn't have done anything anyway."

"Sure I could. I just had to think what to do. If you could spring me out of that jail when Bubba was out to get me, there wasn't a question that I have to return the favor."

"Colby isn't Bubba."

"But they're both evil and want to manipulate the world to suit themselves." She was pulling into a parking spot in front of Kendra's condo. "And we can't let them get away with it." She opened her door. "But that's not tonight. Tonight, you need to go to bed and get a good night's sleep so that we can tackle Colby tomorrow. I'll walk you to your door, then take off for my hotel." She was walking toward the condo entrance. "Unless you'd like me to stay the night?"

"No. And I don't need you to escort me to my door." Though she found it very touching. "I would have let you bail me out if necessary, but I don't need a bodyguard, Beth."

"Sure you do." She smiled as she watched Kendra key herself into the building. "I keep telling you. I'm your muscle." She turned and headed back toward her car. "See you tomorrow . . ."

Kendra shook her head as she watched Beth get into her car and take off. Her relationship with Beth was getting increasingly complicated. Who was protecting whom?

And what difference did it make? It was a dangerous world they were living in right now, and it was only important to survive.

And make sure that Colby did not survive.

But Beth was right, she had to rest so that she would be ready to resume the battle tomorrow.

Shower. Maybe have a cup of tea. Try to go over what she'd seen on the houseboat and see if she would have a breakthrough. Then go to bed and try to get to sleep.

The gully.

Pleasant dreams.

If the nightmare came, it would come. She would not let him make her afraid.

* * *

SHE'D FINISHED THE SHOWER AND washing her hair and was making her tea when her cell phone rang.

Beth checking on her?

No, not Beth.

"Why are you calling, Lynch? Bored? I'm too tired right now to try to entertain you."

"When did you ever make that attempt? And evidently you're keeping yourself too busy to get bored," he said grimly. "I'm surprised you still have your phone. That must mean that they thought better of tossing you into jail."

"Ah, your spies are on the job again." She dropped down in the chair and lifted her cup to her lips. "Or was it Griffin?"

"Both. I got a report that you were being questioned, and I called Griffin and made him fill me in. He wasn't pleased, but he did enjoy the fact that you were up to your neck in trouble and I couldn't do a thing about it."

"That sounds like him. But even if you wanted to help, there was no way you could from Luxembourg."

"Even if I wanted—" He drew a deep breath. "Of course, I'd want to—" He stopped. "Why didn't you tell me that Colby contacted you?"

"You were flying to Europe. What could you have done anyway?"

"How the hell do I know? But you didn't give me the option."

"No one believed it was him anyway. Even Griffin said copycat."

"But you believed it?"

"What difference does that make? Everyone knows I'm obsessed about Colby."

"Stop being flippant. Was it him, Kendra?"

She was silent. "It was Colby, Lynch. I'd swear it."

He muttered a curse. "Do you know? I was hoping you were wrong about him."

"So was I. But hope doesn't always carry the day. Anyway, thanks for not being completely skeptical like the rest of the world."

"The rest of the world doesn't know you the way I do."

"If they did, they'd probably think I was even worse than my reputation. You've seen me at some very bad times, Lynch."

"And a few magnificent ones." He paused. "What's all this DNA business?"

"Colby, backing me in a corner, trying to bring me down before he strikes the final blow."

"Strikes the final blow," he repeated. "That was very matter-of-fact."

"Because it's not going to happen. I'm not going to let Colby have his own way. He's going down." She added, "This conversation isn't heading anywhere. You called to express your concern, and I appreciate it, but there's nothing—"

"Express my concern? You're damn right I'm concerned. I haven't been here more than a day, and you've already been contacted by a serial killer who wants to make you the next victim on his hit list, then came close to being arrested."

"And, of course, none of that would have happened if you'd been here watching my back?"

"Maybe not. I'm really good at watching your back."

She was silent a moment. "Yes, you are. But we both know I can't rely on you to do it. I have no right."

"Rights can be negotiated." He paused. "We can deal."

"You sound like Griffin. He made me promise to re-turn the favor if he got me permission to go into the houseboat."

"He did? That's dangerous. Griffin isn't a man you want to owe."

"I didn't have a choice."

"You have a choice with me," he said quietly. "Take it. Take what I can give. You won't be sorry."

She felt a sudden rush of heat. She could almost see him, the lean strength, the power, the intensity. The words could be taken many ways but there was a note in his voice . . .

"Kendra?"

"What are you talking about?" she said brusquely. "We've been working together for months. I've accepted your help. It's just that there have to be limits."

"Do there? I don't think that I agree. The idea of a lim-itless relationship appeals to me. It's a disciplined world for you right now. You've forgotten how fascinating it can be to slip under the boundaries. That might be where the negotiating comes in." He changed the subject. "Look, I'm working to wrap this situation here up quickly. There are a few sticky angles that I'm having to skim around, and I may be stuck for a day or two."

"Why are you telling me? It's your business to do as you please."

"I'm telling you because if it wasn't a possible hostage situation, I'd be on the next plane."

"Hostage. You didn't tell me that."

"It could go either way. I may have to go in and do some fancy tap dancing. And if I do that, it will be incognito. I won't even be able to take my own phone." He was silent.

"But I'll shove it to someone else if things get more dicey for you. You've got to promise me that you'll tell me right away."

"I don't intend to come running to you if—"

"Promise me."

She knew that tone of voice. He wasn't going to give up. "I'll tell you if I don't believe I can handle it."

He muttered a curse. "And that's almost less than nothing. Okay, remember that he'll strike not only at you but the people close to you. If you don't want to accept help for yourself, do you have the right to not bring in additional troops to save them?"

Beth. Olivia. Her mother.

Lynch was not called the Puppetmaster for nothing. He had found the one argument she couldn't refute. "I'll keep that in mind."

"And isn't it time that you moved into my place?"

"No, it is not. Drop it, Lynch."

He didn't push it. He knew that he'd already won a major battle. "Okay, but remember it's an option."

"How could I forget? Good night, Lynch." She hung up.

She sat there staring down at the phone. The call had been disturbing and annoying and . . . comforting. Not surprising, when Lynch could be all things to all individuals if he wished.

Tonight she'd try to forget the disturbing and remember the comforting. It had been a rough day, and she needed to be soothed and told that everything would be all right.

And he had not done that, but he had said he wanted to watch her back, and that was pretty good, too.

She finished her tea and took the cup to the kitchen. She had planned to go over the items in the houseboat and try to put some clarity to confusion. But she would leave it for the night and go to bed. Maybe everything would be clearer in the morning.

She went back to her bedroom and started to turn out the light.

Then she stopped.

Not yet. One more thing before she risked that nightmare again.

She went into the bathroom and opened the drawer where she kept her toiletries.

Her silverback brush that Olivia had given her last Christmas shimmered in the lights from the vanity.

She looked at it for a moment, then took it out of the drawer. It felt light to the touch. There were a few strands of hair still on the bristles.

It would have been so easy for someone to run a comb through those bristles and take those strands.

Had Colby been here, looking in this mirror, the brush in his hands?

She shuddered. She could almost imagine him standing behind her, smiling.

No!

She threw the brush in the drawer and slammed it closed. She whirled, flipped off the light, and strode back into the bedroom.

She would not imagine what she did not know. She would not let him torment her. He was doing quite enough of that without her help.

She dove into bed and closed her eyes.

Don't think of the gully.

Don't think of that hairbrush.

Think of Lynch. Don't push away any part of what he made her feel. It might save her from Colby tonight.

Take it. Take what I can give. You won't be sorry.
I'm taking it, Lynch. Tonight, I choose you.

KENDRA WAS PERCHED ON THE edge of the sofa, staring intently at her television, when Beth entered the condo the next morning.

"Aha," Beth said. "The only thing that could require that level of concentration is the latest episode of *Real Housewives*. Or maybe *Duck Dynasty*."

"I got up early, and I've been going over the video you shot of Sheila Hunter's houseboat."

"Even more entertaining. I went over it a couple times myself. I have a hunch that you saw more than I did though."

"Not necessarily."

"Does it give you any ideas?"

Kendra paused the video. "Yeah, maybe. At any rate, today we're going to meet with the powerful CEO of a multinational media corporation and ask him a boatload of questions. No problem, right?"

"You've got to be talking about Robert Schultz. I saw the references to him in her phone records. You're going to try to see him?"

Kendra nodded. "Sheila Hunter was in constant contact with him, at all hours of the day and night. I can see it on the call logs Lynch pulled for me."

"You think something was going on between them?"

"*Something* was. It rang a bell with me when I was talking to those cops yesterday. One of them got extremely shifty when I accused him of cheating on his wife."

Beth laughed. "You accused a cop of—"

"Not my finest hour. I kind of lost my patience. Anyway,

it suddenly occurred to me that some of the things that had been wiped clean might have been done to hide evidence of an affair, not a murder."

"What?"

"The main reason that Colby wanted me to go to the houseboat was to see how clever he'd been in planting that DNA. But there might have been something else, and I didn't see anything. Everything was wiped clean. Colby wouldn't have wiped anything clean if he wanted me to see it. So I began to wonder if someone else wiped that crime scene down."

"He could have been hiding evidence of his affair *and* the murder."

"If I didn't know Colby was responsible, I might have thought that myself. I need to talk to Schultz right away."

"Not that I doubt you, but high-powered executives tend be a little busy. How exactly are you going to pull that off?"

"I already have. We're meeting him at Amici Park in half an hour."

"You're not joking."

"No, I have his personal cell number, remember? Plus a bit of embarrassing knowledge. Trust me, it's a potent combination."

IN TWENTY-FIVE MINUTES, KENDRA and Beth were walking on the outskirts of downtown's Amici Park, which on weekdays became the playground for an adjacent elementary school. The small park was located in Little Italy, and it offered one of the few grassy areas for dog walkers in the downtown area.

A slender man in an expertly tailored suit was already there. In his fifties, he had fine features and slightly thinning brown hair. He was leaning against the fence, skimming e-mails on his phone. Kendra approached him. "Robert Schultz?"

"Yes, Ms. Michaels." He put away his phone. "When I suggested this place, I didn't realize it was closed to park goers on school days. We can go somewhere else."

"This will be fine. Our conversation isn't going to last long."

"I hope not." He turned to Beth. "And you are?"

"Helping me," Kendra replied. "Beth Avery."

Schultz nodded. "Which means she's cut from the same cloth." He turned back to Kendra, and said coldly, "I don't usually respond to tactics like yours, Ms. Michaels. I don't appreciate threats."

"You don't usually find yourself in the middle of murder investigations, either."

"I had nothing to do with what happened to Sheila Hunter."

"I believe you."

He stared at her. "Then what's this about?"

"You already know. You wouldn't be here otherwise. I know you were having an affair with her. You spent a lot of time with her in that houseboat. You were paying for it, weren't you? It was billed under one of your midlevel executives, but you were footing that bill."

He looked away. "Why should I talk to you?"

"Because if you don't, I'll make a lot of noise you won't want to hear. I don't care about your affair, Mr. Schultz. I have no interest in telling your story to the world, despite the fact that your girlfriend stooped pretty low to tell mine. But I promise I'll do it if that's what it takes to get the answers I need."

He looked back at her. "I'm a married man. I have

children. And Sheila worked for my company. The last may actually be worse than the first as far as my professional standing is concerned. We had to be very discreet."

Kendra nodded. "You wanted a nice place near your office but not a place where many people would see you coming and going. Almost no one lives on their boats in Harbor Village. I imagine it was a nice spot for you two."

"It was heaven." For the first time, Kendra saw the pain in his eyes. "The place. The woman. Sheila understood me. We had the same values. It was the one place I could relax and enjoy myself. I hated whenever I had to leave."

"The night she was killed . . . I know you were there."

He turned sharply toward her. "I told you I had nothing to do with it."

"And I told you that I believe you. But I know you were there."

He looked down and finally nodded. "I found her. It was horrible. I couldn't believe it."

"She was already dead?"

He nodded.

Beth wrinkled her brow. "But you didn't call the police."

"I couldn't. I couldn't get involved. But I knew the police would put the entire place under a microscope. I wiped my prints off everything, every gift, every trinket that might possibly be linked back to me or my credit-card purchases. I put them in a laundry bag and got the hell out of there."

"Everything," Kendra repeated. "It looked pristine clean. You were in a big hurry. You probably scooped up everything in sight on the chance that it might incriminate you. Is that right?"

He shrugged. "I admit I wasn't being overcareful about picking and choosing. I thought better safe than sorry."

"You don't remember any individual items?"

He shook his head. "It's all pretty much of a blur."

"And where did you put that bag?"

He didn't answer.

"Believe me, I'm not looking for anything to incriminate you, not for murder or adultery. I just have to examine the contents of that bag and see if you threw anything in it that might help me find Sheila's killer."

"And what's to stop you from turning the entire contents over to the police?" he said sharply. "What kind of position would that put me in?"

"It might put you in the position of helping to find the murderer of the woman who understood you, your kind of woman. Remember."

He was silent. "She's dead now. I'm alive."

"Touching," Beth said. "A love affair for the ages."

"I'm a realist," he said harshly. "It's not going to help her for me to ruin my life."

"Okay, suppose I guarantee not to turn the bag over to the police unless I find some evidence that might lead to her killer. And that I promise not to tell anyone the name of the person who removed those items from the houseboat."

"I wouldn't believe you."

"You can believe me. I don't lie." She paused. "And the alternative is that I go to the police right now and tell them that you were her lover and you were there the night she was killed. That would start them digging very deep. How long do you think it would take for them to persuade you to tell them where that bag is now." She looked him in the eyes. "I think I'm your best bet, Schultz."

He scowled. "Neither one is a good option."

She waited.

"Okay. I guess you're right. It's better to take a chance on you than having the police breathing down my neck."

"So where is it?"

"I don't have it. I tossed it that night."

"Tossed it where?" Kendra asked.

"I got in my car and just drove. I was pretty messed up. I kept seeing her on the mast and all that blood . . ."

"Where did you end up?"

"I went to Mission Trails Park outside the city. I used to hike there sometimes. I thought I might bury the bag, or maybe weigh it down and throw it into the lake."

"You *thought* you might," Beth said. "What happened?"

"I drove out there, and I got turned around pretty quickly. It was dark, and the roads looked nothing like they do during the day. I was looking for a place to pull over, but then I was aware of a car behind me, about fifty yards back. Its running lights were on, but the headlights were off."

"Following you?" Kendra asked.

"That's how it looked. No matter how fast or slow I went, it was always right there."

"Did you think it might have been Sheila's killer?" Beth asked.

Schultz waited for an elderly couple to pass by them before he answered, "It crossed my mind. All I could think about was what that murderer had done to Sheila. I was nervous as hell. But the more I thought about it, the less likely it seemed. There's no way I was followed all the way from downtown. I would have seen it earlier."

"So this car continued to follow you with the headlights off?"

Schultz nodded. "And like I said, it was dark. I was having a tough time navigating all those twists and turns with my headlights on. Then I began to think it was a park ranger or maybe a cop. The last thing I needed was to get stopped and caught with a bagful of stuff from my murdered girlfriend's home."

"So what did you do?"

"I waited for a curve in the road and chucked it out the window off a hillside. That way, even if I got stopped, I wouldn't get caught with it. I turned off my own lights when I made the toss, so I was pretty sure I wouldn't be seen doing it."

"And what happened then?"

"I left as quick as I could. I lost sight of the car right after I left the park grounds. I'm guessing it was probably a ranger patrol. I think they were hanging back, trying to see what the hell I was doing there. If I had stopped, they might have gotten in my face. But since I just kept going and exited the park, they didn't bother me."

Kendra nodded. "Maybe. You never went back for the bag?"

"At first, that was my plan, but no. It's a fairly desolate area, far from the major hiking trails. And if it's ever found out there, I don't think there's anything that can necessarily be traced back to Sheila. Or me. I was mainly concerned with its being found in her houseboat."

Kendra leaned toward him. "You have to be able to tell us about at least some of the things you removed from the houseboat."

He thought for a moment. "There were ticket stubs for a few concerts we saw together. I removed gifts I'd given her. Things I'd charged that might be traced back to me. A necklace, a couple bracelets. Several objects I'd given her."

"What kind of objects?" Beth asked.

"Figurines. Little statues. She loved little ceramic shoes. I travel overseas a lot, so I'd buy her things that I'd see." He thought for another moment. "I also cleared out the few pieces of clothing I had there, along with my toiletries."

Kendra nodded. "Guerlain Homme deodorant spray. Creed Green Irish Tweed cologne. Neroli Portofino bar soap."

He stared at her in amazement. "Yes."

"You took them away, but the odors remained. You're wearing the same deodorant and cologne today."

"Amazing," he said.

"The cologne is especially nice. I understand George Clooney also wears that."

"I wouldn't know."

"So you dumped it all?"

"No, the clothes are still in my car. I stuffed the toiletries and the other stuff in a black laundry bag. I had a hard time remembering what I bought her and what was already hers, so if there was doubt, I just scooped it up. Like I said, I was just out of my mind that night." He made a cutting gesture with his hand. "That's it. No more. I'm through."

"Not quite," Kendra said. "I need one more thing from you."

"I think I've done a lot for you already. My lawyer would say too much."

"No, lawyers prefer not to deal with the police if at all possible. I'm much easier." She paused. "But I need you to go with us and help us find the bag."

His reply was immediate and incredulous. "No way in hell."

"I wouldn't ask if wasn't necessary to help find Sheila's killer."

"Why is it necessary? How can it possibly help you find Sheila's murderer?"

"I'm afraid I can't discuss that at the moment."

"After everything I've just shared with you?"

"Unwillingly shared. You're the CEO of a corporation that owns newspapers, television stations, and some of the most popular news Web sites in the world. And just a few days ago, one of those sites held me up for public ridicule and raked me over the coals. That story was written by the woman with whom you claim to have shared your values." She shook her head. "Pardon me if I don't trust you with sensitive information relating to an active homicide investigation."

Schultz opened his mouth to reply, then closed it again. He managed a faint smile. "Point taken."

"So you'll help us?"

He checked his watch. "No, I'm catching a plane for Houston in less than two hours."

"Postpone your trip."

"I can't do that."

"You mean you won't."

"I can't, and I won't. That about covers it. I've told you enough, and I won't run the risk of being caught scrambling over those hills with you. I already avoided that once. I'm not going to go for a replay." He met her eyes. "But I can tell you exactly where I dumped it."

"Where?"

"Not unless you promise me that you won't go until after dark, when you at least have a chance of not being seen."

"No problem. I assure you that we don't want interference either. Where?"

"When you get over there, drive north on Mission Gorge

Road. Just after you pass marker 6, it's down the hill on the left."

Kendra pulled out her phone and tapped in the instructions. "You're positive about this?"

"Yes. I thought I might be going back out there myself, so I was careful to remember exactly where it was. Warning. It still won't be easy making your way down that hill."

"Just as long as we find that bag at the bottom of the slope." She turned and moved back toward her car. "Otherwise, you can expect another visit from us."

CHAPTER 9

THE SUN HAD JUST SET OVER the arid expanse of land just east of the city. The Mission Trails Regional Park was over five thousand square acres, and was popular among hikers and campers. And, apparently, Robert Schultz.

"This probably isn't one of your better ideas," Beth said, as they exited the I-8 freeway. "Rooting around in an unfamiliar wilderness area after dark, searching for a bag of stolen evidence. And what color did he say the bag was?"

"Black."

"Of course it is."

"I'll actually be happy if it's hard to spot."

"Happy?"

"It would improve the chances of that bag's still being there and not having been picked up by a curious hiker."

"And what are the chances of that CEO being totally full of it?"

"I believed him. He knows we can make things uncomfortable for him in a very public way. The threat of public exposure is clearly what has motivated him to make all the decisions he has."

Beth gazed at the dense foliage that suddenly lined the roadside. "Right now, I'm wishing he had made a few different decisions."

"I just hope that when we find that bag, there's something there that makes all this worthwhile. I'm beginning to have my doubts."

"A gift from Eric Colby . . . What could it be?"

"I don't know. It was important to him that I look inside the houseboat myself. He had faith I would see and recognize it, whatever it was. When I went there and didn't come up with anything, I was afraid he might have overestimated me."

"That's not likely. He underestimates you. That's how you got him in the first place."

She grimaced. "But he's had years to prepare for the rematch."

"It won't make any difference." Beth hesitated before continuing. "I've been reading up on the Eric Colby case and how you finally got him."

"A little light reading before bedtime."

Beth shrugged. "I only had to read it, you had to go through it. You actually hid underneath the bodies of his victims and waited for him to walk past. I can't imagine how terrifying that must have been. Then you fractured his skull with a rock."

"That's right."

She hesitated. "If you had it to do over again, would you have . . ." Her voice trailed off.

". . . would I have finished him off?"

"Yes."

Kendra drove in silence for a moment. "I could have done that very easily. The FBI chief you met yesterday, Griffin, thinks I'm feeling guilty for not killing Colby when I had the chance. He thinks that's why I'm so obsessed with him. The truth is . . . Given the information I had at the time, I would have done the same thing all over again. I had every reason to think he could never hurt anyone ever again."

"But with the information you have now?"

"Now . . . I don't know." She thought for a moment. "Sheila Hunter would certainly be alive if I'd finished him off. Just another swing or two with that rock would have done it. When I thought he'd been put to death at San Quentin four months ago, I have to admit that I felt relieved. I have mixed feelings about capital punishment, but it felt good to think that Eric Colby was no longer walking the Earth."

"I completely understand," Beth said thoughtfully. "There are monsters out there, and some of them have given up the right to share the planet with us."

"If you listen to the FBI and the cops, Colby has already been wiped from the face of the Earth." She glanced at Beth. "Which is why I appreciate your believing in me. I've given you very little reason to think that I'm right and everyone else is wrong. I've made a few mistakes since you came on the scene. And yet, here you are. Thank you, Beth."

"And I haven't made any mistakes since you guys got me out of that institution? We're only human. We learn every day. I believe you said something like that to me once."

"And I've had more experience than you. I should have

listened to my own philosophical advice instead of getting so intense and emotional. This Colby business has gotten me completely off track."

"You're not off track as long as it leads to Colby. And you've earned my loyalty and support." She smiled. "Of course, I may be cursing you when we're wandering around that hillside in the dark."

Kendra stiffened as her gaze lifted to the rearview mirror. "We may have a more immediate problem. We're being followed."

"Shit." Beth instinctively glanced back over her shoulder. "Are you sure?"

"I wasn't sure." She moistened her lips. "I didn't want to be sure. I thought it could be my imagination because Schultz was paranoid about being followed. I was going to give it until we made that last turn to decide." She nodded at the headlights in the mirror. "There it is. Brown Chevy. Maybe a Caprice."

"How long has it been following?"

"I'm not certain. Whoever is driving is very good." Her hands tightened on the steering wheel. "A long time. Maybe since the time we left the condo."

"Then no park rangers like Schultz thought were following him."

"No park rangers."

Beth looked back again. "Colby?" she whispered.

That was what Kendra had been thinking. "Possibly." Her heart was beating hard. "We know he might be watching me. Maybe he's decided to take the next step." Was the car getting closer? "Damn, I wish you weren't along."

"Don't *say* that," Beth said. "You only want me along if everything is sunny and safe? I'm in this for the long haul. There's moonlight. Slow down after you take the next curve and I'll try to get a glimpse of the driver when he comes around the curve."

"The headlights will—"

"Just try."

Kendra pressed the accelerator and sped to the next curve. When she rounded the curve, she slowed. She saw the lights before the Caprice made the turn. How would Beth be able to see anything once—"

Then the Caprice made the turn at high speed.

It was almost on top of them!

"Go!" Beth said.

Kendra was already tearing down the road, leaving the Caprice behind.

"I told you that you wouldn't be able to see with those headlights glaring at us."

"But I did." Beth said, looking behind her. "I wasn't sure either, but I found out something. I couldn't make out any of the details of the driver's appearance." She paused. "But I was able to see shapes. *Two* shapes. There are at least two people in that car. Maybe more. I couldn't make out anything about the backseat." She glanced back at Kendra. "Would Colby be traveling with anyone?"

Kendra shook her head. Relief was pouring through her. "He's a loner."

"Then it's not Colby."

"No." Not Colby. No confrontation yet. She glanced up at the rearview mirror. "But whoever they are have stepped up their speed. They don't want to lose us."

"Not rangers, not Colby. Care to guess who—"

"No time for guessing." Kendra weighed her options. Confronting the people in the car was out of the question, especially since she had no idea with whom they were dealing. Giving them the slip also wouldn't be easy, either, on this somewhat isolated road.

Beth squinted at the small roadside sign ahead. "This is marker six."

Kendra pressed hard on the accelerator. "Whoever they are, I don't want to lead them to that bag. We'll double back as soon as we figure out how to lose them."

"Any idea how to do that?"

"I'm working on it."

Kendra poured on another burst of speed, putting a bend in the road between them and their tail. The Caprice was hanging back about a quarter of a mile now, but she'd stretched the gap slightly. She looked ahead, searching . . . There was a small mobile-home park on the right, and beyond that, nothing.

"Hang on," she said. "This is going to be a little rough."

Kendra cut the wheel hard right and spun into the trailer-park entrance. She gave the accelerator another jolt. Her wheels kicked up a cloud of dirt and gravel as they sped toward the back of the park. She braked hard and cut the lights.

Silence.

A few seconds later, the Caprice roared past the entrance.

Kendra drew a deep breath and turned toward Beth. "It won't take them long to realize what we did. They'll be back."

"So what's the plan?"

"You're acting as if I have one. I'm reacting purely on instinct. We'll stay off the road and work our way down the hill from here. We can get back to the marker in just a few minutes."

They threw open the doors and ran the length of the trailer park. They climbed a chain-link fence and worked their way down a steep hillside until they hit the relatively level desert floor.

Kendra motioned back toward the winding road. "This way."

Beth cursed as the low branches scratched her face and caught in her hair. "Not so fast. Where did that moonlight go? It's pitch-black now. I can't see my hand in front of my face. I'm getting mauled here."

"It's okay. Just follow me.

Kendra darted in and out of the bushes and low trees, leading Beth over a clump of boulders that took them past the curve in the road above.

Beth grabbed Kendra's arm to steady herself. "I can't see, dammit. Did that surgery give you night vision, too?"

"Hardly." Kendra was breathing hard, too. "You probably see better than I do."

"Then how are you doing this?"

"Instinct. The air around objects feels differently to my hands and face. And there are aural differences when you're faced with something as opposed to open air. Ask any blind person. It's called acoustic wayfinding. It usually only comes in handy for me these days when I get up for glass of water in the middle of the night."

"It's obvious I've never developed that instinct." She was looking around her. "But I think my eyes are getting used to the dark."

"Good. Believe me, that works better."

"How much farther?"

Kendra glanced up at the road. "We should start looking after another hundred yards or so. Be careful, it looks like there's cactus on the ground here."

They made a wide arc around a clump of cactus plants and pushed on, running alongside the hill that led up to the road fifty feet above.

"Damn." Kendra pointed to the jagged hillside. "I hate to say it, but that bag could have gotten snagged anywhere on the way down."

"Hey, I've got an idea. Let's wait until Schultz gets back into town, and we'll make him climb for it."

"No time. And remember, you're the one who wanted to play detective."

"Don't remind me. You know, I could be playing darts in a central California biker bar right now. More comfortable and less dangerous."

"We both could be. After this is over, I say we—" Kendra stopped in the middle of the path.

Beth stopped with her. "What is it?"

"Get down," Kendra whispered.

They crouched behind a large boulder. Kendra looked up. "Did you see that?"

"I didn't see anything."

"Look!" Kendra pointed to a pair of headlights gliding to a stop on the roadside above. The lights stayed on while two men climbed out of the car and looked down.

Kendra and Beth held their breaths and watched the men for a long moment.

"Who in the hell are these guys?" Beth whispered.

Kendra shook her head. The men were still only shadow figures. "I think the tall one is using binoculars. I don't see a night-vision glow on them, so I think we're okay."

Almost simultaneously, bright flashlights powered on in the men's hands. The high-wattage beams played across the hillside and darted over the brush where Kendra and Beth had been just moments before.

Kendra and Beth retreated behind a cluster of desert shrubs and watched as the flashlights continued to play over the area.

Kendra stiffened. "There it is."

"What?"

She peered into the darkness. "I think I saw the bag. One of the flashlight beams went right over it."

"Show me where."

Kendra pointed to a spot at the bottom of the hill, about twenty yards from where they were hiding. Now that she knew where to look, she could see a reflection from the flashlight beams on the shiny black plastic. "It's there."

"I'll have to take your word for it."

At that moment, both men suddenly started down the hill.

"Shit," Kendra said.

"Go get the bag," Beth said.

"Are you crazy?"

Beth nodded toward the men, who were half sliding down the steep hill. "They're using their flashlights to light their way down. Go now. I'll meet you back at the car."

"And what about those very determined guys who will try to intercept me?"

"Just get the bag and get out of here. They won't be coming after us."

"How do you know?"

"See you back at the car." She disappeared into the bushes.

Kendra tried to stop her, but Beth was already sprinting toward the hill, several yards away from where the two men were still descending. What in hell was she thinking?

But one glance told Kendra that Beth was right about

the men's being focused on climbing down the hill. Now was her chance.

She sprinted toward the spot where the flashlight beam had briefly illuminated the bag's shiny-plastic surface. Nothing but scrub brush and ground-cactus plants. Had it been just a trick of the light?

No. There it was!

She bent low and moved swiftly toward the bag.

She could hear curses and the sound of the men above her half sliding down the hill.

Quick.

She reached it an instant later. Not a trick of light. She picked up the large plastic bag, which was closed by a drawstring. There was lettering on the side that bore the logo of a downtown dry cleaner.

She *had* it.

Whatever the hell it was.

"Hey!"

She'd been spotted. Both flashlight beams swung in her direction!

She jumped to her feet and started running. The bag unbalanced her, and she fell to her knees.

"Get her. She's down!"

She knew that voice.

Stokes.

Dammit, it had been the San Diego PD following them.

Stokes and . . . She couldn't clearly make out the other officer on the slope, but she thought it might be Ketchum.

And there was no way she wanted them to confiscate this bag until she could look through it. She jumped to her feet and started running.

Slipped again.

Tumbled twenty feet. Hit hard.

Cactus. Stinging her face and neck.

But Stokes had slipped, too. He was struggling to get to his feet some distance away from her.

She got up and bolted back the way she and Beth had come.

Keep running. Keep ahead of him.

Screech. Crack.

The sound came from up above, on the road, in a groan of metal against rock. Before Kendra could look up, she was aware of the car's headlight beams suddenly angled downward. She saw Stokes's startled face caught in that beam as he stared up at the road.

Bam.

"No!" Stokes shouted, and started running up the hill as the Caprice rolled off the road.

Kendra stared at it in shock as she watched the car hurtling toward the desert floor.

What had happened?

They won't follow us.

Beth.

Stokes's and Ketchum's shouts and curses were almost as loud as the sounds of their car being pulverized by every stone and tree branch on its journey down. It finally flipped over, smashing whatever metal and glass hadn't already been destroyed.

Run.

Run while the men were still in shock.

Kendra clutched the bag closer to her and darted back toward their car. This time she wasn't nearly as successful at dodging the tree limbs and cactus petals, as the brush tore into her flesh.

It didn't matter. Just keep running.

Almost there.

She climbed the hill and threw herself over the chain-link fence.

"Get in!"

Kendra turned around to see her car waiting there for her, engine running and passenger door open. Beth was behind the wheel. She repeated, "Get in!"

Kendra jumped into the car. Before she could even pull the door shut, Beth peeled out of the lot.

Kendra took a moment to catch her breath. "You do know you totally destroyed their car?"

"Yep, crash, boom, bang. I did good, didn't I? Couldn't have them coming after us, could we? And it serves them right, for walking away with the engine running. For bad guys, they're not very efficient."

"For cops you could say they weren't either."

"Cops?"

"Stokes and Ketchum."

"Oops. Well, how could we know? We were only defending ourselves from unknown attackers."

"I'm sure Stokes will appreciate that defense."

"We'll worry about that later. At least, they won't be on our trail for a little while." She glanced down at the plastic bag in Kendra's lap. "Is that it?"

Kendra patted the bag. "Yes. Let's go back to my place. We'll take a look at it there."

"THAT'S A NASTY BRUISE, KENDRA," Beth said, as they entered the condo over an hour later. "I don't look near as bad as you do. Sit down, and I'll clean it up and find some salve to—"

"I'm fine," Kendra said. "I'll clean up later. I don't know

how long it will be before Stokes decides it's worth their while to come and harass me about what happened tonight."

"What can they do? All they saw was the bag; they don't know what's in it."

"And neither do we. There have to be some items that the police will consider evidence for this case. Not to speak of one destroyed car. Okay, so they never identified themselves before they tailed us or went on the hunt down that hill. But put the car and that bag together, and it will give them their chance to take me in and question me again. That's why we have to hurry." She looked down at her scratched and dirty hands. "On second thought, I'll go and wash up a little before I touch anything. You take everything out of the bag and set them up on the coffee table. Be sure you put on a pair of those evidence gloves in the cabinet before you do it." She headed for the bathroom. "I'll be right back."

Beth was right, she thought as she glanced at herself in the bathroom mirror. Tousled hair, bruised face, and her hands looked as if she'd been plucking briars. She quickly splashed water on her face and hands and ran her fingers through her hair.

Good enough.

"Lots of stuff," Beth said, looking up as Kendra came back into the living room. "Some cheap, some expensive, some kind of weird." She pointed to the corner of the coffee table. "There are all of Schultz's toiletries. I separated them out from the other things. The rest are mostly her figurines, there's a hair barrette and a necklace." She frowned. "I wouldn't have thought Sheila was the type to wear a hair barrette."

"Neither would I. She was far too sleek and sophisticated." She looked down at the amber-and-silver barrette. "Sentimental value?"

"She didn't impress me as being overly sentimental."

"You can never tell about people." Kendra pulled on her gloves and sat down on the couch to survey the array on the coffee table. "And what's weird?"

"Just some keepsakes." She pushed a small, cellophane-wrapped object toward Kendra.

It was a ring wrapped in a red shoestring from a child's tennis shoe.

"Now that is weird. But it looks—" Kendra froze. "My God."

"Kendra?"

She paid no attention. Her hands were moving quickly, frantically over the objects on the coffee table, putting some in front, discarding others.

"Kendra, what are you . . ."

"I have to go." She jumped to her feet. She ran to the closet and grabbed a gray-and-white plastic bag, darted back to the coffee table, and placed the items she'd separated at the front into the bag. "I have to see Griffin."

"At this hour? It's almost midnight."

"Too bad. I have to see him." She grabbed her phone and dialed. "Griffin, Kendra Michaels. I have to see you. Meet me at your office in thirty minutes."

"And why should I do that?" Griffin asked sourly.

This wasn't going to be easy to say. It would be difficult for her to speak these words to anyone. To Griffin, it was excruciatingly difficult. "Because I need you."

Silence. "Amazing."

"Be there." She hung up and headed for the door. "I'll call you, Beth."

"For heaven's sake, tell me what's happening," Beth said. "You're not being fair. Don't leave me like this."

"Sorry." The door was closing behind her. She repeated, "I'll call you."

"GOOD GOD." GRIFFIN'S GAZE TRAVELED over Kendra from her head to her feet. "You look like you fell off a cliff."

"Close. Very close." She dropped down in the visitor's chair. "I'm sure you would have been devastated if that had happened. Again, how would I have ever been able to pay off that favor I owe you?"

"True." He sat back down at his desk. "If you only wish to look at my callous side. Pity. When I have such a complex and interesting personality."

"Too complex for me. I've never been able to see beyond the barriers you made me jump over." She placed the gray plastic bag on the desk. "I even hesitated to bring these to you. But I decided that your professionalism would keep you from letting anything else stand in the way."

"Really?" His gaze was on the bag. "And what do you have for me, Kendra? I'm beginning to be intrigued."

She pulled a pair of evidence gloves from her jacket pocket and tossed them across the desk. "Put these on first."

He smiled and reached for the gloves. "Okay, you definitely have my attention now."

Once he had pulled on the gloves, she placed the bag in front of him. "See for yourself. And think Colby."

She sat back and watched him take the objects out of the bag and set them out in a horizontal row on the desk one by one. Casually at first, then with growing tension, then with scarcely concealed excitement. "Damn," he said softly. "This has got to be what I think it is." His gaze flew up to meet hers. "Tell me it is."

"You know it is." She indicated the first object. A gold compact with a turquoise lotus in the center.

"This belonged to Tiffany Demarco, Colby's third victim. She inherited it from her grandmother. It was the only thing missing from her purse the night her body was found."

Kendra opened the cover on her tablet computer and showed Griffin a grainy, yellowed photograph of the compact. "This was the picture her family gave us. An exact match."

Griffin picked up a hair clip with a blue hummingbird design. "This belonged to the girl in Chula Vista . . ."

Kendra nodded. "Donna Robles. She was wearing two in her hair when she left home on the morning of her nineteenth birthday. Six days later, when her severed head was discovered with the others at the abandoned shoe factory in Carlsbad, she was only wearing one. This is the other."

"Unbelievable."

"It's also a match. As much as I didn't want to pull up that photo, I checked."

He picked up a red shoestring, from which dangled a round gold earring. "What's this?"

"It's a twofer. The earring belonged to Lanie Riedinger, victim number six. She was wearing the other when we found her corpse. The shoelace came from little Stevie Wallach, who had just turned twelve when Colby killed him. His left sneaker was still tied, but the lace had been removed from his right one. A red shoelace."

She sat back in her chair. "There are three others there,

but I won't go in depth into those victims. You'll probably connect them yourself if you study the objects."

"Yes." Griffin leaned on his elbows, staring down at the line of trinkets. "I'm sure I will."

"Trophies, Griffin. Trophies we never found when Colby was caught and sent to prison."

"Where did you get them?"

"Sheila Hunter's houseboat. Colby set them around the place to give me a shock and put a signature to Sheila Hunter's killing."

He frowned. "I didn't see them."

"Because her lover got nervous and scooped up everything in sight and made off with it. I just retrieved it."

He looked at the bruises on her face. "At some cost."

"Yes. It could have been worse." She smiled faintly. "I had a fall, but I survived it."

His gaze went back to the objects before him. "Authentic?"

"We'll have to verify with the families, but I don't believe that Colby is playing games with his toys. I think that he wants me to know that there's no doubt that he's alive and controlling the situation."

"But he's done everything so far to make certain that no one did know that. Hence the fact that you're being thought of as a nutcase. Why now?"

"Maybe he thinks it's time. He's a complete egomaniac, and he's not afraid of anything. He's been hiding out, making his plans. Now, perhaps, he's ready to show everyone how clever he is. This reveal may just be the tip of the iceberg."

"But a fairly powerful revelation."

"That may not be accepted until Colby comes out with

even more irrefutable evidence." She grimaced. "Who's going to believe that these trophies are the real thing? The first question you asked was if they were authentic. It will take some time to verify, and even then, there will be doubters."

"No, the first question was where you got them. I was betting that they were the real McCoy."

"Because you worked those cases. You knew them intimately. That's why I brought them to you."

"And what do you want me to do with them?"

"What's right to do. Verify, then help me to convince San Quentin to admit that there is a possibility that Colby is still alive and a threat."

"Another favor, Kendra?"

"No. A duty, Griffin."

"Ah, such a boring mandate."

"The people Colby has on his kill list aren't going to find it boring."

"And you're first on that list. If it takes as long as you believe to convince everyone he's back, we may not be in time for you."

"I'll take care of myself. That's not why I came to you."

"I know," he said quietly. "I've always appreciated that courage, Kendra. Many of your traits annoy the hell out of me, but that's one I admire."

"I don't want your admiration. I want you to help me. Will you do it?"

"You do know that I won't publicly acknowledge that Colby may be alive until you can bring me stronger evidence than this. I'll have to have public backing before I take that risk."

"I don't care if you're protecting your ass. Just help me get public support."

"That might be possible." He looked back down at the trophies, and said brusquely, "San Diego PD is going to want to get their hands on some of these items. Particularly since they were taken from another one of their crime scenes. I'll have difficulty maintaining control."

"Not true. You always manage to get your own way eventually." She got to her feet. "I brought these to you because I needed you to fast-track the verification and any clues they might yield. Don't you dare give them up to the police. You know how they feel about me. I don't want them buried in their file thirteen. Stall until you get my answers."

He shrugged. "I'll do my best. But it might help if you can schmooze that detective, Stokes, whose iron grip I managed to pluck you from."

"Schmooze? Me? No one would believe it."

He chuckled. "Too true. But you might try explanation and courtesy." His smile faded. "Up to you. It could buy me time."

And so she would do it. Though he didn't realize how difficult those explanations were going to be after that chase through the hills. She wasn't the only one who had bruises.

She turned toward the door. "Then get to work, Griffin. I don't want the humble pie I'm going to eat to be for nothing."

CHAPTER
10

BETH.

Kendra froze after she pressed the elevator button a few minutes later.

Beth was going to kill her.

She swiftly pulled out her phone and dialed. "Beth, I meant to call you on the way to Griffin's office. But then I had to get what I was going to say to him straight in my mind and then—"

"Slow down, Kendra. I'm not interested in excuses. I want to know facts." She paused. "Though I do approve of the fact that you're feeling guilty for treating me so shabbily. After what we went through tonight, I thought we were doing this together."

"Very guilty," Kendra said. "Okay, no excuses, just explanations. What I saw on that coffee table threw me into a tailspin, and I had to talk to someone who knew what I knew." She added, "And you weren't that person, Beth.

You're my friend, but that was another life. I saw that shoe-string, and it all zoomed back to me."

"Facts," Beth repeated. "And I'll decide whether I'm going to forgive you."

"That's fair." She got on the elevator. "It was that red shoestring that sent me spinning. You called it a weird addition, and it was. Colby wanted to catch my attention, and he knew that would do it. Only one shoestring was missing on the shoes of that little boy. No one could find . . ."

She was pulling up at her home by the time she finished telling Beth everything. "And now Griffin wants me to smooth down Stokes, and we both know that's a futile exercise at best."

"Oh, I don't know. I think that Stokes likes you."

"Really? You mean when he's not suspecting me of murder or making me tumble down a hill."

"Well, he at least respects you."

"That's not the same thing." Kendra unlocked her condo and threw open the door. Beth was curled up on the couch and hung up as she saw Kendra. "Not when I'm supposed to persuade him to do what Griffin wants." She plopped down in a chair across from Beth. "But I'll try if it will move things along." She looked at Beth. "So what's the verdict? Am I forgiven for running out on you?"

"This time." She smiled faintly. "You were under extreme duress, or I wouldn't do it. You shouldn't have done that to me, Kendra."

"I know. I'm used to working alone, and I went spiraling backward to that time when there was only me."

"Not Lynch?"

"Lynch is his own person. Just as I am. Sometimes we just . . . come together."

"That's a provocative turn of phrase." She got to her feet. "But I'm not going to pursue it. I'm going back to the hotel and to bed." She gestured to the objects on the table. "I photographed all of them and made a list. I thought you might want to go over them to see if you'd missed anything." She gestured to her computer. "I pulled up Sheila Hunter's coworkers and got addresses and telephone numbers. I'll call them tomorrow and see if I can turn up anything more. You said that Griffin was going to get you that list of people Colby was in contact with during his prison stint. Do you have it?"

"Not yet. I'll nudge him."

"It appears you're making a career out of nudging him."

"Much to his displeasure." She added, "But not this time. There's no one more cynical than Griffin but I think that he believed me about Colby. Colby was a nightmare for Griffin while he was on his rampage. The last thing he wants is for Colby to cause him that headache again. He'll want to put a stop to it before it begins. That's why I had to get to him before the police took over this evidence that might indicate Colby is still alive and kicking."

"And killing."

"And killing," Kendra repeated. "I'll have those files for you before noon tomorrow. Promise."

"See that you do." Beth waved and left the condo.

There had still been a tinge of coolness in Beth's voice when she left, Kendra realized.

And Kendra deserved it. Beth had been with her all the way and risked life and limb, and Kendra had pushed her aside when she had chosen to run to Griffin. Yet Beth was still trying to help in any way she could.

She had to find a way to make it up to her, Kendra

thought wearily. But right now, she was too tired to think how or when.

She glanced at the objects on the table. Nothing more from Colby. She had recognized and collected all of those painful trophies. She carefully put Sheila Hunter's memorabilia back in the black bag and set the bag in the foyer by the door.

Then she headed for the shower. Clean up, get to bed, and hope she got some sleep before Stokes called her or pounded on the door. She had an idea it had to be one or the other. She was lucky that Stokes had probably been too involved with explanations about losing a valuable city vehicle to come after her yet. She should probably go on the offensive and call him and offer the bag. It would look much more cooperative.

But she wasn't up to going on offense or being aggressive right now. She had looked at those trophies, and the memories were still with her.

It was what Colby had wanted, what he had set up, and yet she'd had to fight to get those trophies and give him the satisfaction he wanted.

Damn Schultz. Damn Colby.

And heaven bless the souls of those poor victims he was still using as pawns.

IT WASN'T A TELEPHONE CALL, it was the pounding on the door.

Kendra was having her orange juice the next morning when she heard the door buzzer downstairs. "Good morning, Dr. Michaels," Stokes said coldly. "I guess you were expecting me."

"Oh, yes, come on up."

"I'm on my way."

The words were followed a few minutes later by the impatient pounding on the front door.

"Come in." Kendra stepped aside after answering the door. "I would have been stupid not to think you'd be here to question me." Her gaze went to his face. It was scratched, and there was a purple lump below his left eye. "You look a little worse for wear."

"So do you," he said. "You do know I saw you on that hillside?"

"Yes. Do you expect me to deny it? I was the one being hunted like an animal. Why shouldn't I hide? You didn't identify yourself. I didn't know it was you following me until you started stumbling down that hillside. It could have been anyone."

"Like Eric Colby."

"It was one possibility," she said sarcastically.

"I would have identified myself if you'd—"

"You didn't advise me I was under surveillance, either."

"That went without saying."

"You're right, I should have known you'd tail me. But the rest you didn't handle with any great finesse."

He scowled. "That's what my superintendent told me. You're going to be charged for the destruction of my vehicle."

"How? I was nowhere near it. You saw me at the time that it went off the road."

"You had a Beth Avery with you when you left your condo. She wasn't on that hillside."

"And how are you going to prove it was her? No witness. You left the engine running. It could have been an accident."

"We'll find proof."

"Look, I know that you were probably given a hard time by your superiors. You're still smarting from it. We had no intention of causing you any problem. That's not why we were out there." She turned and grabbed the black plastic bag she had set in the foyer. "This is why we were on that hillside. Take it."

He opened the bag and looked inside. "What is it? It looks like a bunch of bottles and statues."

"That's what it is. It's a collection of objects taken from Sheila Hunter's houseboat the night of her murder."

"By you?"

"Of course not."

"Colby?" he asked scornfully.

"No, though he certainly set them out to be found. Along with a few more important items." She grimaced. "But someone got in Colby's way and spoiled his little surprise for me. Her lover panicked and gathered them up and took them away."

"Because he'd killed Sheila Hunter?"

"No, I told you that was Colby."

"Oh, yes, the ghostly Mr. Colby. Then who stole the things in this bag?"

She shook her head. "I made a deal. In exchange for telling me where he'd hidden the bag, I told him I wouldn't reveal his name."

"Which makes you an accomplice to evidence theft."

"Bullshit. I didn't steal that bag, I found it. And now I'm giving it to you. It should be easy enough for you to pin down who stole these objects without my telling you. You've done checks on all Sheila's associates. He *handled* these objects and I'm sure he didn't do it with gloves on, as Beth and I did. He was too scared."

He was silent, looking down at the plastic bag. "And all the contents are now present and intact?"

"No."

His eyes narrowed on her face. "No?"

"But you can have limited access to them."

"Limited," he repeated softly. "What the hell do you mean?"

"I turned over several objects to Special Agent Griffin to process."

"Evidence from *my* crime scene?"

"Not exactly." She hesitated, then went for it. "Trophies. There were a number of past victims' trophies left at the houseboat by Eric Colby. It was done to taunt me, but there's a possibility they can be verified by the victims' families and offer proof Colby may still be alive."

"And then you'd get what you want."

"It could save lives. Yes, that's what I want. That's what you should want."

"Don't lecture me on what I should want. I like the idea of bringing the bad guys to justice and protecting the family next door. I'm a cop and a damn good one. At least that's what I thought until you showed up on my cases." His eyes were glittering in his taut face. "Since then, I've been called on the carpet twice, and I watched my vehicle crash down a hill. What I want is to find Sheila Hunter's killer and get you out of my life. That's my job, not to prove your crazy theory is correct. Colby is dead."

"He's *alive*, Stokes. If you don't believe me, contact Griffin. He had the same doubts, but he doesn't any longer. Well, that's not true. But he believes enough to start to feel the situation out. Talk to him, help him." She paused, gazing at him urgently, with her entire being focused on convincing him. "Look, you helped me that night at the houseboat. Because you knew that I wanted to find Sheila Hunter's killer. You had some reservations, but you relied on your instincts. Those instincts were right. I'm not guilty of anything but trying to save lives and bring a monster to justice."

He was silent, his face expressionless. "Are you finished?"

What else could she say? "I guess I am."

He turned toward the door. "I'm not going to take you in today, but that might come later." He looked down at the bag in his hands. "You behaved recklessly and without any sense of standard operational procedure. If you destroyed any evidence, you'll have to face the consequences."

"Whatever. But will you work with Griffin? Will you let him try to verify those trophies?"

He opened the door. "I'll talk to him. I'll let him try to convince me that you're not crazy, and Colby is still out there. That's my duty."

"Thank you, Stokes. You're an honorable man."

"Am I? I kind of think you're honorable, too." He looked back at her. "But I don't believe any of this. Colby is stone-cold dead. He can't do anyone any harm now. You might make your life easier if you accept the truth."

"I've already accepted the truth."

He shrugged and walked out of the condo.

She stared after him for a moment. Stokes was being more fair than she'd thought he'd be. He could have caused her a megahassle, and he'd chosen to back down and give her a chance.

Or at least breathing room.

As he'd said, it might not be the end of her problems with the San Diego PD, but maybe it was the start.

And the important thing was that he wasn't going to get in the way of Griffin's work on those trophies.

Providing that Griffin could silver-tongue him into believing that there was even the faintest chance that Colby was still alive. He'd been pretty adamant on the subject.

She reached for her phone to call Griffin and tell him about the challenge she'd set for him.

KENDRA PUNCHED IN THE PHONE number and was surprised when Sam picked up immediately.

"I've been wondering when I'd hear from you again," he answered.

"I've been a little busy, Sam."

"So I gathered. Taunting psychopathic killers is *so* exhausting . . ."

"What?"

"I just ran across your conversation with Colby in that Word file. You told me you'd had some back-and-forth with him, but you neglected to mention that you basically challenged him to come at you. Are you out of your mind?"

"Possibly."

"You have more experience dealing with the sick-and-twisted population than I do, but that seems like some pretty risky behavior."

"He feeds on fear. Strength is the only thing that has ever worked against him."

"Still, it's a little like someone with an allergy sticking their face into a beehive. I wish you wouldn't do it."

"What do you have for me, Sam?"

"Ah, and my concerns for you are summarily dismissed."

"Not at all. Sometimes I need to be told these things."

"But this isn't one of those times?"

"No. I know how dangerous Colby is, believe me. I've seen firsthand what he's capable of doing."

"He's a devious son of a bitch, and I've seen that first-hand."

"What do you mean?"

"I've been poring through the data on your hard drive. It's exactly what I suspected. He was using your laptop's microphone to listen to everything that was being said in the vicinity. Even when you thought your machine was off."

"And my camera?"

"Yeah. Your laptop's webcam, too. At least when the lid was open."

Kendra felt that sickening chill again. The thought of Colby watching her, listening to her conversations . . . "How did he do it? Did he hack in from the Web?"

"No."

"Then how in the hell?"

Sam was silent for a long moment. "That's kind of the scary part, Kendra."

She had an idea where this was going. "Oh, God."

"Yeah. This stuff was loaded onto your computer lo-cally. As in standing right over it. Maybe you left it in your car, or the office . . ."

"No. Whenever I take it out, it goes with me every-where. The only way it could have happened . . ." Kendra could barely make herself say the words. ". . . was here, at home."

"That's what I was afraid of."

Kendra felt sick as her glance moved around her condo. Her hairbrush, her computer . . . Her *home.* Eric Colby had invaded it.

"Kendra?"

"Yes. I'm here. I'm still trying to get my head around this."

"I know." He paused. "Any progress on figuring out who might have helped him?"

"Not yet. We're still working on that."

"And I haven't had any luck in zeroing in on this guy's location. The software he planted in your computer destroys IP-address data as soon as each session is complete. But I think I'm going to try something . . ."

"Try what?"

"I've put your computer back together, and I'm about to go back online with it. I think it will attempt to make contact with whatever computer he's using. I'll monitor the packets, and if a connection is made. I might be able to figure out where he is."

"You really think you can do that?"

"It won't be easy, but geniuses like me thrive on difficulties."

"I'm tempted to knock you off that self-built pedestal, but I don't want to discourage you. I *need* this, Sam."

"I know you do." His voice was grave. "I didn't mean to scare you, but you had to know, Kendra. I'd have a security expert go over your place right away. It must not be that safe."

"I thought it was very secure. I had problems before, and I thought I'd fixed all the possible danger points."

"Evidently you missed a few. Or maybe even just one. That can do it."

"Yes, that can do it." She glanced around her living room again. Where had Colby been in the condo? Had he been sitting on this couch, looking down at her computer. The kitchen? Her bedroom?

Dear God, had she been in the condo at the time?

Had he had the nerve to break into her condo while she was still here? She wouldn't put it past him. As she had told Stokes, he was an egomaniac who would take any chance to prove his superiority. He would have enjoyed the idea of being that close and having her both ignorant and vulnerable.

"You want me to come over and keep you company? I offer everything from sex to tutoring in the fine art of computer games," Sam said. "No charge. Though my services are much in demand."

"No, I want you to concentrate on that computer." She said, "I'll make sure that Colby can't get to me." She added grimly, "And if he does, that he'll regret it. Call me as soon as you come up with anything, Sam."

She hung up and drew a deep breath. It was all very well to claim that she'd keep herself safe, but she was feeling very vulnerable. Okay, call a locksmith and get all the locks changed. Check to see any windows or doors that were problem prone.

Make sure her gun was loaded and on her nightstand. Then go to the closet and get the box Olivia had given her containing all those nasty self-defense mechanisms. A few in her handbag and a few under pillow wouldn't hurt at all.

SAM CUT THE CONNECTION AND pulled off his telephone headset. He was definitely uneasy, but he felt a little better that Kendra was going to take action to make her security arrangements safer. When he'd discovered that Colby had been that close to her computer, it had been a shock.

He should have known that Kendra wouldn't be stupid about taking unnecessary risks. Yet there had been a chance that she would weigh risk against the objective and decide on risk. In many ways, Kendra was the same wild child she'd been in those years just after gaining her sight. She was fearless and big-hearted, with gutsiness to match her amazing mental gifts. If she was still a tad on the reckless side, she embraced life in a way like few others he knew. He'd forgotten how exhilarating it was to be pulled along in her wake.

He walked across the cluttered living room of his one-story Mill Valley home. The house had cost everything he'd made from a recent corporate cybersecurity contract, but it offered him that rare combination of solitude and easy access to the San Francisco nightlife. Redwoods surrounded it in every direction, giving him the feeling of living in a tree house. A nice counterbalance to the piles of circuit boards, hard drives, and other gear filling up every available inch of shelf space. Much of the house was bathed in a CRT glow from a dozen monitors, giving him the status of his various projects.

Sam glanced out at the darkness. He had hoped to meet friends at a bar in the Mission District, but they always understood when he got absorbed in a fascinating project. And Kendra Michaels had brought him a spellbinder.

He looked at her laptop on his dining-room table. It was reassembled and ready to go. So why didn't he just turn it on?

He knew why. Because that thing had been the eyes and ears of a monster.

Stop it, Sam told himself. The monster was on his turf now. Sam checked his network-monitoring system to make sure it was awake and ready to zero in on whoever might reach out to Kendra's laptop once it was back online.

All systems ready.

He placed his finger over the power button and let it

hover while he ran through his mental checklist one last time.

Enough stalling.

He pushed the button. Power on.

Kendra's laptop booted up. In under a minute, the operating system loaded with the computer connected to the Internet.

He glanced over at his monitoring station. Definite online activity under way.

But it was no guarantee that Colby's system was online and waiting to make contact. It could be hours or even days before—

"Hello, Sam."

The gravelly whisper sliced from Kendra's laptop speakers.

He froze.

"You can hear me. Good. I've been waiting for this. Waiting and anticipating."

Sam slowly turned toward Kendra's laptop.

Shit. He was being watched.

"Who is this?" He tried to project strength, but he knew his voice quavered.

"Sam, we're beyond that. Why, I feel like we're old friends." The man spoke slowly, mockingly, still not above a whisper, yet Sam could detect a thread of menace.

"We're not friends. I don't know you."

The man laughed, and Sam's chest tightened. "Well, I know you." Somehow, that laugh was terribly intimidating.

Stay strong. "I don't think so."

"Of course I do, Sam Zackoff. You're Kendra's white knight. One of many."

Sam could feel the sweat break out. The computer was

no longer a faceless tool to be used and conquered. It was the home of the monster.

And the monster knew who he was.

"You think you're going to find me," the man said.

Sam glanced back at his monitoring system. "Maybe I already have . . . Colby."

"See, you do know me." A chuckle. "And maybe I've already found *you.*"

Colby feeds on fear.

So don't speak yet, don't let him hear the fear.

"Beautiful home you have here in the trees. Ridiculously difficult to find at night, but not impossible."

Oh, God.

"And so isolated, Sam. You can do anything out here, and the neighbors will never, ever know . . . By the way, I'm quite fond of your wraparound porch."

Sam's eyes flicked to the front door.

"Did you lock the door? Perhaps you'd better check. Go ahead, I'll wait."

"I don't need to check."

"Such confidence, Sam."

"I designed the security system here myself."

"The thing about security systems, Sam . . . Once they've been penetrated—and they all can be—they can be used to keep the good guys out. Do you know what it's like to be screaming for your life, and knowing that your only salvation is on the other side of your very expensive security system?"

Sam didn't reply.

"No? Perhaps you'll soon know what that's like."

Sam wildly looked around for something he could use as a weapon. A lamp? Maybe the bottle of wine on the side table? Each possibility seemed more ridiculous than the last.

"No gun, Sam? That's right, you rely on brains not violence. Hmm. I suppose you can use that cricket bat behind you . . ."

Sam slammed the laptop lid closed.

More laughter. Dammit, the computer was still powered on.

"Was that necessary, Sam? I was so enjoying the window on your world."

"Sorry to disappoint you."

"It's quite all right. I'm good at carving my own windows."

Sam backed away from the laptop and ejected the flash drive from his network-monitoring system. He stepped to another computer and swiped his finger across the track pad to wake it. He pressed the arrow keys to cycle through views from the four security cameras mounted outside his house.

All clear. Apparently.

Colby's voice still emanated from the closed laptop. "Oh, and I must commend you on the hardwood floors in your hallway and bedroom. Such charm . . ."

Shit.

Sam scooped up Kendra's laptop and moved toward the door. He was tempted to leave it and escape from that bastard. He couldn't do it, he had promised Kendra and that would be more cowardly than he could allow himself. But on the way, he picked up his cricket bat.

"Are you running away, Sam . . ."

"Why are you *doing* this?" Sam was trying to keep the panic from rising in his voice.

"I want Kendra to know that our game isn't finished. Far from it. But for her to take me seriously, someone has to die."

"No, they don't. She takes you seriously."

"Not enough. She needs to get that message loud and clear. Who better to deliver it than her white knight?"

Sam drew a deep breath, threw open the front door, and bolted for his car. On the way he spun around several times, looking for any sign of Colby.

There was none.

He was almost to his car, unlocking it with his keychain remote as he drew near. He dove into the driver's seat after a quick glance to make sure no one was lurking inside.

He locked the door behind him with shaking hands and started the engine.

"Leaving so soon?" Colby whispered from the laptop. "Remember to give Kendra my message, Sam. I'll be very disappointed if you don't. You don't want to disappoint me . . ."

"STRANGE." KENDRA TURNED TO BETH after hanging up from Sam. "He didn't sound . . . I've never heard Sam sound quite like that."

"Like what?"

"I don't know." She frowned. "But I don't like it."

"Did I hear he was coming over?"

"Yes, he drove down from San Francisco. He should be here any minute. He said he was nearby."

"Then you can interrogate him and put your mind at rest." Beth smiled. "And I, for one, do like the idea of his showing up here. I get to meet him at last." She went to the counter and got a cup of coffee. "And thank him."

"He'll just blow you off. He said he enjoyed the idea of breaking into a secured mental institution."

"I don't care. I'm grateful, and he's going to know it." She took a sip of coffee. "Besides, he sounds interesting."

"Oh, no doubt about that. He's completely fascinating, and he makes your mind go as fast as his own. Which is also exhausting to anyone who's not an Einstein or—" She broke off as the buzzer rang. "Sam?" She buzzed him in. "Come on up." She turned back to Beth. "He *must* have been close."

He was banging on the door only a minute later.

"I'll get it." Beth put down her cup and hurried toward the door. She threw it open. "You must be Sam. I'm Beth Avery, and I've been wanting to meet you for—"

"Hello. Where's Kendra?" He brushed her aside and strode into the condo. "It's crazy, Kendra. And you guys shouldn't be answering the door without knowing who's on the other side. You buzzed me in before I even identified myself." He threw his computer and briefcase on a chair. "Do you want to have that nut murder you?"

"I'm glad to meet you, too," Beth said sarcastically. "It's rare indeed you find anyone who is as courteous as you, Sam Zackoff."

"Easy, Beth." Kendra was gazing at Sam. His hair was ruffled and his eyes red and strained. If she wasn't mistaken, his hands were shaking a little. Not the Sam she knew. "I'm sure he didn't mean to be rude. I think . . . there's a problem." She pushed him down on the couch. "Right, Sam?"

"You could say that." He glanced at Beth. "God, you're gorgeous. Could I have a cup of that coffee you're cradling?"

"It might be arranged." Beth moved toward the counter. "Black?"

"No, very strong with cream and sugar."

"Which nullifies the very strong."

"You drink it your way, I'll drink it mine." He closed his eyes. "I'm not up to arguing. I can feel all the sparks she's throwing at me. Kendra, protect me from her."

"Since when do you need protection? Though come to think of it, Beth can be fairly intimidating."

"I knew it." He opened his eyes and drew a deep breath. "Okay, I'm coming out of it. It feels very safe here." His gaze met Kendra's. "Though we both know that's not true."

"I had the locks changed two hours ago. It's safer now than it was." She tilted her head. "And what are you coming out of? And why are you so obsessed with my being safe?"

He made a face. "Actually, I'm obsessed with my own safety at the moment. Not that I'm not concerned about yours but I'm a little off balance, and that leads to an extreme degree of selfish self-preservation."

"Why are you off balance?" Beth handed him his cup of coffee. "Selfish and rude, I noticed. But what's the excuse again?"

"Ouch." He took a sip of coffee. "I'm going to pay, aren't I?"

"Probably not physically," Beth said sweetly. "But we'll see."

Kendra's gaze was on the computer Sam had thrown onto the chair. "Is that . . . mine?"

"No, it's one of my computers I keep in the car. I left my primary computer at home. I was in a hurry." He took a sip of coffee. "I brought your computer, but I left it locked in the trunk of my car. I didn't want it close to me on the way down here. I'll get it later. But maybe not bring it here to you."

"Then why did you even bring it to San Diego?"

"Because I need to work on it. I haven't—I know I promised you that I'd make it happen, but things aren't going precisely the way I'd like." He rubbed his eyes. "But I'll get there, Kendra. Just give me a little time."

"I'll give you as long as you need. You know how grateful I am that you're even trying to locate Colby. I have to find him, Sam."

"I know you do." He paused. "And he knows it, too."

She went still. "What?"

"The bastard knows I'm trying to find him for you." His lips twisted. "He called me your white knight."

"Oh, my God." She dropped down on the couch beside him. "You've seen him, talked to him?"

"Not exactly. He decided to invade my own territory. He probably thought that I'd pay more attention. He didn't need to worry. He had my entire focus from the minute he came online." He shrugged. "He used your computer again, but I got the audio version. It was pretty damn effective."

"I can see it was." She moistened her lips. "What did he say? What happened? Tell me everything."

"I will." He looked down at his coffee. "Though I don't come out looking like a superhero. You deserve to know every word he said." He briefly and concisely related that short, terrifying episode at his home. "That's why I'm here. I wanted to tell you in person what that bastard was threatening you with."

"Another death," Beth said.

"As if I didn't expect it," Kendra said. "I knew he'd never stop." She added grimly. "Not until I stopped him."

"Or he stopped you," Beth said. "So why issue this warning?"

"He wants me to worry, to be afraid, to wonder who's next." She looked at Sam. "And he sent the message through you. Why?"

He shrugged. "I had your computer?"

"No, he could have used another means." She was thinking about it. "He called you my white knight. He knows our background. He issued a not-too-subtle threat."

"He might have meant the death was to be Sam's?" Beth said. "And it would be deliciously malicious to send him as a messenger of his own demise."

"I'm glad you find it delicious," Sam said. "Personally, I'm not high on the whole concept." He set his cup on the coffee table. "And I'm not your white knight, Kendra. I'm just your friend, who is not the least bit brave about this whole mess."

"You're brave to be involved at all."

Sam made a rude sound. "Look, I nearly wet my pants when that creep started playing his games with me."

"Then stop, give me the computer, and I'll give it to the FBI lab to work on."

"And let that son of a bitch win? I had a long time to think on the drive down here. Colby might have sent me as his errand boy because he thought it would bother you to believe I was threatened." He grimaced. "Or he could have thought I was getting too close to finding him and wanted to scare the shit out of me. Which he did. Maybe he wanted me to abandon you."

"Either way I want you out of it." She paused. "Do you believe he was actually there at your house?"

"He wanted me to think so, but now that I've had a longer time to think about it, probably not. He heard you call me the night he first invaded your system. As I recall, you said my first and last name. From there it was a fairly simple matter to learn a few things about me and find my address."

"But he described your place to you," Beth said.

"He described permanent features of my place. The wraparound porch, the hardwood floors in my bedroom and hallway . . . But nothing I brought to the house myself." He picked up Beth's iPad from the dinette table and typed something into the search box. In seconds, an online photo album appeared. He swiped his finger across the screen to show a succession of pictures of his home. "This is from a Bay area real-estate site. There are half a dozen other sites still out there with photos of my house when it was listed for sale last year. That's how I found it. Albums like these are out there for almost any house that goes on the market, and sometimes they're out there for years after they're sold."

Beth nodded approvingly at the photos. "Cool place."

"Thanks."

"So he was bluffing. It's nothing to be comfortable about," Kendra said. "Colby still knows who you are and where you live. And he knows you're helping me track him down."

Sam managed at smile. "I assure you, I'm not exactly comfortable, either."

"So are we any closer to knowing where he actually is?"

"Not unless you're willing to believe he's fled to Antigua."

"Antigua?"

"In the Caribbean. I traced it back to a relay center there. It primarily functions as a clearinghouse for financial transactions of questionable legality. Your friend Colby was content to use it as a means to scare the living shit out of me."

"How would he know to do this?" Kendra asked wonderingly.

Sam shook his head. "It just confirms what I said before. He's had some expert help, and it's been fairly recently. I doubt he went into prison four years ago with the knowledge he would need to pull this off. The technology changes too quickly."

"Antigua," Kendra said. "Another dead end."

"Not necessarily. I had to abandon my session in a bit of panic, so I didn't get to try every way I could to track him."

"There's more you can do?" Kendra asked.

"Maybe." Sam took a deep breath. "But I'd need to draw him out again."

"No," Kendra said sharply. "I can't let you do it."

"Don't fight me too hard. I might give in and run for the hills. It's not something I'd enjoy doing, but it's the only way. I might be able to get a fix on his home location even if he routes through a couple of these relay centers."

"And what if Colby finds out you're doing it? I want you to stop right now."

He shook his head. "Nah, can't do it."

"You certainly can do it."

"Won't do it. I never realized what a coward I was until I came up against Colby. I didn't like the way that made me feel. I'm not going to feel like that again." He smiled. "Or if I do, maybe I won't show it as much. It bothered me that Colby knew I was scared. Presentation is everything, you know."

"No, I didn't know." She stared at him helplessly. "Look, drop it, Sam. It's not worth it to me to have you in danger."

"I'm touched." He took her hand and squeezed it. "But

though it's an incredible surprise, I find it is worth it to me. Imagine that." He got to his feet. "Now if you don't mind, I'll use your bathroom to take a shower and change, then I'll go look for a place to rent for a week or so."

"You're staying in town?" Beth asked.

"Yeah, I like the idea of being close to Kendra. In case she needs me." He grinned. "Or what's more likely—if I need her." His eyes were suddenly twinkling. "How about it? Kendra says you can be intimidating. Want to be my bodyguard?"

"No." She studied him. "You're not at all what I've been imagining since Kendra told me how you helped get the goods on those scumbags who held me at that mental hospital. I was thinking you'd be . . ."

"A white knight? We've already gone down that road. I'm just a fantastically talented computer genius who enjoys challenges." He added, "And one who stayed on the sidelines while Kendra and Eve did all the real work of springing you from that place." He grabbed his bag. "Hell, maybe I was scared then, too. I didn't think so, but I'm having to take a second look at motivations."

"Stop being so hard on yourself, Sam," Kendra said. "And I want you to stay here. There's no reason for you to rent a place."

"Yes, there is. There's no room here for me. I've got to set up a small computer lab. I *will* find Colby. Besides, that means bringing your computer on-site." He shook his head. "I'm not going to expose you to that bastard again. Hell, I don't want to expose myself. But I can't stand the alternative." He headed for the bathroom. "He's messing with my head . . . and my work. And I have to keep your computer functioning in case he sends me . . . or you another message." The bathroom door closed behind him.

"I hate this." Kendra's hands closed into fists at her sides. "Damn *him*. I've never seen Sam that upset. He's right, Colby is messing with his head. He knew just how to reach him."

"His work?" Beth asked.

"He lives for those computers. It was probably almost like a betrayal that Colby could use them against him. It's natural that Sam would want to gain the upper hand in his own arena."

"And possibly dangerous," Beth said quietly. "If Colby was uneasy about Sam's ability to trace him. The threat could be directed at Sam as I suggested. You said he was an egomaniac. It would be the thing an egomaniac might do. Even if he isn't the victim of choice, if he continues to work to find a way to get to Colby, he might end up dead anyway."

Kendra shuddered. Beth was being entirely too logical to be ignored. "I'm not going to be able to convince Sam. You heard him."

She shook her head ruefully. "Then you need to have Griffin lock him up somewhere with a few dozen snipers to watch over him."

"You're joking, but that's not a bad idea," Kendra said. "Except Griffin would immediately try to take over the action and then where—" She stopped as a thought came to her. "But you're definitely on the right track, Beth . . ."

CHAPTER
11

"HEY, I WASN'T EXPECTING THIS." Sam stepped past Kendra into the spacious foyer and looked around. "It's pretty damn incredible. Like a comfortable Taj Mahal. Who lives here?"

"Adam Lynch." She closed the door after Beth entered, and it locked itself. "He'd appreciate the description. He always says that comfort is paramount, luxury is only icing on the cake."

"Beautiful," Beth murmured. "I had no idea your friend Lynch had either the taste or the funds to build a place like this."

"What does he do?" Sam asked. "Stocks? Oil?"

"No, you might say Lynch is in services." She waved her hand, and the lights came on in the entire first floor. "But he does very well."

"Judging by the whizbang-tech security I noticed on the grounds, there are a lot of people who might envy and like to take a little of that cash away," Sam said. "And you seem very much at home here. Sure you're not more than friends?"

"No, sometimes things aren't the way they seem." She smiled. "But what is true is that this place is supersafe, and I'd defy anyone to get to you if you stay behind these walls."

"I don't doubt it. And Lynch will let me stay here?"

"I'm sure he'll agree once I can get in touch with him. He offered me the house."

"You, not me. And if it's so safe, why don't you stay here with me? Think what a good time we could have."

"I want to appear vulnerable to Colby. I need him to act. I don't want this horror to drag on any longer than necessary."

"You changed your locks. I'd say that should convince him you feel vulnerable." He was looking up at the high, coffered ceilings. "Yeah, this house is really cool. The sound should be really great bouncing off those ceilings. You're sure Lynch won't mind if I stay for a couple days? Do you want me to call him?"

"No, he said the situation with which he's dealing is very touchy. He'll see I called, but I didn't even leave a message. If he doesn't get back to me, I'll try to call him later." She turned and moved toward the living room. "Let me show you around the place. You may find it a bit odd, but then that's Lynch." She looked over her shoulder at Beth and Sam. "For instance, you'll see a huge banner photo of Lynch's current girlfriend, Ashley, wearing a bikini and occupying an entire wall. She's a supermodel and gave it to him as a present, and he didn't want to hurt her feelings by removing it. It's right ahead. Brace yourself."

"I am." Beth was looking past Kendra to the living-room wall. "But it's still a shock."

"Shock? Why? I know it's—" Kendra's gaze followed Beth's to the wall, and her jaw dropped. "What?"

"Shock for you, too, evidently," Beth said. "No bikini girl. Just Kendra Michaels. Evidently, Lynch got up his nerve to tell his lady friend that he wanted a fresh face on the wall. It's a wonderful portrait. Did you pose for it?"

"No." It was a mixed-media picture in which Kendra had been portrayed with her eyes closed. Now that the shock was abating, she was beginning to remember where she had seen that portrait. "Lynch and I were questioning an artist in his studio a few months ago, David Warren, and he kept working while he talked to us. I didn't know he was doing me until right before we left his studio. Funny, he said that he knew that it wasn't right until he closed the eyes of the woman in the portrait."

"Strange. He must have sensed . . ."

"What can I say? Warren is an artist. I thought it was a bit weird, too." She shrugged. "Anyway, we left his studio, and that was the last I saw of the portrait."

"But not the last Lynch saw of it," Sam said. "He must have gone back and purchased it." He tilted his head, gazing at the picture. "You know, I might have gone back and done the same thing. The artist really caught you. I wouldn't mind having that around to look at." He grinned. "But then, I'm supposed to be your white knight. It's only right that I should have my lady's portrait." He looked Kendra directly in the eyes. "Colby said I was one of many. Is Lynch a white knight, too?"

"Lynch would laugh at that. He much prefers to be a black knight and run his own show." She cast one more glance at the portrait, then forced herself to turn away. "He probably just liked the work." She moved toward the kitchen. "This kitchen is state-of-the-art, not that you'll cook much. I remember how little you used anything but a microwave."

"And still don't. Just show me the office or study or whatever. I need to know what I have to work with."

Kendra nodded and, for the next fifteen minutes, showed them quickly through the office area before taking them to the guest rooms upstairs.

"That's enough," Sam said impatiently. "I've got the general layout of the place. Now you and Beth leave and let me get to work."

"I believe we're getting kicked out." Kendra was smiling as they started back downstairs. "Come on, Beth. I'm sure that we can find enough of value to do without bothering—"

"No," Beth said flatly, stopping as they reached the bottom of the stairs. "I'm not going with you, Kendra. I'm staying here with Sam."

"What?" Sam said, "You are not."

"Yes, I am." She ignored him, turning to Kendra. "It's where I can be the most useful. There are going to be times when you're going to want to deal with Griffin or Stokes without me. Then I'll be mad as hell if you run out on me like you did before."

"You were going to check on those Colby prison visitor contact files from—"

"I can do that here." She glanced at Sam. "He might even be a help with that."

"I'm flattered you think so," Sam said sarcastically.

"Or he might not. Anyway, I'll have plenty of time to work on it. In between making sure that Sam doesn't do anything foolish that will get him killed."

"I beg your pardon?" Sam said.

"He's pretty safe here, Beth," Kendra said.

"As long as he stays here. I can see him being impulsive and running out to get a cable or hard drive or whatever."

Kendra could see that, too. "Yes."

"If I'm here, I'll go for him. I won't let him do stuff like that."

"Let?" Sam repeated.

"Let." She turned back to him. "Stop being an ass. Kendra would feel terrible if anything happened to you. I have to make sure it doesn't."

"I've taken care of myself for a number of years, Beth."

"And you can take care of yourself for the rest of your life after we get rid of Colby. Until then, you belong to me."

"Really?"

"Don't smirk. This isn't about you, it's about Kendra and the fact that I pay my debts. I owe one to you, and though I'm not sure you deserve—" She stopped. "That's not true. You deserve everything I can do for you. I don't care whether you helped me because it was a challenge, it was *my* life. And you helped give it back to me. So shut up. It's going to happen."

Sam blinked. "I believe it is."

Beth turned back to Kendra. "Don't take chances. Don't worry about us. I'll be in touch every day, and I'll make sure that he works until we get what you need."

Kendra hesitated. Beth's decision had come out of left field, and she wasn't sure that she liked the idea of having her out of sight. Yet what else could she do? Beth was a grown woman and would do what she wanted to do. Give in gracefully. "Thank you. I'm sure you will." She hugged her and turned to Sam. "And you take care of her, too, Sam." She hugged him, and turned toward the door. "I'll let you know what's happening."

"Do that," Beth said absently, her gaze fixed on Sam. "'Bye, Kendra."

Kendra paused at the front door, looking back at them. So different. Beautiful, intelligent Beth, who had been lost and was trying to find herself. Sam who was volatile, worldly, and lively and yet was discovering new things about himself because of the monster in their midst. How would they cope with each other in this forced proximity?

Not her problem. They would have to work it out for themselves. She had her own worries.

That monster in their midst was getting closer all the time.

BETH KEPT TO HER WORD. SHE CALLED Kendra early the next afternoon. "Everything's fine here . . . I guess."

"You guess?"

"I haven't seen Sam for more than a few minutes since you left. He's been closeted in that office except for trips down the hall to the bathroom and to the kitchen to grab a sandwich. I think he slept on the couch in the office." She added sarcastically, "Or maybe hovering from the rafters like a bat over those blasted computers."

"Regretting your decision to stay?"

"No. The reasons are still the same. I'm just facing the reality of Sam Zackoff. As long as I'm here, I'll know he's safe. And I've had time to look over those prison-visitors records, and I've narrowed it down to five possible."

"Five?"

"Evidently, Colby attracted a lot of computer geeks. I don't know why. Maybe they're so removed from reality that they can't differentiate between monsters and ge- niuses."

"No one can deny that Colby is clever. Do you want to send them to me? I'll help you do searches on all of them."

"Let me try to pare it down a little more. I'll get back to you. I'm sure that you have other things to do."

"I've been working with Griffin and visiting the families of those victims and trying to get firm confirmations on those trophies. We've got two so far." She added wearily, "It's very painful, both for us and for them. They never forget, but the sight of those belongings just brings their loss home again."

"But it may help Colby to be caught if you can just get law enforcement to admit he's alive and go after him."

"That's what I tell them, but when the pain is there, it's difficult to think of anything else. Oh well, we've got to do what we think is right."

"It *is* right."

"I know. It just seems as if I'm spinning my wheels. I feel as if Colby is out there watching . . . and waiting."

"Waiting? Waiting for what?"

"I don't know. What he's been waiting for since he managed to escape that prison. My death? Absolutely. But he's not ready for that yet. He's planning something. That's why he sent me that message."

"You've done everything you can to protect Sam. This house is like Fort Knox." Beth added with forced lightness, "And you've got me to keep an eye on him. So maybe Colby is just hunkered down somewhere and gnawing his nails with frustration. I'll enjoy imagining him doing that."

"Me, too," Kendra said. "But send me those names as quick as you can. Okay?"

"You know it." She paused. "You won't change your mind about coming here? Much safer, and I could use the company. I'm not getting any from Sam."

"No. I can't hide away. Colby has to see me moving and coming after him. He has to feel as if there's a chance of getting at me when he's ready."

"I don't like the way you're thinking."

"It's the way he taught me to think. I told you he was waiting. If I hide away, he'll only burrow down until I surface. Or start killing again to force me out." She changed the subject. "But it's making me feel much better to know you and Sam are safe. Stay that way. Keep in touch." She hung up.

Were they safe? Kendra wondered. Lord, she hoped they were. She had done everything she could think to do.

Now, like Colby, she had to wait, and see if that was enough.

"WOW, SAM. I'M DAZZLED. I DON'T know if it will work, but it looks impressive as hell."

Beth was staring at the array of monitors Sam had set up in Lynch's study, tied to a pair of laptops and a stack of black boxes. "I've been wondering what you were doing in here for the past day."

"Setting up. Making adjustments. Trying to find any computer out there that's specifically trying to connect with the software that Colby planted in Kendra's computer. If it just happens once, only once, it can lead us back to Colby. I've been busy."

"And shutting me out."

"Nothing personal. I'm just accustomed to working alone." He glanced soberly at her. "But I appreciated the fact that you were here."

"At your beck and call?"

"Why not?" He grinned. "Hey, what guy wouldn't want

to have a gorgeous woman to meet his every need? You shouldn't complain. You're the one who set it up."

"Not every need," she said dryly.

"Now you're spoiling it. I was having fantasies of—"

"And those fantasies would last only as long as that agile brain of yours wasn't occupied with those computers." She looked around the office. "So tell me about your first and probably only real love."

"Pretty special, huh." Sam smiled proudly as he stepped back from his creation. "Yeah. If Colby makes contact again, I want to be ready."

She looked at the large monitors. "When did you bring all this stuff in?"

"I didn't, actually. I just brought in the laptops. I had them delivered and left on the doorstep."

"That was what was in all those boxes?"

"Yeah, the rest was in the office closet. This guy Lynch must be a real techie."

"You just helped yourself to his gear?"

"Sure, why not? Kendra told us to make ourselves at home."

"Yes, she did," Beth said warily. "And you certainly took her at her word."

"Anyway, I'll feel a lot safer in this place than I did the last time I reached out to Eric Colby." Sam looked at the windows. "Check these out. Glass-clad polycarbonate, almost an inch thick."

"Bulletproof?"

"And even bombproof, up to a point. I've done consulting work with foreign embassies that weren't as secure as this place."

"Who *needs* a house as secure as this?" Beth said.

"Someone who has really pissed off a lot of people." Sam smiled. "My kind of guy. I hope I get a chance to meet him sometime."

"When you do, you can explain to him why you appropriated about twenty thousand dollars' worth of his gear."

"All for the noblest of purposes." Sam sat down at the large mahogany desk. "If it gets us one step closer to finding this monster, who would possibly object?"

"And how close are you?"

"I'm not certain. I've spent a lot of time setting up these network-traffic-analysis rigs. I think I'm ready to find out."

"You are?"

"Yep, that's why I invited you in for the show." He met her eyes, suddenly grave. "I have to work alone, but that doesn't mean I like it. I want you to know that . . . I've liked having you here. But this is the only part I can share. It's all I can give you. If you want to accept it."

"You sound like someone from *Mission Impossible*." She smiled. "It is what it is. Of course I'll accept it. That's why I'm here."

"Good." His hand went to the power switch on Kendra's computer. "Ready to give this a shot?"

Beth leaned forward and pushed his finger into the power button. "Oh, yes. Let's get this asshole."

The indicator lights on Kendra's laptop came to life. Sam punched a button on the HDMI switcher, and the image from the laptop suddenly appeared on one of Lynch's large-screen monitors.

Beth turned back to Sam. "How long will it take?"

"Depends on Colby. Last time, he made contact immediately. It leads me to believe that he has a computer on and waiting for this machine to come online. At least he did then. If that's still true, it can only help us. It's hard to scan the Web like that without leaving some kind of footprint. This time, I'm looking for any sign that his computer is out there looking for us."

"And once it has found us?"

"I'll immediately start tracing the data packets. And if we hit a relay center, I'm ready to start analyzing data traffic patterns from the other side to figure out where it's coming from. He may be smart enough to route himself through several relay centers, but I'm smarter."

Beth nodded. "Not that I doubt you . . . But doesn't the government have entire buildings full of people who do this sort of thing?"

Sam checked one of the monitors. "Yes. And they hire me whenever they fall on their asses."

"Good Lord, what arrogance."

"No, I'm merely supremely sure of myself."

Beth laughed. "And unapologetically."

"Why apologize? For being aware that I'm the best at what I do?"

"You're the only person I've ever met who can swagger while sitting down."

"Another one of my many talents."

She glanced over at him: "So tell me . . . Who do they call when you fall on *your* ass?"

"Hmm. Can't say, because it's never happened. I guess they would just call a priest since the situation would clearly be hopeless."

"Clearly."

Sam suddenly leaned forward. "We've made contact."

Beth tensed. "Can he see and hear us?"

"Not unless we want him to. I've muted the laptop's microphone and camera. Of course, he may not even be there. Just because his computer is on, that doesn't mean that he—"

"Greetings, Sam." That mocking whisper again.

"That's him," Sam said.

"I assume it *is* you, Sam. You're being very rude, not allowing me to see and hear you."

Sam pushed a keyboard combination that opened the microphone. "Of course you can hear me."

"Ah. Good. I trust you gave Kendra my message?"

"I did."

"Fine. Then your part of this is done. I have no further use for you. I must speak to Kendra directly."

"What makes you think she wants to speak to *you*?"

"Is she there?"

"No."

"Too bad. You're wasting time. The clock has started."

"The clock on what?"

The screen flickered, and, suddenly, an image appeared.

Beth leaned close to get a better look. Her eyes widened. "Oh, my God."

KENDRA'S PHONE RANG, AND SHE barely had time to punch the TALK button when she heard Beth on the line, her voice shaking.

"Kendra, open your e-mail now, you hear me? Now! Sam just sent you a link."

"A link? Beth, what's happening?"

"Just do it. Hurry!"

Kendra had already grabbed her tablet computer and opened her e-mail. Three button presses later, she was staring at what appeared to be a live video feed that chilled her to the core.

Detective Martin Stokes, bruised and bloody, tied to a

table. His eyes were wide with fear as he looked at something beyond the range of the camera.

And she had a terrible feeling she knew who he was looking at.

"Kendra, do you see it?"

She couldn't take her eyes from the screen. "Yes."

Sam's voice suddenly cut in. "Kendra, I'm forwarding this to you through my server. I've also sent viewing links to Michael Griffin at the FBI and the San Diego Superintendent of Police. Colby is refusing to talk to anybody but you."

"Can . . . he hear me?"

"I'm going to try and enable two-way communication in three . . . two . . . one . . . now!"

She spoke into her tablet. "Colby . . . It's me. It's Kendra Michaels. I'm the one you want, not him."

Silence. Only Stokes's labored breathing.

Sam had rigged this on the fly, so it was entirely possible that his attempt to provide a two-way communication link was going to be a—

"Hello, Kendra. What a delight it is to be here with you again."

She went still. It was the first time she'd heard Colby's voice since that terrifying morning at San Quentin.

She had hoped never to hear that voice again.

The picture on her screen hadn't changed. Stokes was shirtless and bleeding, tied to what appeared to be an embalming table. "Colby, this is about you and me. You have my attention now. That man has nothing to do with this. He's a cop. He didn't even believe you were still alive."

A long pause.

What was he thinking? Was she making any impact at all?

He finally replied. "To the contrary, Kendra. He has everything to do with this. He disrespected us both when he refused to listen to you about me. He's now paying the price."

"Of course he didn't listen to me, Colby. You were too smart, and you covered your tracks too well. The whole world believed you were dead."

"You didn't believe it, Kendra, even though you wanted to believe it more than anyone on Earth."

"I've met a few dozen victims' family members who wanted to believe it more."

"Possibly. But after today, there will be no doubts, Kendra. This is my gift to you. The whole world will know how right you were. I could have just vanished and let you twist in the wind, espousing your ridiculous theory . . ."

Kendra's phone vibrated. She glanced down and saw a text from Sam. KEEP HIM TALKING. TRYING TO TRACK. FBI AND SDPD ARE IN THE LOOP.

She looked back up. "Don't pretend this is for anyone but you. You enjoyed the hell out of the fact that no one believed me."

"For a little while. But it annoyed me that Stokes couldn't see that such complex planning and clean execution could only originate in a mind like mine. So it's for both of us. I've been planning this for a long time."

"Whatever you planned, it didn't involve this man. Or Sheila Hunter. You didn't know them two weeks ago. Stokes can't possibly matter to you."

"Then should I kill him right now?"

"No! You've made your point."

The screen went black for a moment, then came back. Colby suddenly entered the frame and stepped behind the table. He appeared slightly more muscular than she remembered, and his hair now covered his ears. But his blue eyes were as striking as ever, and his small teeth still gave his angular face a feral quality.

"Only partially." He looked down into Stokes's face. "But he's seen the error of his ways in one important aspect. Admit your mistake, Stokes. Am I still alive?"

Stokes's expression was a mask of anger and terror. "Yes, you bastard, you're alive."

"Excellent." Colby spoke to the camera. "I invite you all to watch as I apply one cut to Detective Stokes's body each five minutes. In exactly one hour, he will die."

"What will that prove?" Kendra voice was strained, frantic. "Don't do it, Colby!"

Colby didn't acknowledge her outburst.

He paused, raised his knife, and stabbed Stokes in the stomach.

Stokes *screamed*.

Then, as the detective gasped and wheezed with pain, Colby stepped out of the frame.

Kendra stared at the screen, stunned and horrified at what she had just seen.

Then she picked up her phone. "Sam, you saw that?" She had to steady her voice. "He meant it. You have to find him. Stokes will die if you don't."

"No pressure," he said hoarsely.

"Of course there's pressure. Do you think I want to put you in that position? If I could do it myself, I would. But it's you, and I can't help—"

"It's okay," Sam interrupted. "I've done some of my most brilliant work under unbelievable pressure. I'll just see that this is one of those times."

Good. Stokes needed Sam's hubris right now. It might be his only chance.

Beth cut in, "Sam just tossed me the phone. Literally. He's working like crazy. I never thought fingers could move across a keyboard that fast."

"Any luck?"

"Some. He traced the data stream to one relay center, and he's working on another."

"And you did say Griffin is clued in."

"Yes, Sam was in touch while you were talking to Colby. I think the entire FBI office is watching that feed. SDPD, too."

"Good."

FBI Field Office
San Diego

GRIFFIN STEPPED OUTSIDE HIS office, where the agents and support personnel were standing around the television monitors. They had just watched Colby plunge his knife into Stokes. The bleeding, shirtless detective was now having difficulty breathing.

The agents slowly turned toward Griffin and away from that hideous picture.

"Stop just standing there. If one more person looks at me with that dumb look on their face, they're fired. You saw it with your own eyes. Eric Colby is alive."

Special Agent Roland Metcalf practically sprinted from his cubicle. He definitely did not have a dumb look on his face. "Who's the hostage?"

"Martin Stokes, SDPD Homicide. He was working the marina murder." Griffin spoke to the other agents as they gathered around. "I've just mobilized the Critical Incident Response Group. We may have a fix on his location within minutes, but we can't count on that. Your analysis of this video must begin *now*. You heard him. Colby has threatened to murder Stokes within the hour."

Metcalf shook his head, and said slowly, "Then Kendra Michaels was right."

"I've been close to believing that ever since she produced those trophies. Now there's no doubt. Metcalf, I need you to organize backup for the CIRG team. If we get the word, we'll need to fly out of here."

"Yes, sir."

Griffin and Metcalf had just begun to coordinate duty assignments when a hush fell over the room.

They turned to see that Colby had stepped back on-screen, still brandishing his large knife. He spoke to the camera. "Fifty-five minutes."

He jabbed Stokes's left side with the knife, and blood spurted as he withdrew it.

CHAPTER 12

SHEER RAGE COURSED THROUGH KENDRA'S veins as she watched Colby's self-satisfied expression on-screen. Stokes writhed in pain, almost appearing to pass out at one point.

She turned from her tablet and activated the speaker-phone function. She was hurriedly pulling on her leather jacket.

"Tell me that you have something for me, Sam."

"Just a few more seconds . . ."

"Stokes is running out of time."

"Colby has run through three different relay centers, and one of them is particularly good at safeguarding its clients' privacy."

"How good?"

Kendra heard a barrage of rapid-fire keyboard clicks, then nothing.

"Sam?"

"Not good enough. I just got it. It comes back to a local IP address, right here in San Diego."

"Where?"

Sam cursed. "It's a customer of a small Internet provider on the east side, Rocketstream."

"Do you have a street address?"

"It doesn't work that way. Only Rocketstream knows which IP address is being used by which customers. They happen to be one of the providers who won't release that information without a court order. Normally, I'd commend them for that, but now I—"

"Court order. Surely, considering the circumstances, they'd be willing to—"

"We don't have time to find out. By the time someone talks to a supervisor and supervisor's supervisor, it could be too late for Stokes." More clicking computer keys. "Their service area is in the Adams North neighborhood. Get the police, your FBI buddies, the cavalry, anyone you can find, and get them over there. I'm going to break about half a dozen laws and hack into Rocketstream's customer database."

"How long will that take?"

"By the time you and the cavalry get over there, hopefully I'll have an address for you." More rapid clicks of the keys. "Go!"

North Mountain View Drive
San Diego

AS KENDRA TURNED ONTO the street that ran alongside Mountain View Park, she spotted the two brown vans that transported the FBI Critical Issue Response Group. A dozen squad cars were also on the scene, flashers on, and obviously awaiting orders.

As she was doing, she thought desperately.

Come on, Sam . . .

Griffin was standing out in the street, coordinating with the San Diego PD SWAT team commander. Kendra skidded to a stop and jumped out of her car.

Griffin moved toward her. "Still waiting for that address."

"From your end or mine?"

"Officially, mine. Your source was right, Rocketstream Internet is requiring a court order. But if you can provide the street address while we work on that, I won't worry too much about how you obtained it."

Kendra held up her phone. "I have an open line to Sam Zackoff. So far he—"

"I'm going to forget I heard that name, just in case he's now doing something terribly illegal. But I did appreciate his forwarding me the feed that Colby is sending out."

"He's forwarding it from my laptop." She added bitterly, "It's a gift from Colby. You know, the man no one believed was still alive."

"They believe it now. And, trust me, this has already changed how a lot of people think of you."

"I don't give a damn about that. I just want to get Stokes back. What's his status?"

Griffin cocked his head over at one of the squad cars, where several detectives had gathered around an iPad.

"That sicko is appearing every five minutes like clockwork to stick him with that hunting knife. Stokes is hanging on, though. He's one tough hombre."

Griffin turned and strode away to speak to the members of his critical-response team.

Kendra grabbed the tablet computer from her car's seat and adjusted the brightness to compensate for the outdoor viewing conditions. She looked at Colby's horror show, and her shaking hands tightened on the tablet. Stokes was tough, but he was now a bloody mess and obviously weaker than he'd been only a few minutes before.

Hang on, Stokes . . .

We're trying so hard.

His mouth twitched. He appeared to be trying to say something.

She reached into her console and pulled out a pair of earphones. She stuffed the rubber tips into her ears and plugged them into her tablet.

The audio feed to Stokes was clearly open. She could hear his jagged breathing and his body shifting on the table, and what sounded like the occasional rumbling of traffic outside. But Stokes had clearly given up on trying to speak.

It wasn't happening. He looked as if it was taking everything he had just to remain conscious.

Damn you, Colby.

She jerked out her earphones just in time to feel her phone vibrating in her pocket. She looked at the screen, and her heart skipped a beat. Yes!

"We got it!" She yelled across the street to Griffin. "It's 620 San Miguel Avenue."

He tensed and repeated the address. "Is that right?"

She nodded. "Go get him."

Griffin smiled and whirled to his team. "We're gone."

SAM LEANED BACK IN THE leather desk chair, limp, and dripping with sweat.

"You did it," Beth said.

He glanced at the video feed of Stokes on Kendra's laptop. "I haven't done it yet. He only has a few minutes left."

"They're already in the neighborhood. They'll make it."

Sam looked down at his phone, where Kendra had just confirmed her receipt of his text. She added, THE TEAM IS EN ROUTE. WILL KEEP YOU POSTED.

"What now," Beth asked.

He shrugged. "We wait."

"To hell with that. We'll meet her there."

He sat up straight. "Seriously?"

"I couldn't be more serious." She turned toward the door. "Let's go."

San Miguel Avenue
San Diego

KENDRA STOOD NEXT TO GRIFFIN AT the south end of San Miguel Avenue, just half a block from the house that Sam had located. It was a street of modest one-story homes, and the entire block was now swarming with uniformed officers and tactical teams.

Kendra looked down at her tablet. "Shit. It's Colby. He's coming back to finish the job." She looked frantically between her tablet and the house.

Colby had glided into position behind the table, brandishing his knife. He smiled. "Time's almost up. Tell me I've been more than fair, Kendra."

She looked frantically back up at the house. "What are they waiting for? Why don't they go in?"

"Any second now," Griffin said.

"We don't have any seconds. Didn't you hear him? Time's almost up."

"I've got a SWAT team at the window in the back. We'll be able to—"

"No!" Kendra was suddenly ice-cold. "Oh, God."

Griffin's eyes flew to her face. "What is it?"

Kendra felt her heart pounding out of her chest. "Colby and Stokes aren't in here."

"What are you talking about? You told me yourself—"

"I don't care what I told you. I know they're not here."

"How do you know?"

"Stop and listen to the video feed. Before I could hear faint traffic noise in the background, and that would be okay. But now you can hear a beeping noise like a delivery truck backing up. There's *nothing* like that sound anywhere around here." She felt as if she was going to throw up. "Dear God, we're in the wrong place."

The officers rammed the door open and swarmed the house.

Colby smiled on the video feed. "Say good-bye to Detective Stokes . . . He really should have believed you, Kendra."

Griffin's radio blared. "The residence is empty. I repeat, the residence is empty."

"Are you watching, Kendra?" Colby asked softly. "Have you figured it out yet?"

And he sliced his blade across Stokes's throat and stepped back to watch as the blood spurted over his face and chest.

"OH, MY GOD." KENDRA STOOD in the doorway, gazing at the huge computer monitor on the wall of the room the agents had just entered. She slumped back against the wall. "No."

"Yes." Griffin moved forward into the room, his hands balled into fists. "Shit. I thought we had him."

"Wrong." She closed her eyes to escape the sight of that lifeless body on the screen. "We were all wrong. He wasn't here. The Stokes feed was probably just a recording on this laptop."

"Kendra!"

She opened her eyes to see Beth coming toward her. She instinctively straightened and tried to block Beth's view of Stokes. "Don't look, Beth. It's too late. We're too late. He dangled the bait, then destroyed it before we could take it."

"Dead?" Beth whispered. She went into Kendra's arms and held her close. "I'm so sorry. I know how you must feel. But none of it was your fault."

"It's my fault for just being alive. Ask Colby." She had been trying to protect Beth, and here was Beth, comforting her. "We were wrong on so many counts. We both thought it might be Sam who was the target. But it was Stokes all the time. And Colby led us up this blind alley." She saw Detective Ketchum standing before that screen and looking up at his dead partner. His face was pale, and he looked sick.

She wondered if she looked the same way. Probably. She felt ghastly.

"It's my fault." Sam had come to stand beside her, his gaze on Stokes. "I don't know why. I swear I did everything right, Kendra. But I should have known it was a red herring. It's got to be my fault."

"We don't know that," she said gently. "You did everything you could."

"It wasn't enough."

"We'll have to go into it later." She pushed him out the door and away from that monitor. "Come on, let's get out of this place. We're no good here. Griffin will come and tell us what's happening with that screen in there."

"Yeah, by all means, let's avoid facing our mistakes," Sam said bitterly. "But it's hard not to stare Stokes in the eye about this one."

"Be quiet, Sam," Beth said curtly. "You heard Kendra, we can't know. I saw how hard you worked, how certain you were. I bet that you didn't do anything wrong."

"I hope you don't lose that bet," Sam said. "It's terrible. I've never seen a man who might have died because of me. He was just lying there, helpless. So helpless. He wasn't allowed to struggle or fight. There's no dignity."

"Colby likes it like that," Kendra said shakily. "Destroys the body, destroys dignity, tries to destroy the soul." They had reached the car, and she leaned against it. "So now you know what you've been fighting."

"I knew before. I just hadn't seen it face-to-face."

"I was looking for you, Kendra." Griffin was coming toward them. "I need to know how this happened. How you could let it happen." He frowned. "You look a little peaked. You okay?"

"Just fine, Griffin." She said, "Why not? It's not as if I have any sensitivity or compassion. It's not as if that man wasn't killed just because Colby thought I had some connection with him. Yes, I'm peaked. Yes, I'm sick." She took a deep breath. "Now tell me what was going on in there."

"You saw it all. It was just the monitor and a small laptop computer behind it. We won't know for sure, but it appears that the room has been wiped clean."

"And we don't even know where Stokes was killed. We probably won't know until we stumble across the body. Or perhaps if Colby deigns to send a message to tell us. Everything at Colby's pleasure."

"That appears to be the way it's going to go."

"No, it's not," she said through set teeth. "We're not going to wait for him to manipulate us. I can't take it any longer. We have to go after him."

"And how do you intend to do that? Please, by all means, tell me," he said sarcastically. "Because I thought this was what was going on. I believe there's a roomful of officers in that room who think it is."

"We've got to do more. *I've* got to do more."

"Come on," Beth took her arm. "Let's go home, Kendra. There's nothing you can do right now. We'll think about it and find some way to—" She broke off and turned to Griffin. "And you're not being either helpful or kind. I know you're frustrated and upset, but do you think she isn't? Stay away from her until you can behave like a decent human being or serve Colby up to her the way he did that detective in there."

Griffin's eyes widened. "I beg your pardon."

"Beg Kendra's pardon. It's what you should do. She's been in this alone and having to beg and plead for help from you." She opened the passenger door and pushed Kendra into the car. "I thought maybe you might be something besides a swellheaded bureaucrat, but now I'm thinking I'm dead wrong. Get in the car, Sam. Let's go."

Griffin was staring at her, frowning. Then as Beth jumped into the driver's seat and started the car, he slowly shook his head. "And I thought you were such a quiet, gentle little thing."

"I'm not a thing. I'm a woman who can be what she wants to be. Just another one of your mistakes, Griffin."

She stepped on the accelerator, and the next moment, she was halfway down the street.

Kendra's lips curved in a ghost of a smile. "He won't

make that mistake again. I didn't need you to defend me, but I thank you anyway, Beth."

"It felt like you needed me. Besides, no one should have to take that kind of abuse when they're in pain. I felt like giving him a karate kick."

"I believe you translated that in verbal terms." She looked back at Sam. "Are you okay? You're very quiet."

"I was just enjoying Beth. I think it's always going to be entertaining to see her effect on the unsuspecting. I needed that right now." He met Kendra's eyes. "You needed it, too. I know you think we failed, and a man died because of it, but I don't believe that's true. I've been going over it in my mind, and I don't think I made a mistake. I just have to get back to my lab and find out what happened."

"Then that's what we'll do." She was trying to think, trying to get over the numbing horror, trying to find hope again. "You're right, we have to take this all apart and see what happened, see how he managed to do this sleight of hand." What a whimsical term for that hideous, deadly act, she thought. "He enjoyed that hour when he was holding us all hostage. I could see it in his expression. That means he won't want it to be over. Colby will be searching for a way to top himself."

"And he'll be in contact again," Sam said. "I'll have another shot at him."

"Maybe," Kendra said. "Who the hell knows how he'll make contact?"

"He likes computers, they've been successful for him, and he thinks that he's beaten us with them," Sam said. "I'd bet that he'll use them again." He turned to Beth. "Find me that computer tech he has on a leash, I have to know how he's going to do it."

"I'm trying. I'm making progress but I haven't had a

chance to—" Beth nodded. "I'll get him for you. Kendra, I'll send you a couple names I thought were promising, and you can do a search. I'll do the other three. Okay?"

"Okay." They'd arrived at her condo, and she opened the passenger door. "I'll get right on it. You're staying with Sam, Beth?"

"Yes, he might need me." She looked at the door of the condo. "It might not be a bad idea for you to change your mind and come back to Lynch's house with us."

"Why?" She got out of the car. "Nothing's changed as far as I'm concerned. Colby doesn't want to end it yet. I told you, he enjoyed that kill. That means I'm relatively safe wherever I am."

"Relatively?"

Kendra shook her head. "It's a word I've lived with since I knew Colby hadn't died in that prison. Yes, he could change his mind in a heartbeat, but we have to play his game." She headed for the front entrance. "Go back to Lynch's and get to work. Send me those computer-expert prospects to work on, and I'll dive in right away. Work may be the only way we'll be able to block the memory of Stokes's face on that monitor."

"I SEE THAT YOU THINK Joseph Northrup might be our man," Kendra told Beth on the phone the next day after going through her hacker prospects. "I agree. Computer degree at MIT. Something of a boy genius and graduated from the university when he was only nineteen. Offered a number of positions at think tanks around the country but evidently he thought he was meant for better things."

"Right," Beth said. "That's why he's at the top of my list. He was arrested for hacking into the stock exchange and manipulating funds. He was paroled after two years and was still considered a hot commodity in the job market. He's held a few jobs in the last six years but dropped out of sight a year ago. Sounds like a firm possibility. How can we find out where he is?"

"I'll check with SDPD and see if they can do it. I imagine they'll be eager to help. They've lost one of their own, and they'll be going after his killer at full force. Our main problem will be to keep them from arresting Northrup before Colby knows we're after him."

"And eliminating a witness who may know where he is."

"He wouldn't allow Northrup to live one day beyond his usefulness. I'll get on it." Kendra hung up, then hesitated before she called the police.

She was reluctant to involve them because of those highly charged feelings she'd mentioned. Northrup might be their only lead to find Colby, and she was frantic not to blow it. But they had to find him fast, and she didn't have the contacts to—

Her phone rang, and she glanced at the ID.

Griffin.

"I'm downstairs," he said when she picked up. "I want to talk. Buzz me in."

"By all means." She buzzed him into the building and was at the door when he arrived at the condo. "What is it, Griffin?"

"I want to apologize." He was scowling as he walked into the foyer. "I didn't take in consideration the fact that you were almost in shock. I was a little rude."

"Yes, you were. But that seldom provokes an apology from you unless it's someone you need something from."

"Accept it graciously. It's all you'll get from me. I've

been going through hell. The media is roasting me alive for not realizing that Colby was still alive. By the way, you're their heroine."

"Today. Tomorrow it may change again," she said. "Is that why you're here, so that you give a press release that you apologized to me?"

"I've already told them that I thought there was a possibility you might be right. After all, I was working on those trophy IDs with you."

"One toe testing the water. You weren't admitting the possibility until there was cast-iron proof."

"Well, now we have it." He waved his hand dismissingly. "Water under the bridge."

"Not necessarily. Is that all that you came to say?"

"No. I wanted to tell you that after we went bust at that house on San Miguel yesterday, I called Quantico. I got one of our top cyberdivision guys in Quantico, Tom Sims, to call Sam Zackoff and team up to figure what really happened yesterday. They worked all night but just came up with the answer only minutes before I got here. Turns out while we were busting our asses to save Stokes, he was already dead. Before we even knew Colby had taken him."

"Are you sure?"

Griffin nodded. "At one point, the screen cut to black for a few moments. When the picture came back, we were seeing a recording, most likely hours old. It was streaming from a hard drive in that house. There was no way Zackoff, or anybody, could have known. The online trail ended right there."

"We never had a chance." All that heartache and hope and agony had been for nothing. "He was playing with us." She was shaking just thinking about it. She turned away. "Okay, you've done your duty. You can leave now."

"Not until I tell you that we have to work together. Look, I've already called Quantico and given Zackoff our prize computer expert to help him. Doesn't that prove I'm going all out? I have to get Colby right away because the media won't be off my ass until I do."

"Not because there might be more murders until he's caught?"

"Of course that's true. But you wouldn't believe it if I gave you any but the most selfish of motives. I have many reasons why I have to move fast on this." He smiled faintly. "So do you. It's time we launched a major campaign in that direction."

"I already have, Griffin."

"Stop being hardheaded. We both know you need me. Work with me."

"So the media can see us arm in arm going after the bad guy."

"Partly." He paused. "I need you, Kendra. Remember the night you came to me and told me that? Now the tables are turned." He added, "We've found Stokes's body."

She stiffened. "Where? When?"

"Two hours ago. On the rooftop of a sleazebag hotel on the south side of the city. A police helicopter spotted it. Colby probably deposited the body there while we were watching his horror show. Forensics is going over both the corpse and the area with a fine-tooth comb, but I want you there."

"It may not do any good. Colby had plenty of time to clean up the scene."

"But you still want to go."

"Of course I do." She grabbed her jacket and headed for the door. "You knew that you'd have me with that bait."

"Yes." He opened the door for her. "But you should still

appreciate the heartfelt apology that went along with it. It was eloquent and even a bit sincere. I don't hand those out every day . . ."

GRIFFIN AND KENDRA CLIMBED THE short flight of steps to the door to the rooftop of the depressing, eight-story hotel. On the few occasions that Kendra had even noticed it, she'd assumed that the establishment had been abandoned years before. Who would stay here?

"This place mostly caters to druggies and prostitutes," Griffin said, as if reading her mind. "It was probably easy for Colby to move around in here without anyone's noticing or caring. Still don't know how he got a corpse on the roof."

Kendra pointed to a laundry cart in the hallway beside the elevator. "I'd start there. See if there's a loading dock behind the building. He could have parked there, put the corpse in the cart, and taken it up the elevator."

Griffin glanced back at the cart. "You could be right." He opened the roof-access door, and Kendra was immediately struck by the roar of helicopters overhead.

"News copters," Griffin said. "Nothing like giving a guy his dignity."

They stepped onto the black asphalt roof and walked past two large water tanks. There, on the roof's far side, was Stokes's body.

The forensic techs were still working, but it was clear they were almost finished with the initial examination. The area was filled with techs, agents, and detectives, all wearing aqua-colored evidence booties as they moved around the scene. Kendra slipped on her own booties and gloves as she moved forward. She forced herself to look at Stokes and flinched.

Torture, terror, and the final ravages of death had completely altered his appearance.

Detach.

Concentrate.

Was there anything about him that could tell her anything?

Only about the fragility of life.

I think you're an honorable man.

Those were practically the last words she had said to him.

And that honorable man had suffered and given his life.

No, it had been taken from him. He hadn't even believed that there was any reason for him to die.

"What are you doing here?"

She turned to see Detective Ketchum coming toward her from across the rooftop. The former belligerence was absent, but it had been replaced by bitterness.

"The same thing you are. Trying to find a way to catch Stokes's killer." She met his gaze. "I'm sorry for your loss, Ketchum. I know this must be rough on you."

"Do you? I went through police academy with him. We came up through the ranks together. I was best man at his wedding. Yeah, you could say it's rough." His eyes were glittering with moisture. "And he'd still be alive if he hadn't met you."

"Knock it off, Ketchum." Detective Starger was suddenly beside him. "You know it wasn't her fault. At least you should if you were thinking straight. Colby is insane, and Stokes just got caught up in his craziness. She told us over and over that Colby was alive, and we should help her catch him."

"Colby killed him as a gift to her. You heard him say it."

"And you heard her try to talk him out of it. We all did." His voice was suddenly hoarse with pain. "I'm hurting, too, buddy. But we've got to focus on the right target."

"Thank you, Detective," Kendra said. "And I'll try to clarify that focus if I can. That's why I'm here."

He nodded jerkily. "I'm grateful for your help. Ketchum will be, too, once he gets a chance to think this through. Stokes always said how smart you were. He admired you, but he was kind of wary of that talent. Let's see if you can make it work for all of us. If you need me, call." He gave Ketchum a nudge away from Kendra. "Come on, we've got work to do."

Ketchum gave her a last glance and let Starger lead him away.

"Not a comfortable encounter." Griffin was behind her. "I thought Ketchum was going to get violent."

"It was possible." She was looking after the two detectives. "Who could really blame him? Colby set me up as a heavy in this kill. Ketchum loved his friend."

"You're being generous."

"No, I'm just trying to understand. I understand Ketchum's anger and hurt far better than your response to Stokes's death." She turned away from him. "Now let me look around and see if I can notice anything on the roof that would make it worth my while to be here." She braced herself and moved across the roof. They hadn't removed Stokes yet, and she wasn't qualified to examine the wounds, but she had to look at his body. And she forced herself to look at that poor, bloody face.

I'm coming to you, Stokes.

With regret and respect and the hope of justice for you.

Bear with me and realize that I know you died an honorable man.

Kendra was standing next to him now.

And she froze. "He was posed."

"I see that."

She crouched beside Stokes for a better look. His bloody fingers were glued together, elbows bent and flat palms facing backward.

Griffin pulled out his phone. "I'll look up the Army field-manual hand-signal guide."

"You don't have to do that," Kendra said. She stood and turned to look down at the city. "I know this one. I expected it. It means 'prepare for another strike.'"

CHAPTER
13

DAMN, IT WAS GOOD TO be home.

Adam Lynch smiled as he turned onto Chester Court and headed toward the end of the street. The mere sight of his house eased a bit of the tension from his neck and back. It had been an intense week in Luxembourg, made all the more harrowing by the rapidly developing Eric Colby case back home. It drove him crazy that he was stuck almost six thousand miles away at the exact same time that Colby appeared to be making a grotesque comeback.

There had been some loose ends to tie up in Luxembourg, but with Colby's reemergence, he'd tossed the responsibility to someone else and headed home. Kendra had been the one to bring the beast down originally, and it was anybody's guess what shape his sick revenge would take now.

But at least Kendra was safe at this moment. She was in the house that he'd built to keep himself safe, and he knew that as long as she was there there, Colby couldn't reach her. He was eager to see her. Only a few more minutes and he—

No, it was late and he wouldn't wake her tonight but wait until they'd both had something resembling a good night's sleep.

The tall gates opened, and he sped up the driveway to the garage. He parked and pressed his thumb against his phone's fingerprint sensor to throw open the lock to his house. He stepped inside and dropped his bags inside the door.

Home. Maybe a few minutes of *Sports Center*, a quick shower, then . . .

He heard something.

A scraping sound from the kitchen.

Kendra?

Perhaps. But he couldn't take the chance. It might not be Colby, but any number of old enemies might have their sights on him.

Lynch slowly, quietly turned back, unzipped his large, checked suitcase, and pulled out his Taurus .45 automatic. He checked the magazine. Fully loaded.

Another sound from the kitchen. Louder this time.

Lynch crept through the dark living room with his gun pointed upward.

Footsteps. Coming his way.

A silhouetted form stepped through the doorway.

Not Kendra.

A man, probably five-ten or five-eleven. He was holding something in his hands.

Lynch took aim. "Freeze!"

"Oh, man. Oh, man. Oh, man."

Lynch cocked his head. His intruder didn't sound like a trained killer . . . More like a scared teenager caught raiding his father's liquor cabinet.

"Whatever is in your hands, drop it."

Without hesitation, the man let go. Lynch saw one of his favorite dinner plates shatter on the floor.

"What in the hell was that?"

"Cheese sandwich."

"What?"

"Auricchio provolone on pumpernickel."

"*My* Auricchio provolone on pumpernickel?"

"That depends," he said warily. "Are you Adam Lynch?"

"You first. Who are you?"

"Sam Zackoff. I'm helping Kendra Michaels. She thought I might be in danger, so she put me up here."

"Suppose we go upstairs and wake her and verify that."

"Upstairs? No one's in the house but Beth Avery. Would she do?"

"No, she would not." Lynch's hand tightened on the gun. "You're telling me that Kendra's not here."

"No, we tried to convince her to come, but she wanted to stay in her own place. She's so damn stubborn. Could you put that gun down now?"

"Not quite yet. You haven't proved shit. Do you have a phone on you?"

"In my pocket."

"Okay, very slowly, take it out and call Kendra. Put the call on speaker."

"What if she doesn't answer?"

Lynch turned on the lamp on the table next to him. His gun still pointed at Sam. "Hope that she does."

Sam slowly reached down and pulled out his phone with

his thumb and forefinger. He punched Kendra's number, then put the phone on speaker.

Kendra answered on the second ring. "Sam, I'd just gotten to sleep. If it's important, start talking. Otherwise, it had better wait until morning to—"

"I kind of think it's important. Adam Lynch is here, and he wants to talk to you. Oh, and as a kind of funny aside, he has a big gun aimed at my chest."

"Oh, shit."

"Hello, Kendra," Lynch spoke from across the room.

"Lynch . . . What are you doing there?"

"Last time I checked, it was still my home. Though I could be mistaken." He put away the gun. "So I assume you're vouching for this guy?"

"Of course. That's Sam Zackoff. He's a flat-out genius. Sam's no threat, and you should get along with him. At least, I'd very much appreciate your not shooting him."

"Thanks, Kendra." Sam grinned. "I'm sure we'll get along fine now that I'm no longer in danger of being mortally wounded by him."

Lynch shrugged. "I wouldn't say *that.*"

Sam's grin faded.

"Sorry about this," Kendra said. "I had no idea you were on your way home, or I would have—" She stopped, and said wearily, "No, I probably wouldn't. Things have been—Do you want me to come up there?"

"It's where you should have been to begin with," Lynch said coolly. "But we'll discuss that later. Go back to sleep. I'll deal with it when I finish here."

He nodded at Sam, who promptly cut the connection.

"I thought you knew," Sam said. "Sorry."

"Ordinarily, it wouldn't be a big deal. I'm just a little wigged out right now."

"I can imagine, coming home and finding a stranger in your kitchen."

"No, actually I'm wigged-out that you were about a millisecond away from being dead on the floor with a bullet in your heart. You don't know how close that came to happening."

"Oh." Sam was taken aback. Then he recovered. "Well, you don't know how close I came to emptying my bowels when I saw you in here with that gun aimed at me. So I guess we're both a little wigged-out."

Lynch smiled. "So what kind of genius are you?"

"Computers. Software, hardware, networking . . . Kendra's psychopathic buddy, Colby, has suddenly gotten very proficient with this stuff, so she called me to help out."

"I'm no genius, but I'm pretty handy in that area myself."

"I figured, with all the gear you have around here. You know how to use all the things I saw in your office?"

"I actually designed some of them. I recently wrote a custom application that lets me crack into anyone's phone within thirty feet or so. I can access their address book, call logs, and personal information." Lynch held up his phone. "As a matter of fact, I've used it to tap into your phone since we've been standing here."

"Really?"

"Yes, it comes in handy. I can even—" Lynch froze as he glanced down at his phone screen. Puzzled, he turned it around to show Sam. In large letters, a warning message read: STAY OUT OF MY PHONE, ASSHOLE."

Sam smiled. "I've written a custom app of my own. It keeps assholes from hacking into my phone."

"And it's obviously very effective."

"I even have a setting that takes the snooper's phone and wipes it clean. Turns it into a brick."

Lynch went still. His face remained almost impassive, but there was the barest flicker of expression. "Indeed?"

"Don't worry, the setting isn't turned on at the moment."

Lynch pocketed his phone. "Small favors, I guess."

"You're welcome."

Lynch suddenly chuckled. "Kendra's right. I think you and I will have a lot to talk about."

"Whew." Sam let out a relieved sign. "I wasn't sure you weren't going to pull out that gun again."

"Suppose we go on to less explosive subjects. How can you get in and out of here without Kendra swiping her finger across her phone screen?"

"I cloned the app and had her swipe her finger on my phone. I modified the software so that her fingerprint registers every time I use it to come or go."

"Hmm. I might have to rethink the security system here."

"It's actually pretty incredible, but of course, *I'm* pretty incredible." Sam paced around the living room. "Kendra called it the Suburban Fortress, but I had no idea how right she was. I don't think even Kendra knows." His eyes were bright with eagerness. "If my calculations are right, this place could withstand an assault of an entire battery of forty-millimeter grenade launchers."

"That's correct. Of course, my neighbors wouldn't be too thrilled about it."

"Expecting an army?"

"Well, I've upset some people who do have small armies at their disposal."

"Two questions. First of all, what people? And second, upset them how? This has to be good."

"I work freelance, so it depends on my employer of the moment."

"I was under the impression that you did government work."

"That's true. But I work for various agencies with different agendas. I've helped bring down crime families here in the U.S., warlords in Africa, and even a corrupt dictatorship."

"Hey, cool. How exactly do you do that?"

Lynch was silent, gazing at him. Zackoff didn't even realize that the questions he was asking could prove both offensive and dangerous. He was like a curious kid probing an intriguing new puzzle. But the answers weren't anything confidential or top secret, and that eagerness was somehow appealing. It wouldn't hurt to go a little further. "How do I do it? Persuasion, mostly. I'm pretty good at convincing people that my goals should be theirs."

"Ah, the Puppetmaster at work."

"Kendra must have told you that. I'm not fond of that name."

"But it sounds like an accurate assessment of your skill set."

"Still, it doesn't make me like it," he said flatly.

Sam held up his hands. "Sorry. See, I'm backing off. But sometimes we have to live with the nicknames we earn."

"And what do people call you?"

Sam rolled his eyes. "My last name is Zackoff. One guess what people have called me my entire life."

"Hmm. That which does not kill us, makes us stronger."

"I never needed schoolyard bullies to make me strong." Sam shrugged. "I entered arrest warrants for them in the local police databases. By the time it all got sorted out, most them spent at least a night in juvie."

Lynch smiled. "Well played. I'll remember to stay on your good side."

"You're already there. Any friend of Kendra's . . ."

Lynch grabbed his suitcase and carry-on bag. "Speaking of whom, I think I'm going to go and get her now."

"Now?"

"You have an objection?"

"It's almost four in the morning. Didn't you just tell her to go back to sleep?"

"I did. I just changed my mind. I'm a tad upset. Why should she sleep when I'm not going to be able to do it? I'll take my bags up to my room, then head over to Kendra's place." He gestured up the stairs. "I assume you didn't take my master bedroom?"

Sam made a face. "Uh, I'll get my things out of there. You weren't even supposed to know about it. I meant to be out the instant I heard you were on your way back. It'll only take a minute."

He bounded up the stairs.

HER PHONE WAS RINGING, KENDRA realized. She had been lying here in bed, unable to sleep after that upsetting conversation with Lynch. He probably hadn't meant her to sleep. He had sounded pissed off when she had spoken to him and Sam. Who could blame him? She had violated the one sanctuary he allowed himself without his permission. Hell, she couldn't please everyone, and keeping Sam safe had been more important than pleasing Lynch.

She snatched the phone from the bedside table and pressed the access.

"I'm downstairs. Buzz me in," Lynch said. "Now."

"Why? You told me to go back to bed. Yet here you are in the middle of the night."

"Buzz me in, Kendra. I'm barely holding on to my control. You don't want to test it."

She was tempted to do just that but pressed the button instead. The she jumped out of bed, grabbed her robe, and strode to the front door.

"I know you have reason to be annoyed with me," she said when she threw open the door. "But I don't appreciate your growling at me. I've had enough trauma for one week."

"So I've heard." He came into the condo and slammed the door. "But I haven't had an easy time of it either, so I'm not in a particularly sympathetic mood."

He jerked her close and kissed her.

Heat. Anger. Sex.

She was too surprised to move.

Then he released her and turned toward the kitchen. "I needed that. Now I'm going to get a cup of coffee. Come on and act the polite hostess and keep me company."

She hesitated, then trailed behind him because she didn't know what else to do. Her lips felt warm, tingling, and her breasts were taut and ready. The response had to be because of the shock of that unexpected caress.

No, she was lying to herself. The chemistry between them had always been there, hot and sexual, like a volcanic undercurrent. An undercurrent that Kendra knew should never be acknowledged if she continued to work with Lynch. It would be a distraction. *He* would be a distraction.

"What kind of coffee do you want?" Lynch called over his shoulder as he put his cup in the automatic coffeemaker.

"I don't want anything. I'm hoping to go back to bed."

"That won't happen right away. Though I'm not going to stay long." He took his coffee to the table and sat down.

"Right now, I need to drink this and have you tell me why you didn't call and tell me what was going on with you. I didn't hear anything until I was hopping the plane out of Luxembourg and got through to my contact in Griffin's office. And that was damn scanty."

"You were having your own problems. You told me so." She sat down across from him. "How did the hostage situation turn out?"

"Touchy. Almost lost one." He shrugged. "But I was able to negotiate my way out with him. I did have to go undercover, as I told you I might. Which is why I didn't have access to my own phone until I got him out."

He looked tired, she thought. His eyes were sunken, and his demeanor had that charged restlessness she had noticed was always present when he'd been stretched too far. "I'm sorry. I'm glad that it worked out."

"So am I." His lips tightened. "Isn't it nice I was able to concentrate because I didn't have to worry about you? I was relieved when I finally got my phone back. I thought for once you'd actually done something I'd asked you to do."

She frowned. "What?"

"No wonder you're puzzled. It never happens, does it?"

"What are you talking about?"

"I drove up to my house feeling confident, even grateful that you'd be there, safe, in a controlled environment I'd created myself. And, lo and behold, who did I find there but Super Sam, the computer man." He took a swallow of coffee. "Interesting man but not who I expected. I thought I was coming home to you."

"I had to find a safe place for him. I left a message for you, but you must have gone undercover already. I meant to call back, but things kept happening." She shook her head. "But why did you believe I was there?"

"You had the key app on your phone. I received an apps text when you activated it. I thought you were doing what I asked you to do." His eyes were glittering in his taut face. "What you should have been doing. My God, when Sam told me what you'd been through, I couldn't believe you were still out here letting Colby take aim at you."

"I was safe here. I changed all the locks. I'm on the alert. Besides, he doesn't want me yet."

"Yeah, Sam said that was the excuse you were using not to stay at my place."

"It's got to be over," she said unevenly. "I can't take any more. I have to draw him out."

Lynch muttered a curse. "The hell you do."

She just looked at him.

"Look, do it some other way. We'll talk about it, explore the options, set a trap."

"I'm doing everything I can. I just can't have him go underground because it's too difficult."

"Too difficult to put your severed head on a pole?"

She smiled faintly. "Something like that."

"Stop smiling. It's not amusing. I can't take this, Kendra."

Her smile vanished. "To hell with you, Lynch. Don't tell me what you can't take. Earlier today, I had to see a man who'd been tortured beyond the boundaries of what a person should be able to bear because Colby decided to give his life to me as a gift. I can't let that happen again."

He was silent. Then he reached over and covered her hand on the table with his own. "*We* can't let it happen again."

Warmth. Comfort. Understanding.

She could feel her throat tighten. Don't break down. She

had held on tight so far. She couldn't let go just because Lynch was here, and everything seemed better, safer.

"Hey, easy." He released her hand and raised his hand to touch her cheek. "We'll be okay. We can take care of this together. Talk to me. Tell me what's happened. Tell me what road we're taking to get this psychopath."

Persuasive, fascinating, coaxing, the Puppetmaster in full force. Only now she thought she could see something deeper, less complex, more sincere. "I'm sure that Sam told you what was happening."

"In brief, from his point of view. I want your point of view. I want to watch your face while you tell me."

"Whatever." She shrugged. "Not a pretty story."

She began to speak.

It wasn't easy, the wounds were too fresh, the memories too horrible. But she got through it without breaking down.

At least she thought she had.

"Ugly." Lynch's fingers touched a tear that was running down her cheek. "Very ugly."

"Yes." She got up and grabbed a tissue from the box on the counter. "And I can't let Stokes die for nothing. I have to find a way to keep Colby from abusing anyone like that again." She dabbed at her cheeks with the tissue. "So there it is. Satisfied?"

"No. I'm not satisfied." He leaned back in the chair with his legs stretched out before him. "I wasn't here."

"You couldn't have done anything."

"Wrong. In case you've forgotten my reputation, I'm not paid exceptionally well for sitting twiddling my thumbs." He frowned thoughtfully. "And it seems first on the agenda is locating Colby's pet computer expert. You say you were going to contact SDPD to help?"

"It seemed a good idea. Even though the police and the FBI will want to run their own show, and I thought it might be dangerous."

"They will, and it would," Lynch said. "I'll handle it. I have contacts both in law enforcement and the underbelly of the criminal hierarcy. I'll tap Zackoff for info on his contacts in the computer field. I'm sure that he has an amazing collection in every category. We should be able to get it done."

Kendra felt a rush of relief. "How long will it take?"

He shook his head. "I'll work fast, but it will take as long as it takes." He paused. "But I won't be stalled by having to worry about you. That would get in my way, and I'm not having it."

She stiffened. "I told you that—"

"You told me you intend to play the sacrificial goat waiting for the tiger. Ain't gonna happen. We'll work something else out."

"You're giving me orders."

"Would I do that? I'm telling you that your being here and not at my house will cause me to constantly keep an eye on you. Which would result in a slowdown to any attempt to go forward. Is that what you want?"

"No." She thought about it. She wasn't sure that he wasn't manipulating her, but there was a possibility that it might be true. Lynch was very protective, and she didn't wish him to have to juggle priorities. "It might be possible."

"Good." He finished his coffee. "Go and dress. Pack up a suitcase and any evidence or info that you have. Then we'll be out of here."

"Right now? There's no rush at the moment. You go on home. I'll come in the morning."

"It's morning now—4:22 A.M." He grinned. "Stop

stalling. I'm not leaving until you walk out that door with me."

And he wouldn't do it, either, she thought ruefully. As long as she'd already acceded to the demand, she might as well give in on this point. "Okay, but I'll follow you. I want my own car."

"Of course you do. I'm not trying to keep you prisoner."

"I wouldn't put it past you," she said dryly. "Just don't try to put an ankle manacle on me."

"Perish the thought." His gaze traveled down her bare legs to her ankles, then her feet. "But it's very tempting. You have very sexy ankles, and I've always liked to see you barefoot. I can remember when you were staying with me after we found out that Colby might be alive. I always looked forward to seeing you pad around, digging your toes in the carpet—"

"Weird. If I'd realized you had a foot fetish, I would have been more careful. I'm glad you let me know."

He sighed. "Talking nether extremities, I've just shot myself in the foot."

"Yes. Better than putting a bullet in my friend, Sam." She headed for the door. "I'll be ready to go in fifteen minutes."

"DOES THAT SUITCASE MEAN WHAT I think it does?" Beth opened the door as Lynch and Kendra approached. She was fully dressed in jeans and shirt though it was only a little before five. She glanced at Lynch. "You're Adam Lynch? You should have gotten here sooner if you have that kind of clout with her. We've been trying to get her to come ever since she brought Sam here."

"No clout. I merely appealed to her reason. I assume

you're Beth Avery." He shook her hand. "Welcome to my home. Or should that be your line?"

She chuckled. "Sam said you were a trifle annoyed that we'd invaded your space. He had to come upstairs and wake me and tell me about it. It sounds like a priceless encounter. I was sorry I missed it when you had him at gunpoint."

"I'm not," Kendra said as she closed the door. "You would probably have tried to put Lynch down, and that wouldn't have been wise. He's no Bubba, either."

Beth was gazing appraisingly at Lynch. "I can see that." She smiled. "It's lucky that I wasn't tested. But it might have been interesting. I've heard a good deal about you from Kendra, Lynch. And I've learned more just by living in your house. I hope you'll forgive us for intruding."

He shrugged. "It's over. You're no longer an intruder. You're now guests. I'm delighted to meet you. Both Zack-off and Kendra shared a few interesting stories regarding your rather unique character."

"Unique. Is that a synonym for weird?" Beth didn't wait for an answer but turned to Kendra. "I'm glad you decided to come. I need someone to help keep Sam in line. Ever since Griffin got his Quantico computer wonder guy to work with Sam, he's been slaving night and day to try to get a clear line to Colby. Sims is very sharp, and I think it's becoming a competition thing."

"Could be," Kendra said. "He always has to be best."

"It sounds like he needs a distraction." Lynch turned and headed for the office. "I'll see what I can do to give it to him."

Beth smiled as she watched him disappear into the office. "A powerhouse," she murmured. "It's no wonder he was able to whisk you back here."

"As he said, he used reason." She wrinkled her nose. "And the faintest tinge of blackmail."

"A powerhouse," Beth repeated as she started for the stairs. "Come on. I'll show you to a guest room." She laughed. "Though you know the house far better than I do. I guess I've kind of taken control since I got here."

"And I'm glad you have." Kendra followed her upstairs. "You've been a godsend, helping with Sam. It lifted a giant weight off my shoulders."

"Then I'm glad I could be here for both of you." She stopped at a door. "Is this room okay?"

"It doesn't matter. They're all great. Lynch made sure of that." She opened the door and glanced inside. Spaciousness. Luxury. Taste. "It will be fine." She turned back to Beth. "He's going to try to find Northrup for us, Beth."

"I figured that might be in the cards." Beth gave her a hug. "I've got a good feeling, Kendra. We're all together and safe. We have a strong lead and smart, innovative people to follow it. Maybe the dark days are over."

"Maybe they are." Her arms tightened around Beth. Lord, she hoped she was right. Sunlight instead of darkness. Life instead of death. It seemed almost too much for which to hope. But Beth was hoping, and she had to follow her star. She gave her another hug and stepped back. "Just let me unpack and take a shower, then I'll be downstairs. I didn't get a chance to even freshen up before I left the condo. Lynch was hovering."

"I can see how that would be distracting." She turned back toward the stairs. "Come on down when you're ready. I'll start breakfast in forty minutes . . ."

Kendra closed the door and stood there for a moment. *Maybe the dark days are over.*

Colby was the quintessence of darkness, and where he was, there would always be darkness.

But Colby was not here now. So shut him out, don't let him make her weak and apprehensive. If she could not be positive, she could at least look forward and not back.

And the future was always what you made of it.

Beth was right. They had all the weapons they needed. They had a chance.

All they had to do was reach out and take it.

HIS CHAMBER HAD NEVER LOOKED more beautiful.

Colby thrust his mop into the twenty-gallon cart and stepped back onto the stairs for a better look. The floor and walls were now coated with a thick coat of warm, dark tar, which seemed to capture and absorb all light. The cream-colored embalming table stood in stark relief, almost appearing to float in the void.

Beautiful. Simply beautiful.

He'd been working all night in his chamber, preparing it for his grand finale. It would certainly be the last time he'd ever use it, and he envisioned a spectacular end for a place that had served him well for so many years.

He touched the wall closest to the stairs. The tar there was already hardening and cool to the touch.

Perfect.

Just as the rest would be perfect.

Colby smiled. He had been patient, and now he would have his reward.

After all these years, it was going to happen.

All he had to do was reach out and take it.

CHAPTER
14

"IT'S ABOUT TIME YOU WOKE UP," Lynch said from the foot of the staircase. "I was about to come up and get you. We have things to do and people to see."

"It's only been two hours," Kendra said as she came down the stairs. "And I'm glad I slept. It's not been happening very much lately."

"No?" He nodded. "I noticed you were looking a little fragile. You've lost a few pounds. Sharing your nights with Colby?"

"More than I would like."

His lips tightened, "More than I would like, too." His fingers touched the dark circles beneath her eyes. "We'll take care of that soon. I'm glad you slept. See, you should have been here from the beginning. You must have felt safer."

"And you're always right?" There might have been an element of truth in his words, but she wasn't about to tell him that his fortress hadn't been the sole reason she had been able to relax. Lynch was here, and that was security in itself. "What things to do and people to see?"

"We need to go to the field office and see Griffin. I want to get a complete report on the investigation into Stokes's abduction and death. They must have facts and possible witness reports by now."

Kendra nodded. "Griffin texted me that they thought Stokes was taken at his home. He was going to text me more later."

"Then he can tell us in person. As well as anything else that's come up." He led her through the living room toward the kitchen. "Coffee, then we're on our way."

"Did you and Sam get together about how to track down Colby's computer ace?"

"Sam has a sort of cult following in San Francisco that he's tapping. Northrup does look promising, but no one's seen him or heard of him since last November, when a source said he was doing a hacking job for a pharmaceutical company. He obviously likes money, so I put out feelers to a money-laundering operation with contacts all over the U.S. He's clever, and he would need to get any fees safely out of the country." He smiled. "Either way, we'll find him. It's only a matter of time."

"Which we do not have."

"Then we'll find a way of hurrying it along. We've only just started the process of—"

"Hey, wait," she interrupted as they were passing by the portrait in the living room. "I meant to ask you. What happened to your beautiful bikini babe?"

He paused and glanced up at Kendra's portrait. "Maybe I'm becoming discriminating."

"Nah."

"Or maybe I like the way your portrait makes me think . . . and remember."

She kept her gaze on the portrait. "How very sensitive. What did your gorgeous Ashley say?"

"She wasn't pleased, but she understood that she has to be tolerant of other women who are less fortunate than she."

"Is that what she said?"

"No, it was implied. Ashley is easy to read."

"When did you buy the portrait?"

"Two days after we saw it together." He grimaced. "The bastard held me up."

"Then why did you give in?"

"Warren knew he had me. I wanted it." He met her eyes. "So I took it."

Heat.

She quickly looked away from him. "Or he took you."

"No, that's not the way it works. In the end, it belongs to me. I can look at it. I can touch it. I can care for it."

"Or destroy it."

He shook his head. "What a waste that would be. No, I believe you're here for the long haul." He took her elbow and nudged her toward the kitchen. "I really don't think I could do without you . . ."

FBI Field Office
San Diego
9:50 A.M.

KENDRA AND LYNCH STEPPED off the FBI field office elevator and walked down the long corridor toward Griffin's office. Kendra glanced around at the busy personnel and was immediately struck by the sense of urgency compared with her other recent visits.

Lynch obviously saw it, too. "There's a psychopath on the loose, and it's being perceived as partially their fault," he said quietly. "They know how bad this has made them look. We can use this to get any amount of cooperation we need from them."

"Spoken like the true Puppetmaster you are."

"Hmm. I really need to stop sharing thoughts like that with you."

"Don't sweat it. I knew when Griffin visited me the day after Stokes was killed that we weren't going to have a problem with them. If it gets us closer to nailing Colby, play whatever games with them you want. Whatever it takes."

"I'm glad to hear you say that. Manipulation doesn't have to be a curse word. It can be just a matter of steering conditions toward a mutually beneficial conclusion."

"Ha. If you dare say that the next time you try to manipulate me, I'll slap you."

He smiled. "I think you would."

"Bet on it. FYI, you should probably keep that little rationalization to yourself."

"Point taken."

Kendra spotted Griffin and several other agents in a large conference room separated from the corridor by floor-to-ceiling glass walls. Griffin waved them in.

Stacks of file folders, reports, and photos covered the long conference table. Agents were hurriedly sorting through the material and pinning especially relevant items on bulletin boards.

Kendra went still when they spotted the hundreds of printed photos stacked in the center of the table.

Photos of *her*. The same photos she had seen papering ever square inch of Colby's cell that day she'd visited him in San Quentin.

They'd made her ill then, and they made her even more so now. Colby had let it be known that he wanted pictures of her, and his numerous correspondents had obliged by sending printed photos from the Web. He'd known that her trail would eventually lead to his cell, and he surmised quite correctly that the collage would creep the hell out of her.

"Sorry you had to see those again," Griffin said. "After Colby's execution, we—"

"You mean supposed execution," Kendra said.

"Yes. Supposed execution."

She wished she didn't take satisfaction from the barely contained anger and frustration that suddenly flashed across his face.

He continued. "We subpoenaed the contents of his prison cell, along with copies of all call and visitor logs. As you know, there was some thought that he might have been responsible for other victims not yet on our radar, and we wanted to have this stuff just in case we needed it down the road. We had it all brought up from our storage facility in National City."

Lynch looked at the stacks of opened mail on the table. "Popular guy for a mass murderer."

Griffin shrugged. "The culture of celebrity. He obviously had help with the computer stuff, so we're still trying to identify as many of his contacts as we can."

"Isn't most of this in the copies and scans you gave me?" Kendra asked.

"Most, but not all. There are notes scribbled on the backs of some of these photos, and we've tracked some more info from the cell phones he was using in prison. We want to make sure we haven't missed anything." Griffin picked up a sheaf of papers from the table. "Your friend, Beth Avery, e-mailed me this fairly detailed memo outlining several possibilities for who may be helping Colby in this area. She zeroed in on Joseph Northrup but indicated there were a few more experts who might be suspect. It's very impressive."

"*She's* very impressive," Kendra said.

"Well, Sims, our computer forensics specialist in Quantico certainly thinks so. I understand he and Zackoff have been in cahoots since I requested help after Stokes's death. But the director wants him to work more closely with Zackoff, so Sims is flying in this morning. He should be arriving around noon. Sims will drop in here first. He wants to see what both our local people and Beth Avery have come up with. Then he'll take a look at the documents and have her explain how she sourced them for her memo."

"It's based almost entirely on this material you've had in your possession for months," Kendra said.

"Okay, I can see you want to rub it in," Griffin said. "And it's your right. We're playing catch-up, I admit that. You've been looking for Colby for months, and we've only been on this for forty-eight hours." He gestured to the piled Colby info on the table. "But we're making progress. You can see we're trying like hell."

"Yes, I can see that." He wanted her to praise him, exonerate him. But there in the conference room, surrounded by Colby's mementos, Kendra felt the walls closing in on her. She tried desperately to push the sensation away from her. She'd had the same reaction when she last saw the man himself at San Quentin.

She drew a deep breath, trying to steady her racing heartbeat.

Power through it. If she let this rattle her, then the monster wins.

She couldn't let that happen.

Lynch did not glance at her, but he gave her arm an unobtrusive squeeze. She felt a rush of gratitude. He alone could see what she was going through, but he wasn't about to blow her lack of control in front of this roomful of agents.

"Fine," Kendra finally said. She pulled out her phone. "I'll text Beth and ask her to be here at noon for the meeting and bring her docs and source materials."

"Thank you."

Lynch quickly turned to Griffin and changed the subject. "Do you know for sure where Stokes was abducted?"

"We have a pretty good idea." Griffin jerked his head toward the doorway. "I'll show you."

They followed him to another conference room just a few yards away. It looked positively barren compared to the room they had just left, but the two bulletin boards were filled with photographs of a home and driveway.

"Stokes never showed up for work that morning, but he'd made a few calls from home between seven thirty and eight." Griffin pointed to a photo of a silver thermal travel mug lying on the driveway. "It looks like he was taken here as he was getting into his car. Autopsy results show that he had a fast-acting muscle relaxant in his system, so it's likely he was caught by surprise and injected with it."

"Was there anyone else at home?" Kendra asked.

"No, he lived alone. Divorced. His wife and three kids live with husband number two in La Jolla."

"None of the neighbors saw anything?" Kendra pointed to some of the other photographs. "These houses look pretty close together."

"Yes, but the driveway at that point has limited visibility. Colby chose his spot well."

"He always has."

Lynch was staring at a pair of blurry photos of a white van. "What's this?"

"Neighbors did report a white van on the street, and one of them even puts it in Stokes's driveway that morning. Traffic cams captured these between 8:15 and 8:25 that morning, with this van moving away from Stokes's neighborhood."

Lynch's eyes narrowed on the grainy photos. "Can't read the license plates, of course."

"Of course. I'll be the first to chip in whenever the hell this city decides to invest in some HD traffic cams. We're trying to round up some security-camera footage in the area to see if we can get a better look at it. It's a Ford Transit with fifty/fifty rear cargo doors and a 130-inch wheelbase. Naturally, there are about a million of those around. And Stokes's neighborhood was just as ordinary. We were lucky that anyone even noticed the van."

Kendra fought back a wave of sadness as she turned back to look at Stokes's modest home. She hadn't known about his failed marriage, and she realized that she actually knew very little about the man. They had only met a few days before, at the scene of that domestic homicide case. It seemed like so much longer ago that she and Stokes had made their introductions and discussed her work on the Van Buren investigation. She'd never imagined that just a few days later he would—

The Van Buren case.

She sharply turned away from the bulletin board.

He'd been so impressed that her lip-reading abilities had blown the case wide open. Is it possible that he—?

"I need to see the video of Stokes's death," she said abruptly. "Right now, Griffin."

Griffin wrinkled his brow. "Once wasn't enough for you?"

"Once is too much for anyone. But I need to look at it again in your A/V lab. It may need to be zoomed in and sharpened. Can you arrange that?"

Griffin still seemed mystified by her request, but he nodded. "Zoomed in, sharpened, forward, backward, or upside down. Any way you want to see it. Do you mind telling me why?"

"It may be nothing, but there's a chance Stokes might have been trying to tell me something. I can't be sure until I look."

"We can go downstairs and have one of the A/V techs pull it up on his console. It's the same guys who are combing security-camera footage for more views of that van. I can pull one of them off for a few minutes."

"Thanks, Griffin. It's worth a shot."

FIFTEEN MINUTES LATER, KENDRA, LYNCH, and Griffin stood in a small, windowless room looking over the shoulder of a chubby, young A/V tech named Nate Copley. Nate sat at his video console, looking up at a flat-panel monitor as he turned a shuttle-wheel control next to his keyboard.

Kendra felt a wrenching pang as Stokes's agonized face appeared on the screen. "It was around five minutes before the end. Please skip as much of this as you can."

"Gotcha," Nate said. "I logged this myself. I hoped I would never have to see it again."

Kendra turned around to avoid the Stokes video as it sped past. Behind them, a tech was at another console, scanning through parking-lot security-camera footage that also happened to capture a busy street. He slowed the footage whenever he saw anything that resembled the elusive white van, then resumed the high-speed scan each time it proved to be nothing.

Nate pointed to his monitor. "Around here?"

Kendra turned back to the monitor. "I think so . . . Go a little slower." She studied the image. "Stop when you see Stokes's head angle slightly to the right. It happens someplace around . . . There!" She touched Nate's shoulder. "Play it at regular speed."

She moved in for a closer view of Stokes's final moments. His face twisted in agony, and his lips moved as if muttering a curse. Yet no sound came out.

He did it again.

"See that?" Kendra said. "Still no sound, but I think his lip movements were identical."

Seconds later he did it once more, then settled back on the table in a state of collapse.

Kendra turned back toward Lynch and Griffin. "Stokes knew I broke the Van Buren case by reading the lips of the murderer on the phone at the crime scene. He might have been trying to tell me something."

She turned toward Nate. "Can you zoom in on his face and play it again?"

He turned back the shuttle dial. "Yes, but it's going to get blurrier. I'll enhance it as much as I can."

He scanned back and used his keyboard controls to zoom in on Stokes's face. He used another control to adjust the sharpness, finally finishing with a setting that was slightly more defined than where they started.

She leaned forward, tensely examining the shape and movement of the detective's mouth.

What are you saying to me, Stokes?

I'm here. I'm listening.

"Play it again, please."

Nate punched a key and leaned back in his chair. "It's now on a loop. It will keep repeating until you tell me to stop it."

Lynch leaned closer to the monitor. "Can you even get a read from this angle?"

"It's not the easiest, but I . . ." She was silent, her gaze on the ever-repeating video. Detach. Focus. Take the movements one at a time. Then bring them together. Her eyes narrowed. "Wingate!"

"What?" Griffin said.

"Hush." She stared at the screen for a moment longer. "That's it. I'm positive."

"Wingate?" Griffin repeated.

"Yes. The 'g' is hardest to pick up, but you can see it bouncing on his throat."

"*You* can see it," Lynch said. "I can only trust you. But what does it mean?"

"I hope it's someone's name," Kendra said. "How the hell do I know? But whatever it is, it was important enough to Stokes to get it out to me even though he was in agony."

"It might be a name," Griffin said. "Though it could be a street, a building, or a development of some kind. Or it could be the raving of a man out of his head with pain."

Lynch shook his head. "Kendra is right, Stokes tried to get it across three times while he was being slowly murdered. And did it in a way that he knew that Kendra could pick up on it yet Colby wouldn't."

Griffin shrugged. "I've learned my lesson. I'm not about to overrule Kendra on anything to do with this case." He picked the phone on the desk next to Nate's workstation. "I'll have my team start a search for it."

"I want to help," Kendra said. "Get me a desk and a computer."

"Right away."

Kendra couldn't take her eyes off Stokes on the monitor screen, still locked in that loop. He was sweating and bleeding, mere minutes away from death. But there he was, still heroically giving his all.

Wingate.

Lynch House
10:25 A.M.

"OKAY, LET INTO that inner sanctum, Sam," Beth called through the door. "I've got a tray, and I'm not going away."

"I'm busy."

"I'm not going away," she repeated. "You very rudely refused to come to breakfast with Lynch and Kendra. Even though I took the trouble to cook. So now you have to eat alone. But you *will* eat, Sam."

"It's not rude to sacrifice myself to finding that son of a bitch. You have a wrong set of values."

"Open the door."

She heard him mumbling, but he was coming toward the door. The next moment, he'd thrown it open and stood scowling at her. "I'm not hungry."

"Your stomach has probably shrunk in the last few days." She sailed into the office, deposited the tray on the coffee table and settled in a corner of the couch. "I haven't been able to get you to eat. Stupid, Sam. Very stupid. I let you get away with it because the pressure was over the top, but now you're back to a steady pace." She poured herself a cup of coffee. "Omelet, bacon, and toast. Eat."

"Why don't you go bother Kendra and Lynch?"

"They went to the FBI office. I just got a text from Kendra. They want me to come in for some kind of forensic computer meeting and bring the research and sources I've pulled together on Colby's possible computer consultants." She grinned mischievously. "Think maybe Griffin wants me to teach his people a thing or two?" She changed the subject. "But before I go anywhere, I want to see you eat."

"So you're going to stay and watch me?"

"Yes, because you'll forget it's there. Then it will get cold and unappetizing, and you won't eat it even when you do remember."

Sam sat down on the couch. "Nag."

"Just doing my job." She smiled. "I told Kendra that it was a competition thing between you and Griffin's fair-haired computer guy."

"Not true. I'm better than he is."

"Without doubt."

He nibbled at his bacon. "But Sims is smart, and I wouldn't want him to think that he can get ahead of me. Just because he's been up there in Quantico with those FBI directors kowtowing to him all those years is no sign that his thinking is any more innovative than mine. That would be embarrassing."

"You'd live through it." She tilted her head. "And you

can't tell me that you couldn't get a job there with all that kowtowing if you wanted it."

"Yeah, Sims has already mentioned it. I told him when I got as old as him, I'd think about it."

"Ouch. How old is he?"

"Oh, fifty or so." His smile was brimming with malicious mischief. "I couldn't resist. He was being patronizing. Can you believe it? Patronizing to *me*."

"Criminal. All I can say is that you'd better come out on top of this horse race."

"I will. In the meantime, Sims is being helpful. We're going at it from two different directions. He's able to request logs from the Internet service providers for Kendra's place, my house, and here, and he has a lot of resources at his disposal to analyze the data and try to figure out where Colby's streams are coming from. I'm actually hacking a lot of those ISPs to find out the same thing. There's some duplication of effort, but we each come up with stuff that the other can't easily find."

"I can see that. He has the full weight of the FBI behind him, and you have the freedom to skirt the law. That makes you a good team."

He scowled at her. "But it's not as if I'm with him night and day. For your information, we haven't been online since yesterday afternoon. We just check in when one of us has had a breakthrough. Then it's natural that we have to work together."

"Perfectly natural," she said solemnly.

"Do I detect sarcasm?" He glanced at his watch. "I don't have time for this."

"You do if I say you do. Eat. It's the quickest way to get rid of me."

He took his fork and began cutting his omelet. "I didn't

really say I wanted to get rid of you. I just don't want you to interfere. I kind of like having you around."

"Sam."

"Okay, I told you that I have privacy issues when I'm working. It's true. But lately, you've been like Old Dog Tray."

"I beg your pardon."

He chuckled. "You know, the dog that lies in front of the fireplace, and you don't notice he's there. But the song says he's the best friend around."

"How flattering . . . I think."

"Look, you're gorgeous and smart, but you don't want me to flatter you. I save that for other women. You want the real thing."

"Old Dog Tray."

"Yeah, because it means something, like the way I feel about Kendra."

"Are you saying that she's Old Dog Tray, too?"

"In a way. We've been together for years, and we know we can count on each other." He looked at her. "We're like that now, aren't we?"

She nodded, smiling faintly. "I believe we've fought our way through to that status."

"Except I don't know how you think sometimes. You know pretty much everything about me, but I don't know—" He grimaced. "I didn't ask Kendra much about how you got into that mental hospital. All I know is that you were imprisoned without cause."

"But you're asking now." She was silent for a moment. "I saw something I shouldn't have seen, and my grandmother wanted to get rid of me."

"Something you shouldn't have seen?"

"Murder," she said baldly. "I was only a teenager, and

I was easy to get rid of. I had a supposed skiing accident, a blow to the head, and she shipped me off to Seahaven, the posh mental hospital that she funded, to be 'cared for' by her tame crew of doctors." She took a sip of her coffee. "And I stayed there for years and years. Until Eve and Kendra came to find me."

"My God." He shook his head. "Your grandmother?"

"She wasn't your usual grandmother. She was beautiful, clever, and ambitious. And our relationship was . . . not warm and fuzzy."

"I'd say that must be an understatement. What a nightmare."

She nodded. "But it's a nightmare I don't allow myself to dwell on. It's over, and I won't let one moment of my present or future be held hostage by it." She said fiercely, "I was a zombie in that place. They were planning on finally killing me when Eve found out she had a sister in that hospital. You can see why I'm grateful to you for helping to spring me." She held up her hand. "So don't you dare downplay what you did for any reason. I'm free, I live my life to the hilt, I learn something new every day." She smiled. "Including bits and pieces of some of that computer know-how you dazzle everyone with. If I stay around long enough, I may even give you a run for your money."

He nodded. "You might at that." He cleared his throat. "And I'd like to be around to see it. You're an extraordinary woman, Beth."

"I'm getting there." She finished her coffee. "Every day, every way, every person I meet." She got to her feet. "You've finished everything but your coffee. I'll let you work on that while you go back to your computers."

"You could stick around."

She threw back her head and laughed. "What a sacrifice. My sad story must have really impressed you. Don't worry, I won't take you up on it. That wouldn't suit either one of us. I don't have time to hold your hand even if you could stand me in here."

"It wouldn't be that bad."

"No, because I wouldn't do it." She picked up the tray and headed for the door. "I'll bring you a pot of coffee before I leave to go to the FBI field office. If you need anything else, let me know." She slanted him a look over her shoulder. "You're a good guy, Sam. And I suppose I have to forgive you for being so rude to me the first time we met."

"It took you long enough."

"I don't forgive easily. Ask my grandmother."

"What do you mean?"

Her smile was both enigmatic and teasing. "As Scheherazade said, that's another tale."

She closed the door behind her.

San Diego FBI Field Office
12:05 P.M.

"BETH AVERY, TOM SIMS." Griffin smiled. "It should be the start of a beautiful friendship. You definitely have something in common."

"You mean someone," Beth said as she shook Sims hand. She had watched him speaking to Griffin's other three local computer experts before Griffin had brought her forward to introduce her. She had been impressed. Confident but not lacking in respect for them or their work. He might be in his fifties as Sam had told her, but he was a young fifty. A lean, fit body, gray-streaked hair, tan skin with just a few wrinkles around his dark eyes, a great smile. "I didn't realize you were going to be at this meeting. But it's obvious now you *are* the meeting. Sam has been talking about you ever since you started working together. I'm very happy to meet you." She grimaced. "But I'll be more happy when you two finally manage to track Colby and aren't working until the wee hours."

"So will my wife. She's becoming very impatient with me," Sims said. "And I'll be happy, too. I'd never admit it to Sam, but I'm not quite as spry as I once was. The tennis helps, but lack of sleep can be hell. If this case weren't so important, I might have delegated it to someone else." He ruefully shook his head. "But I couldn't do it. Sam would have been scornful. And I would have been humiliated."

"I don't know how the two of you managed to get caught up in this rivalry."

"Vanity," Sims said. "I know it's immature. But it's getting the job done. We're making amazing progress."

"I know. Sam told me."

"Sam tells you a lot, doesn't he?" He gazed curiously at her. "He talks about you to me. Did you know that?"

"No, I'm sure it isn't in-depth conversation. I'm just on the peripheral of Sam's life."

"No, the mention is always just in passing. But I could tell that there was a comfortable affection there."

"Like Old Dog Tray?"

"I beg your pardon?"

"Never mind. You would have had to have been there." She grinned. "It was a conversation that Sam obviously kept from you."

His brows rose. "Now that wasn't kind."

"Kind to Sam. Kind to you, too, really." She chuckled.

"And it might be the last break for a while since your director decided the two of you should work side by side. You'll spur each other. Good for finding Colby, not so good for maintaining health and sanity."

"You'll keep us both in line." Sims turned to her and smiled. "And, when all's said and done, it's finding Colby that matters, isn't it?"

She patted the packet of resource materials she'd brought with her. "That's what this is about. Do you want me to go through it with you?"

"How about we do it over lunch? I came right from the airport, and I'm starving."

"Sure." She grinned. "Though we should probably call Sam and invite him. After all, he seems to be your alter ego. Or maybe not, after the way he tried to kick me out of his office today."

"He kicked you out? How rude. Then we definitely won't invite him for lunch." He motioned toward the elevator. "I've always wanted to try Kansas City Barbecue. I'm a *Top Gun* fan, and that's the joint where Maverick and Goose hung out in the film. Before I discovered computers, I wanted nothing more in the world than to be a fighter pilot."

Beth ruefully shook her head. "Boys and their toys."

CHAPTER
15

KENDRA'S PHONE RANG AT 3:32 P.M.

She was still in a conference room at FBI headquarters searching databases that made sense for Wingate. When she saw Griffin's name on the caller ID screen, she immediately punched the talk switch. "Hello, Griffin. Anything on Wingate yet? I've been striking out all day."

He ignored her question. "Is Beth Avery with you?"

"No, not yet. I thought she was still up there in your office with your computer guy. She didn't contact me to tell me anything different."

"Shit," Griffin whispered.

Kendra tensed. "What is it?"

"Beth left with him shortly after noon . . . something about lunch."

"Then it's okay. You scared me, dammit."

"You're not the only one. Look, I just got some disturbing news. Tom Sims isn't supposed to be down here in San Diego at all."

"What?"

"You heard me. There's an uproar in Sims's office. I just had a photo of Tom Sims e-mailed to me. The resemblance of the man who showed up here was close to his description but not close enough. He was an imposter."

"Wait a minute. I'm confused. This Sims doesn't exist?"

"Oh, he exists. But he was still in Washington as of last night. The communication I got late yesterday afternoon telling me that he was being sent down to work more closely with Zackoff was bogus. That message about wanting to meet with Beth Avery and discuss her memo was total bullshit."

"Whoever it was, how could they have known about her memo?"

"That's what I'm trying to tell you. Our system here at the branch office was hacked. I'd bet Sims's and Zackoff's work and communication were also hacked." He paused. "And the real Tom Sims didn't show up at his office in Quantico this morning. That's why his security people went into his computer to see if there might have been foul play. Since he was working on this case, we were number one on their list."

Kendra's mind raced, and the direction was terrifying. Her heart was pounding frantically.

She was seeing the twisted, bloody body of Stokes on that rooftop posed with his warning message.

Prepare for another strike.

Beth!

KENDRA'S PHONE RANG AS SHE DROVE down the 1-8 freeway. She checked the caller ID screen. Sam.

Shit. Sam hadn't been told yet, and she'd been hoping

to speak to him in person. Evidently, she wasn't going to be allowed to do that.

She pressed a button on her steering wheel to answer. "Hi, Sam. I'm on my way back to Lynch's. We need to talk."

"It's about time. I've been trying to get in touch with you guys all day. I'm getting the distinct feeling I'm being frozen out."

"That couldn't be further from the truth. I need you more than ever." She paused. "Beth needs you."

Sam was silent. He knew her well enough to grasp the significance of that sentence and that something was seriously, terribly, wrong. "Kendra, what's going on?"

Kendra hesitated. There was only one way to tell him. "We think Beth has been taken. We think Colby has her."

"Oh, God."

"Yeah."

Sam's voice was suddenly throbbing with anger. "How in the hell could this happen?"

"Beth was supposed to meet Sims and go over the work she's done on Colby's computer contacts. Afterward, she was supposed to bring him to meet you."

"She didn't call me. I've been trying to get hold of her, too."

She drew a deep breath. "It appears it wasn't the real Sims who came here to San Diego. It was someone posing as him. Probably Colby's computer guy. He's taken Beth, and soon, Colby will have her if he doesn't already."

"Shit!" Kendra heard Sam's fist pounding on the desk on his end. "Shit. Shit. Shit."

"Sam, calm down. I'm on my way. Lynch is still with Griffin right now. But we're meeting at Lynch's to figure out our next move."

"We're going to sit around here and talk? We've done enough talking. We need to kill that son of a bitch."

"We need to find him first."

Sam's voice was ragged, but quieter, more determined. "We will. We've got to, Kendra."

"I'll see you in a few minutes."

LYNCH ARRIVED AT THE HOUSE ten minutes after Kendra. "You told Sam? Where is he?"

She nodded at the office. "He objected to talking when he could be working. He said to tell him when he could do anything else. I guess he's right. He's pretty upset."

"Aren't we all? Okay, Sam is working at full steam," Lynch said. "What else can I do?"

"Find that damn imposter," she said. "This computer expert is a tech, not a killer for hire. If he took Beth, we still have a chance of getting her back before he turns her over to Colby." A slim chance, she thought frantically, but still a chance. "Find him or get me a phone number and let me talk to him. Beth is rich as Midas. I can find a way to get him money for ransom. We just have to keep her away from Colby."

"It may be too late." He was heading for the door. "But I'll get with Griffin, and we'll track him down. I'll call you as soon as I hear anything." He looked back at her over his shoulder. "And you let me know if you're contacted."

She watched the door shut behind him. He was expecting her to hear from Colby to tell her he had Beth. He knew as well as she did that it was not likely they'd find Beth before she was handed over to Colby. It was only a desperate move that had made her ask him to go on such a wild-goose chase.

Desperation and a wild hope that something could go right in this nightmare.

Her phone rang.

It could be Griffin.

Or Sam.

No ID.

She slowly answered the phone.

"Hello, Kendra. Are you scrambling wildly to find your pretty little friend?" Colby asked. "I wish I could see you. It would be very satisfying. But I don't expect to be lacking in satisfaction in the near future, so I can accept it."

"Is she *alive*?"

"Oh, yes."

"I want to talk to her."

"Later. Unfortunately, she's not available at present. I'm having her brought to me. You can understand I'm being very cautious with the transfer. I have great respect for you, Kendra."

"Look, Beth is very rich. Even you have to like the idea of that kind of payoff. Don't hurt her, and we can deal."

"I know she's very well off. It was one of the lures I used to bring Northrup into the fold. He's very fond of money."

"Northrup is your computer tech?"

"You guessed it, didn't you? I thought you would. But he was just too clever not to be used. Sadly, he was extremely shy about taking certain important steps." He chuckled. "But Beth Avery's magnificent prospects tipped the scales. He decided that ridding me of Sims would be a small price to pay."

"He killed Tom Sims?"

"Probably not with any great imagination. He mentioned a gun with a silencer and an alley in D.C. I would have been much more inventive, but I was busy with preparations here."

"But he did what you wished and deserves to be rewarded. Let her go, Colby. We'll get the money to you."

"But money isn't what this is all about, Kendra. It's about that wonderfully painful note in your voice. It's about the lamb leading the tiger to slaughter."

"Beth's no lamb. She's a woman you can use to line your pockets. Let her go."

"But you're not denying that you're a tiger, Kendra. I'm preparing a circus where you can perform for me. I'm going to leave you now. I'll be back in touch when I'm ready to turn loose the clowns and have your Beth do a little high-wire acrobatics." He hung up.

And Kendra immediately bent forward, struggling against being sick. She took a deep breath, then sat up straight. Stop being weak. The worst was happening, and she had to cope with it.

Her hand was shaking as she called Lynch. "Colby doesn't have Beth yet. It's Northrup who did the switch with Sims and there's a possibility he might deal if you can get to him in time. But he killed Sims, and there's no way he'd make a deal if the police are involved."

"I take it that Colby called you?"

"Yes. Our only chance is Northrup. Colby wants blood."

"Nothing different there."

It was different because it was Beth's blood he wanted. "Find a way to get to Northrup," she said. "Do anything you need to do."

Lynch was silent a moment. "I'll do what you want. But no time for any manipulation this time, Kendra."

She knew what he was warning her about. Violence and deadliness instead of diplomacy. Skills in which Lynch was equally expert. "Do what you have to do," she repeated.

"I'll get back to you later." He hung up.

She sat there, trying to get her wits together. She should probably call Griffin and tell him about what Colby had told her about the missing Tom Sims.

But there was something else she had to do first. She closed her eyes and braced herself. Dear God, she hated this. Her eyes flicked open, and she reached for her phone. She dialed quickly and listened to it ring. What could she say? How could she explain the unexplainable?

The phone was picked up, and she spoke quickly, "Eve, something terrible has happened." She tried to steady her voice. "And I think you're going to have to drop everything and come out here . . ."

EVE DUNCAN'S EXPRESSION WAS JUST as grim and haggard as Kendra had expected it to be as she exited airport security and moved toward her. Kendra could see the strength and the determination that had made Eve one of the foremost forensic sculptors in the world, but she was also aware of the vulnerability and passion that made her friend intensely human. She had lost her little girl, Bonnie, years ago, and Kendra *hated* the thought that she now had to face the thought of losing a sister she had only just found. Eve gave her a quick hug. "Any news?"

Kendra shook her head. "Nothing." She looked beyond her. "Joe didn't come?"

"I haven't contacted him yet. He's in Mexico City at some police drug-cartel seminar. The cartels are starting to use Atlanta as their home away from home." She strode toward the door. "I have to get my head on straight before

I talk to him. If he sees I'm upset, he'll drop everything and come here."

Kendra knew that was true. Joe Quinn, a police detective with Atlanta PD, had been Eve's lover for many years, and there was nothing he wouldn't do for her. "I can see why he wouldn't want you to be without him during this time."

Eve's lips twisted. "He has a life. I can't lean on him for everything. And from what you say, everything may be over before he gets off the plane."

"I didn't say that." But she'd tried to be as honest as she could with Eve. Her friend would not appreciate sugarcoating. "We're going to get her back, Eve. We're working so hard on several fronts. We have the best police and FBI personnel. Lynch is here and exploring every possibility."

"You'll get her back." Eve's voice was trembling. "But I've been wondering if it will be too late."

"No." She stopped and turned to face her. "I'll do anything to get her back alive, money, a trade, anything."

"Stop that." Eve's eyes were glittering with moisture. "Do you think Beth would tolerate that? Do you think I would?" She took Kendra in her arms and held her close. "No sacrificial lambs. We just have to find a way to get that son of a bitch."

Kendra's voice was muffled against her. "It's my fault, Eve. I should never have let Beth get within a mile of me. I thought I could keep her safe."

"Beth is smart, and I'm sure she knew the risks. She's also stubborn as hell, and she does what she wants." Her voice was uneven. "And why shouldn't she? For years, she was a prisoner in that hellhole of a hospital. It's only for the past months she's been able to reach out and taste everything that life has to offer. Do you know how angry it makes me feel to know that Colby is trying to take that away from her?" She held Kendra at arm's length and looked into her eyes. "It's not your fault. The fault lies with that monster who took her. Now we've got to stop weeping and wailing and get her back."

Kendra nodded. "Maybe a little weeping and wailing. But it won't interfere. I promise." She turned and headed for the door. "Come on and meet Lynch. He's waiting in the car to drive us back to his house. He wouldn't let me come to meet you by myself."

"And I approve," Eve said quietly. "Not only for your protection. You're definitely not going to be a trade, but you're the center, and everything is spinning around you."

And that center was dark and frightening, like a whirlpool that was ready to pull Beth down into its depths.

And in spite of Eve's words, Kendra knew that no matter what the circumstance she could never allow that to happen.

"I WANT TO SEE SAM," EVE said as soon as she stepped into the foyer of Lynch's house. "Where is he, Kendra?"

"Where he always is"—she nodded down the hall—"the office. It's where he set up shop when I brought him here, and since I told him about Beth, he's been working frantically. I haven't been able to get him out of the room to even eat." She smiled faintly. "That's not new, but Beth usually managed to get something down him. Force, persuasion, and persistence, she used them all. She considered Sam her charge." She bit down on her lower lip. "Past tense. I'm using past tense. I won't do that, dammit. She *does* consider Sam her charge."

"From what you told me, they've became very close."

Kendra nodded. "In their very individual ways." She turned and started toward the kitchen. "Go in and see him. I'll go make coffee and sandwiches."

Eve watched her disappear down the hall, then turned and moved toward the office. She knocked, and when she received no answer, she opened the door. "It's Eve, Sam. May I come in?"

"Go away, Eve." He didn't look up from his computer. "Can't you see I'm busy?"

"I'll only be a minute." She came forward. He looked just the same as the night she'd first met him at the mental hospital, when they'd asked him to help free Beth. No, not quite. No breeziness now. His eyes were red and his entire demeanor tense. "Any luck?"

"This isn't about luck. It's about tracing that bastard." He stopped typing but stayed hunched over the computer. "And I *can't* do it. Not in time. It's not like tracing a phone call. There are thousands, maybe millions of computers out there that have been hijacked without the owners even knowing it. They're called zombies. Hacking networks sell access to them to businesses to generate spam, or anybody who will pay them. Colby's messages are going through lots of zombies, different ones each time. That means I have to hack dozens of systems in order to try to track him. It's like trying to untie a big, gnarly, knotted piece of string. There's no *way* that I can do that in time."

Eve stopped before the desk. "Don't *tell* me that. I remember what you did when Kendra asked you to do your magic and save Beth before, when she was at that mental hospital. We were in despair about how to do it. But you were so confident, so sure of yourself. You're going to do the same thing now."

"Am I?" He looked up at her. "It's different now. It was easier. She was only a problem to me then. Now she's . . . Beth."

"And she's my sister." Eve leaned her hands on the desk. "So stop all this nonsense. We're both going to do what has to be done." She stared him in the eye, and said fiercely, "Because I've just found Beth. I never even knew I had a sister. I'm not going to lose her again. Do you understand?"

Sam's eyes widened. "Yeah, I think I do." He made a face. "I was just having a bad moment. I'm okay now."

"Kendra said you've been working your ass off since you came here. I appreciate it. But I'm going to ask you to work even harder." Her voice was firm. "And you'll know I'll work just as hard. I'll match you all the way, Sam. You tell me what to do, and it will be done. I'm no novice. I don't do magic on computers, but I know the Web sites and how to dig for information because of my work as a forensic sculptor. Some people say I have wonderful instincts. I'll use them."

"I don't know what good—"

"Don't analyze, accept," she said. "Kendra's going through the same hell we are. We're all in this together. But I'm not sure how I can help Kendra. So I'm zeroing in on you."

"I don't need—" He stopped as he met her eyes. He smiled. "I can tell Beth is your sister."

"We're nothing alike. For instance, I'm not going to insist you eat. That's up to you. I miss meals myself when it's important to work." She added, "And it's very important to work. So do it, Sam." She turned back toward the door. "I'm going to bring in that pot of coffee Kendra is making. We're going to need it."

* * *

BUZZZZ.

Buzzzz.

Beth tried to open her eyes, but she couldn't summon the strength

Buzzzz.

A giant, buzzing bee was circling her head. At least that's how it sounded.

Time to take a look. If only she could find the energy to open her damned eyes.

Buzzzz.

Through sheer force of will, she raised her eyelids. First the right, then the left. There was just white, blinding light. Nothing else but pain. Her head throbbed, and her mouth stung.

Buzzzz.

It wasn't a bee, she realized. It was the light. Her eyes focused, and she saw there were two bare, fluorescent tubes glowing and buzzing on the ceiling above her.

Buzzzz.

She moved to bring her hands toward her head, but she realized she couldn't. Her hands were pinned by her side, bound by heavy, nylon straps.

She tried to move her legs, but she realized that they, too, were tied.

Tied to what?

She looked down. She was fastened to a cream-colored embalming table. There was an elevated lip and rusty drain between her ankles.

She'd seen this table before, she realized in panic. This was where Detective Stokes had been stabbed over and over by that maniac.

And this was where he had died.

"Hello, Beth." She knew that voice. That low, terrifying voice. "Welcome."

The rest of the room finally slid into focus. What the hell kind of place was this? It was a windowless room, perhaps twelve feet by twelve feet. The walls and floor were covered by a thick, tarlike substance.

Colby stepped closer, smiling at her with those creepy, little, rodentlike teeth. "Your wooziness will pass. You'll want to be awake for this."

"I doubt that," a voice said from behind her. "Full consciousness is rarely desirable when in your presence, Colby." The other man stepped into view.

"Sims," Beth whispered.

The man smiled.

Now she remembered. Sims was in her car looking through her files with her, when he'd suddenly jabbed her with the syringe. They'd been laughing together, then . . . darkness.

"But you're not Sims, are you?" she asked uncertainly.

He now appeared much younger, with no trace of gray in his hair. His face was less full, and his body even appeared thinner.

"Sorry to disappoint you." He carefully peeled off his fake moustache, leaving behind a faint rash above his upper lip. "You seemed to enjoy him so much."

"My young protégé, Joseph Northrup," Colby said. "It took a great deal of coaching, but I so wish I could have seen him proudly stride into the FBI regional office this morning."

Beth was silent a moment, trying to overcome the shock and confusion that was bombarding her.

Colby. Death. She might be going to die. Panic soared through her.

And she might not.

Either way, face it and get through it.

"You hacked Sims's badge?" she asked Northrup.

Northrup shook his head. "Why would I do that when I knew I'd have the genuine article."

"But how would you—" She stopped as the sick realization hit home to her. "You killed him."

Colby smiled. "We couldn't have two Tom Simses walking around, one on each coast, could we? It would have been much too bewildering."

"But why kill—"

"This has all been in the works for a long time," Colby said. "Like pieces of a puzzle falling into place. Only one major difference, though. It was supposed to be Kendra's friend Olivia Moore on that table, but she had the bad manners to leave town just when I needed her."

"Good."

"Ah, so noble. Yet I've discovered nobility fades remarkably fast under the knife. But who knows, you might prove the exception. No matter, you'll still make a suitable replacement." He tilted his head. "Do you know, throughout history, most great works of art are the products of some measure of compromise and improvisation. Depending on the season, Rembrandt substituted burnt umber for burnt sienna pigments for his hand-mixed paints. Mozart would reorchestrate his pieces as he was composing them, based on the availability of talented soloists. Art isn't created in a vacuum."

Beth shook her head in disbelief. "Is that what you think this is. Art?"

"Of course."

"No. That's just what you say to yourself to try and dress up your sick, pathetic compulsion. What you're doing has nothing to do with art."

Colby smiled. "Most people in your position would be doing and saying everything in their power to keep from angering me."

"You don't kill out of anger," Beth said. "I've been studying you, and I know you better than that."

"You know nothing about us," Northrup said.

"You're half-right," Beth said. "I know nothing about you. And no one will ever know anything about you. The history books will have no place for some suck-up toadying pen pal who offered up his computer skills to this homicidal sack of shit. You're even more pathetic."

Northrup's face flushed, and he leaned over her and whispered, "Do you really want to see what I'm capable of?"

Without warning Beth arched her back and snapped her head forward, smashing into Northrup's face.

"Aughh." He howled and stumbled backward away from her. Blood spurted from his broken nose. "You bitch!"

"Interesting. From her background report about being in a mental hospital, I thought she might be much more docile," Colby said, with perhaps a trace of amusement. "It appears that Kendra has chosen someone of her own ilk as a friend. Consequently, you might want to keep your distance from the prisoner, Northrup. Just a suggestion."

Northrup cradled his face. "Is this a joke to you?"

Colby shook his head. "You've made it a joke, Northrup."

"Did you hear that?" Beth said softly to Northrup, "You're the joke."

"I'll kill you!" Northrup staggered back toward her.

Colby blocked his path.

"Stop it," Colby said. "I won't have your lack of control spoiling everything. We have a plan, and we'll keep to it." He turned back to Beth. "And, again, I'm fascinated by your willingness to spit in the face of those who hold your fate in their hands."

"I don't spit. But I might have taken off his nose, an ear, or even a finger or two if you hadn't stopped him." She clicked her teeth.

He chuckled. "Incredible. You're not even trying to bargain."

"Sorry if that deprives you of an erection, but I know that didn't work for the twenty-some-odd people you've already killed. Am I afraid? Of course, I am. Self-preservation doesn't dictate anything else. But I fear death, not you. So why would I want to spend the last minutes of my life groveling to you?"

"I can make those last minutes extremely unpleasant for you."

"You will anyway. You'll want to hurt Kendra, and you believe hurting people close to her will do that. Nothing I can do will change that."

"Quite true." He gave her an admiring nod. "Ironically, my associate here has been lobbying to save your life, at least momentarily. He's been swayed by reports of your extreme wealth. He thinks we can take advantage of this situation to get some of it for ourselves."

"So you want me to write you a check?"

"Oh no. He has some complicated business in mind involving wire transfers and offshore accounts."

"Then he doesn't know you as well as the rest of the world does."

Northrup turned toward Colby, still dabbing at his bloody nose. "You said you'd consider it."

"Sorry, my friend. She's right. There's a certain purity in what I do, and that would only sully it."

"I tell you, it can work," Northrup said.

"That's beside the point."

"Look, I did everything you asked me to do. We've been partners. I told you in the beginning that we'd need money to go somewhere safe and start again."

"Yes, you did. But I've always had funds when I needed them. I'm sorry that you're not similarly blessed." He tilted his head. "But it would probably take even many more fortunes than this woman possesses to satisfy you."

"What the hell? You never said that you wouldn't do it."

"Because you seemed so happy when you talked about it." He smiled. "I like to see you happy, Northrup. You were so talented and being so cooperative."

"You were deceiving me."

"A necessary evil."

Northrup's face was contorted. "I *need* that money. This conversation isn't over."

Colby smiled. "I'm afraid it is."

He whirled around with his hunting knife and cut a clean vertical line down the front of Northrup's torso. As blood and intestines poured from the wound, Northrup staggered back and dropped to the floor. His eyes bulged, and blood trickled from his nose and mouth.

"I'm so very sorry," Colby said. "You've been very helpful, but your usefulness has passed. This isn't a team sport, my friend."

Beth could only watch in horror as Northrup twitched violently as he bled out. In under a minute, he was dead.

Still holding the bloody knife, Colby stepped toward her.

He stopped and stood there silently gazing at her. "You see, it *is* an art," he finally said. "Northrup didn't respect that."

Colby turned and left the room.

"ANY WORD FROM COLBY?" LYNCH asked the minute he walked into the house after leaving Griffin at the FBI field office.

"Not yet," Kendra said. "And I don't know why he's taking so long. It's been ten or twelve hours since he called me." She moistened her lips. "Unless Northrup didn't turn Beth over to him. Dear God, I hope that's it. Anyone would be easier to deal with than Colby."

Lynch shook his head. "I wish I could believe that was true. But Colby has a reputation of maintaining control of every situation. Northrup is an amateur compared to him."

Kendra knew that he was right. "I can still hope. It's better than sitting here thinking about all the sick things he might be doing to her." She rubbed her temple. "I need to do something. Eve is in the office, working with Sam. You're trying to find that van. All I'm doing is tracking every Wingate on the planet and waiting for that damn call." She tried to focus. "What did you find out?"

"Not as much as I'd like. But there's a possibility that might come through." He added quietly, "But I wanted to come back and be with you before you got that call from Colby."

"Because you think I might need a shoulder to cry on?"

"Something like that." He smiled faintly. "Or more likely that he'll try to manipulate you to do what he wants, and I'll need to try to rein you in before you get yourself killed."

"Much more likely." She swallowed to ease the tightness of her throat. "But I keep thinking of Stokes and all the horrible things he did to him. Beth has had such a rough life, she shouldn't have to go through this along—"

"Shh." He was suddenly beside her and pulling her up into his arms. "I didn't say that both options weren't available." His hand stroked her hair as he pushed her head into his shoulder. "This one is far more pleasurable for me. I don't know what the hell Colby has planned for Beth, but I doubt if he'll duplicate Stokes. He probably has something else planned. He may give us a chance to work our way to gutting him."

Lynch wasn't giving her false promises, but he was offering the reality of which they were both aware. Along with the violence and intelligent incisiveness that was his trademark. Strange that explosive combination could offer such comfort . . .

"Okay?" His breath was soft on her ear. "Can I get you something? Glass of wine?"

She didn't want to move away from him. It was good to take this moment to just be—

Her phone rang.

She tensed, then stepped back and away from Lynch.

She quickly reached for her phone.

"Have you missed me?" Colby asked. "I've missed you, Kendra. But I've had a few things to wrap up before I brought us together again." He chuckled. "Besides, I wanted you to have time to wrap a few things up yourself. I wanted the stage set just right. I assume you sent for Eve Duncan to be present at her sister's demise?"

"Eve is here," she said. "If you have Beth, I want to speak to her." She paused. "Northrup delivered her to you?"

"Yes, of course."

Kendra felt her spirits plummet.

"Disappointed? I imagine you had certain hopes in that direction."

"I want to speak to Beth," she repeated.

"Oh, I'll do better than that. I assume you have a computer nearby. Call Zackoff and tell him to tune into your computer I adjusted and send you the video."

Lynch raised his finger, then ran from the living room toward the office.

"You want to show me another hideous display?" she asked. "You're becoming predictable, Colby."

"Perish the thought. I'm always new and fresh. Turn on your computer."

"It's on."

"Then sit back and enjoy the show. Or not really a show yet. More a cozy get-together."

"I don't see anything. What are you—" Then the picture zoomed onto her monitor. Beth lying tied to the embalming table. Memories of Stokes immediately flew back to Kendra. She inhaled sharply and couldn't speak for an instant.

"I thought that might take your breath away," Colby said as he came on camera. "I did quite a good job of making Stokes's death memorable. I'll try to do the same with your friend Beth. But it might be difficult for you to appreciate since you could be dead by the time that she's no longer with us." He smiled down at Beth. "She wants you to talk to her. I know you'll oblige."

"Sure." Beth looked into the camera. "He's a little over-the-top, isn't he, Kendra? This whole scenario is like an old silent movie with little Beth tied on the railroad tracks."

"He hasn't hurt you?" Kendra asked shakily.

"Not yet. But we both know that might come." She

swallowed. "Don't let him play you. Don't look. Don't let him use me to hurt you, okay?"

"I think that's enough," Colby said as he stepped in front of Beth. "I would have stopped her sooner, but she's very eloquent, and that probably served me better."

"What do you want? Is there any way that I can stop you from hurting her?"

"You know what I want. As for that other question, I doubt it. But there may be a way if you're even more clever than I think you are." He smiled. "You're hurting. I can hear it in your voice. That's part of what I want. But the agony has to be excruciating. And pain is always heightened by the anticipation of more pain to come. That's why I allowed you to go so long without showing you your friend."

"I thought you and your computer stooge were just arguing about what to do with her."

"Oh, no, it was all about anticipation. I do admit there was a bone of contention, but I took care of it." He mournfully shook his head. "Unfortunately, Northrup is no longer with us. But he was able to finish up the last of my requests before he departed this plane." He smiled. "But back to anticipation. Even when I was disposing of Stokes, I was thinking that it was too short. That no one had the full experience of my kill. I decided to correct that error with our beautiful Beth. I know if you enjoyed the last twelve hours that you'll be eager to know that I'm going to give you another twenty-four."

"Why?" She stiffened. "What are you going to do to her?"

"How suspicious you are. I'm merely giving you the time you need to be in the frantic state that will make your death totally satisfying to me. I may play with our Beth a bit, but I won't start the final phase of her death until you've gone through sufficient agony. I can see you running around, trying to find her, trying to find me. But, of course, that's not going to happen. I've made sure that I'm very safe. You couldn't find me when Stokes was being butchered, could you? No, you'll try and try, and in the end, when we come together, you'll be broken."

"What do you mean 'play' with her?"

"You'll have to wonder about that, won't you? But it won't be anything compared to the grand finale I'm planning for her and . . . you. Twenty-four hours, Kendra."

The monitor screen went blank.

She stared unseeingly at the screen. Twenty-four hours. Grand Finale.

"Well, that answers the question." Lynch was back in the room. "Colby has her, and Northrup is no longer a player."

"You saw it in the office?"

He nodded. "With Eve and Sam."

"Twenty-four hours. She only has twenty-four hours . . ."

"You're looking at the glass half-empty. *We* have twenty-four hours." His eyes were glittering with fierce vitality. "You've always said Colby was an egomaniac. He doesn't believe that we can upset his foul little apple-cart. He thinks he's safe." His hands fell on her shoulders, and he gave her a slight shake. "But we already have a head start. Hell, twenty-four hours can be a lifetime."

Beth's lifetime.

Kendra shook her head to clear it. She'd been caught up in Colby's malice, Colby's world. She felt a sudden surge of energy and hope as she was drawn back into the world she shared with Lynch.

"You're damn right," she said brusquely. "Twenty-four hours will be enough. We'll make it enough." She headed for the door. "Let's start doing it."

CHAPTER
16

"HOW IS IT GOING?" KENDRA asked, as Eve came into the kitchen where she was working. "I haven't seen anything of you or Sam in hours."

"Busy." Eve reached into the refrigerator and got out a bottle of Red Bull. "I don't how Sam manages to keep going. I guess it's this stuff he keeps drinking. It must be pretty powerful. He gave up coffee last night and has been guzzling this." She got a cup of coffee for herself. "As far as *how* it's going, I don't have any idea. Sam keeps having breakthroughs but not enough, never enough." She rubbed her temple. "Colby's been bouncing his calls and video streams off a lot of different network systems around the world, which makes him difficult to track. Sam thought the last call might have been more direct, so he's been trying to work on that one." She leaned back against the counter and glanced at Kendra's computer and her scratch pad, scrawled with notes. "What about you?"

"Plodding. I've just discovered two more Wingate shipping companies in Los Angeles County and a Wingate funeral home in La Jolla. The funeral home sounds like Colby's style. I'll call Griffin and ask him to send a couple agents to check them out." She grimaced. "Though his men are stretched to the max right now. Do you know how many Wingates are residents of the cities in Southern California? The agents can't even phone them in case they trigger an action on Colby's part. We don't know if it's a name, a company, a ship or—"

"A funeral home," Eve supplied. "I get the picture. Very discouraging."

Kendra shook her head. "I can't be discouraged. I won't let that happen."

Eve nodded. "I feel the same way. We don't have that right." She took her coffee and the bottle of Red Bull and put them on a tray. "Where's Lynch?"

"He set up shop in the living room. He didn't want to disturb me. He's been on the phone for hours. He's been calling every contact he has around the world. He decided that the FBI wasn't enough, so he's pulling in favors from the Justice Department, CIA, Interpol . . . I've never even heard of many of those organizations he works for."

"Bless him," Eve said quietly. "We need all the clout we can get."

"Yes, we do." She smiled faintly. "Though I think he'd be a little surprised that you were raining blessings down on him."

"I'd nominate him for sainthood if he came up with a strong lead." She picked up the tray. "And if it brought us to that crazy bastard, I'd call the Pope and lobby."

"Is there something a little sacrilegious about that thought?"

"It's sacrilegious to think of Colby even near Beth," Eve said. Her hands on the tray were shaking the tiniest bit as she passed Kendra on the way to the door. "I'm trying not to think of it. But I can't keep my eyes off the clock. It's been over twelve hours."

"I know. We still have time, Eve."

She looked over her shoulder. "Yes. But I'd feel better if one of Sam's breakthroughs showed signs of breaking this blasted deadlock." She drew a deep breath. "It will happen. We have to have faith."

Kendra nodded. "And lots of caffeine. I may make another pot of coffee myself."

"Just stay away from the Red Bull." Eve smiled and left the kitchen.

Kendra gazed after her for a moment. In this time of frustration and panic, it was good having Eve here working with her toward a common goal.

But the key word was work. Neither of them had time to devote to anything but finding Beth. She glanced down at her notes and circled the funeral-home reference. It would be—

"Wingate!" Lynch strode into the kitchen. "I just got off the phone. We've got a hit."

She sat up straight. "Finally. Were you talking to Griffin?"

"No, my Justice Department source." Lynch walked across the office and picked up his tablet computer. "Wingate is definitely a name, not a place. Colby has been using that name since he resurfaced." His fingers were racing over the keys. "A James Wingate crossed in from the Mexican border at San Ysidro last week."

It was too good to be true. A name and a connection to Colby. "But how do we know that it's—"

Lynch thrust his tablet computer in front of Kendra's face.

Colby.

At a border pedestrian-inspection station with a beard and longish hair, but definitely Colby. There was no mistaking those piercing eyes and tiny teeth.

"There's surveillance video and about a dozen more photos of him at the border crossing. It's all being sent to Griffin as we speak. Griffin will jump on it with the speed of light."

A lead, a break at last. Excitement was exploding within her. "I think you may just be on your way to sainthood," she murmured.

"What?" he said impatiently.

"Never mind." She couldn't take her eyes from the photos. "Mexico . . . . That's where he's been all these months?"

"Possibly. It would make sense. Under the radar as far as U.S. law enforcement was concerned. Close enough to keep his sights on you until he was ready to strike. The night before Colby crossed over, a fairly well-known identity broker was murdered in Todos Santos. It's a coastal city about thirty miles south of the border. The man was stabbed. Gutted. It could be that Colby bought a new identity from this man, then killed him to wipe out his trail."

"Wingate," Kendra said. She finally made herself look away from Lynch's tablet. "Detective Stokes must have somehow found out that was the name he was using. After he'd been taken, maybe he spotted some paperwork in the van or heard Colby talking to someone."

Lynch nodded. "However he found out, it's impressive that Stokes was able to get it across to us. He was one good cop."

"Yes, he was." Kendra tried to shake the image of Stokes bleeding on that table. She turned back to Lynch. "So what now?"

"Let's get back to the FBI office. With a definite full name to search, this opens up a lot of new investigative possibilities for them. It's logical that one break might lead to another." He said quietly, "And we have you and Stokes to thank for it."

"Excuse me if I'm not ready to start patting myself on the back yet." Kendra checked her watch. Thirteen hours thirty minutes since Colby had set his deadline. What had he been doing to Beth during those hours? She had been trying not to dwell on that while she had been working desperately to find a way to rescue Beth. Colby had said he wanted to break Kendra, and she couldn't let him do it. It would be a defeat for Kendra, and it might be death for Beth. She grabbed her computer and handbag and got to her feet. "Let's go. I have to stop by the office and tell Eve and Sam about this, but we have to hurry. We're running out of time."

Hold on, Beth.

God, I'm praying he's not hurting you.

We're trying so hard.

We'll get to you. I promise.

HE WAS COMING TOWARD HER AGAIN.

Beth couldn't see Colby in the darkness, but she could hear him, smell him.

It was the third time tonight, and she knew what was going to follow.

Tonight. Was it night? She couldn't tell, it was all darkness and the smell of tar.

Her heart was starting to beat hard as helpless panic overwhelmed her.

He had stopped before the end before, but would he do it this time?

"Are you ready, Beth?" Colby asked. "I can practically hear your heartbeat from here. You try so hard to be brave. But it's difficult not knowing, isn't it?

She didn't answer. Her voice might shake, and she didn't want to give him the satisfaction.

"It's such a struggle. You're being deprived of the one thing that is natural to all of us. You can't help but be frightened." He was standing next to her, and she could see his face above her. "But consider it as training. I want you to know what to expect. I'm giving Kendra a taste of anticipation, it's not right that I should deprive you." He lifted his hands and she saw the blur of the white pillow he was holding. "Breathe deep, Beth . . ."

The pillow came down over her face!

She was pinned, unable to shift on the table. She tried desperately to move her head to get away from that smothering hold. It was pure instinct. She knew it was hopeless. Colby was too strong, and he knew just how to use that pillow.

No breath.

No breath.

Her lungs were struggling.

Her heart was pounding, trying to leap from her breast.

Her eyes were bulging.

No breath.

No breath.

No breath.

Dizzy.

Darkness.

This time he was going to do it. This time he wouldn't—

The pillow lifted, and he smiled down at her as she struggled frantically to breathe, to force air into her tortured lungs.

"You're getting weaker. Or were you just more frightened?"

Maybe a little of both, but she wouldn't admit it to him. "Did . . . you enjoy . . . your game?" It didn't matter now that her voice was hoarse and shaking. He would expect it. "I'm not weaker. Cut me loose, and you'll see."

"Why should I do that? Your helplessness is exquisite. It makes the suffering all the more satisfying. You're never certain if I'll let you come back, are you?"

"Aren't you afraid . . . repetition . . . will take that . . . uncertainty . . . away?"

"Oh, no. It will just reinforce it."

"Is that how . . . you're going to kill . . . me? Are you . . . going to smother me?"

"Perhaps. I wouldn't put you through this entertaining training if your death wasn't to have certain similar elements." He stroked the pillow. "I'll leave you now. Try to sleep. It will be interesting waking you . . ."

He was going away.

For a little while, or an hour, or several hours.

Beth drew a deep breath. She would try to sleep because she knew he didn't want her to do it. He wanted her to go through his damn anticipation and dread. Suffer mentally as well as physically.

Sleep.

Rest.

Gather her strength.

For the next time.

* * *

KENDRA AND LYNCH WERE FIVE minutes away from the FBI office when Lynch's text chime sounded from his car stereo system. He pressed a button on his dashboard's touch screen to read the text that had just come in on his phone. "We're taking a detour," he said.

Kendra looked at the text. It read. MEET SPECIAL AGENT METCALF AT BONITA TRUCK RENTALS 1525 12TH STREET. Her gaze flew to Lynch. "Colby's white van?"

"That would be my guess. I told you having a confirmed name could really kick-start things. They've only had twenty-four hours, and they've already identified every place in the city that had rented a Ford Transit cargo van in the last week. But they haven't had time to check names. If this name is attached to the rental, it could score big-time."

Lynch exited and got back on the 1-8 heading east toward downtown. Within fifteen minutes, they were standing in the lobby of Bonita Truck Rentals and Storage on 12th Street. Special Agent Roland Metcalf was already there.

Kendra moved quickly toward him. "What's the story, Metcalf?"

"Colby was here. He rented the van six days ago under the name of James Wingate."

"Address?" Lynch asked.

"The manager's getting it for me now, along with the credit-card info he left. Although I don't know where he got a credit card."

"Probably part of the identity packet he bought in Mexico," Lynch said.

The manager, a bald man with a bushy moustache, emerged from the back room with a canary-yellow copy of the invoice. He nodded his greeting at Kendra and Lynch as he laid the paper on the counter for them to see.

"It was a one-way cross-country rental. The van's due at Star Truck and Van Rentals in Norfolk, Virginia, this weekend."

"Norfolk," Kendra repeated.

Lynch nodded. "They shouldn't count on seeing it there."

"He knew what he was doing as usual," Kendra said, looking at the invoice. "He also has a Norfolk address listed here."

"Bogus, I'm sure," Lynch said. "But you want to have it checked out, Metcalf."

"We're already on it," Metcalf said. He turned toward the manager. "How many copies were there in this invoice?"

"Four. The customer gets the pink copy, we get the other three."

Metcalf nodded down toward the invoice. "I want to take this with me. Will you please round up the other two copies and let me have those, too?"

The manager looked doubtfully at him. "Can't I just make copies for you?"

"No, but feel free to make copies for yourself."

"Uh, don't you need a warrant or something?"

"No time for that," Metcalf snapped. "Your customer is a serial killer, and I know you won't want to be responsible for any other crimes. I need the three originals because his fingerprints may be on one of them. Got it?" Metcalf produced a clear document bag. "And I'd appreciate you handling them very carefully, okay?"

Obviously rattled, the manager nodded and hurried to the back room."

"Nicely done," Kendra murmured.

Lynch pulled out his phone and snapped a photo of the

invoice. "Colby's info may be bogus, but there's something here that might help us." He glanced up at Kendra. "We now have his van's license-plate number."

"Bingo. Success."

He thought for a moment. "Yeah, it very well might." He quickly motioned for her to follow him. "Let's go back to the house. I need to talk to Sam."

Lynch House

"LET ME GET THIS STRAIGHT." Sam pushed away from the desk to stare at Kendra, Lynch, and Eve. "You want me to do an ALPR hack?"

Lynch finished jotting down the license number and slid it across the desk to him. "Can you do it?"

"Of course. The only problem is how long it might take."

"ALPR?" Eve asked.

"Automatic License Plate Reader," Lynch said. "The DEA started using them in border states a few years ago to track possible drug trafficking. Then the Department of Homeland Security started throwing money at local police departments to install them in jurisdictions all over the country. They've given away at least $50 million to do this, probably a lot more. These devices are sometimes clamped on freeway signs, mounted in patrol cars, or even just apps in mobile telephones. They can be anywhere."

"To track terror suspects?" Kendra asked.

"That's the idea, but anybody who's been on an interstate highway in the past few years has had their license plate automatically photographed, logged, and filed away in a database somewhere."

"Several databases," Sam said. "It's kind of a mess right now. Homeland Security is working on combining the license-plate traffic data gathered from thousands of jurisdictions all over the country. One day, they'd like to be able to track any car from one side of the country to the other in real time."

"That's a little scary," Kendra said.

Sam nodded. "The ACLU and other privacy advocates aren't crazy about it. I'm not either. But for Beth's sake, I sure wish they could do that right now."

"You and me both," Eve said. "So what *can* you do?"

Sam studied the license-plate number in his hand. "It depends on how quickly the local ALPR databases are updated with the license-plate numbers they capture. I assume the FBI is doing everything they can on their end?"

"Yes, but I've been part of enough investigations to know how difficult it is to quickly pull this kind of data together from all the various sources: California Highway Patrol, SDPD, San Diego County Sheriff's Department, all the various municipalities . . . Like you say, it's a mess."

"In other words, the FBI doesn't have a Sam Zackoff," Kendra said.

"And they don't have a Tom Sims," Sam said soberly. "But even he would have been at a disadvantage here. There are miles of red tape that any official entity has to wade through for a multijurisdictional project like this."

"My thought exactly," Lynch said. "We don't have time to cut through that tape right now. You know what I'm asking. You went around the system before to track his streaming video message. I want you to do the same thing with this."

Sam leaned back in his chair as he frowned down at the license-plate number. "Not impossible, but when you start crossing swords with Homeland Security, they have a way of getting nasty. And fast. You'd better be ready to smooth things over with them if they come down on us."

Lynch pointed to the walls. "Built to withstand 40mm grenade launchers, remember? I'll try not to test them, but I guarantee I'll buy you all the time you need while I make our explanations."

Sam leaned toward the cobbled-together computer rig that dominated Lynch's office. "I'll see what I can do." He added grimly, "It's not gonna be pretty. I'm going for speed, so I'm not going to even try to cover my tracks when I invade those police departments' networks. Get ready for some hell to rain down."

"YOU'VE HELD UP AMAZINGLY WELL," Colby said as he removed the pillow. "No tears. No begging. I'll have to tell Kendra what a brave little soldier she had for a friend."

"Don't—do—that."

"Why, that was almost begging. Or was it an order? It's difficult to tell when you're panting like that."

"Bastard."

"Ah, it was an order. You don't want Kendra to know how I made you suffer. But that's part of the package, Beth." He laughed, and she could hear him moving away. "A package that is very close to being opened and revealed . . ."

KENDRA'S PHONE RANG.

Sam.

Thank God. They had been waiting for hours for word from him, and she was a nervous wreck.

She punched the access as she showed the ID to Griffin and Lynch. "It's Sam." She spoke into the phone. "Sam,

I just put you on speaker. I hope you're telling me you have something."

"City Heights, off the 1-15 freeway at either University Avenue or El Cajon Boulevard. That's Exit 5A or 5B in City Heights."

Griffin stepped closer to the phone. "What are you basing that on?"

"It's a set of DEA license-plate readers on the Escondido Freeway. If you can get the DEA to give you access, you can see for yourself. Every time that van's license plate has appeared on any of the local ALPR databases, it entered and left the 1-15 freeway at either University Avenue or El Cajon Boulevard. That's Exit 5A or 5B in City Heights."

Griffin turned to Agent Metcalf. "Find us a city plan for that neighborhood. I want architectural details for as many houses and buildings there as you can dig up."

"Including those with basements and cellars," Kendra added.

"Exactly. There aren't many of those around here. But we'll need to go visual with our boots on the ground. House to house, building to building."

"Without alerting Colby," Kendra said.

"That goes without saying. We're not amateurs, Kendra."

"All it takes is one mistake, and Beth is dead."

Lynch stared at a large map of the city that dominated the wall at the end of Griffin's office. "City Heights. It's a large area."

That's what Kendra was thinking.

A very large area.

And Beth only had a little over one hour left on the clock.

Griffin was already on his office phone, ordering the massive increase in manpower needed.

Kendra joined Lynch at the map, her gaze scanning the City Heights area, trying to see something, anything, that would make the search go faster, easier.

She could see nothing.

And she couldn't stay here, helplessly waiting for other people to save Beth. Boots on the ground. She whirled and headed for the door. "Let's get over there."

"ARE YOU READY?" COLBY ASKED.

The words he'd used during all those hours of torture.

"Where's your pillow, you son of a bitch?"

"Not necessary." He smiled down at her. "You've graduated, Beth. I just came to say good-bye."

She went still. "Then do it, damn you."

"Oh, I will." He turned away and went toward the stairs. "Right now."

She stared at him in confusion.

He looked back at her and smiled. "You believe all your training may have been for nothing? No such thing. I'm just adjusting it for another form. Remember the lack of breath. Your lungs struggling. Your heart pounding. The helplessness of not being able to fight what's being done to you."

"I could hardly forget."

"Exactly." He opened a utility box on the wall and then turned a nozzle. "It's time for anticipation to become reality. Sorry I won't be able to see it. But I'll be able to imagine . . .

"I'll be back in a moment. I have a few things to do before I leave you." He turned, opened the door, and was gone.

Gone? What the hell was he doing? It was a complete shock that he—

And then she heard it.

First a trickle, and then a gushing.

Water.

KENDRA'S PHONE RANG WHEN SHE and Lynch had just left the FBI office for City Heights.

Let it be Sam telling her that he'd narrowed down the area where they could find Beth.

"Time's up, Kendra," Colby said.

She stiffened with panic. "No, it's not. You can't do that. I have another forty-five minutes."

"He who holds the power makes the rules, or breaks them. According to what he decides is most amusing." He chuckled. "But, as it happens, I still may slide under the time limit I gave you."

"What are you talking about?"

"I mean, I started your Beth's death gasp, but it won't take effect for a bit. I wanted it to be very slow. Anticipation, you know."

"I don't want to know. What did you do to her?"

"Why, I spent the past twenty-four hours preparing her, and now she's waiting for it to happen." He paused. "But probably not patiently. She fought me to the very end. She didn't want me to tell you how hard she had to struggle."

"Did you hurt her?"

"Yes, not in the way I hurt Stokes, but the mental torment was considerably worse."

"You son of a bitch."

"You mustn't speak to me like that. I'm complimenting your Beth. I actually grew to admire her."

"Then let her go."

"Oh, no, you'll have to go and get her. But we both realize there's a time restraint, and I've put a small obstacle in your path."

"Tell me where she is."

"Suppose I show you. I've grown so fond of all these computer bells and whistles that Northrup installed for me. A picture tells more than a thousand words. Do you have your computer?"

"Yes."

"I thought you would. Turn it on."

She switched on the computer. "You're wasting time. Stop stalling and—"

The picture came in clear and bright.

"Dear God, what are you doing?"

Water. Water gushing. Flooding the floor, lapping against the walls and the shelves and the first rungs of the metal embalming table where Beth lay bound.

"You can see what I'm doing. I made sure of that. I kept Beth in the dark so that she would be disoriented but I wanted you to know instantly what was going on."

"You're going to drown her."

"Yes, some people say that drowning is an easy death. I don't agree. Particularly when you're expecting the suffocation and lung failure. I made certain that Beth would know what to expect."

She closed her eyes as the horror hit home. Then she forced herself to open them and look back at the video. "How long does she have?"

"Perhaps the forty-five minutes I gave you."

"How do I know she's not already dead, like Stokes was?"

"I never promised that the Detective Stokes show was a live broadcast. Trust me, I want you to see your friend die as it happens."

She believed him. Colby was just that sick.

"But give me a number, and I'll have our Beth hold up the same number of fingers so you can have your proof of life."

"Four," Kendra said.

After a few seconds, Beth flashed two peace signs from her restrained hands.

"There you are," Colby said. "But I guarantee you, as clever as your Sam Zackoff may be, I've made sure he won't have time to trace this webcast. Good-bye for now, Kendra. This is the last time we will speak for a while."

"What do you mean?"

"You're wasting time. Good-bye."

He cut the connection.

On her laptop, Kendra watched as Colby waded through the shin-deep water toward Beth. He leaned over her and said something inaudible.

"What in the hell is he doing?" Kendra said.

Colby pinned what appeared to be a rolled-up freezer bag to Beth's sweater. Then he stepped out of the frame.

Kendra's cell phone rang again. She answered it on speaker, this time it really was Sam.

"He called you, didn't he?" Sam asked.

"How did you know?"

"I'm watching it here. I cloned your computer, remember? I'm forwarding it through my server to the FBI and the police. They're in the City Heights area, so now they'll have a description of the clothing he's wearing."

"Providing he doesn't change clothes. Colby thinks of those details."

"But they're also looking for his van. Put them both together and—"

"That's one advantage we do have," Lynch said. "He doesn't know we have the name he's using, or the make and license-plate number of the vehicle he's—"

"None of that is going to do any good if we can't get to Beth in time," Kendra interrupted. "He's *killing* her." She added unsteadily, "Sam, you have to find him. He was so sure that even you wouldn't be able to trace him in time to save her."

"Then I have to prove him wrong, don't I? Because we have to find her." He paused. "But I was thinking while the bastard was spouting off that we may have a third advantage. In the years since Colby went away to jail, much of San Diego County went from water company meter readers . . . to a central-office networked-based system." ˙

"Meaning what?"

"Meaning . . . there's another possibility. I'll call you back." He hung up.

"Another possibility," Kendra repeated. "Let's hope it's a good one. Colby was so sure."

"He's an egomaniac. Of course, he's sure," Lynch said. "That doesn't mean he won't be wrong."

"No," Kendra said. "But it tends to shake the confidence." Her hand was trembling as she reached for her phone again. "I have to call Griffin and make sure he noticed that video shows that Beth is being held in a cellar. I couldn't tell before in the other videos because he only had close-ups. But this time he wanted me to see how helpless she was and the rising water, so he panned around the place. The walls are tarred and there were stairs leading upward. It's a cellar. It will make a difference. We're looking for a house with a cellar."

"Griffin will probably have noticed," Lynch said quietly.

"I have to be certain." She started dialing. "I'm not as confident as Colby. Nothing else must go wrong." But it might go terribly wrong if Sam or Griffin didn't come through for Beth. "Get me to City Heights. I'll ask Griffin to give me addresses of all houses in the area with cellars and eliminate searching any of the others."

SAM PUT DOWN THE PHONE AFTER talking to Kendra and turned to Eve. "Evidently I'm about to be brilliant." He added soberly, "Good wishes and prayers will be appreciated."

"Good. And you'll have them. But I can't stay here and just spin my wheels, Sam." She picked up Kendra's remote key fob from the desk. "Kendra left her car here for me to use. I'm going to City Heights. If that's where Beth is, that's where I need to be."

Sam unplugged his laptop. "Me, too. Let's go. I'll work in the car."

A few minutes later, Eve was driving away from the Lynch house and glanced at Sam in the seat beside her. "Is there anything I can do to help?"

"You can drive as fast as legally or illegally possible to get us to City Heights." His head was bent over his computer. "And let me concentrate on finding one of those houses in the area that's registering a hell of a lot of water pouring out of the pipes into it."

"You can do that?" She made a face. "What am I thinking? Of course you can do it. You're going to hack into the Department of Water and Power usage."

"Well, I'm certainly not going to wait and try to cut

through red tape in that bureaucracy." He was rapidly typing into the computer. "It could take days . . ."

And they had only minutes, Eve thought. It had terrified her when she had seen Beth bound on that table when they had watched Colby's video to Kendra. Beth had looked so . . . helpless.

It was still terrifying her.

She drove slowly, watching the GPS, waiting for Sam to say something.

Finally, she couldn't stand it any longer. She swerved onto the shoulder of the congested 1-15 freeway and glanced over at Sam. "Anything?"

He angled his laptop screen out of the sun's glare. "Hacking into the Department of Water site was no problem, but there are seven possibilities in the immediate area. Six of them are probably swimming pools being filled."

"Welcome to Southern California," Eve said.

"Right. But the seventh has to be Beth, wherever she is." His fingers flew over the keyboard. "I'm checking each of these addresses against Google Earth. That'll give me an overhead satellite shot and show if there's a pool on the property. So far I'm two for two."

The car shook as they rolled over raised reflector strips on the shoulder.

"Sorry," Eve said. "El Cajon Boulevard is just ahead. Should I still get off there?"

"Yes, and turn right." He squinted at the screen. "Three for three."

His phone rang. "Kendra." He tapped his headset to answer. "Kendra, I know I told you I'd call you back. I got distracted. Where are you?"

"Where do you think I am? Heading for City Heights. Sam, Beth's not got much—"

"I'm working on it. I'm getting near the area now. Stand by for an address. Shit! Another pool."

"What?"

"Nothing. Look, I've tapped into the water-usage meters, and I'm eliminating the swimming pools. And . . . I'm now five for five. Why can't we get a break? I hope I'm right about this being the right neighborhood."

"You'd better be. Half of the police department and all of FBI's local tactical response team are there breaking down doors."

"Damn. It seems like they're all pools. Only two to go. Cross your fingers. We're running out of options. I don't know where we can possibly go after—" He stopped. "Oh, my God."

"Sam?"

"This has to be it! It's a small two-story commercial building. I think it used to be a bakery, with maybe an apartment above."

"Where?" Kendra asked.

"At 4276 Euclid Avenue, just south of El Cajon. Tell the cops—4276 Euclid. We're almost there."

"Five minutes." Kendra hung up.

"I've got it." Eve gunned the engine.

Two right turns and two minutes later, Sam and Eve were approaching the former bakery, which was already surrounded by police cars with flashers blazing.

"Dear God," Eve whispered.

She was looking at the water pouring over the sidewalk from the two-story building. She jammed her foot on the brake.

Sam threw open his door. "It doesn't mean anything. We can't give up. I know it looks bad but . . . Come on!"

Sam and Eve ran down the narrow side alley to a door that had obviously just been rammed open by the police officers. Water was rushing from the open doorway.

Eve pushed past the half dozen cops. Two of whom tried to stop her.

One officer said, "You can't go in there, ma'am."

"The hell I can't. My sister's in there."

Another one of the officers grabbed her arm and shined his flashlight toward a descending cellar stairway that was already entirely underwater.

"It's too late," he said gently. "That water was rushing too fast and filled up that stairwell in just seconds."

Eve tried to break free. "No. We have to bring her up."

"I'm sorry. We need to wait for—"

"Let me go!"

"Ma'am, we've just radioed for the dive team. They're on their way."

"And we're supposed to wait? How long? Ten minutes? Twenty? It'll be too late, dammit."

"I'm afraid it's too late now."

Eve tried to wrench herself free as more police officers restrained her. She desperately exchanged a quick glance with Sam, and her eyes narrowed.

He understood.

He glanced toward the open cellar door, then gave her a tiny, almost imperceptible nod.

Eve yelled hysterically, and swung her arm. The rest of the police officers joined the fray, trying to restrain her. She threw herself back, giving Sam just the opening he needed.

He took a deep breath and dove into the water!

Sam heard the cops yelling behind him as he kicked his way down into the darkness of the submerged cellar. A couple of them splashed on the top couple of steps, but none followed.

They weren't crazy. Not like he clearly was.

The water was *cold*. It was now completely dark, and he couldn't see his own hand in front of his face. It was then he realized he had no orientation of the strange place, not even a clue of which direction Beth and that embalming table might lie.

Wait!

He fished in his pocket and pulled out his keys. A tiny, flat xenon flashlight was on the ring, useful for seeing door locks at night and computer motherboards in dim corners of his workshop.

And it just might save his life.

He squeezed the flashlight between his thumb and forefinger, and a wide-angle beam illuminated the ceiling and side wall.

Bizarre. In just a few seconds, he'd already become disoriented to the point that he couldn't tell up from down. He spun around, trying to keep a fix on where the stairs were. He couldn't let himself lose track of how to get the hell out of there.

If he ever got out. His lungs were already aching.

He went deeper and kicked, looking for some sign of the embalming table he'd seen in Colby's videos. Again he'd become disoriented, finding himself almost face-to-face with one of the black-as-coal walls.

Where in the hell was—?

He turned around and saw her. Only inches from him, facing him.

Beth.

No!

Beth's eyes were closed, and she was floating upright, her feet still strapped to the table. Her wrists were now free of restraints, but Beth's struggle had left bruises and scrapes all over her lower arms.

She'd never had a chance. She was motionless, and her long hair floated around her beautiful face.

Oh, God.

Beth.

I'm sorry, Beth. I should have worked faster, found you sooner . . .

His oxygen-starved lungs burned . . . Could he even make it out of here?

I won't leave you. I'll get you out of this awful place, Beth. I won't leave without you . . .

He dove down and saw that her ankle restraints were buckled underneath the table. No way she could've reached them, he realized. He released the buckles, then gripped her arms and yanked her free of the table.

He held her tight as he kicked toward the stairway. He could feel her long hair brush, cling, to his face.

I've got you. You're getting out of here, Beth. I won't leave you in this pit where he put you to die.

His chest was throbbing, about to explode. He was getting light-headed.

Where were those damned stairs? Was he even on the right side of the room?

He touched the wall with his fingertips and kicked harder. There. There were the stairs.

He gripped Beth tighter and kicked upward. Then, finally, he could see light from the doorway. Several flashlight beams speared downward.

Kick harder. Just a few more yards.

God, I'm sorry, Beth. Forgive me. Someone else should have been here for you. I failed you. I should have been faster . . .

He finally broke the surface, gasping and gulping air. Several strong hands gripped him and Beth and dragged them through the doorway and out into the alley. There were now over a dozen cops and a paramedic unit there. Kendra and Lynch were getting out of their car parked down the alley and hurrying toward them. Kendra's expression was stricken as her gaze fell on Beth.

I tried, Kendra.

The paramedics converged on Beth, while Sam stood up and staggered away. Kendra was there beside the ambulance, kneeling beside the paramedics.

Sam leaned against the building and watched the paramedics work on Beth. Too late, he wanted to tell them. Can't you see? It's too late.

He was vaguely aware that Eve had walked over and was standing next to him. She tucked a blanket around his shoulders. Then she silently put her hand on his.

Only then did Sam realize he was crying. "It was so damn dark down there. I wasn't fast enough. I wanted to save her."

Eve nodded, wiping tears from her own face. "Sam . . . in her entire life, no one ever did more for her than you did. No one."

"It wasn't enough." He shook his head. "Hell, I'm not even a very good swimmer. I spend all my time with computers. I should have been stronger, better for her."

"Sam, you were *there* for her. You gave everything you had."

"But it didn't keep her from—"

Eve stiffened. "Hush." Eve suddenly whirled to face the paramedics. "I think I heard . . ."

Sam's gaze followed Eve's. He couldn't see anything past the paramedics surrounding Beth.

But he heard it, too.

A cough, or gurgle or . . . something.

It couldn't be. She was dead.

Wasn't she?

He was running toward the ambulance.

Beth was lying where they had placed her. Her eyes were still closed. She didn't look any different than a few minutes ago.

But the medics were working furiously over her now.

Kendra had jumped to her feet and was standing right beside them. "A cough. Didn't I hear her cough?"

"Step back, ma'am."

"Please, just say yes or no. Then I'll get out of your way."

"Yes," he said. "We have a heartbeat. But that doesn't mean much right now. We have to stabilize her and get her to the hospital. Then we'll see what we have."

"She's alive?" Sam said wonderingly.

Eve turned, grabbed his arm, and pulled him back away from the ambulance. The tears were pouring down her cheeks. "Come on. Let's get out of their way and let them work."

"She's alive?"

Kendra was suddenly there beside them. She nodded, her expression luminous, and gave him a hug. "Yes, she's alive, Sam."

CHAPTER
17

"WHAT'S HAPPENING?" LYNCH strode down the ER corridor toward Kendra. "She's still unconscious? I thought she was recovering."

"So did we," Kendra said. "That paramedic warned me she wasn't out of the woods, but I didn't want to believe him." She nodded soberly at the ER doors. "I believe him now. They can't seem to wake her."

"I thought it was too good to be true." Sam turned away from the window. "She was dead when I found her. It would take a miracle to bring her back."

Kendra shook her head. "Not a miracle. And according to the specialist to whom I just spoke, she wasn't dead. Very close. Her heart had probably even stopped. But you said she'd managed to free her arm restraints but not those on her ankles and that would have made her able to breathe until the water was almost up to the ceiling. She would have been able to breathe until the chamber was filled, only minutes before the water overflowed through the cellar doorway."

"Minutes," Sam repeated. "Why didn't she drown?"

"You," she said simply. "When drowning, the heart stops beating after about three minutes. But it's possible to revive someone without brain damage for about seven minutes. Judging by the way the water was rushing out of the cellar and into the streets, you and Eve must have arrived on the scene almost at the time her heart stopped beating."

"But we don't know if I got her out in time to make that seven-minute deadline," Sam said.

She wanted to comfort him, reassure him, but she couldn't lie. "No, we don't know. You did everything you could, but we can't even be sure what went on in that cellar before you got there."

"She fought," he said hoarsely. "Her arms were bruised . . . she fought those ties until she managed to slip out of them. Maybe the water helped. But it was probably too late for her to free her ankles. That son of a bitch had her pinned and helpless."

The vision of Beth struggling desperately in that water was unbearable for Kendra. It must have been even more wrenching for Sam, who had seen it. Her hand grasped his arm. "She's still fighting, Sam. And she may win."

"When will we know?"

She shook her head. "They're still evaluating. Using all their fancy machines."

"Even if she lives . . . You said seven minutes without brain damage."

She nodded. "But we don't know that either. They can see there's swelling to the brain, but they don't know how much or if there was damage. The doctors will let us know as soon as they do. Dr. Jordkol appears to know what he's doing."

"Yeah, maybe." He turned back to look out the window.

She gazed at him helplessly.

"Come on. I'll buy you a soda." Lynch took her arm and guided her toward the soda machine. "There's nothing you can say to him right now. He's feeling guilty as hell."

"I know. But there's no reason. He did everything. He was a hero." She took the Diet Coke he handed her. "It doesn't make sense."

"No more than your feeling guilty."

"That's different. I was responsible for setting her up for Colby. I even brought Sam into it."

"Hush." His fingers touched her lips. "In the end, everyone is responsible for themselves and their choices."

"And I chose to involve people who got terribly hurt in the process." She changed the subject. "Has Griffin found any sign of Colby?"

He shook his head. "They've scoured the house and the neighborhood, and the only thing they found was the corpse of an old lady on the top floor of the house and Northrup in a closet in the cellar."

"No sighting of the van?"

Lynch shook his head. "Not yet. Griffin said he'd come and bring us up to date as soon as he knew something."

"Someone has to have seen him." She shook her head numbly. "He couldn't have just done that to Beth and vanished."

"You know he had it all planned," Lynch said. "There's a good chance that's exactly what he did. Turned on the water, then left the house and probably the area."

"And we just missed him?"

He nodded. "He wouldn't have known that we were that

close." He looked at the ER room. "Though he probably does now. The media was all over Griffin when they got wind of what happened at City Heights."

"Not close enough." She looked at Eve, who had gone over to stand beside Sam. "She's been wonderful with Sam. She's hurting so much herself but she's been there for him through all of this. She called Joe Quinn when she got to the hospital and told him what was happening, but since then she's been Sam's anchor."

"You weren't doing a bad job yourself when I walked in."

She shrugged. "He's my friend, but Eve is better than I am at that kind of conversation. In case you haven't noticed, I have a habit of saying the wrong thing."

"Not when you care about someone." He turned away. "Of course, I don't have firsthand proof of that statement. Go sit down. I'll go call Griffin again, and then I'll be back with you."

"You don't have to sit with me."

"It's my pleasure. Well, now that was the wrong phrase. There's no pleasure connected to this. But it's definitely my privilege." He strolled down the hall. "Fifteen minutes, Kendra."

She watched him leave and felt suddenly alone.

Ridiculous.

She was just very vulnerable at the moment. She glanced at Eve and Sam. They were all vulnerable because of that very special woman in the ER.

And they might as well cling together until they knew what Beth's fate was to be. If she was awkward and said the wrong thing, so be it.

She moved across the room toward the window where Eve and Sam stood.

* * *

LYNCH WASN'T BACK IN FIFTEEN MINUTES, it was closer to an hour when he came back to the waiting room. "Sorry, when I called Griffin, he was in the middle of something and had to call me back. He's on his way here now."

"What was happening?" Kendra asked. "Colby?"

"Maybe. He wanted to confirm, then get back to us."

Her gaze narrowed on his face. "It is Colby. Have they caught him?"

"If they had, I'd be the first to tell you." He glanced at the ER room. "Beth?"

Kendra shook her head. "No word yet. I don't like it." She paused. "Any more than I like you changing the subject. Why aren't you talking to me?"

"Because I thought Griffin should take the heat. I get enough of it from you. Besides, I hoped he might know more by the time he got here."

"More about what? Why should—"

"Hello, Kendra." Griffin was striding down the corridor toward them. "How is Beth Avery? Better, I hope."

"We don't know. I'm sure she'd feel better to know that Colby has been caught." She paused. "Or shot down like the animal he is. I hope that's what you're going to tell me."

"I'm afraid not. I know you're upset about this, and so am I. But you have to remember that Colby has been evading the law for a long time, and he's gotten very good at it."

"I don't have to remember anything," she said fiercely. "Except that Beth may be dying or brain-dead before this day is over. I don't care if you're upset because the media is roasting you alive. I want Colby found."

"We're trying to do that," Griffin said soothingly. "It's

not a question of Colby's being on the run, that would make things easier, he'd make mistakes. Every action he's taken since he turned on that water has been deliberate and well thought-out."

"What actions?"

"We've just got a report that the credit card belonging to Tom Sims, the FBI computer head, who was killed in D.C., was used to purchase groceries and clothes in San Ysidro, just across from the Mexican border."

"What?"

"Sims's credit card was missing when his body was found in that alley."

"You think Colby is on his way back to Mexico?"

"I have to consider the possibility." He reached into his pocket. "Particularly since he left this charming farewell note for you."

"Note?"

"Don't you remember? He pinned it to Beth Avery's sweater before he left her. It was in a waterproof freezer bag." He handed her a printed sheet of paper. "I had it copied for you."

She slowly took the note.

The words were typically Colby.

Kendra

Your little friend was a delight, but you are without peer. I can hardly wait for the day when we'll come together. But I'm a patient man as you might have noticed. I know you're getting close. You are so very clever. So it's time to shift, to do a little dance, and come at you at a different time and place. But be assured, the dance will continue.

Or perhaps you might choose to come at me

again. I'll be on familiar ground, and you'll be the
stranger. That might even be more enjoyable . . .

Colby

"He said nothing about Mexico," she said. "He just hinted."

"We're checking border-patrol videos, and we'll continue to do so. But you don't have to have ID or passport to go into Mexico. It's returning that you have to have ID and documents. It would be the easiest place for him to go to try to purchase new documents and stage his next attack on you."

"But if he hears that Beth is still alive, he might decide to come back faster and finish the job."

"Naturally, we'll furnish her protection until we're sure that it's not necessary."

"You mean when she dies," she said baldly.

"I didn't say that."

"No, you didn't," she said. "And maybe I'm being unfair. It's hard for me to tell right now. I want to know when you get that photo of Colby crossing the border."

"I'll e-mail it to Lynch. You're a little occupied at the moment."

"Do that." She turned and crossed the room to tell Eve and Sam Griffin's news.

And continue to wait for news of her own.

Wouldn't the doctors ever come out of that ER?

DOCTOR JORDKOL CAME OUT OF the ER forty-five minutes later. He didn't come to Kendra but directly to Eve. Kendra didn't expect anything else. Eve was family, next of kin.

"We believe Ms. Avery is out of danger for the time being," he said. "It was touch-and-go for a while, but she has a strong heartbeat now." He added soberly, "However, she's still unconscious, and we prefer that she stay that way for at least the next few days. We'll probably put her in a medically induced coma for at least tonight."

"Why?" Eve asked.

"We prefer to keep the brain activity down so that we can monitor it."

"You're checking for brain damage," Eve said. "Are there indications?"

He hesitated. "Perhaps. It's difficult to tell with the swelling. But you mustn't give up hope of a normal recovery."

"There's no question of that," Kendra said. "When will we know?"

"When the swelling goes down enough for us to bring her out of the coma. Tomorrow at the earliest."

"May we visit her?" Eve asked.

He shrugged. "Of course, just don't expect a response." He nodded, turned, and strode down the hall.

"Not warm," Kendra said.

"I don't care as long as he's good," Eve said. "And right about a possible normal recovery. I'm scared."

Kendra nodded. "But she's out of danger."

"Temporarily." Sam spoke for the first time from where he stood by the wall. "He didn't seem too optimistic."

"It appears it's going to be a long haul," Lynch said. "May I make a suggestion? Why don't you all go back to my place and take a shower and change clothes? You look like you're been through a tornado. Then decide what's going to be the order of sitting with Beth? I'm sure she wouldn't want you all hovering over her."

"She'd laugh at us," Sam said suddenly.

Kendra looked at him and nodded. How well Sam had

gotten to know Beth. "I'll stay with her and wait until you get back and—"

"No," Eve said firmly. "I'm pulling rank. I'll stay with my sister." She pulled out Kendra's remote key fob and handed it to her. "You heard me. Get out of here."

She turned on her heel and went toward the nurses' station.

"Well, that appears to be settled," Lynch said. "She obviously has a mind of her own."

Kendra nodded. "I'll come back to relieve her in an hour or two."

"Because you're responsible?" Lynch said. "We've already discussed that."

"I want to go and sit with Beth," Sam said abruptly.

Kendra looked back at him. "Eve has first call, Sam. She's family."

"I want to do something for her."

"And you will," she said gently. "And you have. But look at you. Your clothes have dried on you, your hair is in spikes. That can't be comfortable. If one of the nurses saw you with Beth, they'd probably kick you out."

"Like you're doing?"

She nodded. "Go home, clean up, get something to eat. Then come back and sit with Beth. That way, if she happens to wake up, you won't scare her. Okay?"

"She won't wake up. You heard the doctor."

"I'd rather believe in Beth."

He didn't speak. Then he nodded. "Me too." He turned and walked toward the exit.

She watched him until he was out of sight. Then she turned to Lynch. "You've cleared the decks so that Eve and Sam are probably going to spend most of the night with Beth. Why did you do it?"

"Me? I was merely arranging things so that it would be easiest for you. Though how you could think I could judge how things would fall into place, I have no idea."

"You threw an idea out there and watched everyone pick up the ball in the way you thought they'd react. Manipulation."

"A small talent, but my own. Okay, I'll admit to manipulation if it's for your sake."

"And why is it for my sake?"

"You'd want to be free, and it wouldn't be possible if you felt bound to watch over Beth."

"Of course I want to watch over Beth." Her gaze narrowed on his face. "And why would I need to be free?"

He took out his phone. "Because ten minutes ago, Griffin wired me this photo." He handed the phone to her. "He crossed over the border into Mexico."

Colby.

Wearing a hat, but the camera had caught his profile. It was unmistakable.

Her gaze flew to Lynch's face. "How long ago?"

"An hour or so," he said. "I know Mexico very well. I have contacts there. He'll be looking for new documents, and I know where he can find them. If his head start isn't too great, I'll be able to track him."

"Not without me."

"I knew that would be your attitude. I would either have to take you with me, or you'd try to find him alone." He shrugged. "So I freed you up." He took her elbow. "I'll walk you to your car. I'll take the Ferrari back to my house. Follow me, and we'll take your car. The Ferrari is a little too showy for Mexico."

"Unless you're a drug lord. But you probably have the same problem here in the States."

"That stung a bit. You must be feeling a little better."
He held the door open for her. "I thought that taking action would make you function with your usual verve."

"You mean planning on killing Colby would excite
me?" She walked across the parking lot with him. "Not
excite. That's not what I'm feeling. Beth asked me once if
I had it to do over again would I kill Colby instead of sending him to prison. I told her I had mixed feelings. But I
don't any longer. When I saw Beth lying there struggling
to live, when I saw what he'd done to her, it was all over. I
can't stand the thought of his ever having the power to do
that again. And I wouldn't trust the police or a jury or the
prison board to make certain that he was put safely away."
She met his eyes. "I have to do it myself."

"With a little help from your friends." He stopped beside her car. "Don't shut me out, Kendra." He gently
touched her hair. "You don't have to feel responsible for
me. Your way is the way I want to go."

Warmth. Strength. Safety,

Why should she feel safe with Lynch when no one
would ever call him a safe man?

Because her world was not safe, and it was good to have
a companion in that world.

"Then that's the way we'll go . . . for a little while." She
unlocked her keyless car with her remote fob and stuffed
it into her pocket. She slipped into the driver's seat. "I'll
see you back at the house."

He nodded and turned and trotted across the lot toward
his Ferrari.

BE ASSURED THE DANCE *will continue.*

Kendra gripped her steering wheel as she entered the
freeway that would take her to Lynch's house. Colby's mes-

sage was clearly meant to terrify her, to make her live in constant fear.

She wouldn't let that happen.

You lose, Colby. The whole world is looking for you now. You'll be the one looking over your shoulder, studying each face you see for that fatal flash of recognition.

And one of those times, you'll see me there.

Maybe tonight. Maybe tomorrow.

Kendra hoped it would be that soon. She needed to get back to Beth. She had already begun compiling a mental list of world-class neurologists. She had met and worked with many of them in her years of music-therapy work, and she'd make sure Beth received the finest care possible.

As Kendra drove out of the city and traffic thinned out, she felt the slightest bit of tension draining away. There would be plenty of time to worry in the coming hours—or even days—but for now, Beth was resting and hopefully healing.

Sleep well, Beth. We'll be there for you when you wake.

And I hope to give you news that will—

"Hello, Kendra. What a wonderful night for a drive."

Colby!

Something cold and sharp snapped around her neck.

The steering wheel slid through her fingers, and the car careened toward the center divider!

Kendra frantically pulled the wheel hard right, narrowly missing the wall.

Her eyes flew to the rearview mirror.

The rear seatback was now down, opening a pathway from her trunk.

A thin wire was taut around her neck, beaded with blood. *Her* blood.

And there was Eric Colby himself, blue eyes piercing straight through her.

Shock. Panic.

How in the hell could this be happening?

He smiled. "Nice recovery, Kendra." He tightened the wire until she gasped with pain. "No use ending this party before it's even begun."

"Party?" Every word was agony as it put pressure on the wire. "It's more . . . of a game to you. You can't win, Colby."

"But I already have."

"There's nowhere for you to go. Nowhere."

"Let's classify that as my problem." He tugged on his wire, cutting even deeper into her throat.

She gagged as the pain grew in intensity. "Why now? You probably think . . . you could have . . . killed me days ago."

"Months ago, Kendra. Don't fool yourself."

"Then why didn't you?"

He smiled again. "I had time in prison and my sojourn in Mexico to decide exactly what I wanted for you. It all had to go according to plan." He loosened the wire slightly, making it easier for her to speak.

"And it was part of your plan to try to fool us when you crossed into Mexico tonight? How did you get back across the border to the U.S.?"

"As I said, all according to plan. I bought two sets of documents before I left Mexico. Wingate and Childress. I saved the Victor Childress identity to return for our grand finale."

"What a convoluted plan it turned out to be. Is it worth it to you?"

"Absolutely. Surely, you didn't think a quick and uninspired kill was the way I wanted to go with you."

"Of course not. You always liked to torture your victims first."

"Much more interesting, no?"

"No." She started to shake her head, then stopped as the wire bit deeper. "Just sad."

"Hmm. Maybe sometimes. A twinge, now and then."

Kendra looked back at Colby. He was, as always, supremely confident and self-satisfied. "So what is your great plan for me?"

"All in good time. First, I need you to lower your window and toss your mobile phone out. You won't need it where you're going."

"Just take it, it's all yours. The phone's there . . . on the console."

"Nice try, but your friends are far too technologically astute. I know they can use it to track you. So do as I say. Out the window, Kendra."

She lowered her window and tossed out her phone. In the side view mirror, she saw it strike sparks on the freeway.

"Perfect. Thank you."

"Do you know where we're going, or am I just supposed to drive all night?"

"Oh, I definitely know where we're headed. And deep down in your soul, so do you. It's a special place for both of us."

"I doubt that."

"Do I really need to tell you?" he asked softly.

No, he didn't. The awful realization had sunk home. Of course that's where he'd take her. "We're going to Coachella Valley. We're going back to the gully."

"Ah, I knew it would come to you. I knew this day would come. I've known it for four years, from the day I woke up in that hospital with a fractured skull. Did you know I've had a terrible ringing in my ears ever since that night? It has never quite gone away, a constant reminder of you, Kendra."

Weapons. How could she get hold of a weapon? Her gun was in the glove box, but there was no way she could reach it.

"I'm sure that night hasn't quite faded for the families of those two FBI agents you murdered there, either."

"The honored dead. Those people should thank me. I made those men heroes."

"You slaughtered them."

"I saved them from an ordinary, mediocre existence. Those men didn't have it in them to rise to the great heights of human achievement. Not like you do, Kendra. I was their only hope for an extraordinary life, and I delivered it to them."

"What's disgusting is that I know . . . you're not saying this to goad me. You really believe it."

"Of course I do. I never say anything I don't believe. Think about it: Do you know anyone more honest than I am?"

Kendra's eyes darted around the front seat. If only she had Olivia's nasty box of tricks . . .

"You know the way, Kendra. And just know that if you manage to flag a police officer during our journey, I will kill him. And our fair city will have yet another fallen hero to mourn . . . and I will have made another ordinary life extraordinary. Do you doubt me?"

"No. Not for a second."

"Good girl."

KENDRA AND COLBY DIDN'T TALK for the remainder of their long drive to Coachella Valley, with Colby keeping his wire taut and painful against her throat the entire way. Kendra broke the silence as they turned and took the slow climb up Rock Road. "You haven't been back here since that night, have you?"

"No. How did you know?"

"Because I've been here many times in the past few months. I knew you'd be drawn to this place, so I kept coming back to look for some sign of you here. I never saw any, but I knew you'd be back someday."

"Correct as always, Kendra. Unfortunately for you. It has to end here. It's a compliment to you and your abilities that I know I can't let you live." He paused. "And you didn't only visit this place searching for me, did you? How many times did you dream of the gully, Kendra?"

"Too many times."

"I knew it, I felt it."

Kendra looked ahead to the hillside where she had seen Colby murder those two brave FBI agents. And just below it was the gully where she'd had her own horrible confrontation with him.

The wire around her neck loosened slightly, and as she glanced in her rearview mirror, she realized that Colby was also looking ahead and remembering that night. "You could have just gone away, Colby. No one was looking for you."

"No one but you."

Kendra picked up speed as she climbed the curvy mountain road, her headlights darting back and forth like machetes clearing the landscape. She could see the wooden roadside barrier and the dark waters of the quarry below. "No one was listening to me. You could have just stayed away and lived out the rest of your days as a free man."

"I still can."

"How?"

"This world has a short attention span. It got even shorter in just the few years I was away, with all of our texts, news bursts, alerts, and twenty-four-hour news cycles. There's always another atrocity to push the last one aside, then another after that. No one will be looking for me in a few months. I'll be a faint, unpleasant memory. Then I'll be back, doing what I've always done, rescuing people from their mediocre lives."

Dear God, his words held a terrible truth that could lead to an even more terrible reality. She could actually see it all coming to pass.

No. No. No.

Kendra took a deep breath. She couldn't let it happen. "No, Colby. Not again. Never again."

No weapons.

Only one way.

She spun the wheel hard left. The next moment, the car broke through the roadside barrier that separated them from the Coachella Quarry.

She heard Colby curse as her car became airborne in the darkness. The car plummeted thirty feet, then struck the still, deep water with a bone-crunching force that hit her at the exact same moment as the air bag. Her entire body throbbed with pain.

Water. Water everywhere, rising over her legs and stomach . . .

But she was alive!

But where was Colby . . . ?

Move. Get the hell out. Now.

She clawed through the air bag, trying to reach her seatbelt latch.

Success.

Her hands flew to her throat, where Colby's wire still dangled. She slid her fingers underneath to loosen it, then slowly lifted the wire over her chin, her nose, her forehead . . ."

Zippp.

It suddenly closed over her head and fingers.

Pain. Sharp, excruciating pain . . .

She looked back at Colby. With no seat belt and no air bag, his face had borne the brunt of their impact. Blood dripped from his chin and nose, and he'd lost several front teeth.

He braced himself against the backseat and pulled on the wire.

She pushed upward on the wire as it cut into her scalp. Her hands were a bloody mess. Just a little bit more . . .

The water rose more quickly now, and the car listed to the left. She unlocked the door and leaned against it.

It didn't budge. The pressure was just too great.

She looked desperately into her rearview mirror.

Colby had his knife out. He raised it with his right hand while keeping her head pulled back with his wire.

No, dammit.

She kicked the drivers-side window. Water flooded inside, blasting Colby back into his seat.

This was her chance. She tore off the wire and scrambled through the window just as the water pressure equalized. Her car was now almost entirely submerged.

Just another few feet, and—

Colby grabbed her foot!

She kicked, but his grip was too strong.

Slice.

He cut her ankle.

God, the pain . . .

Slice.

He'd cut her again. She wriggled her foot, kicking madly.

She was free!

She positioned her foot. She took aim. Gotta make it count . . .

Contact!

She struck Colby's already-shattered face. Even underwater, she could hear his anguished scream.

With one final kick, she propelled herself out the window, just before her car rolled over onto its driver's side and landed on the rocky bottom.

Kendra turned for a last look. A full moon shimmered through the water and bathed her car in an ethereal glow. The car's dashboard was still lit, and inside she could see Colby moving.

He was scrambling for the passenger door, she realized. If he got it open, he might escape.

And it would all begin again.

Not this time, Colby.

She swam back toward the car, fighting through the pain of her injuries. She floated over to the passenger-side door, watching Colby for a long moment.

Then he saw her. He smiled maliciously as they locked eyes.

He reached for the door handle. And in that moment Kendra dug out the remote key fob of her keyless car that she'd shoved into her pocket back at the hospital. She dangled it over the window, in front of his face.

Then she pressed it, and the door locked.

Thunkkk.

Colby was smiling mockingly as he reached out and pulled on the passenger-door handle.

It didn't open.

Child-safety locks, she wanted to tell him. For her young clients, but they'd never been more useful than they were at this moment.

Colby couldn't believe it. He kept trying to open the door.

Panicked, Colby pounded on the window. For the first time, she saw fear in his eyes. Absolute terror.

Still, only a tiny percentage of the terror he had brought into the world, she thought.

How does it feel, Colby? Remember Beth?

Colby's eyes bulged, and in one magnificent burst, his lungs exploded with water. Kendra watched, transfixed, as he thrashed on the seat.

He went still.

Eric Colby was dead. His striking blue eyes were still wide open, reflecting the shimmering, water-filtered moonlight.

She couldn't believe it.

Yes, she could. Because *she* had done it. As she had promised herself she would.

Kendra turned, and, the next minute, she broke the surface and started to swim toward the bank.

LYNCH ARRIVED AS THE EMTS were lifting Kendra into the ambulance on the road above the quarry.

"You look a total mess." He climbed inside the ambulance and sat beside her.

"You should have seen the other guy," Kendra said. "And I mean that. You would have enjoyed it."

"I bet I would." His hand stroked her cheek. "I nearly went crazy when I found out that you were missing. I told you not to shut me out."

"No choice. I called you as soon as I got my hands on a phone, didn't I?" Her eyes closed. "I'm tired. I don't want to talk any more right now."

"And you won't. We'll get you to the nearest hospital and have them look at that throat. It looks nasty."

"No." She opened her eyes. "They keep saying that's what they're going to do, but I want to go to the same hospital as Beth. Don't let them take me anywhere else."

"Whatever you say." He smiled. "Anything you want."

"That's right." Her eyes closed again. "I can't fight anymore right now. Do it for me, okay?"

"Now. Tomorrow. Forever. Just give me my orders."

"Very sappy, Lynch."

"I guess I was. It's the situation. Just go to sleep. I'll take care of it."

Yes, Lynch would take care of it.

She let go of everything and drifted off . . .

Alvarado Hospital Medical Center

EVE WAS BESIDE HER when she woke the next time.

"Hi," Kendra said drowsily. "You're not supposed to be with me. You were sitting with Beth . . ."

"That was yesterday." Eve smiled. "And I'm still watching out for her. But the doctors kicked me out while they did some more tests, so I decided to come down and check on you."

"Yesterday?" She looked at the daylight streaming into the hospital room. "I'm fine, but I shouldn't have slept this long."

"You were in pretty bad shape when they brought you in. Cuts, bruises, shock. The doctors decided to give you a sedative while they were working on you." She wrinkled her nose. "Probably at Lynch's suggestion. He was very protective."

"He said he'd take care of it," Kendra said dryly. "I should have known it would be in the way he decided was best."

"I might have made the same decision," Eve said quietly. "You're going to have a zillion conflicting emotions after getting rid of Colby."

Kendra didn't doubt it. She was already feeling strangely at a loss, as well as bewildered and sad and angry. "Maybe a zillion, but none of them will be regret. Not after what he did to Beth."

"Beth . . ." Eve suddenly jumped to her feet. "Care to take a trip up to see her?"

"Now?" she asked, startled.

"Right now." Eve was wheeling a wheelchair up to the bed and helping Kendra to sit up. "You'll have to ride. The nurses would have a fit if they saw me helping you down the hall."

"I could wait until—"

"No, you can't." She was tucking Kendra into the wheelchair. "Now hush while I sneak you upstairs."

Two minutes later, they were getting off the elevator, and Eve was wheeling Kendra toward Beth's room.

"Eve, something is going on."

"How perceptive. Anyone could tell that. It doesn't take a Kendra Michaels." Eve stopped at the door. "Yes, it is." She opened the door. "At about four this morning, Beth woke up on her own. She smiled at me and said my name, then drifted back to sleep."

"Oh, thank God." Kendra was suddenly afraid. "Not unconscious? Not a coma?"

"She was still under sedation. But she has woken twice since then, and they say she's in a normal sleep now."

She moistened her lips. "How . . . normal?"

"Recognition. She knew me. She knew the year, the date. I don't know what else the doctors found when they tested her. They say there's still swelling." She smiled. "But hope, Kendra. Gigantic hope."

"Why didn't you tell me right away when I woke up?"

"I wanted to get all the results first." She grimaced. "Okay, I wanted to stage a big surprise with all the trimmings. But I couldn't wait. I had to share it."

"May I sit with her for a while?"

"Until the nurses find you fled the coop and call out security." She wheeled her next to Beth's bed. "Which might not be too long. I'll keep watch from the door."

Beth looked pale and fragile, but her breathing was steady, and she didn't have that terrible remoteness that had so frightened Kendra.

It's over, Beth. Come back to us, and you won't have to be afraid.

But Beth was never afraid. Even when she should have been during that horrible time with Colby.

"Kendra?" Beth's eyes were opening. Her voice was weak but steady. "You look . . . terrible. You need to see one of these doctors they have . . . bustling around here."

"I'll consider it." She covered Beth's hand with her own. "You were keeping them pretty busy, but they might have a little time in the near future."

"Now . . ."

"Stop bossing me." It was wonderful having Beth boss her or do anything that was blessedly normal. "I have something to tell you before Eve has to smuggle me out of here. It's something you have to know . . ."

Alvarado Hospital Medical Center
Two Days Later

"BETH WANTS TO SEE YOU." Eve smiled at Sam, but her tone was stern. "Now stop waffling and go in and talk to her."

"I wasn't waffling," Sam protested. "I just don't like hospitals, and she's been busy with all of you trying to—"

"Make her feel as if we're glad that she's alive and getting better?"

"She knows that I'm glad she's alive."

"Yes, she does. Because I told her exactly how you were responsible for keeping her that way."

"Oh, shit."

"I do believe you're embarrassed. Sorry, you can't avoid facing Beth. Now go in and take it on the chin."

Sam hesitated, then squared his shoulders and opened the door and swaggered into Beth's hospital room.

Beth was lying with eyes closed, expression peaceful, her dark hair free and shining on the pillow.

For an instant, Sam felt his heart race with fear. She looked the same as she had underwater when he'd realized that she was dead.

Only she wasn't dead. Though he didn't know how the hell she'd escaped. Miracle. No matter what explanations they gave, it was a miracle.

"Why are you just standing there?" Her eyes had opened. "Come over here."

"I thought you were sleeping." He made a face as he walked over to the bed. "Or dead. You scared me."

"I was pretty scared myself. Though I couldn't let Colby know that. He would have enjoyed it too much." She reached out and took his hand. "He's really dead?"

"Kendra must have told you."

"Yes, but it begs reinforcement, and I couldn't talk about him very much to Kendra. She's feeling guilty as hell, and I only want her to forget I was ever down in that cellar."

"We all want to forget it," Sam said. "But it ain't gonna happen."

She was silent. "No, you're right. It will be with me forever but I've got to find something in that memory to heal, not hurt." She looked down at his hand. "They tell me you played the big hero and saved me."

"Damn straight. I was bloody wonderful."

"You always were over-the-top. This is the second time you stepped up to rescue me. I suppose you expect me to thank you and swear eternal gratitude."

"It would be the gracious thing to do. But it would probably embarrass me. I'm such a modest soul."

She made a rude noise.

"That's typical. And so unfair."

"Eternal gratitude . . . What a concept." Her eyes were suddenly shining with mischief. "Personally, I'm a fan of the old proverb. If you save a person's life, they are your responsibility forever."

"There's something very wrong about that."

"I've always thought so, but I'm beginning to like the idea." She grinned. "I've never really had anyone responsible for me before. It could be a good fit. Unless you manage to turn the tables at some point."

"That philosophy is too confusing. I'm opting out."

"No." Her hand closed on his. "No matter how we work it, there's no opting out. I'm Old Dog Tray, remember."

"Yeah." He smiled down at her. "I don't mind your hanging out and snoozing in front of a fireplace, but no more cellars. Okay?"

"Okay." She lifted his hand and pressed her lips to it. "Whatever you say . . . my dear friend." She released it and closed her eyes. "Get out of here. I have to get well fast. There's a life to live out there. I have things to do . . ."

EPILOGUE

Seahaven Behavioral Health Center
Santa Barbara, California
Two Months Later

KENDRA'S GAZE WAS SEARCHING the crowd. "Where's Beth, Sam? I don't see her."

Sam grinned and gestured with his champagne glass across the crowd at the slight hill overlooking the shore. "She's up there in the rocks, where she can get the best view. Just follow the bird of paradise."

As she headed for the rocks, Kendra's gaze traveled around the small crowd of guests, who looked as if they were dressed for a garden party. That's what Beth had wanted, when she'd called Kendra and told her that she wanted her here for this very special occasion.

"Make it a celebration," she'd said. "Wear something floaty and happy. Something that reminds you of a butterfly."

"My dear Beth. I don't have any butterfly clothes. It's not my style."

"Then it should be. Who is more of a butterfly than you, Kendra? Think about it."

"I'll think about you," she said. "You're the true butterfly." She sighed. "And I'll attempt to find something in that theme that doesn't make me look ridiculous."

"Thank you. I just had the same argument with Eve." She hung up the phone.

After much searching, Kendra had found a copper-colored maxi dress that was appropriately floaty and met the compromise. She'd decided she might even wear it again. Or not. It didn't matter. It would make Beth happy.

Kendra caught sight of Eve talking to Lynch and Joe Quinn across the wide green lawn. Eve had found a dress in dark blue and peacock that was simple but sophisticated and still managed to float a little. They had all obeyed Beth's orders and tried to give her what she wanted.

"Here, Kendra," Beth called. She had seen Kendra and was smiling at her as Kendra made her way toward her. Beth was dressed in scarlet-and-orange chiffon that made her dark hair shimmer in contrast and was unashamedly bold and dazzling.

"Hey, quite a spread, isn't it? And the champagne is great." She patted the rock next to her. "Come on and have a prime seat at the event." She looked at the hospital across the lawn. "They have the explosives ready to go. I told them to wait until it was fully dark."

Kendra dropped down beside her. From here she could see the surf striking the rocks below and feel the moist wind in her hair. The setting was breathtaking, only the purpose of the place had been somber and frightening. "You're really going to blow it up. You're sure you want to do this, Beth?"

"Positive. I've been thinking about doing it since you and Eve sprung me from the place. Buy the damn hospital, get rid of all the monstrous memories, and donate the land for a park, where all the memories will be happy ones. But I had to brace myself and make sure that was the way I wanted it to go. For some reason, I was reluctant, maybe I was even afraid. It had been my home and prison for so many years." She smiled. "But one thing Colby did for me during that last hideous day was to erase all doubts. I was trying to celebrate life before he came along, but he gave me the crowning lesson." She lifted her champagne glass. "Here's to living every day and every minute with joy." She glanced at the hospital, then at the guests scattered at the tables. "And being grateful to people who love you and live them with you."

"I'll drink to that." Eve was suddenly there beside them. She gave Beth a kiss on the cheek. "This is a very good thing." She took a sip of her champagne. "Now afterward, wouldn't you like to come home with me for a while?"

Beth chuckled. "You always try, don't you?"

"Well, I was a little shaken when I was called out here this time. I'm all for letting you live your own life. But I prefer you *live* it."

"My fault," Kendra said quietly. "It won't happen again, Eve."

Eve chuckled. "Good Lord, I'm not blaming you. If there's one thing I've learned about Beth, it is that she'll do as she wishes." She sighed. "I just wish she'd wish to come home with me."

"Soon," Beth said. "I still have some growing up to do."

"That goes on forever, Beth," Eve said gently.

"Maybe. But everyone else had a head start." She looked to the west. "The sun's down, it should be dark in a few minutes."

"Is it time?" Kendra asked.

Beth looked for a long time at the hospital. Then she lifted her hand and gave the signal. "Yes, it's time."

She got to her feet and lifted her glass with Kendra and Eve on either side of her. "Let's watch the fireworks. They promised me it would be splendid. Better than the Fourth of July."

And the next moment proved that to be true. The hospital blew in a fiery explosion that lit up the night sky.

"Oh, yes," Beth whispered. "Celebration."

Read on for an excerpt from Iris Johansen's upcoming book

HIDE AWAY

Available in hardcover in April 2016 from St. Martin's Press

CHAPTER 1

Community Hospital of the Monterey
Carmel, California

SHE WAS ALONE.

She mustn't panic. After all, she was eleven years old and had been taught to take care of herself. She had always been told that someday she might have to face this.

Cara Delaney leaned back against the door after leaving Eve Duncan's hospital room and tried to smother the fear that was surging through her. Her heart was beating hard and her throat was tight. They were going to send her away. It was all very well to tell herself she had known that it might happen someday, but it still came as a shock. She wasn't ready to face it yet.

But she'd better get ready. She'd been on the run most of her life and should have been prepared for the day that there would be no one here to help her. Her sister, Jenny, had been killed; Elena, who had cared for Cara since she was born, had been killed. Now Cara was the only one left, and if Eve had decided she didn't want her, she'd have to find a way to face the loneliness and protect herself.

What was she thinking? Cara thought in sudden disgust. She had been feeling so sorry for herself that she had forgotten that it was Eve that she was supposed to be worrying about. It was Eve who had to be taken care of as Cara had promised. Jenny had died so that Cara could live and so had Elena. Now it was Cara's turn to give back.

She drew a deep breath and opened her hands, which had been clenched into fists. She could work through this, she just couldn't give up. There had to be a way . . .

"Cara?"

Margaret Douglas was walking down the corridor toward her, a concerned look on her face. Margaret was Eve's friend, and she had taken over Cara's supervision to keep her out of the hands of Child Services. She had been kind to Cara since Eve had been in the hospital, and Cara liked her. But Cara didn't want kindness now.

She wanted to go back into that room from which Joe Quinn had sent her and start the battle to keep her place at Eve's side.

WHAT ON EARTH HAD HAPPENED to Cara, Margaret thought. Her gaze was fixed worriedly on the child's face as she came down the hall toward her. Cara's lips were tight, and there was a tension about the muscles of her shoulders. Maybe it was just the accumulated trauma of the last days that had finally hit home. What wouldn't be wrong with an eleven-year-old child who had gone through what Cara had suffered in the last few days, much less her short life, Margaret thought bitterly. She and her sister, Jenny, were the daughters of Juan Castino, the kingpin of a drug cartel in Mexico City, and they had been kidnapped as an act of vengeance by Salazar, the leader of a rival drug cartel. Jenny had been killed, and Cara had been taken on the run by her nurse, Elena, for eight long years. Just a few days ago, Elena had been murdered by a hit man, James Walsh, hired by Salazar to find them. Cara had later been cornered by Walsh, who had come close to killing her. Only Eve's intervention had

prevented it, but it had landed her in this hospital with a concussion. Yes, Cara had every reason to look tense.

"Hey, what's the problem?" Margaret stopped in front of
Cara and smiled gently. "Anything I can do to help?"

Cara shook her head. "I don't think so. I think it has to be
me. Something has gone wrong. I could tell when Joe Quinn
came into Eve's room and sent me out here. It's probably
about me. He said it wasn't and that I didn't do anything
wrong. But what else could it be?" Her hazel eyes were glittering with moisture. "Eve said they were going to take me
home with them for a while. But Joe probably thinks that the
reason Eve was hurt was because of me. He's right, you
know."

Margaret reached out and gently touched the child's dark
hair. "You don't know that he's upset with you, Cara. Joe is
very fair. He knows that Eve does what she thinks is right,
and nothing stops her. Yes, she was hurt trying to save your
life. But Joe was there almost immediately afterward, and he
was concerned for you as well as Eve." She cupped Cara's
thin shoulders in her hands. "We were all concerned. It was
a nightmare finding you and trying to keep you safe from
that horrible man. There was no way Eve was going to
stop."

"I know," Cara whispered. "Jenny said to trust Eve, that
she would never stop until I was safe."

Margaret stiffened. "Jenny? Cara, your sister, Jenny is—"
She hesitated. There was no other way to put it. "Jenny isn't
with us. She died eight years ago."

Cara nodded. "I know that, but she . . . I dream about
her." She looked at Margaret defiantly. "And she doesn't
seem . . . Do you think I'm crazy?"

"Who, me?" She brushed the hair back from Cara's face.
So much intensity in that small face, those wide-set hazel
eyes that were more green than brown. The winged brows
and pointed chin. In the few days since she'd come to know
the child, she'd become aware of how much emotion and intensity lay behind that usually reserved expression. Intensity

and strength. Strange to think of a child as being strong, but Cara's life had been different from that of other children. She'd had to be strong and enduring to bear the constant change and terror of being on the run. Even now when Walsh, the man who'd been hunting her had been killed, she knew she wasn't safe, that there might be another killer on the horizon. That life had made Cara mature beyond her years, and Margaret was constantly finding out new and different facets to her character. "I'm the last one to think anyone is crazy because of a few dreams. A lot of people think I'm a little weird because I don't march to their drummers."

"You don't seem weird," Cara said. "You seem . . . nice."

"One doesn't exclude the other. You seem nice, too." She stepped back. "And a dream can just be a memory."

"Yeah," Cara nodded. "But it seems like more." She paused. "I think Eve dreams about Jenny, too."

"It wouldn't surprise me. Eve has a kind of sensitivity to people like us. That's why I get along so well with her." She added gently, "I know this is all strange to you, Cara. *We're* strange to you. It's only been a couple days since you met all of us. We blew into your life at a time when everything was terrible and scary. You even lost your best friend, Elena, to that monster who was hunting you. You probably don't know whom to trust or how to react to all of us. You don't know where you're going next."

"You're wrong. I know where I'm going." Cara looked over her shoulder at the door of Eve's room. "I'm going with her. I have to take care of her. She needs me."

Margaret's brows rose. "Really? Everyone needs affection. But other than that, Eve's pretty strong, Cara."

"I have to take care of her," she repeated. "I promised Jenny."

"In that dream you had?"

She didn't answer directly. "I promised her." She went on in a rush, "And, like I said, Eve was going to let me stay with her and Joe for a while. She said so." She was frowning. "But when Joe came into the room a few minutes ago, I could tell that he was upset. Maybe he changed his mind."

"I doubt it." She tilted her head curiously. "What would you do if he did?"

"I'd go with her anyway. I'd find a way." Her gaze was still fixed on the door. "I have to take care of her."

Determination, intensity, and total commitment. Margaret shook her head with amazement. All of them had been so focused on finding and saving Cara during these last weeks that they had been thinking of her as helpless. She might have been in danger, but there was nothing helpless about this child. "Well, soon she'll be out of the hospital and on her way home. She won't need taking care of." She smiled. "Though I'm sure that she'll still want your company, Cara. You're jumping to conclusions. Come on, let's go to the waiting room, and I'll buy you a soda."

She thought Cara was going to refuse, but then the girl turned away from Eve's door. "Okay. I can't do anything right now anyway."

"Very sensible," Margaret said, as they strolled down the hall. "There's probably not going to be anything to do anyway. Maybe it's your imagination."

"No," Cara said soberly. "It's not imagination." She glanced back over her shoulder at Eve's door. "Joe was . . . tense. Something *is* wrong . . ."

Mexico City, Mexico

SOMETHING WAS WRONG, Alfredo Salazar thought impatiently. In his last report, Walsh had told him that he had located Castino's kid and that bitch, Elena Pasquez, who had hidden her all these years, and that they'd be dead within days.

Why the hell hadn't he heard from him? It was making

him damn uneasy. He'd been losing faith in James Walsh lately, but there was no doubt he was an expert once he set his sights on a victim. What could have gotten in his way?

Or who?

He reached in his desk drawer and pulled out the dossiers he'd compiled from the reports Walsh had given him.

Eve Duncan. Joe Quinn. Cara Delaney.

There were other dossiers but none as important as those three.

Eve Duncan, forensic sculptor who had restored the skull of Jenny Castino after her bones had been recently unearthed. He glanced at her photo. Not to his taste. Slim, red-brown hair with hazel eyes. An attractive, interesting face, but he preferred exotic and voluptuous. Evidently she was brilliant because she was considered one of the world's most gifted forensic sculptors.

Also very determined and stubborn. He'd warned Walsh that he should get rid of her before she got in his way. But she was an artist, a sculptor, and not equipped to go up against an enforcer of Walsh's capabilities.

He glanced at the Joe Quinn dossier. Brown hair, brown eyes, strong jaw. Detective with the ATLPD, ex-FBI, ex-SEAL. He had lived with Eve Duncan for a number of years and was said to be extremely loyal to her. He was undoubtedly deadly and capable of interfering with Walsh.

He glanced at the photo of the child. Cara had only been three when Walsh had taken her from the Castino home. Her sister Jenny had been nine, but they'd had the same high cheekbones and winged brows. That damn Eve Duncan had reproduced Jenny's features almost exactly when she'd been sent that skull of the skeleton buried in northern California and found by the Sheriff's Department. Now Walsh was sure that she was trying to locate Jenny's sister, Cara.

Which could mean disaster for Salazar.

And he wasn't about to sit here and wait any longer for word from Walsh. If he hadn't completed the kill, it was time he was taken out himself.

He reached for his phone.

It rang before he could dial.

Ramon Franco.

Which did not bode well. When Salazar had begun to have his doubts about Walsh's efficiency, Franco was the young man Salazar had sent to shadow him and make certain he was performing effectively.

"Walsh is dead," Ramon Franco said harshly as soon as Salazar picked up the call. "Killed. I just found out last night, and I've been scrambling to get information. I told you that you should have sent me to take care of that kid. He bungled the kill, and now there are police all over the place. We'll be lucky if they don't trace anything back to you."

Son of a bitch!

Salazar's hand tightened on the phone as the fury tore through him. "That can't happen. I've spent eight years covering Walsh's incompetence. I won't let that bastard's death toss me into Castino's jaws for him to chew up. Who killed him?"

"Eve Duncan."

So he had been wrong. Evidently the artist had a few more lethal skills than her credentials suggested. He had warned Walsh that she was a possible problem when the woman had gone on the hunt for him after he had stolen her reconstruction of Castino's daughter's skull. Now she was no longer a problem; she was a major pain in the ass. "For God's sake, Duncan is only a forensic sculptor, and she managed to put down Walsh? How many people has Walsh killed over the years? He should have been able to squash her like a bug. How did it happen?"

"It could have been an accident. Her statement to the police claimed they were fighting on the high ledge of a cave, and he backed off and fell to his death." He added, "Or she might have outsmarted him. Castino's other daughter, Cara, was in the cave, and you told me she was the target."

"The last target," Salazar said bitterly. "And Walsh couldn't even manage to find and kill an eleven-year-old kid."

"He found her in that cave, but he couldn't finish the job. Eve Duncan got in the way. He managed to kill her nursemaid, Elena Pasquez, but no one else. I would never have let that happen."

"And when the police start digging into who that kid really is, they'll toss her back to her father, Castino, and he'll go after me. He's just waiting for a chance to break the coalition agreement."

"Then we have to make sure he doesn't have a reason to do it until we're strong enough to bury him and all the rest of the men in his damn cartel. Give me the word, and I'll erase Walsh's death and that little girl as if they'd never existed." His voice was suddenly impassioned. "You haven't been fair to me. Haven't I always been loyal to you? From the time I was twelve, I did everything you told me to do. No kill was too hard. Yet you sent me here to Carmel to watch that bumbler, Walsh, just to make sure he was going to be able to finish the kill on the Castino kid. It was a job for a beginner. I may be young, but I'm no beginner."

"No, I know you're not." He tried to make his tone soothing. Franco's tone bordered on insolence, and he was tempted to cut him down to size, but he might need him. He was the man on the spot, with all contacts in place. Better to handle Ramon Franco with kid gloves. The young recruits always lacked discipline, but they were also the ones most eager to prove themselves in blood. He was only nineteen, but his kill record with the cartel was impressive. He was quick, lethal, and totally vicious. "That's why I trusted you to watch Walsh. I never knew when I would have to have someone good enough to take over. Walsh had the experience, but he was going downhill, and I couldn't trust him." He paused. "Not like you, Franco. I see myself in you."

"You do?" Franco was silent, then said haltingly, "I'm honored, sir. It's just that I don't understand. You told me so little about what was going on with Walsh. I felt . . . like an errand boy."

Which was exactly how Salazar saw him. But circumstances dictated the errand boy be promoted until Salazar could take charge himself. "I don't want any of my other men to be jealous of you. Particularly not now. I'd rather you concentrate on getting me out of the mess Walsh made up there in Carmel. You're going to have to dance a fine dance to save the situation. But you're a smart boy, and I know that you can do it for me."

"I'm a man, not a boy."

"Of course you are. But it's not a bad thing that others believe you to be a boy, so they won't suspect how very deadly you can be. I've seen you use that ploy before."

"Sometimes."

"Often. Do you think I haven't been watching you? Use your brains and that smile the ladies like so much."

"Then tell me what I need to know. Tell me what Walsh knew, what I should have known from the beginning."

A definite touch of arrogance, Salazar noticed. "You know the beginning. You grew up with it. The drugs, the vice, that son of a bitch, Juan Castino, constantly moving into my territory. He acted as if his cartel was the only one in Mexico, and every time anyone came close to taking him down, he managed to come out on top. I had the brains and the plans but Castino had the contacts and was always just ahead of me. If I hadn't managed to form a mutual coalition of all the cartels in Mexico, he would have eaten me alive. I can rein him in as long as he knows I have the backing of the coalition behind me."

"Until we find a way to kill him. That's the best way. Don't worry. I'll do it for you."

So simple, so incredibly naïve. "I know you will. But it has to be staged very carefully. I can't let any of the other cartels know that I'm getting ready to jump Castino." He paused. "Or that I yielded to temptation eight years ago to twist the knife and make him hurt. They might turn against me."

"Because you arranged with James Walsh to kidnap Castino's two little girls and their nanny and kill them? They all probably wish they'd had the balls to do it."

"They'd chop me up and serve me to Castino. And then move into my territory and split it up." His voice was laden with frustration. "It was going to be so simple. Walsh would kill them, and there would be no bodies or anything to connect me to it. I'd be able to sit back and watch Castino suffer, then, when the time was right, I'd make sure he joined his little girls in the grave yard. But Walsh screwed it up. He left me hanging and vulnerable if Castino finds out I paid Walsh to kill them. We have to fix it, Franco."

"I can do it if I work fast. I don't think that Castino knows anything yet. The kid's name on the police report is Cara Delaney, and Walsh is only suspected of being a serial killer. Nothing about Castino."

Hope and relief shot through Salazar. "You're certain?"

"I paid a good deal of your money to bribe a look at those reports. No mention of Castino . . . or you."

"Yet."

"As you say. But there may be a way to keep you safe if we work fast. Eve Duncan hasn't made a statement yet. She's in a local hospital being checked out for concussion, and her lover, Joe Quinn, isn't letting her be interviewed."

"Where's the kid?"

"She's being taken care of by a friend of Duncan's, Margaret Douglas."

"Not at Child Services? They're big on Welfare shit in the U.S."

"No, I'm sure. I knew you'd want to know where you could put your hands on her."

"Oh, yes." His hands around her throat to end this nightmare. "Then it appears you may have a multitude of targets in the near future. You need to find out how much Duncan knows about Cara Castino . . . and me. I have to know I'm safe from Duncan before I move forward again."

"You'll be safe. It's only a question which target I hit first." His voice was suddenly eager. "You tell me, and it will be done. Duncan? Quinn? The kid?"

"You're moving too fast. I want you to go to that hospital and report back to me. Do you understand?"

"If I took out Duncan, it would stop the—"

"Report back to me," Salazar repeated. "Is that clear?"

"Yes, sir." He was silent. "I didn't mean to argue. You're the *Pez Gordo*, the big boss. I'm just concerned."

He was concerned because if Salazar and his cartel fell, he could be part of the collateral damage, Salazar thought cynically. It was obvious Franco was very ambitious. "Then it's time to use that concern in the way I told you."

"I'll leave for the hospital right away. I won't disappoint you." He hung up.

Franco was moving fast and was eager to please but Salazar still wasn't sure that he would obey instructions if an opportunity presented itself.

Oh well, Franco was a superb assassin, and Salazar was just angry enough with the way Eve Duncan had spoiled his plans that he was willing to take a chance that Franco wouldn't pay her a fatal visit in her hospital room without taking appropriate precautions. Salazar rather liked the idea of Duncan's lying helplessly in that bed in her room while Franco moved around that hospital like a lethal buzz saw.

But if Franco decided to do it, he'd damn well better do it right.

Community Hospital of the Monterey

"CARA HAS GOOD INSTINCTS," Eve Duncan said as she turned back to Joe after watching the child walk out of her hospital room. "You're not easy to read, Joe. I'm glad that whatever you're upset about wasn't about her. Though I'm not sure she believed you. It would have been difficult explaining a sudden change of heart. Do you know, I'm starting to look forward to having Cara staying with us for a while?" She shook her head. "Remember, we were talking on the day Jane left for London about my life may be changing? Then all of this happened. Do you suppose Cara is the change?"

"Not necessarily."

Eve went still. She couldn't miss that jerky roughness in his tone. "What are you talking about? What *is* wrong?"

"Not wrong. Strange. Bizarre." He shook his head. "I don't know what else."

"Stop playing around with words. Talk to me."

"I don't know how to say it."

"Just tell me."

"The hospital has the results from all the tests they've been running on you. The doctor stopped me in the hall to go over them."

"The results? Joe, I know you've been ramrodding everything connected to my treatment since you brought me to this hospital, but that's going a little too far. Why go over them with you and not with me?" She tried to smile. "Some terrible disease popped up that he thought you should break to me?"

"God, I'm not doing this right. No terrible disease. You're very healthy and ready to go home. He just didn't want you to leave the hospital without knowing."

"Joe, what are you trying to tell me?"

"In my completely clumsy and inadequate fashion." He reached out and took her hand. "I'm trying to tell you that you're going to have a child, Eve."

"YOU'RE JOKING," EVE SAID DAZEDLY. "It's some kind of mistake?"

"No." Joe's hand tightened around her own. "And no. To both questions. I wouldn't have dared come in here if I hadn't made sure the doctor had checked and double-checked. You're pregnant." His teeth bit his lower lip. "And that goes to show how upset I am. *We're* pregnant. I can't quite take it in either. I went into shock when the doctor told me."

"Tell me about it," she said weakly as she sat up in the bed. "It wasn't supposed to happen. I thought it couldn't happen. It wasn't as if we weren't careful."

"I didn't think so either," Joe said. "We did everything right. Or maybe we didn't. But I don't know how we could have done anything different." He shook his head. "I'm a little confused on that point at the moment."

"Me, too." She met his gaze. "I . . . feel lost. I can't quite grasp it." She reached up and ran a hand through her hair. "How . . . long?"

"Barely. A few weeks. You must have conceived before we left the Lake Cottage to come out here to California."

"I remember when I was pregnant with Bonnie, I didn't know for months."

"Things have changed since you were sixteen. They can tell within five or six days now."

She nodded dazedly. "The whole world has changed. My whole life has changed. I'm not the same person."

"Yes, you are. You've just been tempered by experience." He lifted her palm to his lips. "And this particular experience may do some more very intricate tempering. Just don't let it throw you. We'll think about it, then make decisions."

"Decisions." No, she couldn't make decisions right now. Her head was whirling, and all she could think about was the fact that in nine months she would bear a child. It was impossible. No, it was going to happen. "How do you feel about it?"

"As dazed as you." He grinned. "Kind of . . . primitive. I've never fathered a child of my own. I suppose that's a natural reaction. I . . . like it." His smile faded. "I never suggested it to you. After all you've gone through, I thought that it had to come from you. I know what you went through when you lost your Bonnie when she was killed. After we adopted Jane, I believed that might be the way we should go."

"So did I." She moistened her lips. "And now I'm wondering why we never talked about having a child of our own. Did I just bury my head in the sand? My God, Joe, I must have sensed you'd feel like this. Was I so afraid that I avoided facing it?"

He didn't answer.

Because he knew it was true, she realized. She was his center, and he wouldn't allow her to be hurt even if it meant being cheated himself. "You should have spoken to me about it."

He shook his head. "I have you. That's enough, more than enough." He leaned forward and kissed her. "Now stop fretting about me, you have thinking to do."

"Thinking," she repeated. "You said decision. You know I won't have an abortion. I couldn't do that."

"That's not what I meant. You told me once that you'd intended to adopt Bonnie out to a good home before she was born. Then, when you saw her, you changed your mind."

Eve stared at him in shock. "You'd consent to me doing that?"

"I have no idea. I doubt it. Every instinct is shouting no, but I just had to bring it up because you'd once considered it. You were a teenager then, poor, virtually alone, and Bonnie was illegitimate. Now you're older, but you have a career that obsesses you, and family would get in the way." He met her gaze. "Whatever your decision, it has to be made with your whole heart. After that, we'll work out what we need to do individually to meet both our own goals. We'll find a way to blend them together."

"Joe . . ."

"Hush." He squeezed her hand before releasing it. "I'm going to go and see about your release papers. You rest awhile then I'll send Margaret in to help you dress." He paused. "Do you want me to tell her?"

She shook her head. "It's not real to me yet. How can I make it real to anyone else?"

"What about Cara? Do you still want to take her into our home for a while?"

"Of course I do. What are we supposed to do? Let her go back to Mexico and be torn apart in all those cartel wars? She's just a child, and she's already lost her sister and Elena, her best friend. You know that Salazar won't stop hunting her because Walsh is dead. We've got to keep her safe until we can find a way to get rid of Salazar."

"And Juan Castino, her loving father," Joe said grimly. "You're right, she's a pawn. She wouldn't stand a chance if immigration sends her back to Mexico." He turned toward the door. "I just thought that you might want me to handle it myself. You may be a little busy for a while."

"I believe the word is occupied," Eve said dryly.

"Whatever." He glanced back at her. "I wasn't sure that you'd be prepared for the hassle. We're going to have to whisk Cara away from here, keep her real identity from the authorities, and get her to Atlanta. Then I'll get to work on bringing down Salazar's cartel. That should keep him too busy to pay attention to Cara in the near future."

"I agree. But most of those arrangements are in your court."

"It will overflow."

She nodded. "Then I'll face it then." She smiled. "And a challenge will be good for me. It will keep me from . . . It will distract me."

"I doubt it."

The next moment, he was gone.

He was probably right, she thought. Nothing was going to distract her from this news that had shaken her world. But she had always found that hard work and putting her own problems at the end of the agenda could be a salvation.

But did she need salvation? Why had the word even occurred to her?

All she needed was to adjust to a situation that happened to millions of women every year.

So adjust.

She closed her eyes and leaned her head back on the pillow. Sort out what she really felt and examine it.

Shock.

A natural reaction.

Disbelief.

Also natural.

Fear.

A pregnancy was never easy when you were older.

Of course, there was an element of—

No, don't hide behind that easy answer. There was something else behind it.

Bonnie. Her little girl who had been her entire life during those seven short years before her death. Bonnie. The pain and agony that had almost killed Eve after she'd been taken.

The fear that agony could come back if she allowed herself to love another baby as she had Bonnie. She had dearly loved her adoptive daughter, Jane, but that had been another relationship entirely. Jane had been ten when they'd found each other and with a maturity that had made them more best friends than mother and daughter. So different from Bonnie. She had been responsible for her from the instant of her birth, and she had lost her. Could she bear the constant worry that another child would be taken from her?

Coward. She was a coward. Mothers faced that threat every single day.

Did you know what a coward I am, Joe? Is that why you never asked?

Well, there was no asking now. It was a fact. Stunning. Life-changing. Inevitable.

Magical.

The word had come out of nowhere.

Because that was the final emotion she had felt when Joe had told her she was going to have a child.

Magic. Joyous, rich, heady, magic.

She slowly looked down at her abdomen. Flat. No sign that someone was growing, taking on more life with every second. She reached out tentatively and touched the skin of stomach.

What's happening? It's a crazy world out here, are you sure you want to trust me to take you through it?

Was she expecting an answer from this baby, who had

just barely been conceived? Of course not, the question was really for herself. She had lost Bonnie. She would have to do better to prove herself to this child.

Her hand dropped away from her abdomen.

Later. We'll have to work on this. We're just starting out. We have a long way to go.

She sat up in bed and swung her legs to the floor. Time to start living life and not trying to avoid it. She went to the closet and started to take down her clothes.

"Hey, I'm supposed to do all that." Margaret had come into the room. "Joe said I should give you a little while to rest, and here you are ready to jump into your clothes."

Eve smiled affectionately at her. Margaret had been a tower of strength during the last days when they had been hunting for Cara, then Eve's time in the hospital. But then Margaret had shown remarkable strength from the moment Eve had met her. She was young and full of life and possessed instincts and a knowledge of animals that was as unusual as her ability to deal with people.

"I want to get out of here." Eve headed for the bathroom. "And I've done nothing but rest since I got here. I had a mild concussion, and Joe insisted on having those doctors run every test under the sun to make sure I was okay."

"Typical Joe Quinn," Margaret said. "He was a trifle . . . brief when he was talking to me. Is everything okay?"

"Everything's fine."

"Then you might tell Cara. She's not too sure."

Eve stopped at the bathroom door. "She thinks I'm abandoning her?"

"No, it's not gotten that far yet. But who could blame her? She doesn't really know any of us. She's known since she was three years old and her sister, Jenny, was killed almost in front of her eyes, that she had to run and keep on running just to stay alive. Her nurse, Elena, taught her she mustn't trust anyone." She added grimly, "And with good reason. Elena died trying to protect her. Now Cara is alone, and she's trying to come to terms with taking care of herself." She shrugged. "Though she seems more concerned with taking care of you. Do you know she dreams about Jenny?"

"Yes."

"And she told me she thinks you dream about her, too. Do you?"

"Not exactly."

Margaret gazed at her, waiting. When Eve didn't go on, she said. "Okay, you don't want to talk about it. I understand. Well, I don't really, but I would if you'd trust me. I thought that those reports from 'confidential sources' you told our Sheriff Nalchek you received were a trifle suspect when we were hunting down Walsh." She suddenly chuckled. "Though he'd think what I'm guessing now is far more weird than suspect." She took Eve's suitcase out of the closet. "Go on, get dressed. Call if you need me. I'll pack you up, and we'll be set to go as soon as you're ready."

"Thanks, Margaret," Eve said quietly. "Thanks for everything. We would never have found Cara if you hadn't helped. You've been there for me since the beginning of this nightmare."

"Not quite." She tilted her head. "And that sounds remarkably like good-bye. Is it?"

"I prefer *au revoir.*" She hesitated. "What Joe and I are doing isn't exactly legal in taking Cara back to Atlanta with us. It's morally right, but you could still get in trouble. You and the Immigration Department aren't on the best of terms."

"We're fine with each other as long as I'm smart enough to avoid them."

And Eve knew Margaret had made a science of avoiding them and keeping under the radar. Eve had never been told why Margaret felt that was necessary and could only be grateful that she occasionally dropped into their lives. "And you might be caught in the cross fire if they find out that we're keeping Cara from her legal father."

"Who is a murderer, drug lord, and general scumbag."

"Joe and I will be working on clearing up her situation,

but it will take time. In the meantime, Salazar will be a danger."

"Then I should be there to—"

"No, Margaret," Eve said firmly. "You have too much to lose. I won't have you stuck in a jail while they decide whether or not to deport you." She made a face. "Though I don't even know where they'd send you. You haven't been very forthcoming on that score."

"It's my life, my problems." Margaret shook her head. "I can't convince you, can I?" She shrugged. "Then I won't try. If you need me, get in touch." She started packing Eve's bag. "Do you need to know where to get phony documents for Cara? I know a few good places and some people who will—"

"No," Eve said. "You're out of this. Joe has managed to block any investigation on Cara's background, but there are still problems. It will be a very tentative fix, but as long as they think Cara is an orphan after the death of her supposed Aunt Elena, we may get away with it. We're hoping that Sheriff Nalchek will smooth things over with Child Services and persuade them to let us have temporary custody. He's well thought of in this area."

"He'll do it. He's like you. He won't want a child in danger."

"I believe you're right. We'll have to see. Everything is a little bewildering right now."

"Eve." Margaret was studying her face. "You're sure everything is okay? You look a little . . . unusual."

"Do I?" Trust Margaret to sense a truth that had only just been revealed to Eve. Unusual? The world was shaking. Everything was changing. She didn't know how she was going to cope. But she would do it.

She had to do it.